D1538950

Mademoiselle de Maupin

This is the golden book of spirit and sense,
　　The holy writ of beauty; he that wrought
　　Made it with dreams and faultless words and thought
That seeks and finds and loses in the dense
Dim air of life that beauty's excellence
　　Wherewith love makes one hour of life distraught
　　And all hours after follow and find not aught.
Here is that height of all love's eminence
Where man may breathe just for a breathing-space
　　And feel his soul burn as an altar-fire
　　To the unknown God of unachieved desire,
And from the middle mystery of the place
　　Watch lights that break, hear sounds as of a quire,
But see not twice unveiled the veiled God's face.

A. C. Swinburne

MADEMOISELLE DE MAUPIN

by THEOPHILE GAUTIER

WITH THE PREFACE BY THE AUTHOR,
AN INTRODUCTION FOR THE MODERN READER BY
JACQUES BARZUN
AND HAND-COLORED ILLUSTRATIONS BY
ANDRÉ DUGO

THE HERITAGE PRESS, NEW YORK

THE NONESUCH PRESS, LONDON

1944

INTRODUCTION *for the* MODERN READER

BY JACQUES BARZUN

We all know what French novels are—or we think we do: something in yellow covers which will not bear looking into, unless one is looking for naughty things. From *Candide* to *Madame Bovary,* and from Gautier to Anatole France and Maupassant, the odor of forbidden fruit lures the foreign reader and persuades him that the French public requires strong doses of voluptuous excitement from literature as well as from life. For half a century, *Mademoiselle de Maupin* has served foreigners as the proof of this erroneous conclusion no less than as a contraband satisfaction.

The fact is that in France Gautier's novel has always had a rather grudging and limited approval. On its appearance in 1835, it was hailed as a masterpiece by Balzac and Victor Hugo and generally condemned by the rest of the critical press. It sold poorly, waited decades before being reprinted, was attacked once again in 1880 as having helped to demoralize the victim in a *cause célèbre,* and has since then been coldly treated by a prevailingly anti-romanticist literary opinion. Only in English-speaking lands, and there chiefly, as I have said, for hole-and-corner reading, has the novel become a popular success. One notes a large turnover in second-hand copies, which dealers' catalogues regularly supply with one of those insinuating three-line descriptions more suggestive than anything in the book, or indeed in any book.

But if one is not hunting for titillating *curiosa,* what is Gautier's novel really worth? What did the author want to accomplish in writing it, and what kinds of pleasure does he afford us? The answers are very simple: the worth of the novel lies in its varied substance and literary finish; the author wanted to tell us about himself and his tastes under guise of a casual fiction, mainly humorous; and the pleasures thus yielded are stylistic, narrative, and psychological.

Gautier was a romanticist; and we think we know what that means, pretty much as we know what French novels are like. We generalize from a few striking facts. But the alert reader of *Mademoiselle de Maupin* will find that if this is a romantic book, his idea of romanticism must be broadened; he will find that there is more to romantic art than a preoccupation with airy fancies and brisk adventure. For one thing—and it is significant—if the reader tackles the novel in French, he will discover that throughout the author refers to his own fancy or folly as *romanesque* (novel-like), never as *romantique*. Romanticism does include those charming, vaporous images and daydreams which the young hero imparts at the outset to his friend Silvio; but these form only the upper air of the romantic universe. To Gautier and his generation, the task of the writer was to record in firm artistic shape a sum of experience ranging from hopes and fears and superstitions, at one end of the scale, to the plainest facts and least palatable realities at the other. Thus the *demoiselle* who gives her name to the book is a "romantic" girl in the usual sense of the word, but she is no less truly romantic when she observes the brutal and sordid aspects of her first night at the inn.

Gautier was only a boy of twenty-three when he wrote the greater part of this first novel, but his "experience" as I have defined the word was already considerable. Having led a troop of militant youth in defense of the new literary school, he was a public character. He had struggled as a journalist for five years, published three books, studied, painted, and loved with precocious versatility.

Since *Mademoiselle de Maupin* is certainly a love story, it is not amiss to stress the three or four love affairs which Gautier had had—not exactly one after the other—with women of diverse and distinguished personalities. He had also dealt, as he bluntly admits in the novel, in purchased love, and likewise in *amourettes* with working girls. Most of the time, however, he lived at home in sober and contented harmony with his parents, or in industrious intimacy with fellow artists. Yet the quest that he describes in his novel is the search for a mistress; not for an impossible, but at least for a highly "improbable she", whose improbability, when he finds her, is heightened by male attire. Was it restlessness, swagger, or surviving *naïveté* that prompted the choice of such a theme? I take it that first novels are likely to be autobiographical, but I suggest that, while expressive of a yearning usual enough at twenty-three, Gautier's simple plot is also an apt literary device.

For the description of the ideal mistress enables the author to elaborate his view of life's meaning. The riddle of existence was nearly as puzzling in post-Napoleonic Europe as it is now, and Gautier propounds an answer from which he never departed: the world of the senses is the gateway to the world of art, and art is the justification of life. Whereas society is built on self-seeking and falsehood, art is built on solid truths and self-devotion. Art, Love, Nature—this, for him, is the Trinity of the Real.

We can see it in *Mademoiselle de Maupin,* where love is treated in what must be called a very modern manner. Its sexual expression, its humor, its distortion into vanity, disgust, loneliness and perversity, are plainly, even violently emphasized. But Gautier's idea of love transcends the "realistic" discovery that if you let your beloved fall asleep on your arm, you will get a cramp. Like an Elizabethan, our author does not blink the gross or ridiculous physical truth, but he perceives simultaneously with it something intangible, elusive—yet vivid and permanent—beyond the physical. It is because this "ideal" is also a reality that Rosette's complete submission to d'Albert does not seem perfect love to either of them. Neither the sensual-physical nor the ideal-sentimental suffices by itself. The romantic requires that both merge into a completer experience. Remember the circumstances of the single happy kiss exchanged by the first pair of lovers, and recall how in Maupin's great erotic scene her lover requests her to pose like a model while he judges her with a painter's eye. This is no affected appeal to the "objectivity" of the studio. It is Gautier's vision of combined passion and contemplation. His whole book is an artfully artless blend of adventure and scene painting, with the narrator at the same time steadily engaged in analyzing himself—fiction on three levels. No wonder the book seemed strange to generations as yet ignorant of Proust!

Like Proust's, too, the novel is one of reminiscence. I do not mean only the use of Gautier's real ladyloves in fashioning Rosette, Théodore, and the young page. I mean the extraordinary resonance of remembered art. Hardly a paragraph fails to bring up an echo of ancient or modern literature, or of Renaissance painting, or of the "new music" of his own times. This may well account for the distaste of those French critics who find the story "cold" in spite of its physical ardor. For Gautier makes no secret of his allusiveness and, again in a very modern manner, boldly uses names and scenes from Balzac, phrases from George Sand, and finally, the plot of Shakespeare's *As You Like It*—itself a great example of art based on other art. Young men of genius are often tempted to set out in this way, and they are likely to succeed in eking out first-hand experience with second-hand because of the very strength of imagination which makes them young geniuses.

It would be idle to enumerate all of Gautier's real and bookish interests. Only the reader who is in a hurry to know "how it all ends" will miss their recurrence: solitude, luxury, art, scenery, horseflesh, old houses, fencing, costumes, melancholy brooding, jolly cynicism, mockery of the Philistine, defiance of convention, faith in friendship and love. All these are woven into a pseudo-autobiography as free from egotism as it is from literal truth.

This last aspect of the work must not be overlooked. Our author asks of his reader a capacity to modulate swiftly in accompaniment to his own rapid transitions. He demands also the gift of generous interpretation.

When Gautier says that life is for pleasure only, we must remember how disinterested his own hero chooses to be, how he rejects *easy* pleasure, how exacting and indeed ethical his tastes are. Similarly, Gautier's humor employs a great number of stops, through which blow the strong breath of his physical vitality. Beside youthful cynicism (sometimes close to obvious) you find wit, horseplay, clownish melancholy and that boisterous laughter of common sense which triumphs by exaggeration. The same romantics who could act *il penseroso* were full of zest for satiric hoaxing and caricature. It was they who cleared Rabelais' reputation and justified his "bad taste".

The reader needs no further caution about taking Gautier's tale too narrowly, but he may find some interest in two matters of historical fact— one relating to the genuine Mademoiselle de Maupin, the other to the meaning of the Preface, which even French critics have the habit of calling "brilliant" without saying why it is so.

The historic Mademoiselle de Maupin lived in the late sixteen hundreds, the classical age of Louis XIV, where she cut an unforgettable swath as a duellist, actress, lover of either sex, and male impersonator. Among her titles to fame she is said to have been the first contralto heard on the Paris stage and to have despatched by the skill of her sword three gallants in one evening, at convenient intervals after the curtain had rung down on her show. Though Gautier has drawn from her all he needed for his variations on love, he has toned down, not exaggerated, history. It suited him to use an authentic personage, partly because his contemporaries had recently read a "true" account of the seventeenth-century heroine, partly because he and his romanticist friends were fond of history. It was to them a measure of mankind's variety. Balzac and others had treated similar abnormalities and, like Shelley, they had found them in history, against which critics are powerless. The facts notwithstanding, the guardians of morality cried out that the family, the state, and religion were in danger.

This brings us to the preface, intentionally antedated May 1834. Its traditional brilliancy must probably be taken for granted by the American reader of 1943, for until a translator of the caliber of Scott Moncrieff gives us a rendering as fluid and electrical as Gautier's prose, it will always seem rather stiff and not a little obscure. The reason is that it is—or was—a fantasia on the eternal subject of morality in art, which Gautier had special cause for treating topically.

By 1834, the bourgeois monarchy of Louis Philippe had hardly begun to feel the ground solid under its feet. The four years since the revolution that brought it to power had witnessed a series of insurrections, scandals, epidemics, threats of European war, and violent public controversies about the regime. Rightly or wrongly, the government associated the "new literature" with revolt; official favors went to the old guard—the "safe and sane" in art and criticism. The romanticists—Hugo, Balzac, Dumas, Vigny, Berlioz, Stendhal, Delacroix—existed on sufferance and were subjected to daily insult and derision by the sober journals, the clerical party, and the academic clique. A high point in persecution was reached in 1833 when Hugo was denied access to the *Théâtre Français*, a virtual censorship instituted, and Gautier involved in a literary lawsuit. He had "resuscitated" the hitherto neglected poet François Villon and the journal that printed his article was accused of glorifying thieves and debauchees.

Gautier was not sufficiently well-known to take a leading role in the verbal and legal brawl that followed, but he kept his ears open and collected notes. The Preface to *Mademoiselle de Maupin* was the product of his rage and reporter's skill. Slowly and carefully—as was his wont in composing— he put together a sort of "address to the jury" in which every person, idea, platitude, illogicality, or vulgar motive that had come forth during the previous two years of literary strife is scarified. Scorn, irony, extravagant reductions to the absurd rush by in a torrent of words which must be heard rather than read. The inquisition is complete—even to the advertisements of rubber goods (then a novelty) which in the "enemy newspapers" surrounded the announcement of new books.

So much is made of detail that the argument suffers. Gautier's "principles" lack consistency, as one would expect in a fencing display aimed at diversely placed opponents. What still interests us today is to find the slogans of Art-above-Morality, Art for Art's Sake, and life for the distilling of choice pleasures, struck off at white heat by a young swashbuckler (he was not born, but conceived, at the Château d'Artagnan) in the year 1834. We had thought these ideas a product of the new wisdom of the nineties— not the eighteen-thirties—the work of Oscar Wilde, Pater, Huysmans and the Goncourt brothers, not of Gautier and his peers.

Perhaps there is a moral in this discovery, even if there is none in the work of art containing it. But I doubt whether it is the obvious moral that nothing is new under the sun. Rather it is that 1834 is but a recent yesterday. Make allowance for certain adjectives and a few local allusions, swallow the historical germ of the fiction, and you feel yourself reminded at every turn of the latest views on sex, unconscious memory, bourgeois stupidity, and artistic discipline. And there is the added piquancy of finding these set forth with all the freshness of vigorous and carefree youth—that of the author as well as that of the century.

PREFACE

BY

THE AUTHOR

ONE of the greatest burlesques of the glorious epoch at which we have the good fortune to live, is unquestionably the rehabilitation of virtue undertaken by all the journals of every hue, red, green, or tri-coloured.

Virtue is assuredly very respectable, and we have no wish to fail in respect to her, God forbid! good and worthy woman that she is! We think that her eyes are brilliant enough through their spectacles, that her leg is neatly gartered, that she takes her snuff in her gold box with all imaginable grace, that her little dog bows like a dancing-master. We think all this. We will even acknowledge that for her age, she is, in point of fact, not so much amiss, and that she carries her years as well as can be. She is a very agreeable grandmother—but she is a grand-mother. It seems to me natural, especially at twenty years of age, to prefer some little immorality, very spruce and coquettish, and very good-natured, with her hair a little uncurled, her skirt short rather than long, an enticing foot and eye, her cheek lightly kindled, laughter on her lips, and her heart in her hand. The most monstrously virtuous journalists cannot be of a different opinion, and if they say the con-trary, it is very probable that they do not think it. To think one thing and write another happens every day, especially in the case of virtu-ous people.

x

I remember the jokes launched before the Revolution (that of July, I mean) against the unfortunate and virginal Viscount Sosthène de la Rochefoucauld, who lengthened the skirts of the dancers at the Opera, and with his own patrician hands applied a modern plaster to the middle of all the statues. Viscount Sosthène de la Rochefoucauld has been far surpassed. Modesty has been greatly improved upon since that time, and we now indulge in refinements which he would not have dreamed of.

For my own part, not being accustomed to look at statues in certain places, I thought, like other people, that the vine leaf carved by the chisels of the superintendent of the fine arts was the most ridiculous thing in the world. It appears that I was wrong, and that the vine leaf is among the most meritorious of institutions.

I have been told—I refused to believe it, so singular did it seem to me—that people existed, who, standing before Michael Angelo's "Last Judgment," saw nothing in it but the episode of the licentious prelates, and veiled their faces, as they cried out against the abomination of the desolation!

Such people, too, know nothing of the romance of Rodrigo save the verse about the snake. If there is any nakedness in a picture or a book they go straight to it, like swine to the mire, without troubling themselves about the full-blown flowers, or the beautiful golden fruit which hang in every direction.

I confess that I am not virtuous enough for that. The impudent abigail Dorine may safely display her plump breast before me. I shall certainly not take out my pocket-handkerchief to cover the bosom that cannot be seen. I shall look at her breast as at her face, and, if it is white and well-formed, I shall take pleasure in it; but I shall not try whether Elmire's dress is soft, nor push her in a saintly way towards the edge of the table, as did the pitiful Tartuffe.

The great affectation of morality which reigns at present would be very laughable, if it were not very tiresome. Every feuilleton becomes a pulpit, every journalist a preacher, and nothing but the tonsure and the little collar is wanting. Rainy weather and homilies are the order of the day; we protect ourselves from the one by not going out except in a carriage, and from the other by reading Pantagruel again with bottle and pipe.

Good heavens! what exasperation! what fury! Who has bitten you? Who has stung you? What the deuce is the matter with you, that you make such an outcry, and what has this poor vice done to you, that he has so much of your ill-will, he who is such a good fellow and so easy-going, and who only asks to amuse himself without annoying other people, if that be possible? Do with vice as Serre did with the gendarme: embrace each other, and let all this come to an end. Believe me, it will do you good. Why, good heavens! worthy preachers, what would you do without vice? You would be reduced to beggary from to-morrow, if people became virtuous to-day.

The theatres would be closed this evening. What subjects would you have for your feuilletons? No more balls at the opera-house to fill your columns; no more novels to cut up; for balls, novels, and comedies are veritable pomps of Satan, if we are to believe our Holy Mother the Church. The actress would send away her lover, and could no longer pay you for your praise. People would cease to subscribe to your papers; they would read Saint Augustine, and go to church and tell their beads. That might perhaps be all very well, but most certainly you would gain nothing by it. If people were virtuous, what would you do with your tirades against the immorality of the century? You see that vice is good for something after all.

But it is the fashion now to be virtuous and Christian; people have taken a turn for it. They affect Saint Jerome as formerly they affected Don Juan; they are pale and macerated, they wear their hair apostle-wise, they walk with clasped hands and with eyes fixed on the ground; they have a Bible open on the mantelpiece, and a crucifix and some consecrated boxwood by the bed; they swear no longer, smoke little, and scarcely chew at all.

Then they are Christians, and speak of the sacredness of art, the lofty mission of the artist, the poetry of Catholicism, Monsieur de Lamennais, the painters of the Angelic school, the Council of Trent, progressive humanity, and a thousand other fine things. Some infuse a little Republicanism into their religion, and these are not the least curious. They couple Robespierre and Jesus Christ in the most jovial fashion, and, with a seriousness worthy of praise, amalgamate the Acts of the Apostles and the decrees of the *holy* Convention, to use the sacramental epithet; others, as a last ingredient, add a few Saint-Simonian ideas. Such persons are complete down to the ground; they cannot be excelled. It is not given to human absurdity to go further—*has ultra metas,* &c., they are the pillars of Hercules of burlesque.

Christianity is so much in vogue, owing to the prevalent hypocrisy, that neo-Christianity itself enjoys a certain favour. They say that it even possesses an adept, including Monsieur Drouineau.

An extremely curious variety of the moral journalist, properly so-called, is the female-family journalist.

He pushes chaste susceptibility as far as anthropophagy, or to within little of it.

His manner of procedure, though simple and easy at first sight, is none the less facetious and superlatively diverting, and I think that it is worth preserving for posterity—for our children's children, as the perukes of the so-called "grand century" would say.

First, in order to pose as a journalist of this species, a few little preparatory utensils are needful—such as two or three wedded wives, a few mothers, as many sisters as possible, a complete assortment of daughters, and female cousins without number. Next there is required a theatrical piece or a novel, a pen, ink, paper, and a printer. It might, perhaps, be as well to have an idea and several subscribers, but with a good deal of philosophy and shareholders' money, it is possible to do without them.

When you have all this you may set up as a moral journalist. The two following recipes, suitably varied, are sufficient for the editing:—

MODELS OF VIRTUOUS ARTICLES
ON A FIRST PERFORMANCE

"After the literature of blood, the literature of mire; after the Morgue and the galleys, the alcove and the lupanar, after rags stained by murder, rags stained by debauchery; after, &c. (according to necessity and the space available, this strain may be continued from six lines up to fifty or more)—this is justice. See whither forgetfulness of wholesome doctrine and romantic licentiousness lead us: the theatre has become a school for prostitution, into which it is impossible to venture, without trembling, in the company of a woman you respect. You come trusting to an illustrious name, and you are obliged to withdraw at the third act, with your young daughter, quite disconcerted and out of countenance. Your wife hides her blushes behind her fan; your sister, your female cousin, &c." (The titles of relationship may be diversified; it is enough if they are those of females.)

Note.—There is one who has pushed this morality so far as to say: "I will not go to see this drama with my mistress." That man I admire and love; I carry him in my heart, as Louis XVIII carried the whole of France in his bosom; for he has had the most triumphant, colossal, irregular, and luxorian idea that has entered the brain of man, out of all the numerous droll ideas conceived in this blessed nineteenth century.

The method of giving an account of a book is very expeditious, and within the reach of every capacity: —

"If you wish to read this book, shut yourself up carefully at home; do not let it lie about on the table. If your wife or your daughter were to open it, she would be lost. It is a dangerous book, and it counsels vice. It would, perhaps, have had a great success in the time of Crè-billon, in the *petites maisons,* at the delicate suppers of the duchesses; but now that morals are purified, that the hand of the people has overthrown the worm-eaten structure of the aristocracy, &c., &c., that—— that——that——there must be in every work an idea——a religious and moral idea, which——a view, lofty and profound, answering to the needs of humanity; for it is deplorable that young writers should sacrifice the most holy things to success, and employ an otherwise estimable talent in lewd pictures which would make a captain of dragoons blush. (The virginity of the captain of dragoons is the finest discovery, next to that of America, which has been made for a long time.) The novel we are reviewing recalls 'Thérèse Philosophe,' 'Félicia,' 'Compère Mathieu,' and the 'Contes de Grécourt.' " The virtuous journalist has immense erudition in the matter of filthy novels. It would be curious to know why.

It is frightful to think that, by order of the newspapers, there are many honest manufacturers who have only these two recipes to live on, they and the numerous family that they employ.

Apparently I am the most enormously immortal personage to be found in Europe or elsewhere, for I see nothing more licentious in the novels and comedies of to-day than in the novels and comedies of former times, and I cannot well understand why the ears of the gentlemen of the press should have suddenly become so Jansenically delicate.

I do not think that the most innocent journalist dare say that Pigault-Lebrun, the younger Crébillon, Louvet, Voisenon, Marmontel, and all other makers of romances and novels, do not surpass in immorality, since immorality there is, the most disordered and licentious productions of Messrs. So-and-so, whom I do not mention by name out of regard for their modesty.

It would need the most signal bad faith not to acknowledge it.

Let it not be objected that I have here adduced names little or imperfectly known. If I have not alluded to illustrious and monumental names, it is not that they do not support my assertion with their great authority.

Except for the difference in merit, the romances and tales of Voltaire are assuredly not much more susceptible of being given as prizes to little boarding-school Misses than are the immoral tales of our friend the lycanthropist, or even the moral tales of the mealy-mouthed Marmontel.

What do we see in the comedies of the great Molière? The holy institution of marriage (to adopt the style of catechism and journalist) mocked and turned into ridicule in every scene.

The husband is old, ugly, and eccentric; he wears his wig awry, his coat has gone out of fashion, he has a bill-headed cane, his nose is daubed with snuff, his legs are short, and his abdomen is as big as a budget. He sputters, speaks only folly, and acts suitably to his words; he sees nothing and hears nothing; his wife is kissed to his very beard, and he does not know what is going on. This lasts until he has been well and duly proved a cuckold in his own eyes and in the eyes of the whole highly edified house, which applauds enthusiastically.

Those who applaud the most are those who are married the most.

Marriage in Molière is called George Dandin or Sganarelle.

Adultery, Damis, or Clitandre; there is no name sweet and charming enough for it.

The adulterer is always young, handsome, well-made, and a marquis, at the least. He enters humming the latest couranto in an aside; he makes one or two steps on the stage with the most deliberate and triumphant air in the world; he scratches his ear with the rosy nail of his coquettishly opened little finger; he combs his beautiful fair hair with his tortoise-shell comb, and adjusts the legs of his trousers, which are of great size. His doublet and hose are hidden beneath aigulets and bows of ribbon, his neck-band is by the best maker; his gloves smell better than benjamin and civet; his plumes have cost a louis the spray.

How fiery his eye and how blooming his cheek! how smiling his mouth! how white his teeth! how soft and well-washed his hands!

He speaks, and we have nothing but madrigals and perfumed gallantries delivered in a fine affected style, and with the best air; he has read romances and knows poetry; he is valiant and ready to draw; he scatters gold with open hand. Thus Angélique, Agnès, and Isabelle, can scarcely restrain themselves from leaping upon his neck, well-bred and great ladies though they be, and the husband is duly deceived in the fifth act, fortunate if he has not been so from the first.

This is the manner in which marriage is treated by Molière, one of the loftiest and weightest geniuses that have ever lived. Do people think that there is anything stronger in the speeches in "Indiana" or "Valentine"?

Paternity is still less respected, if that be possible. Look at Orgon, look at Géronte, look at all of them.

How they are robbed by their sons and beaten by their valets! How they are exposed, without pity for their age, their avarice, and their obstinacy, and their imbecility! What jestings! what mystifications! How they are shouldered out of life, these poor old men who are slow about dying, and will on no account give up their money! How the eternity of parents is spoken of! What speeches against heredity, and how much more convincing they are than all the Saint-Simonian declamations!

A father is an ogre, an Argus, a gaoler, a tyrant, a something which at the very most is only good for delaying a marriage, during three acts, until the final denouement. A father is as ridiculous as the most ridiculous husband. A son is never ridiculous in Molière, for Molière, like all authors of all possible times, paid court to the youthful generation at the expense of the old.

And the Scapins, with their cloaks striped in Neapolitan fashion, their cap on their ear, and their feather sweeping the flies—are they not very pious people, very chaste, and deserving of canonisation? The galleys are full of worthy people, who have not done a quarter of what they do. The cheatings of Trialph are petty in comparison with theirs. And the Lisettes and Martons, what wantons, ye gods, are they! The courtesans of the streets are far from being so sharp as they are, so ready to give a smutty reply. How well they understand how to deliver a note! how well they keep watch during a rendezvous! They are, on my word, precious girls, and give excellent advice.

'Tis a charming society that moves and walks through these comedies and imbroglios. Duped guardians, cuckolded husbands, libertine attendants, cunning valets, young ladies madly in love, debauched sons, adulterous wives—are they not all quite equal to the melancholy young beaux, and the poor, weak, oppressed, and impassioned young women of the dramas and novels by our fashionable authors?

And withal the denouements, minus the final dagger-blow and minus the necessary cup of poison, are as happy as those in fairy tales, and everybody, even the husband himself, is always as pleased as possible. In Molière virtue is always disgraced and thrashed; it wears the horns, and offers its back to Mascarille; morality may just, perhaps, put in a single appearance at the end of the piece, under the somewhat homely personification of police-officer Loyal.

In all that we have just said we have had no intention of chipping the corners of Molière's pedestal; we are not foolish enough to try to shake this bronze colossus with our puny arms; we simply wished to demonstrate to the pious journalists, who are shocked by recent romantic works, that the ancient classics, which every day they recommend us to read and imitate, far surpass them in wantonness and immorality.

With Molière we might easily join both Marivaux and La Fontaine, those two very opposite expressions of the French character, and Regnier, and Rabelais, and Marot, and many others. But our intention is not to construct here, *à propos* of morality, a course of literature for the use of the virgins of the feuilleton.

It seems to me that they should not make so much ado about so little. We are, happily, no longer in the time of the fair Eve, and we cannot in conscience be as primitive and patriarchal as they were in the Ark. We are not little girls preparing for their first communion, and when we play at Crambo we do not answer "cream-tart." Our artlessness is tolerably knowing, and our virginity has been about town for a long time. These are among the things which we cannot have twice, and do what we may, we cannot recover them; for there is nothing in the world that goes more quickly than a virginity which departs and an illusion which takes to flight.

Perhaps after all there is no great harm done, and the knowledge of everything is preferable to the ignorance of everything. It is a question that I leave to be discussed by those who are more learned than I. The world has, at all events, passed the age when we can counterfeit modesty and bashfulness, and I think it too old a grey-beard to be able to play the child and virgin without making itself ridiculous.

Since her marriage with civilisation, society has lost the right of being ingenuous and bashful. There are certain blushings which are still admissible at bed-time on the part of the bride, and which can be of no further service on the morrow; for the young woman perhaps remembers the young girl no longer, or, if she does, it is a very indecent thing, and seriously compromises her husband's reputation.

When I chance to read one of the fine sermons which have taken the place of literary criticism in the public prints, I am sometimes seized with great remorse and apprehension, I who have on my conscience sundry small jokes somewhat too highly spiced, such as a young man with life and spirit may have to reproach himself with.

Besides these Bossuets of the Café de Paris, these Bourdaloues of the balcony at the Opera, these Catos at so much a line, who scold the century in such fine fashion, I, in fact, look upon myself as the most terrible rascal that has ever polluted the face of the earth, and yet, heaven knows, the nomenclature of my sins, capital as well as venial, with the margins and spaces strictly observed, would scarcely, in the hands of the most skilful bookseller, make up one or two octavo volumes a day, which is little enough for one who makes no pretension of going to paradise in the next world, and of winning the Monthyon prize or of carrying off the rose in this.

Then, when I think that I have met with rather a large number of these dragons of virtue beneath the table, and even elsewhere, I get a better opinion of myself, and estimate that, with all the faults that I may have, they have another, which is, in my eyes, the very greatest and worst of all, and that is hypocrisy.

If we looked carefully, we might perhaps find another little vice to add, but it is one so hideous, that in truth I scarcely dare name it. Come close, and I will whisper its name into your ear: it is envy.

Envy, and nothing else.

It is this that goes creeping and winding through all these paternal homilies. However careful it may be to conceal itself, it may from time to time be seen gleaming above metaphors and figures of rhetoric with its little flat viper's head; it may be surprised licking its venom-blued lips with its forked tongue; it may be heard hissing in the shade of an insidious epithet.

I know perfectly well that it is insufferable conceit to pretend that you are envied, and that it is almost as nauseous as a coxcomb vaunting his good fortune. I am not so boastful as to believe that I am hated and envied; that is a happiness which is not given to everybody, and it will probably be long before I have it. Thus I shall speak freely and unreservedly, as one quite disinterested in the matter.

One thing which is certain and easy of demonstration to those who might doubt its existence, is the natural antipathy of the critic to the poet, of him who makes nothing to him who makes something, of the drone to the bee, of the gelding to the stallion.

You do not become a critic until it has been completely established to your own satisfaction that you cannot be a poet. Before descending to the melancholy office of taking care of the cloaks, and noting the strokes like a billiard-marker or a servant at the tennis-court, you long courted the Muse and sought to win her virginity; but you had not sufficient vigour to do so, your breath failed you, and you fell back pale and worn to the foot of the holy mountain..

I can understand this hatred. It is painful to see another sit down at a banquet to which you have not been invited, and sleep with a woman who would have nothing to say to you. With all my heart, I pity the poor eunuch who is obliged to be present at the diversions of the Grand Seignior.

He is admitted into the most sacred depths of the Oda; he conducts the Sultanas to the bath; he sees their beautiful bodies glistening beneath the silver water of the great reservoirs, streaming with pearls and smoother than agates; the most hidden beauties are unveiled to him. His presence is no restraint—he is a eunuch. The Sultan caresses his favourite before him, and kisses her on her pomegranate lips. His position is, in truth, a very false one, and he must feel greatly embarrassed.

It is the same with the critic who sees the poet walking in the garden of poesy with his nine fair odalisques, and disporting idly in the shade of large green laurels. It is difficult for him not to pick up the stones on the highway to cast them at him, and, if he be skilful enough to do so, wound him behind his own wall.

The critic who has produced nothing is a coward, like an Abbé who courts the wife of a layman. The latter can neither retaliate nor fight with him.

I think that the history of the different ways of depreciating any work for a month past would be at least as curious as that of Teglath-Phalasar or Gemmagog who invented pointed shoes.

There are materials enough for fifteen or sixteen folios, but we will take pity on the reader and confine ourselves to a few lines—a benefit for which we expect more than eternal gratitude. At a very remote epoch, which is lost in the mist of ages, very nearly three weeks ago, the romance of the middle ages flourished principally in Paris and the suburbs. The coat of arms was held in great honour; head-dresses, *à la* Hennin, were not despised, parti-coloured trousers were esteemed; the dagger was beyond all price; the pointed shoe was worshipped like a fetich. There was nothing but ogives, turrets, little columns, coloured glass, cathedrals, and strong castles; there was nothing but damozels and squires, pages and varlets, vagrants and veterans, gallant knights and fierce castellans; all being things which were certainly more innocent than innocent pastimes, and which did nobody any harm.

The critic had not waited for the second romance in order to begin his work of depreciation. No sooner had the first appeared than he had wrapped himself up in his cloth of camel's hair, poured a bushel of ashes on his head, and then, assuming that loud and doleful tone of his, begun to cry out: —

"Still the middle ages, always the middle ages! who will deliver me from the middle ages, from these middle ages that are not the middle ages? Middle ages of cardboard and baked clay, which have nothing of the middle ages but their name. O the iron barons in their iron armour, with their iron hearts in their iron breasts! O the cathedrals with their ever full-blown roses, and their flowered glass, their lace-work of granite, their open trefoils, their gables cut like a saw, their stone chasubles embroidered like a bride's veil, their tapers, their chants, their glittering priests, their kneeling people, their droning organs, and their angels hovering and flapping their wings beneath the vaulted roofs! How have they spoiled my middle ages, my middle ages so delicate and bright! How have they hidden them beneath a coating of coarse badigeon! What loud over-colouring! Ah! ignorant daubers, who think that you have produced colour by laying red upon blue, white upon black, and green upon yellow; you have seen nothing of the middle ages but their shell. You have not divined the soul of the middle ages, no blood circulates beneath the skin with which you clothe your phantoms, there is no heart in your corselets of steel, there are no legs in your trousers of wool, there is neither body nor breast

XXI

behind your emblazoned skirts. They are garments having human form, and that is all. Then away with the middle ages, as they have been made by the fabricators (the word is out! the fabricators!) The middle ages are unsuitable now; we want something else."

And the public, seeing the journalists barking against the middle ages, was seized with a great passion for these poor middle ages, which they pretended that they had slain at a blow. The middle ages invaded everything, assisted by the obstruction of the papers; dramas, melodramas, romances, novels, poems, there were even vaudevilles of the middle ages, and Momus repeated feudal jollities.

By the side of the romance of the middle ages sprouted the carrion romance, a very agreeable kind, largely consumed by nervous women of fashion and *blasé* cooks.

The journalists very soon scented it out, as crows do the quarry, and with the beaks of their pens they dismembered and wickedly put to death this poor species of romance, which only sought to prosper and putrefy peaceably on the greasy shelves of circulating libraries. What did they not say? What did they not write? Literature of the Morgue or the galleys, nightmare of the hangman, hallucination of drunken butchers and hot-fevered convict-keepers! They benignly gave us to understand that the authors were assassins and vampires, that they had contracted the vicious habit of killing their fathers and mothers, that they drank blood in skulls, used tibias instead of forks, and cut their bread with a guillotine.

And yet, seeing that they had often breakfasted with them, no one knew better than they did that the authors of these charming butcheries were honourable men of family, gentle, and mixing in good society, white gloved, fashionably short-sighted, more ready to feed on beef-steaks than on human cutlets, and more accustomed to drink Bordeaux than the blood of young girls or new-born infants. And from having seen and touched their manuscripts, they knew perfectly well that they were written with most virtuous ink upon English paper, and not with blood from the guillotine upon the skin of a Christian flayed alive.

But do or say what they might, the age was disposed for carrion, and the charnel-house pleased it better than the boudoir; the reader could only be captured by a hook baited with a little corpse beginning to turn blue. A very conceivable thing; put a rose at the end of your line, and spiders will have time enough to spin their webs in the bend of your arm—you will not take the smallest fry; but fasten on a worm or a bit of old cheese, and carp, barbel, perch, and eels will leap three feet out of the water to snap it. Men are not so different from fish as people seem generally to believe.

You would have thought that the journalists had become Quakers, Brahmins, Pythagoreans, or bulls, they had suddenly taken such a horror to redness and blood. Never had they been seen so melting, so emollient; it was like cream and whey. They admitted two colours only, sky-blue and apple-green. Pink was only tolerated, and they would have led the public, had it allowed them, to feed on spinach on the banks of the Lignon side by side with the sheep of Amaryllis. They had changed their black dress-coat for the turtledove-coloured jacket of Celadon or Silvander, and surrounded their goose-quills with tufts of roses and favours after the fashion of the pastoral crook. They allowed their hair to flow down like a child's, and they had manufactured virginities, according to Marian Delorme's recipe, in which they had succeeded as well as she did.

They applied to literature the article of the Decalogue: "Thou shalt not kill."

The smallest dramatic murder was no longer permitted, and the fifth act had become impossible.

They deemed the dagger extravagant, poison monstrous, and the axe without excuse. They would have had dramatic heroes live to the age of Melchisedec, although it has been recognised from time immemorial that the end of all tragedy is to kill, in the last scene, a poor devil of a great man who cannot help himself, just as the end of all comedy is to unite matrimonially two fools of lovers each about sixty years of age.

It was about this time that I threw into the fire (after taking duplicates, as is always done) two superb and magnificent dramas of the middle ages, one in verse and the other in prose, the heroes of which were quartered and boiled in the middle of the stage—an incident which would have been very jovial and somewhat unprecedented.

In order to conform to their ideas, I have since composed an ancient tragedy, in five acts, called "Heliogabalus," the hero of which throws himself into the water-closet, an extremely novel situation which has the advantage of introducing a decoration not as yet seen on the stage. I have also written a modern drama far superior to "Antony," "Arthur, or the Fatal Man," in which the providential idea occurs in the shape of a Strasburg *pâté de foie gras*, which the hero eats to the last crumb after effecting several rapes, and this joined to his remorse gives him an abominable attack of indigestion, of which he dies. A moral termination, if ever there was one, proving that *God is just*, and that vice is always punished and virtue rewarded.

As to the monstrous kind, you know how they have treated it, how they have settled Hans of Iceland, the man-eater; Habibrah, the Obi; Quasimodo, the bell-ringer; and Triboulet, who was only a hunchback; —all that strangely swarming family—all those gigantic creatures that my dear neighbour makes crawl and skip through the virgin forests and cathedrals of his romances. Neither grand features like Michael Angelo's, nor curiosities worthy of Callot, nor effects of light and shade after the manner of Goya—nothing could find favour in their eyes; they sent him back to his odes when he composed romances, and to his romances when he composed dramas—tactics common with journalists, who always prefer what a man has done to what he does. Happy the man, nevertheless, who is recognised by the feuilleton writers as superior in all his works, excepting of course that one with which they are dealing, and who would only have to write a theological treatise or a cookery book to have his stage deemed admirable!

As for the romance of the heart, the ardent and impassioned romance whose father is the German Werther, and whose mother is the French Manon Lescaut, we have alluded, at the beginning of this preface, to the moral scurf which is desperately attached to it under pretence of religion and good morals. Critical lice are like bodily lice, which desert corpses to seek the living. From the corpse of the romance of the middle ages the critics have passed to the body of this other, whose skin is hard and healthy and might well injure their teeth.

We think, in spite of all the respect that we have for the modern apostles, that the authors of the so-called immoral novels, without being married to the same extent as the virtuous journalists, have commonly enough a mother, and that many of them have sisters, and are abundantly provided with female relations; but their mothers and sisters do not read novels, even immoral ones; they sew, embroider, and busy themselves with household matters. Their stockings, as Monsieur Planard would say, are perfectly white; you may look at their legs, they are not *blue;* and Chrysale, good man, who had such a hatred for learned women, might hold them up as an example to the learned Philaminte.

As to the *spouses* of these gentlemen, since they have so much of them, I certainly think that, however virginal their husbands may be, there are sundry things which they ought to know. It may be indeed that they have been taught nothing. In that case, I understand the anxiety to keep them in this precious and blessed state of ignorance. God is great, and Mahomet is His prophet! Women are inquisitive; Heaven and morality grant that they may satisfy their curiosity in a more legitimate fashion than did their grandmother Eve, and ask no questions of the serpent!

As for their daughters, if they have been to a boarding-school, I do not see what these books could teach them.

It is as absurd to say that a man is a drunkard because he describes an orgie, or a debauchee because he recounts a debauch, as to pretend that a man is virtuous because he has written a moral book; every day we see the contrary. It is the character who speaks and not the author; the fact that his hero is an atheist does not make him an atheist; his brigands act and speak like brigands, but he is not there-fore a brigand himself. At that rate it would be necessary to guillotine Shakespeare, Corneille, and all the tragic writers; they have commit-ted more murders than Mandrin and Cartouche. This has, neverthe-less, not been done, and I think that it will be long before it is done, however virtuous and moral criticism may come to be. It is one of the manias of these narrow-brained scribblers to substitute always the author for the work and have recourse to personalities, in order to give some poor scandalous interest to their wretched rhapsodies, which they are quite aware nobody would read if they contained only their own individual opinions.

We find it hard to understand the purport of all this bawling, the good of all this temper and despair, and who it is that impels the miniature Geoffreys to constitute themselves the Don Quixotes of morality, and, like true literary policemen, to seize and cudgel, in the name of virtue, every idea which makes its appearance in a book with its mobcap awry or its skirt tucked up a little too high. It is very singular.

Say what they will, the age is an immoral one (if this word signifies anything, of which we have strong doubts), and we wish for no other proof than the quantity of immoral books it produces and the success that attends them. Books follow morals, and not morals books. The Regency made Crébillon, and not Crébillon the Regency. Boucher's little shepherdesses had their faces painted and their bosoms bare, because the little marchionesses had the same. Pictures are made according to models, and not models according to pictures. Some one has said somewhere that literature and the arts influence morals. Whoever he was, he was undoubtedly a great fool. It was like saying green peas make the spring grow, whereas green peas grow because it is spring, and cherries because it is summer. Trees bear fruits; it is certainly not the fruits that bear the trees, and this law is eternal and invariable in its variety; the centuries follow one another, and each bears its own fruit, which is not that of the preceding century; books are the fruits of morals.

By the side of the moral journalists, under this rain of homilies as under summer rain in some park, there has sprung up between the planks of the Saint-Simonian stage a theory of little mushrooms, of a novel and somewhat curious species, whose natural history we are about to give.

These are the utilitarian critics. Poor fellows! Their noses are too short to admit of their wearing spectacles, and yet they cannot see the length of their noses.

XXVI

If an author threw a volume of romance or poetry on their desk, these gentlemen would turn round carelessly in their easy chair, poise it on its hinder legs, and balancing themselves with a capable air, say softly:—

"What purpose does this book serve? How can it be applied for the moralisation and well-being of the poorest and most numerous class? What! not a word of the needs of society, nothing about civilisation and progress? How can a man, instead of making the great synthesis of humanity, and pursuing the regenerating and providential idea through the events of history, how can he write novels and poems which lead to nothing, and do not advance our generation on the path of the future? How can he busy himself with form, and style, and rhyme in the presence of such grave interests? What are style, and rhyme, and form to us? They are of no consequence (poor foxes! they are too sour). Society is suffering, it is a prey to great internal anguish (translate—no one will subscribe to utilitarian journals). It is for the poet to seek the cause of his uneasiness and to cure it. He will find the means of doing so by sympathising from his heart and soul with humanity—(philanthropic poets! they would be something uncommon and charming). This poet we await, and on him we call with all our vows. When he appears, his will be the acclamations of the crowd, his the palm, his the crown, his the Prytaneum."

Well and good! But as we wish our reader to remain awake until the end of this blissful preface, we shall not continue this very faithful imitation of the utilitarian style, which is, in its nature, tolerably soporific, and might, with advantage, take the place of laudanum, and Academic discourses.

No, fools, no, goitrous cretins that you are, a book does not make gelatine soup; a novel is not a pair of seamless boots; a sonnet, a syringe with a continuous jet; or a drama, a railway—all things which are essentially civilising and adapted to advance humanity on its path of progress.

By the guts of all the popes past, present, and future, no, and two hundred thousand times no!

We cannot make a cotton cap out of a metonymy, or put on a comparison like a slipper; we cannot use an antithesis as an umbrella, and we cannot, unfortunately, lay a medley of rhymes on our body after the fashion of a waistcoat. I have an intimate conviction that an ode is too light a garment for winter, and that we should not be better clad in strophe, antistrophe, and epode than was the cynic's wife who contented herself with merely her virtue as chemise, and went about as naked as one's hand, so history relates.

However, the celebrated Monsieur de La Calprenède had once a coat, and when asked of what material it was made, he replied, "Of Silvandre." *Silvandre* was the name of a piece which he had just brought out with success.

Such arguments make one elevate one's shoulders above the head, and higher than the Duke of Gloucester's.

People who pretend to be economists, and who wish to reconstruct society from top to bottom, seriously advance similar nonsense.

A novel has two uses—one material and the other spiritual—if we may employ such an expression in reference to a novel. Its material use means first of all some thousands of francs which find their way into the author's pocket, and ballast him in such a fashion that neither devil nor wind can carry him off; to the bookseller, it means a fine thoroughbred horse, pawing and prancing with its cabriolet of ebony and steel, as Figaro says; to the papermaker, another mill beside some stream or other, and often the means of spoiling a fine site; to the printers, some tons of logwood for the weekly staining of their throats; to the circulating library, some piles of pence covered with very proletarian verdigris, and a quantity of fat which, if it were properly collected and utilised, would render whale-fishing superfluous. Its spiritual use is that when reading novels we sleep, and do not read useful, virtuous, and progressive journals, or other similarly indigestible and stupefying drugs.

Let any one say after this that novels do not contribute to civilisation. I say nothing of tobacco-sellers, grocers, and dealers in fried potatoes, who have a very great interest in this branch of literature, the paper employed in it being commonly of a superior quality to that of newspapers.

XXVIII

In truth, it is enough to make one burst with laughing to hear the dissertations of these Republican or Saint-Simonian utilitarian gentlemen. I should, first of all, very much like to know the precise meaning of this great lanky substantive with which the void in their columns is daily truffled, and which serves them as a Shibboleth and sacramental term—utility. What is this word, and to what is it applicable?

There are two sorts of utility, and the meaning of the vocable is always a relative one. What is useful for one is not useful for another. You are a cobbler, I am a poet. It is useful to me to have my first verse rhyme with my second. A rhyming dictionary is of great utility to me; you do not want it to cobble an old pair of boots, and it is only right to say that a shoe-knife would not be of great service to me in making an ode. To this you will object that a cobbler is far above a poet, and that people can do without the one better than without the other. Without affecting to disparage the illustrious profession of cobbler, which I honour equally with that of constitutional monarch, I humbly confess that I would rather have my shoe unstitched than my verse badly rhymed, and that I should be more willing to go without boots than without poems. Scarcely ever going out and walking more skilfully with my head than with my feet, I wear out fewer shoes than a virtuous Republican, who is always hastening from one minister to another in the hope of having some place flung to him.

I know that there are some who prefer mills to churches, and bread for the body to that for the soul. To such I have nothing to say. They deserve to be economists in this world and also in the next.

Is there anything absolutely useful on this earth and in this life of ours? To begin with, it is not very useful that we are on the earth and alive. I defy the most learned of the band to tell us of what use we are, unless it be to not subscribe to the "Constitutionnel," nor any other species of journal whatsoever.

Next, the utility of our existence being admitted *a priori*, what are the things really useful for supporting it? Some soup and a piece of meat twice a day is all that is necessary to fill the stomach in the strict acceptation of the word. Man who finds a coffin six feet long by two wide more than sufficient after his death does not need much more room during his life. A hollow cube measuring seven or eight feet every way, with a hole to breathe through, a single cell in the hive, nothing more is wanted to lodge him and keep the rain off his back. A blanket properly rolled around his body will protect him as well and better against the cold than the most elegant and best cut dress coat by Staub.

With this he will be able, literally, to subsist. It is truly said that it is possible to live on a shilling a day. But to prevent one's-self from dying is not living; and I do not see in what respect a town organised after the utilitarian fashion would be more agreeable to dwell in than the cemetery of Père-la-Chaise.

Nothing that is beautiful is indispensable to life. You might suppress flowers, and the world would not suffer materially; yet who would wish that there were no more flowers? I would rather give up potatoes than roses, and I think that there is none but an utilitarian in the world capable of pulling up a bed of tulips in order to plant cabbages therein.

What is the use of women's beauty? Provided that a woman be medically well formed, and in condition to bear children, she will always be good enough for economists.

What is the good of music? of painting? Who would be foolish enough to prefer Mozart to Monsieur Carrell, and Michael Angelo to the inventor of white mustard?

There is nothing truly beautiful but that which can never be of any use whatsoever; everything useful is ugly, for it is the expression of some need, and man's needs are ignoble and disgusting like his own poor and infirm nature. The most useful place in a house is the water-closet.

For my own part, may it please these gentlemen, I am one of those to whom superfluity is a necessity—and I like things and persons in an inverse ratio to the services that they render me. I prefer a Chinese vase, strewn with dragons and mandarins, and of no use to me whatever, to a certain utensil which is of service to me, and of my talents the one I esteem the most is my incapacity for guessing logogriphs and charades. I would most joyfully renounce my rights as a Frenchman and a citizen to see an authentic picture by Raphaël, or a beautiful woman naked—Princess Borghese, for instance, when she posed for Canova, or Julia Grisi entering her bath. I would willingly consent, so far as I am concerned, to the return of the anthropophagous Charles X, if he brought me back a hamper of Tokay or Johannisberger from his Bohemian castle, and I would deem the electoral laws sufficiently wide, if some streets were more so and some other things less. Although I am no dilettante, I would rather have the noise of fiddles and tambourines than that of the bell of the President of the Chamber. I would sell my breeches for a ring, and my bread for preserves. It appears to me that the most fitting occupation for a civilised man is to do nothing, or to smoke analytically his pipe or cigar. I also highly esteem those who play skittles and those who make good verses. You see that the utilitarian principles are far from being mine, and that I shall never be a contributor to a virtuous journal, unless, of course, I become converted, which would be rather comical.

Instead of offering a Monthyon prize as the reward of virtue, I would rather, like that great but misunderstood philosopher Sardanapalus, give a large premium to any one inventing a new pleasure; for enjoyment appears to me to be the end of life and the only useful thing in the world. God has willed it so, He who has made women, perfumes, light, beautiful flowers, good wines, frisky horses, greyhound-bitches, and Angora cats; He who did not say to His angels, "Have virtue," but "Have love," and who has given us a mouth more sensitive than the rest of our skin to kiss women, eyes raised on high to see the light, a subtle power of smell to breathe the soul of flowers, sinewy thighs to press the sides of stallions, and to fly as quick as thought without railway or steam-boiler, delicate hands to stroke the long head of a greyhound, the velvety back of a cat, and the smooth shoulders of a creature of easy virtue, and who finally has granted to us alone the triple and glorious privilege of drinking when without thirst, of striking a light, and of making love at all seasons, a privilege which distinguishes us from brutes far more than the custom of reading papers and fabricating charters.

Good heavens! what a foolish thing is this pretended perfectibility of the human race which is continually being dinned into our ears! One would think, in truth, that man is a machine susceptible of improvements, and that some wheel-work in better gear or a counterpoise more suitably placed would make him work in a more convenient and easy fashion. When they succeed in giving man a double stomach so that he may ruminate like an ox, or eyes at the other side of his head that, like Janus, he may see those who put out their tongues at him behind, and contemplate his *indignity* in a less inconvenient position than that of the Athenian Venus Callipyge, when they plant wings upon his shoulder-blades that he may not be obliged to pay three-pence for an omnibus, and create a new organ for him, well and good: the word *perfectibility* will then begin to have some meaning.

After all these fine improvements, what has been done that was not done as well and better before the flood?

Have people succeeded in drinking more than they drank in the times of ignorance and barbarity (old style)? Alexander, the doubtful friend of the handsome Hephæstion, did not drink so badly, although in his time there was no "Journal of Useful Knowledge," and I do not know of any utilitarian who would be capable of draining the great drinking vessel that he called the cup of Hercules, without becoming oïnopic and more swelled out than the younger Lepeintro or a hippopotamus.

Marshal de Bassompiere, who emptied his great funnel-shaped boot to the health of the thirteen cantons, appears to me singularly worthy in his way and difficult to improve upon.

What economist will enlarge our stomachs so as to contain as many beef-steaks as did the late Milo of Crotona who ate an ox? The bill of fare of the Café Anglais, of Véfour's, or of any other culinary celebrity that you will, appears to me very meagre and œcumenical, compared with the bill of fare of Trimalcio's dinner. At what table do they now serve up a sow and her twelve young ones in a single dish? Who has eaten sea-eels and lampreys fattened on man? Do you really believe that Brillat-Savarin has improved on Apicius?

Could that great tripe-man of a Vitellius fill his famous Minerva's shield at Chevet's, with brains of pheasants and peacocks, tongues of flamingoes, and livers of scarus? Your oysters from the Rocher de Cancale are truly rarities beside the Lucrine oysters, which had a sea made expressly for them. The little suburban villas of the Marquises of the Regency are wretched country-boxes in comparison with the villas of the Roman patricians at Baiæ, Capræe, and Tibur. Should not the Cyclopean magnificence of those great voluptuaries who built eternal monuments for the pleasures of a day make us fall flat on the ground before the genius of the ancients, and strike out for ever from our dictionaries the word *perfectibility?*

Have they invented a single capital sin the more? Unfortunately, there are but seven as before, a very moderate number of falls for the upright man per day. I do not even think that after a century of progress, at the rate we are going, any lover will be able to repeat the thirteenth labour of Hercules. Can a man be agreeable to his divinity even once oftener than in the time of Solomon? Many very illustrious, learned men, and very respectable ladies, hold quite the contrary opinion, and maintain that amiability is decreasing. Well, then, what is the use of speaking of progress? I am quite aware that you will tell me that we have an Upper and a Lower Chamber, that we hope that everybody will soon be an elector, and the number of representatives doubled or tripled. Do you think that there are not enough mistakes in French made as it is on the national tribune, and that there are too few for the evil work they have to plot? I can scarcely understand the utility which consists in penning two or three hundred provincials in a wooden hut, with a ceiling painted by Monsieur Fragonard, to have them jumble and blunder any number of petty laws which are either atrocious or absurd. What matters it whether it be a sabre, an aspergill, or an umbrella that governs you? It is always a stick, and I am astonished that men of progress should dispute about the choice of cudgel to tickle their shoulders, when it would be much more progressive and less expensive to break it and throw the pieces to all the devils.

The only one among you who has common-sense is a madman, a great genius, an idiot, a divine poet far above Lamartine, Hugo, and Byron; he is Charles Fourrier, the phalansterian, who is all this in himself alone: he alone has displayed logic with boldness enough to follow out its consequences to the end. He affirms without hesitation that men will soon have a tail fifteen feet long, with an eye at the extremity. This would certainly be progress, and would admit of our doing a thousand fine things previously impossible, such as killing elephants without striking a blow, swinging on trees without swings as conveniently as the best conditioned ape, doing without umbrella or parasol by spreading the tail over our heads like the squirrels, who get on very agreeably without gamps, together with other prerogatives which it would take too long to enumerate. Many phalansterians even pretend that they already have a small one, which is ready to become larger, if God but grant them life.

Charles Fourrier has invented as many species of animals as Georges Cuvier the great naturalist. He has invented horses three times as big as elephants, dogs as large as tigers, fishes capable of satisfying more people than Jesus Christ's three fishes, which the incredulous Voltairians think were April ones, and I a magnificent parable. He has built towns, beside which Rome, Babylon, and Tyre were but mole-hills; he has piled Babels one upon the other, and raised spires to the clouds more infinite than any of those in John Martin's engravings; he has conceived I know not how many orders of architecture and new condiments; he has designed a theatre which would appear grand even to the Romans of the Empire, and drawn up a bill of fare which Lucius or Nomentanus might perhaps have found sufficient for a dinner of friends; he promises to create new pleasures, and to develop our organs and senses; he is to render women more beautiful and voluptuous, and men more robust and vigorous; he guarantees you against children, and proposes to reduce the number of the world's inhabitants, so that everybody may be at his ease, which is more reasonable than to urge the proletarians to produce others only to cannonade them afterwards in the streets when they multiply overmuch, and to send them bullets instead of bread.

Progress is possible only in this way. All the rest is bitter mockery, witless buffoonery that is not even good enough to dupe gaping idiots.

The phalanstery is truly an improvement on the Abbey of Thélème, and it definitively relegates the terrestrial paradise to the number of

completely superannuated and old-fashioned things. The "Thousand and One Nights," and the "Tales of Madame d'Aulnoy," can alone wrestle successfully with the phalanstery. What fertility! What invention! There is sufficient in it to supply with the marvellous three thousand cart loads of romantic or classic poems; and our versifiers, Academicians or not, are very sorry *trouvères* if we compare them with Monsieur Charles Fourrier, the inventor of impassioned attractions. The idea of making use of impulses, which up to the present people have sought to repress, is most assuredly a lofty and powerful one.

You say that we are progressing! If a volcano were to open its jaws to-morrow at Montmartre, and make a winding sheet of ashes and a tomb of lava for Paris, as Vesuvius did formerly for Stabia, Pompeii, Herculaneum, and if after some thousands of years the antiquaries of the time were to dig and exhume the corpse of the dead town, what monument pray would still be standing to witness to the splendour of the great buried building, the Gothic Notre-Dame. They would obtain a fine idea of our arts by clearing out the Tuileries as touched up by Monsieur Fontaine! The statues of the Pont Louis XV would have a fine effect when transferred to the museums of the day! And if there were not the pictures of the ancient schools, and the statues of antiquity, or of the Renaissance heaped up in that long, shapeless interior, the gallery of the Louvre; if there were not the ceiling by Ingres to prevent a belief that Paris had been but an encampment of barbarians, a village of Welches or Topinamboux, the things obtained from the excavations would be of a very curious nature. Sabres belonging to the National Guard, firemen's helmets, and coins struck with an unformed stamp, that is what they would find instead of the beautiful, curiously-chased armour which the middle ages have left beneath their towers and ruined tombs, and the medals which fill the Etruscan vases and pave the foundations of all the Roman structures. As to our wretched furniture of veneered wood, all those miserable boxes, so bare, so ugly, so insignificant, which are called chests of drawers and writing-tables, and all our formless and fragile utensils, I hope that time would have sufficient pity for them to destroy them without leaving a trace behind.

Once upon a time we took a fancy to build a grand and magnificent monument. We were first of all obliged to borrow the plan from the ancient Romans; and even before it was finished our Pantheon gave way on its legs, like a rickety child, and stumbled, like a pensioner dead drunk, so that it was necessary to furnish it with crutches of stone, without which it would have fallen pitifully at full length before the whole world, and provided the nations with food for laughter for more than a hundred years. We wished to set up an obelisk in one of our squares; we had to go and filch it from Luxor, and we were two years bringing it home. Old Egypt bordered her highways with obelisks, as we do ours with poplar trees; she carried bunches of them under her arms as a kitchen-gardener carries his bundles of asparagus, and cut out a monolith in the sides of her mountains of granite more easily than we shape a tooth-pick or an ear-pick. Some centuries ago they had Raphaël, they had Michael Angelo; now we have Monsieur Paul Delaroche, and all because we are making progress.

You boast of your opera; ten operas such as yours would dance the saraband in a Roman circus. Monsieur Martin himself, with his tame tiger and his poor lion, gouty and asleep, like a subscriber to the "Gazette," is something very wretched beside an ancient gladiator. What are your benefit performances which last until two o'clock in the morning when we think of these plays which lasted a hundred days, of those representations in which veritable vessels veritably fought in a veritable sea; in which thousands of men conscientiously cut themselves to pieces;—turn pale, O heroic Franconi!—in which, when the sea had retired, there came the desert, with its tigers and roaring lions, terrible supers who served only for once, in which the leading part was filled by some robust Dacian or Pannonian athlete whom it would often have been very difficult to recall at the conclusion of the piece, and whose sweetheart was some beautiful and dainty Numidian lioness that had been fasting for three days? Does not the elephant funambulist appear to you superior to Mademoiselle Georges? Do you think that Mademoiselle Taglioni dances better than Arbuscula, and Perrot better than Bathyllus? I am persuaded that Roscius might have given points to Bocage, excellent as the latter is. Galeria Coppiola played a young girl's part at more than a hundred years of age. It is right to say that the oldest of our young ladies is scarcely more than sixty, and that Mademoiselle Mars is not even progressing in that direction. They had two or three thousand gods in whom they believed, and we have only one in whom we scarcely believe at all. It is progression of a strange sort. Is not Jupiter something more than Don Juan, and a very different kind of seducer? In truth, I know not what we have invented or even improved upon.

Next to the progressive journalists, and as if to serve as an antithesis to them, there come the *blasé* journalists, who are usually twenty or two-and-twenty years of age, who have never left their own neighbourhood, and have as yet slept only with their charwoman. Everything tires them, everything is too much for them, everything wearies them; they are surfeited, *blasé*, worn out, inaccessible. They know beforehand what you are going to tell them; they have seen, felt, experienced, heard all that it is possible to see, feel, experience, and hear; the human heart has no recess so secret that they have not turned their lantern upon it. They tell you with marvellous self-assurance: "The human heart is not like that; women are not made so; this character is untrue;" or, perhaps, "What! always love and hate; always men and women! Cannot people speak of something else? But man is worn threadbare, and women still more so, since Monsieur de Balzac has concerned himself with them.

" 'Who will deliver us from men and women?'

"You think, sir, that your fable is new? It is so in the same way that the Pont-Neuf is; nothing in the world is more common; I read it somewhere or other when I was at nurse or elsewhere; it has been dinned into my ears for ten years past. Moreover, learn, sir, that there is nothing that I do not know, that everything is used up so far as I am concerned, and that were your idea as virginal as the Virgin Mary, I should none the less affirm that I had seen her prostitute herself on the roadsides with the pettiest of scribblers and poorest of pedants."

These journalists have been the cause of Jocko, of the Monstre Vert, the Lyons of Mysore, and a thousand other fine inventions.

They are continually complaining of being obliged to read books, and see pieces at the theatre. *Apropos* of a paltry vaudeville, they will talk to you of almond-trees in flower, balmy limes, the breeze of spring, and the fragrance of the young foliage; they set up for lovers of nature after the fashion of young Werther, and yet have never set foot out of Paris, and could not tell a cabbage from a beet. If it is winter, they speak of the charms of the domestic hearth, the crackling fire, and irons, slippers, dreaming, and dozing; they will not fail to quote the famous line from Tibullus,

"Quam juvat immites ventos audire cubantem:"

whereby they will give themselves the most charming little appearance in the world, at once disillusioned and ingenuous. They pose as men who have ceased to be influenced by the work of man, whom dramatic emotion leaves as cold and hard as the knife with which they mend their pen, and who nevertheless cry, like J. J. Rousseau, "Voilà la pervenche!"* They profess a fierce antipathy to Gymnase colonels, American uncles, cousins male and female, sensitive old growlers, and romantic widows, and try to cure us of the vaudeville by proving to us every day in their feuilletons that all Frenchmen are not born clever. We do not, indeed, consider this a great evil, but the contrary, and we are delighted to acknowledge that the extinction of vaudeville or comic opera in France (national species) would be one of the greatest blessings from heaven. But I should like to know what kind of literature these gentlemen would allow to take its place. It is true that it could not be worse.

Others preach against bad taste, and translate the tragic Seneca. Lastly, to bring up the rear, a new battalion of critics has been formed of a kind not seen before.

Their critical formula is the most convenient, extensible, malleable, peremptory, superlative, and triumphant that a critic has ever conceived. Zoilus would certainly have profited by it.

Hitherto, when it was wished to depreciate a work, or discredit it in

*"Look at the periwinkle" (the flower), *i.e.* "the summer is coming."— *Translator's Note.*

the eyes of the patriarchal and ingenuous subscriber, false or per-
fidiously isolated quotations were made; phrases were maimed and
verses mutilated in such a fashion that the author even would have
thought himself the most ridiculous person in the world; he was
charged with imaginary plagiarisms; passages in his book were compared with passages in ancient and modern authors with which they
had not the least connection; he was accused in kitchen style, and
with many solecisms, of not knowing his own language, and of pervert-
ing the French of Racine and Voltaire; it was seriously affirmed that
his work had a tendency towards anthropophagy, and that its readers
would infallibly become cannibals and hydrophobes in the course of
the week; but all this was poor and behind the time, as brazen-faced
and fossilised as possible. The accusation of immorality, dragged as it
had been through feuilletons and "variety" columns, was becoming
insufficient, and so unserviceable, that scarcely any paper but the
"Constitutionnel," a pure and progressive one, as is known, had the
desperate courage still to employ it.

Then was invented criticism of the future, prospective criticism.
Can you not see at once how charming it is, and how it is the product
of a fine imagination? The recipe is simple, and may be imparted to
you. The book to be considered fine and worthy of praise is one that
has not yet appeared. The book that appears is bound to be detestable.
To-morrow's will be superb—but it is always to-day. Such criticism
is like the barber who had the following words for a sign written in
large characters:—

SHAVING GRATIS HERE TO-MORROW

All the poor devils who read the placard promised themselves for
the morrow the unspeakable and sovereign delight of having a shave
for once in their lives without loosening their purse-strings, and for
joy of it their beards grew half-a-foot on their chins in the course of
the night preceding the lucky day; but when they had the napkin
round their necks, the barber asked them whether they had any
money, and requested them to shell out, or he would treat them after

the fashions of nutters and apple-gatherers in Le Perche; and he swore his most sacred oath that he would cut their throats with his razor if they did not pay. And when the poor beggars, in miserable and pitiful plight, quoted the placard and the sacrosanct inscription, the barber said: "Ho, ho! my fine fellows, you are no great scholars, and would do well to go back to school! The placard says: 'To-morrow.' I am not so simple and whimsical as to shave gratis to-day; my fellow-barbers would say that I was ruining the trade. Come again next time, or the week when two Sundays come together, and you will find yourselves well off. May I become a green leper if I don't shave you gratis, on the word of an honest barber."

Authors who read a prospective article jeering at an actual work, always flatter themselves that the book that they are writing will be the book of the future. They try to comply, as far as is possible, with the critic's ideas, and become social, progressive, moralising, palin-genesical, mythical, pantheistical, buchezistical, believing that they will thereby escape the tremendous anathema; but they fare as did the barber's customers—to-day is not the eve of to-morrow. The often promised to-morrow will never shine upon the world; for this formula is too convenient to be abandoned so soon. While decrying the book of which they are jealous, and which they would fain annihilate, they put on the gloves of the most generous impartiality. It looks as though they asked nothing better than to approve and to praise, and yet they never do so. This recipe is far superior to that which might be called the retrospective, and which consists in extolling only ancient works, which are no longer read and which trouble nobody, at the expense of modern books which occupy attention and wound self-love more directly.

We said, before beginning this review of the critics, that the mate-rials might furnish fifteen or sixteen folio volumes, but that we should content ourselves with a few lines. I am beginning to fear that these few lines must be each two or three thousand fathoms long, and re-semble those great pamphlets which are so thick that a gunshot could not pierce them, and which bear the treacherous title—A word about the Revolution, a word about this or that. The history of the deeds and jests, and multiple loves of the divine Madeleine de Maupin would run a serious risk of being put off, and it will be understood that an entire volume is not too much to worthily sing the adventures of this fair Bradamant. Hence, wishful though we be to continue the blazonry of the illustrious Aristarchuses of the age, we shall content ourselves with the unfinished sketch we have just obtained, adding a few reflections on the good-nature of our gentle brethren in Apollo, who, stupid as the Cassander of pantomime, stand still to receive blows from harlequin's wand and kicks in the rump from the clown, without stirring any more than if they were images.

It is as though a fencing-master should cross his arms behind his back during a bout, and receive all his adversary's thrusts in his unguarded breast, without essaying a single parry.

It is like a pleading in which the king's attorney had the sole right of speech, or a debate in which reply was not allowed.

The critic advances this or that. He lords it, and makes a great display. Absurd, detestable, monstrous; it is like nothing; it is like everything. A drama is produced, and the critic goes to see it; he finds that it corresponds in no respect to the drama which he had fabricated in his head on the suggestion of the title; and so, in his feuilleton, he substitutes his own drama for the author's. He gives large doses of erudition; he disburdens himself of all the knowledge he has obtained the day before in some library, and treats like negroes people to whom he should go to school, and the least of whom might teach men more able than he.

Authors endure this with a magnanimity and forbearance that seems really inconceivable to me. What, after all, are these critics whose tones are so peremptory and words so short, that one might take them for true sons of the gods? They are simply men who have been at college with us, and who have evidently profited less by their studies than we, since they have never produced a work, and can do nothing but bespatter and spoil the works of others like veritable stymphalian vampires.

Would it not be something to criticise the critics? for these fastidious grandees, who make such an affectation of being haughty and hard to please, are far from possessing the infallibility of our Holy Father. There would be enough to fill a daily paper of the largest size. Their blunders, historical or otherwise, their forged quotations, their mistakes in French, their plagiarisms, their dotage, their trite and ill-mannered pleasantries, their poverty of ideas, their want of intelligence and tact, their ignorance of the simplest things which make them ready to take the Piræus for a man and Monsieur Delaroche for a painter, would provide authors with ample materials for taking their revenge, without involving any work but that of underlining the passages with pencil and reproducing them word for word; for the critic's patent is not accompanied by that of a great writer, and mistakes in language or taste are not to be avoided merely by reproving such in others. The critics prove this every day.

If Châteaubriand, Lamartine, and others of the same kind were to criticise, I could understand people kneeling and adoring; but that Messrs. Z. K. Y. V. Q. X., or some similar letter between A and Ω, should play the part of petty Quintilians and scold you in the name of morality and polite literature, is something which always revolts me, and makes me indulge in unparalleled rage. I would fain have a police regulation forbidding certain names from jostling certain others. It is true that a cat may look at a king, and that Saint Peter of Rome, giant as he is, cannot prevent these Transteveronians from polluting him in strange sort below; but I none the less believe that it would be insane to write along monumental reputations:

COMMIT NO NUISANCE HERE

Charles X alone really understood this quotation. By ordering the suppression of the newspapers, he did a great service to the arts and to civilisation. Newspapers are a species of courtiers or jobbers who interpose between artists and public, between king and people. We know what fine results have followed. These perpetual barkings deaden inspiration and fill heart and intellect with such distrust, that we dare not have faith either in a poet or government; and thus royalty and poetry, the two greatest things in the world, become impossible, to the great misfortune of the people, who sacrifice their welfare to the poor pleasure of reading every morning a few broadsheets of bad paper, soiled with bad ink and bad style.

There was no art criticism under Julius II, and I am not acquainted with any feuilleton on Daniel de Volterre, Sebastian del Piombo, Michael Angelo, or Raphaël, nor on Ghiberti delle Porte or Benvenuto Cellini; and yet I think that for people who had no newspapers, and who knew neither the word *art* nor the word *artistic*, they had for all that a fair amount of talent, and did not acquit themselves badly in their calling.

The reading of newspapers prevents the existence of true scholars and true artists. It is like a daily debauch which makes you come enervated and strengthless to the couch of the Muses, those hard and difficult maidens who require their lovers to be vigorous and quite fresh. The newspaper kills the book, as the book has killed architecture, and as artillery has killed courage and muscular strength. We are not aware of what pleasures newspapers deprive us. They rob everything of its virginity; owing to them we can have nothing of our own, and cannot possess a book all to ourselves; they rob you of surprise at the theatre, and tell you all the catastrophes beforehand; they take away from you the pleasure of tattling, chattering, gossiping and slandering, of composing a piece of news or hawking a true one for a week through all the drawing-rooms of society. They intone their ready-made judgments to us, whether we want them or not, and prepossess us against things that we should like; it is owing to them that the dealers in phosphorus boxes, if only they have a little memory, chatter about literature as nonsensically as country Academicians; it is also owing to them that all day long, instead of artless ideas or individual stupidity, we hear half-digested scraps of newspaper which resemble omelettes raw on one side and burnt on the other, and that we are pitilessly surfeited with news two or three hours old and already known to infants at the breast; they blunt our taste, and make us like those peppered-brandy drinkers and file and rasp swallowers, who have ceased to find any flavour in the most generous wines, and cannot apprehend their flowery and fragrant bouquet.

If Louis-Philippe were to suppress the literary and political journals for good and all, I should be infinitely grateful to him, and would rhyme him on the spot a fine disordered dithyramb with bold verses and cross rhymes, signed: "Your very humble and very faithful subject, &c." Let it not be imagined that literature would no longer engage attention; at a time when there were no newspapers, a quatrain used to occupy all Paris for a week and a first performance for six months.

It is true that we should lose the advertisements and the eulogies at fifteen-pence a line, and notoriety would be less prompt and less startling. But I have devised a very ingenious method for replacing the advertisements. If my gracious monarch suppresses the journals between the present time and the publication of this glorious romance, I shall certainly make use of it, and I promise myself wonders from it. The great day being come, twenty-four criers on horseback, and in the publisher's livery, with his address on their backs and breasts, carrying in their hands banners embroidered on both sides with the title of the romance, and each preceded by a drummer and a kettle-drummer, will traverse the town, and, stopping in the squares and at the cross-ways, cry in a loud and intelligible voice: "To-day, and not yesterday, nor to-morrow, is published the admirable, inimitable, divine, and more than divine romance, 'Mademoiselle de Maupin,' by the very celebrated Théophile Gautier, which Europe, and even the other parts of the world and Polynesia, have been expecting so impatiently for a year and more. It is being sold at the rate of five hundred copies a minute, and the editions are following one another every half hour; the nineteenth has been reached already. A picket of municipal guards is before the door of the shop, restraining the crowd and preventing all disorder."

Surely this would be quite equal to a three-lined advertisement in the "Débats" or the "Courier Français," among elastic belts, crino-lined collars, feeding-bottles with indestructible teats, Regnault's jujubes, and cures for toothache.

May 1834

MADEMOISELLE DE MAUPIN

I

"*You complain,* my dear friend, of the scarcity of my letters. What would you have me write, except that I am well, and that I have ever the same affection for you? These are things of which you are quite aware, and which are so natural, considering my age, and the excellent qualities to be discerned in you, that it is almost ridiculous to send a wretched sheet of paper on a journey of a hundred miles with no more information than that. All my seeking is in vain, I have no news worth relating; my life is the most uniform in the world, and nothing comes to disturb its monotony. To-day is followed by to-morrow, just as yesterday was followed by to-day; and, without being so conceited as to play the prophet, I can in the morning boldly predict what will befall me in the evening.

"Here is the plan of my day: I get up—that is of course, and is the beginning of every day; I breakfast, fence, go out, come in again, dine, pay visits or read something, and then I go to bed, just as I did the day before; I fall asleep, and my imagination, not having been excited by new objects, affords me but trite and hackneyed dreams as monotonous as my real life. This is not very diverting, as you see. Nevertheless, I am better pleased with such an existence than I should have been six months ago. I am dull, it is true, but it is in a peaceful and resigned fashion, not devoid of a certain sweetness, which I should be ready enough to compare to those wan and tepid autumn days in which we find a secret charm after the excessive heat of summer.

"Although I have apparently accepted this kind of existence, it is nevertheless scarcely suitable for me, or at least it has very little resemblance to that of which I dream, and to which I consider myself adapted. It may be that I am mistaken, and that I really am suited only to this mode of life; but I can scarcely believe it, for if this were my true destiny, I should have fitted myself into it with greater ease, and should not have been bruised by the sharp corners of it at so many places and so painfully.

"You know what an overpowering attraction strange adventures have for me, how I worship everything that is singular, extravagant, and perilous, and how greedily I devour novels and books of travels. There is not, perhaps, on earth a fancy more foolish or more vagrant than mine. Well, through some fatality or other, it so happens that I have never had an adventure and have never made a journey. So far as I am concerned, the circuit of the world is the circuit of the town in which I live; I touch my horizon on all sides; I rub shoulders with the real; my life is that of the shell on the sand-bank, of the ivy round the tree, of the cricket on the hearth; in truth, I am surprised that my feet have not yet taken root.

"Love is painted with bandaged eyes; but it is destiny that should be depicted thus.

"I have as valet a species of clown, heavy and stupid enough, who has roved as much as the north wind, who has been to the devil, and I know not where besides, who has seen with his own eyes all those things about which I have formed such fine ideas, and who cares as much for them as he does for a glass of water; he has been placed in the strangest situations, and he has had the most astonishing adventures that one could have. I make him talk sometimes, and am maddened to think that all these glorious things have befallen a booby, who is capable of neither feeling nor reflection, and who is good for nothing but his usual work,—brushing clothes and cleaning boots.

"It is clear that this rascal's life ought to have been mine. As for him, he thinks me very fortunate, and is lost in wonder to see me melancholy, as I am.

"All this is not very interesting, my poor friend, and is scarcely worth the trouble of writing, is it? But since you insist on my writing to you, I must relate my thoughts and feelings, and give you the history of my ideas, in default of events and actions. There will, perhaps, be little order and little novelty in what I shall have to tell you, but you must lay the blame on yourself alone. I shall be obeying your own wish.

"You have been my friend from childhood, and I was brought up with you; our lives were passed together for a long time, and we are wont to tell each other our most secret thoughts. I can therefore, without blushing, give you an account of all the nonsense that passes through my idle brain. I shall neither add, nor deduct a single word, for I have no false pride with you. And so I shall be scrupulously exact, even in trifling and shameful matters; I shall certainly not veil myself before *you.*

"Beneath this winding sheet of indifferent and depressing languor of which I have just told you, there sometimes stirs a thought, torpid rather than dead, and I do not always possess the sweet, sad calm that melancholy gives. I have relapses, and I fall again into my old perturbations. Nothing in the world is so fatiguing as these purposeless whirlwinds and these aimless flights. On such days, although I have nothing to do any more than on others, I rise very early, before the sun, so persuaded am I that I am in a hurry, and that I shall not have the necessary time. I dress myself with all speed, as if the house were on fire, putting on my garments at random, and bewailing the loss of a minute. Any one seeing me would suppose that I was going to keep a love appointment or look for money. Not at all. I even do not know whither I am going; but go I must, and I should believe my safety compromised if I remained. It seems to me that I am called from without, that my destiny is at that moment passing in the street, and that the question of my life is about to be decided.

"I go down with an air of wild surprise, my dress in disorder, and my hair uncombed. People turn and laugh when they meet me, and think that I am a young debauchee, who has spent the night at the tavern or elsewhere. Indeed I am intoxicated, though I have drunk nothing, and I have the manner of a drunkard, even to his uncertain gait, now fast and now slow. I go from street to street, like a dog that has lost his master, seeking quite at a venture, very troubled, very much on the alert, turning at the least noise, gliding into every group, heedless of the rebukes of the people I run up against, and looking about me everywhere, with a clearness of vision which at other times I do not possess. Then it suddenly becomes evident to me that I am mistaken, that it is assuredly not there, that I must go further, to the other end of the town, I know not where, and I set off as if the devil were carrying me away. My toes only touch the ground, and I do not weigh an ounce. Truly I must present a singular appearance with my preoccupied and frenzied countenance, the gesticulations of my arms and the inarticulate cries I utter. When I think of it in cold blood, I laugh heartily in my own face; but this, I would have you know, does not prevent me from doing just the same on the next occasion.

"If I were asked why I rush along in this way, I certainly should be greatly at a loss for an answer. I am in no haste to arrive, since I am going nowhere. I am not afraid of being late, since I have no engagement. There is no one waiting for me, and I have no reason for being in a hurry here.

"Is it an opportunity for loving, an adventure, a woman, an idea or a fortune, something which is wanting to my life, and which I seek without accounting to myself for it, but impelled by a vague instinct? Is it my existence which desires to complete itself? Is it the wish to emerge from my home and from myself, the weariness of my present life and the longing for another? It is something of this, and perhaps all of this put together. It is always a very unpleasant condition, a feverish irritation, which is usually succeeded by the dullest atony.

"I often have an idea, that if I set out an hour earlier, or had increased my pace, I should have arrived in time; that, while I was passing down one street, the object of my search was passing down the other, and that a block of vehicles was sufficient to make me miss what I have been pursuing quite at random for so long. You cannot imagine the sadness and the deep despair into which I fall when I see that all this ends in nothing, and that my youth is passing away with no prospect opening up before me; then all my idle passions growl dully in my heart, and prey upon themselves for lack of other food, like beasts in a menagerie that the keeper has forgotten to feed.

"In spite of the stifled and secret disappointments of every day, there is something within me which resists and will not die. I have no hope, for hope implies desire, a certain disposition for wishing that things should turn out in one way rather than in another. I desire nothing, for I desire everything. I do not hope, or rather I hope no longer;—that is too silly,—and it is quite the same to me whether a thing happens or not. I am waiting, and for what? I do not know, but I am waiting.

"It is a tremulous waiting, full of impatience, broken by starts and nervous movements, as must be that of a lover who awaits his mistress. Nothing comes; I grow furious, or begin to weep. I wait for the heavens to open, and an angel to descend with a revelation to me, for a revolution to break out and a throne to be given me, for one of Raphaël's virgins to leave the canvas and come to embrace me, for relations, whom I do not possess, to die and leave me what will enable me to sail my fancy on a river of gold, for a hippogriff to take me and carry me into regions unknown. But, whatever I am waiting for, it is assuredly nothing usual and commonplace.

"This has reached such a pitch, that, when I come in, I never fail to say: 'No one has come? There is no letter for me? No news?' I know perfectly well that there is nothing, and that there can be nothing. It is all the same; I am always greatly surprised and disappointed on receiving the customary reply: 'No, sir, nothing at all.'

5

"Sometimes—but this is seldom—the idea takes a more definite form. It will be some beautiful woman whom I do not know, and who does not know me, whom I have met at the theatre or at church, and who has not heeded me in the least. I go over the whole house, and until I have opened the door of the last room—I scarcely dare tell you, it is so foolish—I hope that she has come, and that she is there. This is not conceit on my part. I have so little of the coxcomb about me, that several women, whom I believed very indifferent to me, and without any opinion in particular respecting me, have, so others tell me, been greatly prepossessed in my favour. It has a different origin.

"When I am not dulled by weariness and discouragement, my soul awakes and recovers all its former vigour. I hope, I love, I desire, and so violent are my desires, that I imagine that they will draw everything to them, as a powerful magnet attracts particles of iron, even when they are at a great distance from it. This is why I wait for the things I wish for, instead of going to them, and frequently neglect the most favourable opportunities that are opened up to my hopes. Another would write the most amorous note in the world to the divinity of his heart, or would seek for an opportunity to approach her. As for me, I ask the messenger for the reply to a letter which I have not written, and spend my time constructing the most wonderful situations in my head for bringing me in the most favourable and most unexpected light under the notice of her whom I love. A book might be made larger and more ingenious than the 'Stratagems of Polybius' of all the stratagems which I imagine for introducing myself to her and revealing my passion. Generally, it would only be necessary to say to one of my friends: 'Introduce me to Madame So-and-so,' and to pay a compliment drawn from mythology and suitably punctuated with sighs.

"To listen to all this, one would think me fit for a madhouse; nevertheless, I am a rational fellow enongh, and I have not put many of my follies into practice. All this passes in the recesses of my soul, and all these absurd ideas are buried very carefully deep within me; on the outside nothing is to be seen, and I have the reputation of being a placid and cold young man, indifferent to women, and without interest in things belonging to his years; which is as remote from the truth as the judgments of the world usually are.

"Nevertheless, in spite of all my discouragements, some of my desires have been realised, and, so little joy has been given me by their fulfilment, that I dread the fulfilment of the rest. You remember the childish eagerness with which I longed to have a horse of my own; my mother has given me one quite recently; he is as black as ebony, with a little white star on his forehead, with flowing mane, glossy coat, and slender legs, just as I wished him to be. When they brought him to me, it gave me such a shock, that I remained quite a quarter of an hour very pale and unable to compose myself. Then I mounted, and, without speaking a single word, set off at full gallop, and for more than an hour went straight across the country in an ecstasy difficult to conceive. I did the same every day for a week, and I really do not know how it was that I did not kill him or at least break his wind. By degrees all this great eagerness died away, I brought my horse to a trot, then to a walk, and now I have come to ride him with such indifference, that he often stops and I do not notice it. Pleasure has become habit more quickly than I could have thought possible.

"As to Ferragus—that is the name I have given him—he is really the most charming animal that one could see. He has tufts on his feet like eagle's down; he is as lively as a goat and as quiet as a lamb. You will have the greatest pleasure in galloping him when you come here; and, although my mania for riding has passed away, I am still very fond of him, for he is a horse of an excellent disposition, and I sincerely prefer him to many human beings. If you only heard how joyfully he neighs when I go to see him in the stable and with what intelligent eyes he looks at me! I confess that I am touched by these tokens of affection, and that I take him by the neck and embrace him with as much tenderness, on my word, as if he were a beautiful girl.

"I had also another desire, more keen, more eager, more continually awake, more dearly cherished, and for which I had built in my soul an enchanting castle of cards, a palace of chimeras, that was often destroyed but raised again with desperate constancy: it was to have a mistress—a mistress quite my own—like the horse. I do not know whether the fulfilment of this dream would have found me so soon cold as the fulfilment of the other; I doubt it. But perhaps I am wrong, and shall be tired of it as soon. Owing to my peculiar disposition, I desire a thing so frantically, without, however, making any effort to procure it, that if by chance, or otherwise, I attain the object of my wish, I have such a moral lumbago, and am so worn out, that I am seized with swoonings, and have not energy enough left to enjoy it: hence things which come to me without my wishing for them generally give me more pleasure than those which I have coveted most strongly.

"I am twenty-two years old, and I am not virgin. Alas! no one is so now at that age, either in body, or, what is much worse in heart. Besides consorting with the class of females who afford us pleasure for payment, and are not to be counted any more than a lascivious dream, I have gained over several virtuous or nearly virtuous women, neither beautiful nor ugly, neither young nor old, such as are to be met with by young fellows who have nothing regular on hand and whose hearts are unoccupied. With a little good-will, and a pretty strong dose of romantic illusions, you can call this having a mistress, if you like. For myself, I find it impossible; I might have a thousand of the kind, and I should still believe my desire as unfulfilled as ever.

"I have not, therefore, as yet had a mistress, and my whole desire is to have one. It is an idea that torments me strangely; it is not an effervescence of temperament, a boiling of the blood, the first burst of puberty. It is not *woman* that I want, but *a* woman, a mistress; I desire one, and shall have one shortly; if I did not succeed, I confess to you that I should never get over it, and that I should have an inward timidity, a dull discouragement, which would exercise a serious influence upon the rest of my life. I should consider myself defective in certain respects, inharmonious or incomplete, deformed in mind or body; for after all my requirement is a just one, and nature owes it to every man. So long as I have not attained my end, I shall look upon myself merely as a child, and I shall not have the confidence in myself which I ought to have. A mistress is to me what the *toga virilis* was to the young Roman.

"I see so many beautiful women in the possession of men who are ignoble in every respect, and scarcely fit to be their lackeys, that I blush for them, and for myself. It gives me a pitiful opinion of women to see them wasting their affection on blackguards who despise and deceive them, instead of giving themselves to some loyal and sincere young fellow who would esteem himself very fortunate, and would worship them on his knees; to myself, for instance. It is true that men of the former species obstruct the drawing-rooms, show themselves off before every one, and are always lounging on the back of some easy chair, while I remain at home, my forehead pressed against the window pane, watching the river stream and the mist rise, while silently erecting in my heart the perfumed sanctuary, the marvellous temple in which I am to lodge the future idol of my soul. A chaste and poetical occupation, and one for which women are as little grateful to you as may be.

"Women have little liking for dreamers, and peculiarly esteem those who put their ideas into practice. After all, they are right. Obliged by their education and their social position to keep silence and to wait, they naturally prefer those who come to them and speak, and thus relieve them from a false and tiresome position. I am quite sensible of this; yet never in my life shall I be able to take it upon me, as I see many others do, to rise from my seat, cross a drawing-room, and say unexpectedly to a woman: 'Your dress becomes you like an angel,' or: 'Your eyes are particularly bright this evening.'

"All this does not prevent me from positively wanting a mistress. I do not know who it will be, but I see none among the women of my acquaintance who could suitably fill this dignified position. I find that they possess very few of the qualities I require. Those who would be young enough are wanting in beauty or intellectual charm; those who are beautiful and young are basely and forbiddingly virtuous, or lack the necessary freedom; and then there is always some husband, some brother, a mother or an aunt, somebody or other, with big eyes and large ears, who must be wheeled or thrown out of the window. Every rose has its worm, and every woman has a swarm of relations who must be carefully cleared away, if we wish to pluck some day the fruit of her beauty. There is not one of them, even to country cousins of the third degree, whom we have never seen, that does not wish to preserve the spotless purity of their dear cousin in all its whiteness. This is nauseous, and I shall never have the patience to pull up all the weeds, and lop away all the briars which fatally obstruct the approaches to a pretty woman.

"I am not fond of mammas, and I like young girls still less. Further, I must confess that married women have but a very slight attraction for me. They involve a confusion and a mingling which are revolting to me; I cannot tolerate the idea of division. The woman who has a husband and a lover is a prostitute for one of them, and often for both; and, besides, I could never consent to yield the first place to another. My natural pride cannot stoop to such a degradation. I shall never go because another man is coming. Though the woman were to be compromised and lost, and we were to fight with knives each with a foot upon her body, I should remain. Private staircases, cupboards, closets, and all the machinery for deception would be of little service with me.

"I am not much smitten with what is called maidenly ingenuousness, youthful innocence, purity of heart, and other charming things which in verse are most effective; that I call simply nonsense, ignorance, imbecility, or hypocrisy. The maidenly ingenuousness which consists in sitting on the very edge of an easy chair, with arms pressed close to the body, and eyes fixed on the point of the corset, and in not speaking without permission from its grand-parents, the innocence which has a monopoly of uncurled hair and white frocks, the purity of heart which wears its dress high up at the neck because it has as yet neither shoulders nor breast to show, do not, in truth, appear wonderfully agreeable to me.

"I do not care much for teaching little simpletons to spell out the alphabet of love. I am neither old enough nor depraved enough for that; besides, I should succeed badly at it, for I never could show anybody anything, even what I knew best myself. I prefer women who read fluently, we arrive sooner at the end of the chapter; and in everything, but especially in love, the end is what we have to consider. In this respect, I am rather like those people who begin a novel at the wrong end, read the catastrophe first of all, and then go backwards to the first page. This mode of reading and loving has its charm. Details are relished more when we are at peace concerning the end, and the inversion introduces the unforeseen.

"Young girls then, and married women are excluded from the category. It must, therefore, be among the widows that we are to choose our divinity. Alas! though nothing else is left to us, I greatly fear that neither will they afford us what we wish.

"If I happened to love a pale narcissus bathed in a tepid dew of tears, and bending with melancholy grace over the new marble tomb of some happily and recently departed husband, I should certainly, and in a very short while, be as miserable as was the defunct during his lifetime. Widows, however young and charming they may be, have a terrible drawback which other women are without; if you are not on the very best terms with them, and a cloud passes across the heaven of your love, they tell you at once with a little superlative and contemptuous air—

" 'Ah! how strange you are to-day! It is just like what *he* was. When we quarrelled, he used to speak to me in the very same way; it is curious, but you have the same tone of voice and the same look; when you are out of temper, you cannot imagine how like my husband you are; it is frightful.'

"It is pleasant to have things of this sort said to your very face! There are some even who are impudent enough to praise the departed one like an epitaph, and to extol his heart and his leg at the expense of your leg and your heart. With women who have only one or more lovers, you have at least the unspeakable advantage of never hearing about your predecessor, and this is a consideration of no ordinary interest. Women have too great a regard for what is appropriate and legitimate not to observe a diligent silence in such an event, and all matters of the kind are consigned to oblivion as soon as possible. It is an understood thing that a man is always a woman's first lover.

"I do not think that an aversion so well founded admits of any serious reply. It is not that I consider widows altogether devoid of charm, when they are young and pretty and have not yet laid aside their mourning. They have little languishing airs, little ways of letting the arms droop, of arching the neck and of bridling up like unmated turtle-doves; a heap of charming affectations sweetly veiled beneath the transparency of crape, a well-ordered affectation of despair, skilfully managed sighs, and tears which fall so opportunely and lend such lustre to the eyes!

"Truly, next to wine—perhaps even before it—the liquid I love best to drink is a beautiful tear, clear and limpid, trembling at the tip of a dark or a blonde eye-lash. What means are there of resisting that? We do not resist it; and then black is so becoming to women! A white skin, poetry apart, turns to ivory, snow, milk, alabaster, to everything spotless that there is in the world for the use of composers of madrigals; while a dark skin has but a dash of brown that is full of vivacity and fire.

"Mourning is a happy opportunity for a woman, and the reason I shall never marry, is the fear lest my wife should get rid of me in order to go into mourning for me. There are, however, some women who cannot turn their sorrow to account, and who weep in such a way that they make their noses red, and distort their features like the faces that we see on fountains; this is a serious danger. There is need of many charms and much art to weep agreeably; otherwise, there is a risk of not being comforted for a long time. Yet notwithstanding the pleasure of making some Artemisia faithless to the shade of her Mausolus, I cannot really choose from among this swarm of lamenting ones her whose heart I shall ask in exchange for my own.

"And now I hear you say: Whom will you take then? You will not have young girls, nor married women, nor widows. You do not like mammas, and I do not suppose that you are any fonder of grandmothers. Whom the deuce *do* you like? It is the answer to the charade, and if I knew it, I should not torment myself so much. Up to the present, I have never loved any woman, but I have loved and do love— *love*. Although I have had no mistress, and the women that I have had have merely kindled desire, I have felt, and I am acquainted with love itself. I have not loved this woman or that, one more than another; but some one whom I have never seen, who must live somewhere, and whom I shall find, if it please God. I know well what she is like, and, when I meet her, I shall recognise her.

"I have often pictured to myself the place where she dwells, the dress that she wears, the eyes and hair that she has. I hear her voice; I should recognise her step among a thousand, and if, by chance, some one uttered her name, I should turn round; it is impossible that she should not have one of the five or six names that I have given her in my head.

"She is twenty-six years old, neither more nor less. She is not without experience, and she is not yet satiated. It is a charming age for making love as it ought to be, without childishness and without libertinism. She is of medium height. I like neither a giantess nor a dwarf. I wish to be able to carry my goddess by myself from the sofa to the bed; but it would be disagreeable to have to look for her in the latter. When raising herself slightly on tiptoe, her mouth should reach my kiss. That is the proper height. As to her figure, she is rather plump than thin. I am something of the Turk in this matter, and I should scarcely like to meet with a corner when I expected a circumference; a woman's skin should be well filled, her flesh compact and firm, like the pulp of a peach that is nearly ripe: and the mistress I shall have is made just so. She is a blonde with dark eyes, white like a blonde, with the colour of a brunette, and a red and sparkling smile. The lower lip rather large, the eyeball swimming in a flood of natural moisture, her breast round, small, and firm, her hands long and plump, her walk undulating like a snake standing on its tail, her hips full and yielding, her shoulders broad, the nape of her neck covered with down; a style of beauty at once delicate and compact, graceful and healthy, poetic and real; a subject of Giorgione's wrought by Rubens.

"Here is her costume: she wears a robe of scarlet or black velvet, with slashings of white satin or silver cloth, an open bodice, a large ruff *à la* Medici, a felt hat capriciously drawn up like Helena Systerman's and with long feathers curled and crisp, a golden chain or a stream of diamonds about her neck, and a quantity of large, variously enamelled rings on all her fingers.

"I will not excuse her a ring or a bracelet. Her robe must be literally of velvet or brocade; at the very most, I might permit her to stoop to satin. I would rather rumple a silk skirt than a linen one, and let pearls and feathers fall from the hair than natural flowers or a simple bow; I know that the lining of a linen skirt is often at least as tempting as that of a silk one, but I prefer the silk one.

"Thus, in my dreams, I have given myself as mistresses many queens, many empresses, many princesses, many sultanas, many celebrated courtesans, but never a commoner or a shepherdess; and amid my most vagrant desires, I have never taken advantage of any one on a carpet of grass or in a bed of serge d'Aumale. I consider beauty a diamond which should be mounted and set in gold. I cannot imagine a beautiful woman without a carriage, horses, serving-men, and all that belongs to an income of four thousand a year: there is a harmony between beauty and wealth. One requires the other: a pretty foot calls for a pretty shoe, a pretty shoe calls for a carpet, and a carriage, and all the rest of it. A beautiful woman, poorly dressed and in a mean house, is, to my mind, the most painful sight that one could see, and I could not feel love towards such a one. It is only the handsome and the rich who can make love without being ridiculous or pitiable. At this rate few people would be entitled to make love: I myself should be the first to be excluded; but such is nevertheless my opinion.

"It will be in the evening, during a beautiful sunset, that we shall meet for the first time; the sky will have those clear yellow and pale-green orange-coloured tints that we see in the pictures of the old masters; there will be a great avenue of flowering chestnut trees and venerable elms filled with wood-pigeons—fine trees of fresh dark green, giving a shade full of mystery and dampness; a few statues here and there, some marble vases with their snowy whiteness standing out in relief on the ground of green, a sheet of water with the familiar swan, and, quite in the background, a mansion of brick and stone, as in the time of Henri IV, with a peaked slate roof, lofty chimneys, weather-cocks on all the gables, and long narrow windows.

"At one of these windows, the queen of my soul, in the dress I have just described, leaning with an air of melancholy on the balcony, and behind her a little negro holding her fan and her parrot. You see that nothing is wanting, and that the whole thing is perfectly absurd. The fair one drops her glove; I pick it up, kiss it, and bring it to her. We enter into conversation; I display all the wit that I do not possess; I

14

say charming things; I am answered in the same way, I rejoin, it is a display of fireworks, a luminous rain of dazzling words. In short, I am adorable—and adored. Supper-time arrives; I am invited, and accept the invitation. What a supper, my dear friend, and what a cook is my imagination! The wine laughs in the crystal, the brown and white pheasant smokes in the blazoned dish; the banquet is prolonged far into the night, and you may be quite sure that I do not end the latter at my own home. Is not this well conceived? Nothing in the world can be more simple, and it is truly very astonishing that it has not come to pass ten times rather than once.

"Sometimes it is a large forest. The hunt sweeps by; the horn sounds, and the pack giving tongue crosses the path with the swiftness of lightning; the fair one, in a riding habit, is mounted on a Turkish steed as white as milk, and as frisky and mettlesome as possible. Although she is an excellent horsewoman, he paws the ground, caracoles, rears, and she has all the trouble in the world to hold him in; he gets the bit between his teeth and takes her straight towards a precipice. I fall there from the sky for the purpose, check the horse, take the fainting princess in my arms, restore her, and bring her back to the mansion. What well-born woman would refuse her heart to a man who has risked his life for her? Not one; and gratitude is a cross-road which very quickly leads to love.

"You will, at all events, admit that when I go in for romance, it is not by halves that I do so, and that I am as foolish as it is possible to be. It is always so, for there is nothing in the world more disagreeable than folly with reason in it. You will almost admit that when I write letters they are volumes rather than simple notes. In everything, I like what goes beyond ordinary limits. That is the reason why I am fond of you. Do not laugh too much at all the nonsense I have scribbled to you: I am laying my pen aside in order to put it into practice; for I ever come back to the same refrain: I want to have a mistress. I do not know whether it will be the lady of the park or the beauty of the balcony, but I bid you good-bye that I may commence my quest. My resolution is taken. Should she, whom I seek, be concealed in the remotest part of the kingdom of Cathay or Samarcand I shall manage to find her out. I will let you know of the success or failure—I hope it will be the success—of my enterprise. Pray for me, my dear friend. For my own part, I am putting on my finest coat, and am leaving the house determined not to return without a mistress in accordance with my ideas. I have been dreaming long enough; to action now.

"*P.S.*—Send me some news of little D——; what has become of him? No one here knows anything about him, and give my compliments to your worthy brother and to the whole family."

II

"**Well!** *my friend,* I have come in again without having been to Cathay, Cashmere, or Samarcand; but it is right to say that I have not a mistress any more than before. Yet I had taken myself by the hand and sworn my greatest oath that I would go to the end of the world—and I have not even been to the end of the town. I do not know how it is, but I have never been able to keep my word to any one, even to myself: the devil must have a hand in it. If I say, 'I shall go there to-morrow,' I am sure to remain where I am; if I purpose going to the wine shop, I go to church; if I wish to go to church, the roads become as confused beneath my feet as skeins of thread, and I find myself in quite a different place; I fast when I have determined on an orgie, and so on. Thus I believe that my resolve to have a mistress is what prevents me from having one.

"I must give you a detailed account of my expedition; it is quite worthy of the honours of narration. That day I had spent two full hours at least at my toilet. I had my hair combed and curled, the small amount of moustache that I possess turned up and waxed, and with my usually pale face animated somewhat by the emotion of desire, I was really not so bad. At last, after looking at myself carefully in the glass in different lights to see whether I had a sufficiently handsome and gallant appearance, I went resolutely out of the house, with lofty countenance, chin in air, and one hand on my hip, looking straight before me, making the heels of my boots rattle like an anspessade, elbowing the townsfolk, and with quite a victorious and triumphal mien.

"I was like another Jason going to the conquest of the Golden Fleece. But, alas! Jason was more fortunate than I: besides the conquest of the fleece he at the same time effected the conquest of a beautiful princess, while, as for me, I have neither princess nor fleece.

"I went away, then, through the streets, noticing all the women, and hastening up to them and looking at them as closely as possible when they seemed worth the trouble of an examination. Some would assume their most virtuous air, and pass without raising their eyes. Others would at first be surprised, and then, if they had good teeth, would smile. Others again would turn after a little to see me when they thought I was no longer looking at them, and blush like cherries when they found themselves face to face with me.

"The weather was fine, and there was a crowd of people out walking. And yet, I must confess, in spite of all the respect I entertain towards that interesting half of the human race, that which it is agreed to call the fair sex is devilishly ugly: in a hundred women there was scarcely one that was passable. This one had a moustache; that one had a blue nose; others had red spots instead of eyebrows. One was not badly made, but her face was covered with pimples. A second had a charming head, but she might have scratched her ear with her shoulder. A third would have shamed Praxiteles with the roundness and softness of certain curves, but she skated on feet that were like Turkish stirrups. Yet another displayed the most magnificent shoulders that one could see; but as a set off, her hands resembled for shape and size those enormous scarlet gloves which haberdashers use as signs. And generally, what fatigue was there on these faces! how blighted, etiolated, and basely worn by petty passions and petty vices! What expressions of envy, evil curiosity, greediness, and shameless coquetry! And how much more ugly is a woman who is not handsome than a man who is not so!

"I saw nothing good—except some grisettes. But there is more linen than silk to rumple in that quarter, and they are no affair of mine. In truth, I believe that man, and by man I also understand woman, is the ugliest animal on earth. This quadruped who walks on his hind legs seems to me singularly presumptuous in assigning quite as a matter of right the first rank in creation to himself. A lion, or a tiger, is handsomer than man, and many individuals in their species attain to all the beauty that belongs to their nature. This is extremely rare among men. How many abortions for one Antinoüs! how many Gothones for one Phyllis!

"I am greatly afraid, my dear friend, that I shall never embrace my ideal, and yet there is nothing extravagant or unnatural in it. It is not the ideal of a third-form schoolboy. I do not require globes of ivory, nor columns of alabaster, nor traceries of azure; and in its composition I have employed neither lilies, nor snow, nor roses, nor jet, nor ebony, nor coral, nor ambrosia, nor pearls, nor diamonds; I have left the stars of heaven in peace, and I have not unhooked the sun out of season. It is almost a vulgar ideal, so simple is it; and it seems to me that with a bag or two of piastres I might find it ready made and completely realised in no matter which bazaar of Constantinople or Smyrna; it would probably cost me less than a horse or a thoroughbred dog. And to think that I shall never attain to this—for I feel that I shall never do so! It is enough to madden one, and I fall into the finest passions in the world against my fate.

"As for you—you are not so foolish as I am, and you are fortunate; you have simply given yourself up to your life without tormenting yourself to shape it, and you have taken things as they come. You have not sought happiness, and it has sought you; you are loved, and you love. I do not envy you—you must not think that, at least—but when I reflect on your bliss, I feel less joyous than I ought to be, and I say to myself with a sigh that I would gladly enjoy similar felicity.

"Perhaps my happiness has passed close to me, and in my blindness

I have not seen it. Perhaps the voice has spoken, and the noise of the storms within me has prevented me from hearing.

"Perhaps I have been loved in obscurity by some humble heart that I have disregarded and broken. Perhaps I have myself been the ideal of another, the lode-star of some soul in suspense, the dream of a night and the thought of a day. Had I looked to my feet, I might perhaps have seen some fair Magdalene, with her box of odours and her sweeping hair. I passed along with my arms raised towards the heavens, desiring to pluck the stars which fled from me, and disdaining to pick up the little Easter daisy that was opening her golden heart to me in the dewy grass. I have made a great mistake: I have asked from love something more than love, and that it could not give. I forgot that love was naked; I did not understand the meaning of this grand symbol. I have asked from it robes of brocade, feathers, diamonds, sublimity of soul, knowledge, poetry, beauty, youth, supreme power—everything that is not itself. Love can offer itself alone, and he who would obtain from it aught else is not worthy to be loved.

"I have without doubt hastened too much: my hour has not come; God, who has lent me life, will not take it back from me before I have lived. To what end give a lyre without strings to a poet, or a life without love to a man? God could not do such an inconsistent thing; and no doubt He will, at His chosen time, place in my path here whom I am to love, and by whom I am to be loved. But why has love come to me before the mistress? Why am I thirsty, yet without the spring at which to quench my thirst? or why can I not fly like the birds of the desert to the spot where there is water? The world is to me a Sahara without wells or date-trees. I have not a single shady nook in my life where I can screen myself from the sun: I endure all the fervor of passion without its raptures and unspeakable delights; I know its torments, and am without its pleasures. I am jealous of what does not exist; I am disquieted by the shadow of a shadow; I heave sighs which have no motive; I suffer sleeplessness which no worshipped phantom comes to adorn; I shed tears which flow to the ground without being dried; I give to the winds kisses which are not returned; I wear out my eyes trying to grasp in the distance an uncertain and deceitful form;

I wait for what is not to come, and I count the hours anxiously, as though I had an appointment to keep.

"Whoever thou art, angel or demon, maid or courtesan, shepherdess or princess, whether thou comest from the north or from the south, thou whom I know not, and whom I love! oh! force me not to wait longer for thee, or the flame will consume the altar, and thou wilt find in the place of my heart but a heap of cold ashes. Descend from the sphere where thou art; leave the crystal skies, consoling spirit, and come thou to cast the shadow of thy mighty wings upon my soul. Come thou, woman whom I will love, that I may close about thee the arms that have been open for so long. Let the golden doors of the palace wherein she dwells turn on their hinges; let the humble latch of her cottage rise; let the branches in the woods and the briars of the wayside untwine themselves; let the enchantments of the turret and the spells of the magicians be broken; let the ranks of the crowd be opened up to suffer her to pass through.

"If thou comest too late, O my ideal! I shall not have the power left to love thee. My soul is like a dovecote full of doves. At every hour of the day there flies forth some desire. The doves return to the cote, but desires return not to the heart. The azure of the sky becomes white with their countless swarms; they pass away, through space, from world to world, from clime to clime, in quest of some love where they may perch and pass the night: hasten thy step, O my dream! or thou wilt find in the empty nest but the shells of the birds that have flown away.

"My friend, companion of my childhood, to you alone could I relate such things as these. Write to me that you pity me, and that you do not reckon me a hypochondriac; afford me comfort, for never did I need it more: how enviable are those who have a passion which they can satisfy! The drunkard never encounters cruelty in his bottle. He falls from the tavern into the kennel, and is more happy on his heap of filth than a king upon his throne. The sensualist goes to courtesans for facile amours or shameless refinements. A painted cheek, a short petticoat, a naked breast, a licentious speech, and he is happy; his eye grows white, his lip is wet; he attains the last degree of his happiness, he feels the rapture of his coarse voluptuousness. The gamester has need but of a green cloth and a pack of greasy and worn-out cards to obtain the keen pangs, nervous spasms, and diabolical enjoyments of his horrible passion. Such people as these may be sated or amused; but that is impossible for me.

"This idea has so taken possession of me that I no longer love the arts, and poetry has no longer any charm for me. What formerly transported me, makes not the least impression on me.

"I begin to believe that I am in the wrong, and that I am asking more from nature and society than they can give. What I seek has no existence, and I ought not to complain for having failed to find it. Yet if the woman of our dreams is impossible to the conditions of human nature, what is it that causes us to love her only and none other, since we are men, and our instinct should be an infallible guide? Who has given us the idea of this imaginary woman? From what clay have we formed this invisible statue? Whence took we the feathers that we have placed on the back of this chimera? What mystic bird placed unnoted in some dark corner of our soul the egg from which there has come forth our dream? What is this abstract beauty which we feel but cannot define? Why, in the presence of some woman who is often charming, do we sometimes say that she is beautiful, while we think her very ugly?

"Where is the model, the type, the inward pattern which affords us the standard of comparison?—for beauty is not an absolute idea, and it can be estimated only by contrast. Have we seen it in the skies,—in a star,—at a ball, under a mother's shadow, the fresh bud of a leafless rose? Was it in Italy or in Spain? Was it here or was it there, yesterday or a long time ago? Was it the worshipped courtesan, the fashionable singer, the prince's daughter? A proud and noble head bending beneath a weighty diadem of pearls and rubies? A young and childish face stooping among the nasturtiums and bindweeds at the window? To what school belonged that picture in which this beauty stood out white and radiant amid the dark shadows? Was it Raphaël who caressed the outline that pleases you? Was it Cleomenes who polished the marble that you adore? As you in love with a Madonna or a Diana? Is your ideal an angel, a sylphid, or a woman?

21

"Alas! it is something of all this, and yet it is not this.

"Such transparency of tone, such freshness so charming and full
of splendour, such flesh wherein runs so much blood and life, such
beautiful flaxen hair spreading itself like a mantle of gold, such sparkling smiles and such amorous dimples, such shapes undulating like
flames, such force and such suppleness, such satin gloss and such rich
lines, such plump arms and such fleshy and polished backs—all this
exquisite health belongs to Rubens. Raphaël alone could fill lineaments so chaste with that pale amber colour. What other, save he,
curved those long eye-brows so delicate and so black and spread the
fringes of those eye-lashes so modestly cast down? Do you thing that
Allegri goes for nothing in your ideal? It is from him that the lady of
your thoughts has stolen the dull, warm whiteness that enraptures
you. She has stood for long before his canvases to surprise the secret
of that angelic and ever full-blown smile; she has modelled the oval
of her face on the oval of a nymph or a saint. That line of the hip which
winds so voluptuously belongs to the sleeping Antiope. Those fat,
delicate hands might be claimed by Danaë or Magdalene.

"Dusty antiquity itself has provided many of the materials or the
composition of your young chimera. Those strong and supple loins
around which you twine your arms with so much passion were sculptured by Praxiteles. That divinity has purposely suffered the top of
her charming little foot to pass through the ashes of Herculaneum that
your idol may not be lame. Nature has also contributed her share.
Here and there in the prism of desire you have seen a beautiful eye
beneath a window-blind, an ivory brow pressed against a pane, a
smiling mouth behind a fan. From a hand you have divined the arm,
and from an ankle, the knee. What you saw was perfect; you supposed
the rest to be like what you saw, and you completed it with portions of
other beauties obtained elsewhere.

"Even the ideal beauty realised by the painters did not satisfy you,
and you have sought from the poets more rounded curves, more
ethereal forms, more divine charms, and more exquisite refinements.
You have besought them to give breath and speech to your phantom,
all their love, all their musing, all their joy and sadness, their melan-

choly and their morbidness, all their memories and all their hopes, their knowledge and their passions, their spirit and their heart. All this you have taken from them, and to crown the impossible you have added your own passion, your own spirit, your own dream, and your own thought. The star has lent its ray, the flower its fragrance, the palette its colour, the poet his harmony, the marble its form, and you your desire.

"How could a real woman, eating and drinking, getting up in the morning and going to bed at night, however adorable and full of charm she might otherwise be, compare with a creature such as this? It could not reasonably be expected, and yet it is expected and sought. What strange blindness! It is sublime or absurd. How I pity and how I admire those who pursue their dream in the teeth of all reality, and die content if they have but once kissed the lips of their chimera! But what a fearful fate is that of a Columbus who has failed to discover his world, and of a lover who has not found his mistress!

"Ah! if I were a poet my songs should be consecrated to those whose lives have been failures; whose arrows have missed the mark, who have died without speaking the word they had to utter and without pressing the hand that was destined for them; to all that has proved abortive and to all that has passed unnoticed, to the stifled fire, to the barren genius, to the unknown pearl in the depths of the sea, to all that has loved without return, and to all that has suffered with pity from none. It would be a noble task.

"Plato was right in wishing to banish you from his republic, O ye poets! for what evil have you wrought upon us! How yet more bitter has our wormwood been rendered by your ambrosia! and how yet more arid and desolate seems our life to us after feasting our eyes on the vistas which you open up to us of the infinite! How terrible a conflict have your dreams waged against our realities, and how have our hearts been trodden and trampled on by these rude athletes during the contest!

"We have sat down like Adam at the foot of the walls of the terrestrial paradise, on the steps of the staircase leading to the world which you have created, seeing a light brighter than the sun's flashing

23

through the chinks of the door, and hearing indistinctly some scattered notes of a seraphic harmony. Whenever one of the elect enters or comes forth amid a flood of splendour, we stretch our necks trying to see something through the half-opened portal. The fairy architecture has not its equal save in Arab tales. Piles of columns with arches super-posed, pillars twisted in spirals, foliage marvellously carved, hollowed trefoils, porphyry, jaspar, lapis-lazuli—but what know I of the trans-parencies and dazzling reflections, of the profusion of strange gems, sardonyx, chrysoberyl, aqua marina, rainbow-tinted opals, and azerodrach, with jets of crystals, torches that would make the stars grow pale, a lustrous vapour, giddy and filled with sound—a luxury perfectly Assyrian!

"The door swings to again, and you see no more. Your eyes, filled with corrosive tears, are cast down on this poor earth so impoverished and wan, on these ruined hovels and on this tattered race, on your soul, an arid rock where nothing living springs, on all the wretchedness and misfortune of reality. Ah! if only we could fly so far, if the steps of that fiery staircase did not burn our feet; but, alas! Jacob's ladder can be ascended only by angels!

"What a fate is that of the poor man at the gate of the rich! What keen irony is that of a palace facing a cottage—the ideal facing the real, poetry facing prose! What rooted hate must wring the heart-strings of the wretched beings! What gnashings of teeth must sound through the night from their pallet, as the wind brings to their ears the sighs of theorbos and viols of love! Poets, painters, sculptors, musicians, why have you lied to us? Poets, why have you told us your dreams? Paint-ers, why have you fixed upon the canvas that impalpable phantom which ascended and descended with your fits of passion between your heart and your head, saying to us: 'This is a woman'? Sculptors, why have you taken marble from the depths of Carrara to make it express for ever, and to the eyes of all, your most secret and fleeting desire? Musicians, why have you listened during the night to the song of the stars and the flowers, and noted it down? Why have you made songs so beautiful that the sweetest voice saying to us, 'I love you,' seems hoarse as the grinding of a saw or the croaking of a crow? Curse you

for impostors!—and may fire from heaven burn up and destroy all
pictures, poems, statues, and musical scores——But this is a tirade
of interminable length, and one which deviates somewhat from the
epistolary style. What a dose!

"I have given myself up nicely to lyrics, my dear friend, and I have
now been writing bombast for some time absurdly enough. All this is
very remote from our subject, which is, if I remember rightly, the
glorious and triumphant history of the Chavelier d'Albert in his pursuit of the most beautiful princess in the world, as the old romances
say. But in truth the history is so meagre that I am obliged to have
recourse to digressions and reflections. I hope that it will not be always so, and that the romance of my life will before long be more
tangled and complicated than a Spanish imbroglio.

"After wandering from street to street, I determined to go to one of
my friends who was to introduce me to a house where, I was told, a
world of pretty women were to be seen—a collection of real ideals,
enough to satisfy a score of poets. There were some to suit every taste
—aristocratic beauties with eagle looks, sea-green eyes, straight noses,
proudly elevated chins, royal hands, and the walk of a goddess; silver
lilies mounted on stalks of gold; simple violets of pale colour and sweet
perfume, with moist and downcast eye, frail neck, and diaphanous
flesh; lively and piquant beauties, affected beauties, and beauties of
all sorts; for the house is a very seraglio, minus the eunuchs and the
kislar aga.

"My friends tell me that he has already had five or six flames there
—quite as many. This seems to me prodigious in the extreme, and I
greatly fear that I shall not be equally successful; De C—— pretends
that I shall, and that I shall succeed beyond my wishes. According to
him, I have only one fault, which will be cured by time and by mixing
in society: it is that I esteem woman too much and women not enough.
It is quite possible that there may be some truth in this. He says that
I shall be quite lovable when I have got rid of this little oddity. God
grant it! Women must feel that I despise them, for a compliment which
they would think adorable and charming to the last degree in the
mouth of another, angers and displeases them as much as the most

25

cutting epigram when it proceeds from mine. This has probably some connection with what De C—— objects to in me.

"My heart beat a little faster as I ascended the staircase, and I had scarcely recovered from my emotion when De C——, nudging me with his elbow, brought me face to face with a woman of about thirty years of age, rather handsome, attired with heavy luxury and an extreme affectation of childish simplicity, which, however, did not prevent her from being plastered with red paint like a coach wheel. It was the lady of the house.

"De C——, assuming that shrill, mocking voice so different from his customary tones, and which he makes use of in society when he wishes to play the charmer, said to her, with many tokens of ironic respect, through which was visible the most profound contempt:

" 'This is the young fellow I spoke to you about the other day—a man of the most distinguished merit. He belongs to one of the best families, and I think that it cannot but be agreeable to you to receive him. I have therefore taken the liberty to introduce him to you.'

" 'You have certainly done quite right, sir,' replied the lady, mincing in the most exaggerated fashion. Then she turned to me, and, after looking me over with the corner of her eye after the manner of a skilled connoisseur, and in a way that made me blush to the tops of my ears, said, 'You may consider yourself as invited once for all, and come as often as you have an evening to throw away.'

"I bowed awkwardly enough, and stammered out some unconnected words, which could not have given her a lofty opinion of my talents. The entrance of some other people released me from the irksomeness inseparable from an introduction, and De C——, drawing me into a corner of the window, began to lecture me soundly.

" 'The deuce! You are going to compromise me. I announced you as a phœnix of wit, a man of unbridled imagination, a lyric poet, everything that is most transcendent and impassioned, and there you stand like a blockhead without uttering a word! What a miserable imagination! I thought your humour more fertile than that. But come, give your tongue the rein, and chatter right and left. You need not say sensible and judicious things; on the contrary, that might do you harm. Speak—that is the essential thing—speak much and long.

Draw attention to yourself; cast aside all fear and modesty. Get it well into your head that all here are fools or nearly so, and do not forget that an orator who would succeed cannot despise his hearers enough. What do you think of the mistress of the house?'

" 'She displeases me considerably already; and, though I spoke to her for scarcely three minutes, I felt as bored as if I had been her husband.'

" 'Ah! is that what you think of her?'

" 'Why, yes.'

" 'Your dislike to her is then quite insurmountable? Well, so much the worse. It would have been only decent to have courted her if but for a month. It is the proper thing to do, and a respectable young fellow cannot be introduced into society except through her.'

" 'Well! I'll pay court to her,' I replied with a piteous air, 'since it is necessary. But is it so essential as you seem to think?'

" 'Alas! yes, it is most indispensable, and I am going to explain the reasons to you. Madame de Thémines is at present in vogue; she has all the absurdities of the day after a superior fashion, sometimes those of to-morrow, but never those of yesterday. She is quite in the swim. People wear what she wears, and she never wears what has been worn already. Furthermore she is rich, and her equipages are in the best taste. She has no wit, but much jargon; she has keen likings and little passion. People please her, but do not move her. She has a cold heart and a licentious head. As to her soul—if she has one, which is doubtful —it is of the blackest, and there is no wickedness or baseness of which it is incapable; but she is very dexterous, and she keeps up appearances just so far as is necessary to prevent anything being proved against her. She will grant her favours to a man without ado, but will not write him the simplest note. Accordingly her most intimate enemies can find nothing to say about her except that she rouges too highly, and that certain portions of her person have not in truth all the roundness that they seem to possess—which is false.'

" 'How do you know?'

" 'What a question! in the only way one knows things of the kind, by finding out for myself.'

" 'Then you've been intimate with Madame de Thémines?'

" 'Certainly! Why not? It would have been most unbecoming if I had not had her. She has been of great service to me, and I am very grateful for it.'

" 'I do not understand the nature of the services she can have rendered you.'

" 'Are you really a fool then?' said De C——, looking at me with the most comical air in the world. 'Upon my word, I am afraid so. Must I tell you the whole story? Madame de Thémines is reputed, and deservedly so, to have special knowledge on certain subjects, and a young man that she has taken up and favoured for a while may present himself boldly everywhere, and be sure that he will not remain for long without having an affair on hand, and two rather than one. Besides this unspeakable advantage, there is another no less important, which is, that as soon as the women of the world here see that you are the recognised lover of Madame de Thémines, they will make it a pleasure and a duty, even if they have not the least liking for you, to carry you off from a woman who is the fashion as she is. Instead of the advances and proceedings that would have been necessary, you will not know where to choose, and you will of necessity become the object of all the allurements and affections imaginable.

" 'Nevertheless, if she inspires you with too great a repugnance, do not take her. You are not exactly obliged to do so, though it would have been polite and proper. But make a choice quickly, and attack her who pleases you most, or who seems to afford you most facilities, for delay would lose you the benefit of novelty, and the advantage it gives you for a few days over all the cavaliers here. All these ladies have no conception of those passions which have their birth in intimacy, and develop slowly with respect and silence. They are for thunderbolts and occult sympathies—something marvellously well imagined to save the tedium of resistance, and all the prolixity and repetition which sentiment mingles with the romance of love, and which only serve to delay the conclusion uselessly. These ladies are very economical of their time, and it appears so precious to them that they would be grieved to leave a single minute unemployed. They have a desire to oblige mankind, which cannot be too highly praised, and they love their neighbour as themselves, which is quite according to the Gospel, and very meritorious. They are very charitable creatures, who would not for anything in the world cause a man to die of despair.

" 'There must be three or four already smitten in your favour, and I would advise you in a friendly way to pursue your point with spirit over these instead of amusing yourself gossiping with me in the embrasure of a window, which will not advance you to any great extent.'

" 'But, my dear De C——, I am quite new to this kind of thing. I am utterly without the power to distinguish at first sight a woman who is smitten from one who is not; and I might make strange blunders if you did not assist me with your experience.'

" 'You are really as primitive as you can be. I did not think that it was possible to be as pastoral and bucolic as that in the present blessed century! What the devil do you do, then, with the large pair of black eyes that you have there, and that would have the most crushing effect if you knew how to make use of them?

" 'Just look yonder a moment at that little woman in rose, playing with her fan in the corner near the fireplace. She has been eyeing you for a quarter of an hour with the most significant fixity and assiduity. There is not another in the world who can be indecent after such a superior fashion, and display such noble shamelessness. She is greatly disliked by the women who despair of ever attaining to such a height of impudence, but to compensate for this, she is greatly liked by the men, who find in her all the piquancy of a courtesan. She is in truth charmingly depraved, and full of wit, spirit, and caprice. She is an excellent preceptor for a young man with prejudices. In a week she will rid your conscience of all scruples, and corrupt your heart in such a way that you will never be a subject for ridicule or elegy. She has inexpressibly practical ideas about everything; she goes to the bottom of things with a swiftness and certainty that are astonishing. She is algebra incarnate, is that little woman. She is precisely what is needed by a dreamer and an enthusiast. She will soon cure you of your vapourish idealism, and she will do you a great service. She will moreover do it with the greatest pleasure, for it is an instinct with her to disenchant poets.'

"My curiosity being aroused by De C——'s description, I left my retreat, and gliding through the various groups, approached the lady, and looked at her with much attention. She was perhaps twenty-five or twenty-six years of age. Her figure was small, but well made, though somewhat inclined to embonpoint. Her arm was white and plump, her hand noble, her foot pretty and even too delicate, her shoulders full and glossy, and her bosom small, but what there was of it very satisfactory, and giving a favourable idea of the remainder. As to her hair, it was splendid in the extreme, of a blue black, like that of a jackdaw's wing. The corner of her eye was turned up rather high towards the temple, her nose slender with very open nostrils, her mouth humid and sensual, a little furrow in the lower lip, and an almost imperceptible down where the upper was united to it. And with all this there was such life, animation, health, force, and such an indefinable expression of lust skilfully tempered with coquetry and intrigue, that she was in short a very desirable creature, and more than justified the eager likings which she had inspired and still inspired every day.

"I wished for her; but I nevertheless understood that, agreeable as she was, she was not the woman who would realise my desire, and make me say, 'At last I have a mistress!'

"I returned to De C—— and said to him: 'I like the lady well enough, and I shall perhaps make arrangements with her. But before saying anything definite and binding, I should be very glad if you would be kind enough to point me out these indulgent beauties who had the goodness to be smitten with me, so that I may make a choice. It would please me, too, seeing that you are acting as demonstrator to me here, if you would add a little account of them with the nomenclature of their qualities and their defects, the manner in which they should be attacked, and the tone to adopt with them in order that I may not look too much like a provincial or an author.'

" 'Willingly,' said De C——. 'Do you see that beautiful melancholy swan, displaying her neck so harmoniously, and moving her sleeves as though they were wings? She is modesty itself—everything that is chastest and most maidenly in the world. She has a brow of snow, a heart of ice, the looks of a Madonna, the smile of a simpleton, her dress is white, and her soul is the same. She puts nothing but orange-blossoms or leaves of the water-lily in her hair, and she is connected with the earth only by a thread. She has never had an evil thought, and she is profoundly ignorant of how a man differs from a woman. The Holy Virgin is a Bacchante beside her, which, however, does not prevent her from having had more lovers than any other woman of my acquaintance, and that is saying a good deal. Just examine this discreet person's bosom for a moment; it is a little masterpiece, and it is really difficult to show so much while hiding more. Say, is she not, with all her restrictions and all her prudery, ten times more indecent than that good lady on her left, who is making a grand show of two hemispheres, which, if they were joined together, would make a map of the world of natural size, or than the other on her right, whose dress is open almost to her stomach, and who is parading her nothingness with charming intrepidity?

" 'This maidenly creature, if I am not greatly mistaken, has already computed in her head the amount of love and passion promised by your paleness and black eyes, and what makes me say so is the fact that she has not once, apparently, at least, looked towards you; for she can move her eyes with so much art, and look out of the corner of them so skilfully, that nothing escapes her; one would think that she could see out of the back of her head, for she knows perfectly well what is going on behind her. She is a female Janus. If you would succeed with her you must lay swaggering and victorious manners aside. You must speak to her without looking at her, without making any movement, in an attitude of contrition, and in suppressed and respectful tones. In this way you may say to her what you will, provided it be suitably veiled, and she will allow you the greatest freedom at first of speech, and afterwards of action. Only be careful to look at her with tenderness when her own eyes are cast down, and speak to her of the sweets of platonic love and of the intercourse of the soul, while employing the least platonic and ideal pantomime in the world! She is very sensual and very susceptible; embrace her as much as you like; but, when most freely intimate with her, do not forget to call her *madame* two or three times in every sentence. She quarrelled with me because when I was most intimate with her I addressed her familiarly when saying something or other. The devil! a woman is not virtuous for nothing.'

" 'I have no great desire to hazard the adventure, after what you have told me. A prudish Messalina! the union is monstrous and strange.'

" 'It is as old as the world, my dear fellow! It is to be seen every day, and nothing is more common. You are wrong not to have fixed upon her. She has one great charm, which is, that with her a man always seems to be committing mortal sin, and the least kiss appears perfectly damnable, while in the case of others he scarcely thinks the sin a venial one, and often even thinks nothing of it at all. That is why I kept her longer than any other mistress. I should have had her still if she had not left me herself. She is the only woman who has anticipated me, and I have a certain respect for her on that account. She has little voluptuous refinements of the most exquisite delicacy, and she possesses the great art of making it appear that she has wrested from her what she grants very willingly—a circumstance which gives each of her favours a peculiar charm. You will find in the world ten of her lovers who will swear to you on their honour that she is the most virtuous creature in existence. She is just the contrary. It is a curious study to anatomise virtue of that kind on a pillow. Being forewarned you will not run any risk, and you will not have the awkwardness to fall really in love with her.'

" 'And how old is this adorable person?' I asked, for, examining her with the most scrupulous attention, I found it impossible to determine her age.

" 'Ah! how old is she? That is just the mystery, and God alone knows. I who pique myself on telling a woman's age to within a minute have never been able to find out. I merely estimate approximately that she is perhaps from eighteen to thirty-six years of age. I have seen her in full dress, in dishabille, and less scantily clad, and I can tell you nothing with respect to this. My knoweldge is at fault; the age which she seems particularly to be is eighteen, yet that cannot be the case. She has the body of a maiden and the soul of a gay woman, and to become so deeply and so speciously depraved, much time or genius is necessary; it is needful to have a heart of bronze in a breast of steel; she has neither one nor the other, and I therefore think that she is thirty-six; but practically I do not know.'

" 'Has she no intimate friend who could give you information on this point?'

" 'No. She arrived in this town two years ago. She came from the country, or from abroad, I forget which—an admirable situation for a woman who knows how to turn it to account. With such a face as hers she might give herself any age she liked, and date only from the day that she arrived here.'

" 'Nothing could be more pleasant, especially when some impertinent wrinkle does not come to give you the lie, and time, the Great Destroyer, has the goodness to lend himself to this falsification of the certificate of baptism.'

"He showed me some others who, according to him, would favourably receive all the petitions that it might please me to address to them, and would treat me with most particular philanthropy. But the woman in rose at the corner of the fire-place, and the modest dove who served as her antithesis, were incomparably better than all the rest; and if they had not all the qualities which I required, they had, in appearance at least, some of them.

"I conversed the whole evening with them, especially with the latter, and was careful to cast my ideas in the most respectful mould. Although she scarcely looked at me, I thought that I saw her eyes gleam sometimes beneath their curtain of eyelashes, and, when I ventured some rather lively gallantries, clothed, however, in most modest guise, a little blush, checked and suppressed, pass two or three lines below her skin, similar to that produced by a rose-coloured liquid when poured into a semi-opaque cup. Her replies were, in general, sober and circumspect, yet acute and full of point, and they suggested more than they expressed. All this was intermingled with omissions, hints, indirect allusions, each syllable having its purpose, and each silence its import. Nothing in the world could have been more diplomatic and more charming. And yet, whatever pleasure I may have taken in it for the moment, I could not keep up a conversation of the kind for long. One must be perpetually on the alert and on one's guard, and what I like best of all in a chat is freedom and familiarity.

"We spoke at first of music, which led us quite naturally to speak of the Opera, next of women, and then of love, a subject in which it is easier than in any other to find means of passing from the general to the particular. We vied with each other in making love; you would have laughed to listen to me. In truth, Amadis on the poor Roche was but a pedant without fire beside me. There was generosity, and abnegation, and devotion enough to cause the deceased Roman, Curtius, to blush for shame. I really did not think myself capable of such transcendent balderdash and bombast.

"I playing at the most quintessential Platonism—does it not strike you as a most facetious thing, as the best comedy scene that could be presented? And then, good heavens! the perfectly devout air, the little, demure, and hypocritical ways that I displayed! I looked most innocent, and any mother who had heard me reasoning would not have hesitated at all in letting me go about with her daughter, and any husband would have entrusted his wife to me. On that evening I appeared more virtuous, and was less so than ever in my life before. I thought that it was more difficult than that to play the hypocrite, and to say things without in the least believing them. It must be easy enough, or I must be very apt to have succeeded so agreeably the first time. In truth, I have some fine moments.

"As to the lady, she said many things that were most ingeniously detailed, and which, in spite of the appearance of frankness which she threw into them, denoted the most consummate experience. You can form no idea of the subtlety of her distinctions. That woman would saw a hair into three parts lengthways, and would disconcert all the angelic and seraphic doctors. For the rest, she speaks in such a manner that it is impossible to believe that she has even the shadow of a body. She is immaterial, vaporous, and ideal enough to make you break your arms, and if De C—— had not warned me about the ways of the animal, I should assuredly have despaired of success, and have stood piteously aside. And when a woman tells you for two hours, with the most disengaging air in the world, that love lives only by privations and sacrifices, and other fine things of the sort, how the devil can you decently hope to persuade her some day to place herself in such a situation with you as will enable you to discover whether you are both made alike?

"In short, we separated on very friendly terms, with reciprocal congratulations on the loftiness and purity of our sentiments.

"The conversation with the other one was, as you may imagine, of quite an opposite description. We laughed as much as we spoke. We made fun very wittily of all the women who were there; but I am mistaken when I say: 'We made fun of them very wittily.' I should have said that 'she' did so, for a man can never laugh effectively at a woman.

For my part, I listened and approved, for it would have been impossible to draw a more lively sketch, or to colour it more highly. It was the most curious gallery of caricatures that I have ever seen. In spite of the exaggeration, one could see the truth underlying it. De C——was quite right; the mission of this woman is to disenchant poets. She has about her an atmosphere of prose in which a poetical thought cannot live.

"She is charming and sparkling with wit, yet beside her one thinks only of base and vulgar things. While speaking to her I felt a crowd of desires incongruous and impracticable in the place where I was, such as to call for wine and get drunk, to place her on one of my knees and madly kiss her, to raise the hem of her skirt and see whether her ankle was slender or just the reverse, to sing a ribald refrain with all my might, to smoke a pipe, or to break the windows—in short, to do anything. All the animal part, all the brute, rose within me; I would willingly have spat on the Iliad of Homer; and I would have gone on my knees to a ham. I can now quite understand the allegory of the companions of Ulysses being changed into swine by Circe. Circe was probably some lively creature like my little woman in rose.

"Shameful to relate, I experienced great delight in feeling myself overtaken by brutishness; I made no resistance, but assisted it as much as I could—so natural is depravity to man, and so much mire is there in the clay of which he is formed.

"Yet for one moment I feared the canker that was seizing upon me, and wished to leave my corrupter; but the floor seemed to have risen to my knees, and it was as though I were set fast in my place.

"At last I took it on me to leave her, and, the evening being far advanced, I returned home much perplexed and troubled, and without very well knowing what to do. I hesitated between the prude and her opposite. I found voluptuousness in one and piquancy in the other, and after a most minute and searching self-examination, I found, not that I loved them both, but that I wished sufficiently for them both, for one as much as for the other, to dream about them and be preoccupied with the thought of them.

"To all appearance, my friend, I shall gain over one of these women, and perhaps both; and yet I confess to you that the possession of them will only half satisfy me. It is not that they are not very pretty, but at sight of them nothing cried out within me, nothing panted, nothing said, 'It is they.' I did not recognise them. Nevertheless, I do not think that I shall meet with anything much better so far as birth and beauty are concerned, and De C—— advises me to go no further. I shall certainly take his advice, and one or other of them will be my mistress, or the devil will take me before very long; but at the bottom of my heart a secret voice reproaches me for being false to my love, and for stopping thus at the first smile of a woman for whom I care nothing, instead of seeking untiringly through the world, in cloisters and in evil places, in palaces and in taverns, for her who, whether she be princess or serving-maid, nun or courtesan, has been made for me and destined to me by God.

"Then I say to myself that I am fancying chimeras, and that it is after all just the same whether I sleep with this woman or with another; that it will not cause the earth to deviate by a hair's breadth from its path, or the four seasons to reverse their order; that nothing in the world can be of smaller moment; and that I am very simple to torment myself with such crotchets. This is what I say to myself; but it is all in vain! I am not more tranquil nor resolved than before.

"This, perhaps, results from the fact that I live a great deal with myself, and that the most petty details in a life so monotonous as mine assume too great an importance. I pay too much attention to my living and thinking. I hearken to the throbbing of my arteries, and the beatings of my heart; by dint of close attention I detach my most fleeting ideas from the cloudy vapour in which they float, and give them a body. If I acted more I should not perceive all these petty things, and I should not have time to be looking at my soul through a microscope, as I do the whole day long. The noise of action would put to flight this swarm of idle thoughts which flutter through my heart, and stun me with the buzzing of their wings. Instead of pursuing phantoms I should grapple with realities; I should ask from women only what they can give—pleasure; and I should not seek to embrace some fantastic ideal attired in cloudy perfections.

"This intense straining of the eye of my soul after an invisible object has distorted my vision. I cannot see what is for my gazing at what is not; and my eye, so keen for the ideal, is perfectly near-sighted in matters of reality. Thus I have known women who are declared charming by everybody, and who appear to me to be anything but that. I have greatly admired pictures generally considered bad, and odd or unintelligible verses have given me more pleasure than the most worthy productions. I should not be astonished if, after offering up so many sighs to the moon, staring so often at the stars, and composing so many elegies and sentimental apostrophes, I were to fall in love with some vulgar prostitute or some ugly old woman. That would be a fine downfall! Reality will perhaps revenge herself in this way for the carelessness with which I have courted her. Would it not be a nice thing if I were to be smitten with a fine romantic passion for some awkward cross-patch or some abominable trollop? Can you see me playing the guitar beneath a kitchen window, and ousted by a scullion carrying the pug of an old dowager who is getting rid of her last tooth?

"Perhaps, too, finding nothing in the world worthy of my love, I shall end by adoring myself, like the late Narcissus of egotistical memory. To secure myself against so great misfortune, I look into all the mirrors and all the brooks that I come across. In truth, with my reveries and aberrations, I am tremendously afraid of falling into the monstrous or unnatural. It is a serious matter, and I must take care.

"Good-bye, my friend; I am going directly to see the lady in rose, lest I should give myself up to my customary meditations. I do not think that we pay much attention to entelechia, and I imagine that anything we may do will have no connection with spiritualism, although she is a very spiritual creature: I carefully roll up the pattern of my ideal mistress, and put it away in a drawer, that I may not use it as a test with her. I wish to enjoy peacefully the beauties and the merits that she possesses. I wish to leave her attired in a robe that suits her, without trying to adapt for her the vesture that I have cut out beforehand, and at all hazards for the lady of my thoughts. These are very wise resolutions; I do not know whether I shall keep them. Once more, good-bye."

III

~~~~~~~~~~~~~~~

I am the established lover of the lady in rose; it is almost a call or a charge, and gives one stability in society. I am no longer like a school-boy seeking good luck among the grandmothers, and not venturing to utter a madrigal to a woman unless she is a centenarian. I perceive that since my installation people think more of me, that all the women speak to me with jealous coquetry, and put themselves very much about on my account. The men, on the contrary, are colder, and there is something of hostility and constraint in the few words that we exchange. They feel that they have in me a rival who is already formidable, and who may become more so.

"I have been told that many of them had criticised my manner of dress with bitterness, and said that it was too effeminate; that my hair was curled and glossed with over much care; that this, joined to my beardless face, gave me the most ridiculously foppish appearance; that for my garments I affected rich and splendid materials which had the odour of the theatre about them, and that I was more like an actor than a man—all the commonplaces in fact that people utter in order to give themselves the right of being dirty and of wearing sorry and badly-cut coats. But all this only serves to whitewash me, and all the ladies think that my hair is the handsomest in the world, and that my refinements in dress are in the best taste, and they seem very much inclined to indemnify me for the expense I have gone to on their account—for they are not so foolish as to believe that all this elegance is merely intended for my own personal adornment.

"The lady of the house seemed at first somewhat piqued by my choice, which she had thought must of necessity have fallen upon herself, and for a few days she harboured some bitterness on account of it (towards her rival only; for she has always spoken in the same way to me), which manifested itself in sundry little 'My dears,' uttered in that sharp, jerky manner which is the exclusive property of women, and in sundry unkind opinions respecting her toilet given in as loud a tone as possible, such as: 'Your hair is dressed a great deal too high, and does not suit your face in the least;' or, 'Your bodice is creased under the arms; whoever made that dress for you?' or, 'You look very wearied; you seem quite changed;' and a thousand other small observations, to which the other failed not to reply when an opportunity presented itself with all the malice that could be desired; and if the opportunity did not come soon enough, she herself provided one for her own use, and gave back more than she had received. But another object diverting the attention of the slighted Infanta, this little wordy war soon came to an end, and things returned to their usual order.

"I have told you summarily that I am the established lover of the lady in rose, but that is not enough for so exact a man as you. You will no doubt ask me what she is called. As to her name, I will not tell it to you; but if you like, to facilitate the narrative, and in memory of the colour of the dress in which I saw her for the first time, we will call her Rosette; it is a pretty name, and it was thus that my little puss was called.

"You will wish to know in detail—for you love precision in matters of this kind—the history of our loves with this fair Bradamant, and by what successive gradations I passed from the general to the particular, and from the condition of simple spectator to that of actor; how from being an indifferent onlooker I have become a lover. I will gratify your wish with the greatest pleasure. There is nothing sinister in our romance. It is rose-coloured, and no tears are shed in it save those of pleasure; no delays or repetitions are to be met with in it; and everything advances towards the end with the haste and swiftness so strongly recommended by Horace; it is a truly French romance.

"Nevertheless, do not imagine that I carried the fortress at the first assault. The Princess, though very humane towards her subjects, is not so lavish of her favours as one might think at first. She knows the value of them too well not to make you buy them; and she further knows too well the eagerness given to desire by apt delay, and the flavour given to pleasure by a show of resistance, to surrender herself to you all at once, however strong the liking may be with which you have inspired her.

"To tell you the story in full I must go a little further back. I gave you a sufficiently circumstantial narrative of our first interview. I had one or two more in the same house, or perhaps three, and then she invited me to go and see her; I did not wait to be pressed, as you may well believe; I went at first with discretion, then somewhat oftener, then oftener still, and at last whenever I felt so inclined, and I must confess that that happened at least three or four times a day. The lady, after a few hours' absence, always received me as if I had just returned from the East Indies; I was very sensible of this, and it obliged me to show my gratitude in a manner marked with the greatest gallantry and tenderness in the world, to which she responded to the best of her ability.

"Rosette, since we have agreed to call her so, is a woman of great sense, and one who understands men admirably; and although she delayed the conclusion of the chapter for some time, I was never once out of temper with her. This is truly wonderful, for you know the fine passions I fall into when I have not at once what I desire, and when a woman exceeds the time that I have assigned her, in my head, for her surrender.

"I do not know how she managed it, but from the first interview she gave me to understand that she would be mine, and I was more sure of it than if I had had the promise written and signed with her own hand. It will be said, perhaps, that the boldness and ease of her manners left the ground clear for the rashness of hopes. I do not think that this can be the true reason: I have seen some women whose extraordinary freedom excluded in a measure the very shadow of a doubt, who have yet not produced this effect upon me, and with whom I have experienced timidity and disquietude when they were at the least out of place.

"What makes me much less amiable with the women whom I wish to overcome than with those about whom I am unconcerned, is the passionate waiting for the opportunity, and the uncertainty in which I am respecting the success of my undertaking: this makes me gloomy, and throws me into a delirium, which robs me of many of my talents and much of my presence of mind. When I see the hours which I had destined for a different employment escaping one by one, anger seizes me in spite of myself, and I cannot prevent myself from saying very sharp and bitter things, which are sometimes even brutal, and which throw things back a hundred leagues. With Rosette I felt nothing of all this; never, even when she was resisting me the most, had I the idea that she wished to escape my love. I allowed her quietly to display all her little coquetries, and I endured with patience the somewhat long delays which it pleased her to inflict on my ardour. Her severity had something smiling in it which consoled you as much as possible, and in her most Hyrcanian cruelties you had a glimpse of a background of humanity which hardly allowed you to have any serious fear.

"Virtuous women, even when they are least so, have a cross and disdainful appearance which to me is intolerable. They always look as if they were ready to ring the bell and have you kicked out of the house by their lackeys; and I really think that a man who takes the trouble to pay his addresses to a woman (which as it is, is not so agreeable as one would fain believe) does not deserve to be looked at in that way.

"Our dear Rosette has no such looks—and, I assure you, that it is to her advantage. She is the only woman with whom I have been myself, and I have the conceit to say that I have never been so good. My wit is freely displayed, and by the dexterity and the fire of her replies she has made me discover more than I credited myself with, and more, perhaps, than I really have. It is true that I have not been very logical; that is scarcely possible with her. It is not, however, that she has not her poetical side, in spite of what De C—— said about it; but she is so full of life, and force, and movement, she seems so well off in the atmosphere in which she is, that one has no wish to leave it in order to ascend into the clouds. She fills real life so agreeably, and makes such an amusing thing of it for herself and others, that dreamland has nothing better to offer you.

"What a wonderful thing! I have known her now for nearly two months, and during that time I have felt weary only when I was not with her. You will acknowledge that it is no ordinary woman that can produce such an effect, for usually women produce just the reverse effect upon me, and please me much more at a distance than when close at hand.

"Rosette has the best disposition in the world, with men, be it understood, for with women she is as wicked as a devil. She is gay, lively, alert, ready for everything, very original in her way of speaking, and always with some charming and unexpected drolleries to say to you. She is a delicious companion, a pretty comrade whom one is fond of, rather than a mistress, and if I had a few years more and a few romantic ideas less, it would be all one to me, and I should even esteem myself the most fortunate mortal in existence. But—but—a particle which announces nothing good, and this little limiting devil of a word is unfortunately more used than any other in all human languages;—but I am a fool, an idiot, a veritable ninny who can be satisfied with nothing, and who is always conjuring up difficulties where none exist, and I am only half happy instead of being wholly so. Half is a good deal for this world of ours, and yet I do not find it enough.

"In the eyes of all the world I have a mistress whom many wish for and envy me, and whom no one would disdain. My desire is therefore apparently fulfilled, and I have no longer any right to pick quarrels with fate. Yet I do not seem to have a mistress; I understand by reasoning that such is the case, but I do not feel it to be so, and if some one were to ask me unexpectedly whether I had one, I believe I should answer 'No.' Nevertheless, the possession of a woman who has beauty and wit constitutes what at all times and in all lands has been and is called having a mistress, and I do not think that any other mode exists. This does not prevent me from having the strangest doubts on the subject, and it has gone so far that if several persons were to conspire to affirm to me that I am not Rosette's favoured lover, I should, in spite of the palpable evidence to the contrary, end by believing them.

"Do not imagine from what I have told you that I do not love her, or that she displeases me in any way. On the contrary, I love her very much, and I find her, as all the rest of the world will find her, a pretty, piquant creature. I simply do not feel that she is mine, and that is all. And yet no woman has ever made herself more engaging, and if ever I have understood what voluptuousness is, it was in her arms. A single kiss from her, the chastest of her endearments, makes me quiver to the soles of my feet, and sends all my blood flowing back to my heart.

Account for all this if you can. It is just as I tell you. But the heart of man is full of such absurdities, and if it were necessary to reconcile all its contradictions, we should have enough to do.

"What can be the origin of this? In truth I do not know.

"I see her the whole day, and even the whole night if I wish. I give her all the caresses that I please when we are by ourselves both in town and country. Her complaisance is inexhaustible, and she enters thoroughly into all my caprices, however whimsical they may be. One evening I was seized with a fancy to fondle her roughly in the drawing-room, with the lustre and candles lighted, a fire on the hearth, the easy chairs arranged as if for a great evening reception, she dressed for a ball with her bouquet and fan, all her diamonds on her fingers and neck, plumes on her head, and in the most splendid costume possible, while I myself was dressed like a bear. She consented to my whim. When all was ready the servants were greatly surprised to receive an order not to allow anybody to come up; they did not seem to understand it in the least, and they went off with a dazed look which made us laugh greatly. Without doubt they thought that their mistress was distinctly mad, but what they did or did not think was of little moment to us.

"It was the drollest evening of my life. Imagine to yourself the appearance I must have presented with my plumed hat under my paw, rings on all my claws, a little sword with a silver guard, and a sky-blue ribbon at the hilt. I approached the fair one, and after making her a most graceful bow, seated myself by her side, and laid siege to her in all due form. The affected madrigals, the exaggerated gallantries which I addressed to her, all the jargon of the occasion was singularly set off by passing through my bear's muzzle, for I had a superb head of painted cardboard, which, however, I was soon obliged to throw under the table, so adorable was my deity that evening, and so greatly did I long to kiss her hand, and something better than her hand. The skin followed close on the head, for, not being accustomed to play the bear, I was greatly stifled in it and more so than was necessary.

"The ball costume had then a fine time of it, as you may believe; the plumes fell like snow around my beauty, her round white shoulders were scarcely confined by the sleeves, her bosom heaved above her corset, her feet emerged from her shoes. The necklaces became unstrung, and rolled on the floor, and I think that never was more fresh a dress more piteously crushed and rumpled; the dress was of silver gauze, with a lining of white satin. Rosette displayed on this occasion a heroism which was quite beyond that of her sex, and which gave me the highest opinion of her. She looked on at the wreck of her toilet as though she was a disinterested spectator, and not for a single instant did she show the least regret for her dress and her laces; on the contrary, she was madly gay, and even assisted herself in the ill-treatment to which her finery was subjected by me at the height of my frenzy.

"Do you not think this fine enough to be recorded in history beside the most splendid deeds of the heroes of antiquity? The greatest proof of love that a woman can give her lover is not to say to him: 'Take care not to rumple me or stain me,' especially if her dress is new. A new dress is a stronger motive for a husband's security than is commonly believed. Rosette must worship me, or she possesses a philosophy superior to that of Epictetus.

"However, I think that I paid Rosette the worth of her dress in caresses—a coin which is not the less esteemed and prized that it does not pass current with the shopkeepers. So much heroism as she displayed well deserved a reward, and, like a generous woman, she well repaid what I bestowed on her. I experienced a mad delight, such as I did not believe myself capable of feeling. Those sounding kisses mingled with piercing laughs, those quivering and impatient caresses, all that irritating enjoyment, that incomplete pleasure, a hundred times keener than if it had been without impediment, had such an effect upon my nerves that I was seized with acute spasms, from which I recovered with difficulty.

"You cannot imagine the tender and proud air with which Rosette looked at me, and the manner, full of joy and disquietude, in which she busied herself about me. Her face still radiated the pleasure which she felt at producing such an effect upon me, while at the same time her eyes, bathed in gentle tears, bore witness to the fear that she experienced at seeing me ill, and the interest that she took in my health.

Never has she appeared to me so beautiful as she did at that moment. There was something so maternal and so chaste in her look, that I totally forgot the more than Anacreontic scene which had just taken place, and, kneeling before her, asked permission to kiss her hand. This she granted me with singular gravity and dignity.

"Assuredly such a woman is not so depraved as De C—— pretends, and as she has often seemed to myself. Her corruption is of the mind, and not of the heart.

"I have quoted this scene to you from among twenty others, and it seems to me that after this a man might, without extreme conceit, believe himself to be a woman's lover. Well, it is what I do not do. I had scarcely returned home when the same thought again took possession of me, and began to torment me as usual. I remembered perfectly all that I had done and seen done. The most trivial gestures and attitudes, all the most petty details, were very clearly delineated in my memory; I recalled everything, to the lightest inflections of voice and the most fleeting shades of enjoyment; and yet I did not seem to realize that all these things had happened to myself rather than to another. I was not sure that it was not an illusion, a phantasmagoria, a dream, or that I had not read it somewhere, or even that it was not a tale composed by myself, just as similar ones had often been made by me. I was afraid of being the dupe of my own credulity and the butt of some hoax; and in spite of the witness borne by my lassitude, and the material proofs that I had slept elsewhere, I would have been ready to believe that I had put myself under my bedclothes at my usual time, and had slept till morning.

"I am very unfortunate in not having the capacity to acquire the moral certainty of a thing, the physical certainty of which I possess. Generally the reverse happens, and it is the fact that proves the idea. I would fain prove the fact to myself by the idea; I cannot do so; though this is singular enough, it is the case. The possession of a mistress depends upon myself up to a certain point, but I cannot bring myself to believe that I have one while having her all the time. If I have not the necessary faith within me, even for something so evident as this, it is as impossible for me to believe in so simple a fact as it is for another to believe in the Trinity. Faith is not acquired; it is purely a gift, a special grace from Heaven.

"Never has any one desired so strongly as myself to live the life of others, and to assimilate another nature; never has any one succeeded less in doing so. Whatever I may do, other men are to me scarcely anything but phantoms, and I have no sense of their existence; yet it is not the desire to recognise their life and to participate in it that is wanting in me. It is the power, or the lack of real sympathy for anything. The existence or non-existence of a thing or person does not interest me sufficiently to affect me in a sensible and convincing manner.

"The sight of a woman or a man who appears to me in real life leaves no stronger traces upon my soul than the fantastic vision of a dream. About me there moves, with dull humming sound, a pale world of shadows and semblances false or true, in the midst of which I am as isolated as possible, for none of them acts on me for good or evil, and they seem to me to be of quite a different nature. If I speak to them, and they reply to me with something like common-sense, I am as much surprised as if my dog or my cat were suddenly to begin to speak and mingle in the conversation. The sound of their voices always astonishes me, and I would be very ready to believe that they are merely fleeting appearances whose objective mirror I am. Inferior or superior, I am certainly not of this kind.

"There are moments when I recognise none save God above me, and others, when I judge myself scarcely the equal of the wood-louse beneath its stone, or the mollusc on its sand-bank; but in whatever state of mind I may be, whether lofty or depressed, I have never been able to persuade myself that men were really my fellows. When people call me 'Sir,' or in speaking about me, say, 'this man,' it appears very singular to me. Even my name seems to me but an empty one, and not in reality mine, yet no matter in how low a tone it be pronounced amidst the loudest noise, I turn suddenly with a convulsive and feverish eagerness for which I have never been able to account to myself. Can it be the dread of finding in this man who knows my name, and to whom I am no longer one of the crowd, an antagonist or an enemy?

"It is especially when I have been living with a woman that I have most felt the invincible repugnance of my nature to any alliance or mixture. I am like a drop of oil in a glass of water. It is in vain that you turn and move the latter; the oil can never unite with it. It will divide itself into a hundred thousand little globules which will reunite and mount again to the surface as soon as there is a moment's calm. The drop of oil and the glass of water—such is my history. Even voluptuousness, that diamond chain which binds all creatures together, that devouring fire which melts the rocks and metals of the soul, and makes them fall in tears, as material fire causes iron and granite to melt, has never, all powerful as it is, succeeded in taming and affecting me. Yet my senses are very keen, but my soul is to my body a hostile sister, and the hapless couple, like every possible couple, lawful or unlawful, live in a state of perpetual war. A woman's arms, the closest bonds on earth, so people say, are very feeble ties, so far as I am concerned, and I have never been further removed from my mistress than when she was pressing me to her heart. I was stifled, that was all.

"How many times have I been angered with myself! How many efforts have I made not to be as I am! How have I exhorted myself to be tender, amorous, impassioned! How often have I taken my soul by the hair, and dragged her to my lips in the midst of a beautiful kiss! Whatever I did she always retreated as soon as I released her. What torture for this poor soul to be exposed to these mad caprices of mine, and to sit everlastingly at banquets where she has nothing to eat!

"It was with Rosette that I resolved, once for all, to try whether I was not decidedly unsociable, and whether I could take sufficient interest in the existence of another to believe in it. I pushed my experiments to the point of exhaustion, and I did not become much clearer amid my doubts. With her, pleasure is so keen that often enough the soul is, if not moved, at least diverted, and this somewhat prejudices the exactness of my observations. But after all I came to see that it did not pass beyond the skin, and that I had only an epidermic enjoyment in which the soul took no part save from curiosity. I have pleasure, because I am young and ardent; but this pleasure comes to me from myself and not from another. The cause of it is in myself rather than in Rosette.

"My efforts are in vain, I cannot come out of myself. I am still what I was, something, that is to say, very wearied and very wearisome, and this displeases me greatly. I have not succeeded in getting into my brain the idea of another, into my soul the feeling of another, into my body the pain or joy of another. I am a prisoner within myself, and all invasion is impossible. The prisoner wishes to escape, the walls would most gladly fall in, and the gates open up to let him through, but some fatality or other invincibly keeps each stone in its place, and each bolt in its socket. It is as impossible for me to admit any one to see me as it is for me to go to see others, I can neither pay visits nor receive them, and I live in the most mournful isolation in the midst of the crowd. My bed perhaps is not widowed, but my heart is so always.

"Ah! to be unable to increase one's self by a single particle, a single atom; to be unable to make the blood of others flow in one's veins; to see ever with one's own eyes, and not more clearly, nor further, nor differently; to hear sounds with the same ears and the same emotion; to touch with the same fingers; to perceive things that are varied with an organ that is invariable; to be condemned to the same quality of voice, to the return of the same tones, the same phrases, and the same words, and to be unable to go away, to avoid one's self, to take refuge in some corner where there is no self-pursuit; to be obliged to keep one's self always, to dine with it, and go to bed with it; to be the same man for twenty new women; to drag into the midst of the strangest situations in the drama of our life a reluctant character whose *rôle* you know by heart; to think the same things, and to have the same dreams: what torment, what weariness!

"I have longed for the horn of the brothers Tangut, the cap of Fortunatus, the staff of Abaris, the ring of Gyges; I would have sold my soul to snatch the magic wand from the hand of a fairy, but I have never wished so much for anything as, like Tiresias the soothsayer, to meet on the mountain the serpents which cause a change of sex, and what I envy most in the monstrous and whimsical gods of India are their perpetual *avatars* and their countless transformations.

"I began by desiring to be another man; then, on reflecting that I might by analogy nearly foresee what I should feel, and thus not experience the surprise and the change that I had looked for, I would have preferred to be a woman. This idea has always come to me when I had a mistress who was not ugly—for to me an ugly woman is simply a man—and at particular moments I would willingly have changed my part, for it is very provoking to be unaware of the effect that one produces, and to judge of the enjoyment of others only by one's own. These thoughts, and many others, have often given me, at times when it was most out of place, a meditative and dreamy air, which has led to my being accused, really most undeservedly, of coldness and infidelity.

"Rosette, who very happily does not know all this, believes me the most amorous man on earth; she takes this impotent transport for a transport of passion; and to the best of her ability she lends herself to all the experimental caprices that enter my head.

"I have done all that I could to convince myself that I possess her. I have tried to descend into her heart, but I have always stopped at the first step of the staircase, at her skin or on her mouth. In spite of the particular intimacy of our relations, I am very sensible that there is nothing in common between us. Never has an idea similar to mine spread its wings in that young and smiling head; never has that heart, full of life and fire, that heaves with its throbbing so firm and pure a breast, beaten in unison with my heart. My soul has never united with that soul. Cupid, the god with hawk's wings, has not kissed Psyche on her beautiful ivory brow. No! this woman does not belong to me.

"If you knew all that I have done to compel my soul to share in the love of my body, the frenzy with which I have plunged my mouth into hers, and steeped my arms in her hair, and how closely I have strained her round and supple form! Like the ancient Salmacis enamoured of the young Hermaphrodite, I strove to blend her frame with mine; I drank her breath and the tepid tears caused by voluptuousness to overflow from the brimming chalice of her eyes. The more she drew me towards her, and the closer our embraces, the less I loved her. My soul, seated mournfully, gazed with an air of pity on this lamentable marriage to which he was not invited, or veiling her face in disgust, wept silently beneath the skirt of her cloak. All this comes perhaps from the fact that in reality I do not love Rosette, worthy as she is of being loved, and wishful as I am to love her.

"To get rid of the idea that I was myself, I devised very strange surroundings, in which it was altogether improbable that I would encounter myself, and not being able to cast my individuality to the dogs, I endeavoured to place it in such a different element that it would recognise itself no longer. I had but indifferent success, and this devil of a self pursues me obstinately; there are no means of getting rid of it. I cannot resort to telling it like other intruders that I am out, or that I have gone to the country.

"When my mistress has been in her bath, I have tried to play the Triton. The sea was a very large tub of marble. As to the Nereid, what was seen of her accused the water, all transparent as it was, of not being sufficiently so for the exquisite beauty of what it concealed. I have been with her, too, at night by the light of the moon in a gondola accompanied by music.

"This would be common enough at Venice, but it is not at all so here. In her carriage, flying along at full gallop, amid the noise of the wheels, with leaps and joltings, now lit up by the lamps, and now plunged into the most profound darkness, I have loaded her with caresses and found a pleasure therein which I advise you taste. But I was forgetting that you are a venerable patriarch, and that you do not go in for such refinements. I have come into her house through the window with the key of the door in my pocket. I have made her come to me at noon-day; and, in short, I have compromised her in such a fashion that nobody now (myself, of course, excepted) has any doubt that she is my mistress.

"By reason of all these devices, which, if I were not so young, would look like the expedients of a worn-out libertine, Rosette worships me chiefly and above all others. She sees in them the eagerness of a petulant love which nothing can restrain, and which is the same notwithstanding the diversity of times and places. She sees in them the constantly reviving effect of her charms, and the triumph of her beauty; truly, I wish that she were right, and to be just, it is neither my fault nor hers that she is not.

"The only respect in which I wrong her is that I am myself. If I were

51

to tell her this, the child would very quickly reply that it is just my greatest merit in her eyes; which would be more kind than sensible.

"Once—it was at the beginning of our union—I believed that I had attained my end, for one minute I believed that I had loved—I did love. Oh! my friend, I have never lived save during that minute, and had that minute been an hour I should have become a god. We had both gone out on horseback, I on my dear Ferragus, she on a mare as white as snow, and with the look of a unicorn, so slim were its legs and so slender its neck. We were following a large avenue of elms of prodigious height; the sun was descending upon us lukewarm and golden, sifted through the slashings in the foliage; lozenges of ultramarine sparkled here and there through the dappled clouds, great lines of pale blue strewed the edge of the horizon, changing into an apple-green of exquisite tenderness when they met with the orange-coloured tints of the west. The aspect of the heavens was charming and strange; the breeze brought to us an odour of wild flowers that was ravishing in the extreme. From time to time a bird rose before us, and crossed the avenue singing.

"The bell of a village that was not visible was gently ringing the *Angelus,* and the silver sounds, which reached us weakened by the distance, were infinitely sweet. Our animals were at a walk, and were going so equally side by side, that one was not in advance of the other. My heart expanded, and my soul overflowed my body. I had never been so happy. I said nothing, nor did Rosette, and yet we had never understood each other so well. We were so close together that my leg was touching the body of Rosette's horse. I leaned over to her and passed my arm about her waist; she made the same movement on her side, and laid back her head upon my shoulder. Our lips clung together; oh! what a chaste and delicious kiss! Our horses were still walking with their bridles floating on their necks. I felt Rosette's arm relax, and her loins yield more and more. For myself I was growing weak, and was ready to swoon. Ah! I can assure you that at that moment I thought little of whether I was myself or another. We went thus as far as the end of the avenue, when the noise of feet made us abruptly resume our positions; it was some people of our acquaintance, also on horse-

back, who came up and spoke to us. If I had had pistols, I believe that I should have fired upon them.

"I looked at them with a gloomy and furious air, which must have appeared very singular to them. After all, I was wrong to become so angry with them, for they had, without intending it, done me the service of interrupting my pleasure at the very moment when, by reason of its own intensity, it was on the point of becoming a pain, or of sinking beneath its own violence. The science of stopping in time is not regarded with all the respect which is its due. Sometimes when toying with a woman you pass your arm around her waist; it is at first most voluptuous to feel the gentle warmth of her frame, to come almost in contact with her soft and velvety flesh, the polished ivory of her skin, and to watch the heaving of her swelling and quivering breast. The fair one falls asleep in this amorous and charming position; the curve of her body becomes less pronounced, her breast becomes calm; her sides heave with the larger and more regular respiration of sleep; her muscles relax, her head rolls over in her hair.

"Your arm, however, is pressed more than before, and you begin to perceive that it is a woman and not a sylphid; yet you would not take away your arm for anything in the world, and for this there are many reasons. First, it is rather dangerous to awake a woman who has fallen asleep beside you; you must be prepared to substitute for the delicious dream that she has been having a reality more delicious still. Secondly, by asking her to raise herself that you may withdraw your arm, you tell her indirectly that she is heavy and in your way, which is not polite, or perhaps you give her to understand that you are weak or fatigued—a most humiliating thing for you, and one which will prejudice you infinitely in her mind. Thirdly, you believe that as you have experienced pleasure in this position, you may do so again by maintaining it, and in this you are mistaken. The poor arm finds itself caught beneath the mass that oppresses it, the blood stops, the nerves twitch, and the numbness pricks you with its millions of needles. You are a sort of little Milo of Crotona, and the surface of your couch and the back of your divinity represent with sufficient exactness the two parts of the tree which are joined together again. Day comes at last to release you from this martyrdom, and you leap down from this rack with more eagerness than any husband displays in descending from the nuptial stage.

"Such is the history of many passions.

"It is that of all pleasures.

"Be that as it may, in spite of the interruption, or by reason of it, never did such voluptuousness pass over my head; I really felt myself to be another. The soul of Rosette had entered in its integrity into my body. My soul had left me, and filled her heart as her own soul filled mine. No doubt they had met on the way in that long equestrian kiss, as Rosette afterwards called it (which by the way annoyed me), and had crossed each other, and mingled together as intimately as is possible for the souls of two mortal creatures on a grain of perishable mud.

"The angels must surely embrace one another thus, and the true paradise is not in the sky, but on the lips of one we love.

"I have waited in vain for a similar moment, and I have tried, but without success, to provoke its return. We have very often gone to ride in the avenue of the wood during beautiful sunsets; the trees had the same verdure, the birds were singing the same song, but the sun looked dull to us, and the foliage yellowed; the singing of the birds seemed harsh and discordant, for there was no longer harmony within ourselves. We have brought our horses to a walk, and we have tried the same kiss. Alas! our lips only were united, and it was but the spectre of the old kiss. The beautiful, the sublime, the divine, the only true kiss that I have ever given and received in my life had disappeared for ever. Since that day I have always returned from the wood with a depth of inexpressible sadness. Rosette, gay and playful as she usually is, cannot escape from the impression of this, and her reverie is betrayed by a little, delicately wrinkled pout, which at the least is worth her smile.

"There is scarcely anything but the fumes of wine, and the brilliancy of wax-candles that can recall me from these melancholy thoughts. We both drink like persons condemned to death, silently and continually, until we have reached the necessary dose; then we begin to laugh and to make fun most heartily of what we call our sentimentality.

54

"We laugh—because we cannot weep. Ah! who will cause a tear to spring in the depths of my exhausted eye?

"Why had I so much pleasure that evening? It would be very difficult to say. Nevertheless I was the same man and Rosette the same woman. It was not the first time that either of us was out riding. We had seen the sun set before, and the spectacle had only affected us like the sight of a picture which is admired according as its colours are more or less brilliant. There are more avenues of elms and chestnut trees than one in the world, and it was not the first that we were passing through. Who, then, caused us to find in it so sovereign a charm, who metamorphosed the dead leaves into topazes, and the green leaves into emeralds, who had gilded all those fluttering atoms, and changed into pearls all those drops of water scattered on the sward, who gave so sweet a harmony to the sounds of a usually discordant bell, and to the caroling of sundry little birds? There must have been some very searching poetry in the air, since even our horses appeared to be sensible of it.

"Yet nothing in the world could have been more pastoral and more simple. Some trees, some clouds, five or six blades of wild thyme, a woman, and a ray of the sun falling across it all like a golden chevron on a coat of arms. I had, further, no sensation of surprise or astonishment! I knew where I was very well. I had never come to the place before, but I recollected perfectly both the shape of the leaves and the position of the clouds; the white dove which was crossing the sky was flying away in the same direction—the little silvery bell which I heard for the first time had very often tinkled in my ear, and its voice seemed to me like the voice of a friend; without having ever been there I had many times passed through the avenue with princesses mounted on unicorns; my most voluptuous dreams used to resort thither every evening, and my desires had given kisses there precisely similar to that exchanged by Rosette and myself.

"The kiss had no novelty to me, but it was such a one as I had thought that it would be. It was perhaps the only time in my life that I was not disappointed, and that the reality appeared to me as beautiful as the ideal. If I could find a woman, a landscape, a piece of architecture, anything answering to my intimate desire as perfectly as that minute answered to the minute of my dreams, I should have no reason to envy the gods, and I would very willingly resign my stall in paradise. But in truth, I do not believe that a man of flesh could withstand such penetrating voluptuousness for an hour—two kisses such as that one would pump out an entire existence, and would make a complete void in soul and body. This is not a consideration that would stop me, for, not being able to prolong my life indefinitely, I am indifferent to death, and I would rather die of pleasure than of old age or weariness.

"But this woman does not exist. Yes, she does exist. It may be that I am separated from her merely by a partition. It may be that I have jostled her yesterday or to-day.

"What is lacking in Rosette that she is not that woman? She lacks my belief in her. What fatality is it that causes me ever to have for my mistress a woman whom I do not love. Her neck is smooth enough to hang on it necklaces of the finest workmanship; her fingers are tapering enough to do honour to the finest and richest rings; rubies would blush with pleasure to sparkle at the rosy extremity of her delicate ear; her waist might gird on the cestus of Venus; but it is love alone who can knot his mother's scarf.

"All the merit that Rosette possesses is in herself, I have lent her nothing. I have not cast over her beauty that veil of perfection with which love envelops the loved one; the veil of Isis is transparent beside such a one as that. Nothing but satiety can raise a corner of it.

"I do not love Rosette; at least the love, if any, which I have for her has no resemblance to the idea that I have formed of love. Still my idea is perhaps not correct. I do not venture to give any decision. However, she renders me quite insensible to the merit of other women, and I have never wished for anybody with any consistency since possessing her. If she has cause to be jealous of any, it is only of phantoms, and they do not disquiet her much. Yet my imagination is her most formidable rival; it is a thing which, with all her acuteness, she will probably never find out.

"If women knew this! Of what infidelities is not the least volatile lover guilty towards his most worshipped mistress! It is to be presumed that the women pay us back with interest; but they do as we do, and say nothing about it. A mistress is an obligato, which usually disappears beneath its graces and flourishes. Very often the kisses she receives are not for her; it is the idea of another woman that is embraced in her person, and she often profits (if such can be called a profit) by the desires which are inspired by another. Ah! how many times, poor Rosette, have you served to embody my dreams, and given a reality to your rivals! How many the infidelities in which you have been the involuntary accomplice! If you could have thought at those moments when my arms clasped you with so much intensity, when my lips were united most closely to yours, that your beauty and your love counted for nothing, and that the thought of you was a thousand leagues away from me! If you had been told that those eyes, veiled with amorous languor, were cast down only that they might not see you and so dissipate the illusion that you merely served to complete, and that instead of being a mistress you were but an instrument of voluptuousness, a means of deceiving, a desire impossible of realisation!

"O celestial creatures, beautiful virgins, frail and diaphanous, who bend your pervinca eyes and clasp your lily hands on the golden background of the pictures of the old German masters, window saints, missal-martyrs who smile so sweetly amid the scrolls of arabesques, and emerge so fair and fresh from the bells of flowers! O beautiful courtesans lying veiled by your hair only, on beds strewn with roses, beneath broad purple curtains with your bracelets and necklaces of huge pearls, your fans and your mirrors where the west hangs in the shadow a flaming spangle! brown daughters of Titian, who display so voluptuously to us your undulating hips, your firm and compact limbs, your smooth bodies, and your supple and muscular frames! ancient goddesses, who rear your white phantom in the shadows of the garden! —you form a part of my seraglio; I have possessed you all in turn. Saint Ursula, on Rosette's beautiful hands I have kissed thine; I have played with the black hair of the Muranese, and never had Rosette more trouble in dressing her hair again; maidenly Diana, I have been with thee more than Actæon, and I have not been changed into a stag: I have replaced thy beautiful Endymion! How many rivals who are unsuspected, and on whom no vengeance can be taken! Yet they are not always painted or sculptured!

"Women, when you see your lover become more tender than is his wont, and strain you in his arms with extraordinary emotion; when he sinks his head into your lap, and raises it again with humid and wandering eyes; when enjoyment only augments his desire, and he stifles your voice with kisses, as though he feared to hear it, be certain that he does not know even whether you are there; that he is keeping tryst at this moment with a chimera which you render palpable, and whose part you play. Many chamber-maids have profited by the love inspired by queens. Many women have profited by the love inspired by goddesses, and a vulgar enough reality has often served as a socle for an ideal idol. That is the reason why poets usually take trollops for their mistresses. A man might live ten years with a woman without having ever seen her; such is the history of many great geniuses whose ignoble or obscene connexions have astonished the world.

"I have been guilty only of infidelities of this description towards Rosette. I have betrayed her only for pictures and statues, and she has shared equally in the betrayal. I have not the smallest material trespass on my conscience to reproach myself with. I am in this respect as white as the snow on the Jungfrau, and yet, without being in love with any one, I would wish to be so with some one. I do not seek an opportunity, and I should not be sorry were it to come; if it came I should perhaps not avail myself of it, for I have an intimate conviction that it would be the same with another, and I had rather it were thus with Rosette than with any other; for, putting the woman on one side, there remains to me at least a pretty companion, full of wit, and very agreeably demoralised; and this consideration is not one of the least that restrain me, for, in losing the mistress, I should be grieved to lose the friend."

IV

wwwwwwwwww

"**Do you know** that for nearly five months — yes, for quite five months — for five eternities, I have been Madame Rosette's established Celadon? It is perfectly splendid. I should never have believed that I was so constant, nor, I will wager, would she have believed it either. We are, in truth, a couple of plucked pigeons, for only turtle doves could display such tenderness. What billing! What cooing! What ivy-like entwinings. What a twofold existence! Nothing in the world could have been more touching, and our two poor little hearts might have been put on one cartel, pierced by the same spit, with a gusty flame.

"Five months *tête-à-tête*, so to speak, for we have been seeing each other every day and nearly every night—the door always closed to everybody; is it not enough to make one shudder to think of it! Well, to the glory of the peerless Rosette, it must be said that I have not been overmuch wearied, and that this period will no doubt prove to have been the most agreeable in my life. I do not believe that it would be possible to occupy a man devoid of passion in a more sustained and amusing manner, and God knows what a terrible idleness is that which proceeds from an empty heart! It would be impossible to form any idea of this woman's resources. She commenced by drawing them from her intellect, and then from her heart, for she loves me to adoration. With what art does she profit by the smallest spark, and how well she knows how to convert it into a conflagration! how skilfully she directs the faintest movements of the soul! how well can she turn languor into tender dreaming! and by how many indirect paths can she guide the mind that is wandering from her back to herself again! It is wonderful! And I admire her as one of the loftiest geniuses that can exist.

"I came to see her very cross, in a very bad temper, and seeking a quarrel. I know not how the sorceress managed it, but at the end of a few minutes she had obliged me to pay her compliments, although I had not the least wish to do so, and to kiss her hands and laugh with all my heart, although I was terribly angry. Is such tyranny conceivable? Nevertheless, skilful as she is, the *tête-à-tête* cannot last much longer; and, during the past fortnight, I pretty often chanced to do what I had never done before, to open the books that are on the table, and read a few lines in the intervals of conversation. Rosette noticed it, and was struck with dismay, which she was scarcely able to conceal, and she sent away all the books out of the room. I confess that I regret them, although I cannot ask for them again.

"The other day—frightful symptom!—some one called while we were together, and instead of being furious, as I used to be at the beginning, I experienced a kind of joy. I was almost amiable; I kept up the conversation which Rosette was trying to let drop so that the gentleman might take his leave, and, when he was gone, I volunteered the remark that he was not without wit, and that his society was agreeable. Rosette reminded me that two months before I had thought him stupid, and the silliest nuisance on earth, to which I had nothing to reply, for I had indeed said so. I was nevertheless right, in spite of my recent contradiction: for the first time he disturbed a charming *tête-à-tête*, and the second time he came to the assistance of a conversation that was exhausted and languishing (on one side at least), and for that day spared me a scene of tenderness somewhat fatiguing to go through.

"Such is our position. It is a grave one—especially when one of the two is still enamoured, and clings desperately to what remains of the other's love. I am in great perplexity. Although I am not in love with Rosette, I have a very great affection for her, and I should not like to do anything that would cause her pain. I wish to believe, as long as possible, that I love her.

"In gratitude for all those hours to which she has given wings, in gratitude for the love which, for my pleasure, she has bestowed on me, I wish it. I shall deceive her, but is not an agreeable deception better than a distressing truth? for I shall never have the heart to tell her that I do not love her. The vain shadow of love on which she feasts appears so adorable to her, she embraces the pale spectre with such intoxication and effusion that I dare not cause it to vanish; yet I am afraid that in the end she will perceive that, after all, it is but a phantom. This morning we had a conversation, which I am going to relate in dramatic form for the sake of greater fidelity, and which makes me fear that we cannot prolong our union very long.

"The scene represents Rosette's room. A ray of sun is shining through the curtains; it is ten o'clock. Rosette has one arm beneath my neck, and does not move for fear of waking me. From time to time she raises herself a little on her elbow, and, holding her breath, bends her face over mine. I see all this through the grating of my eyelashes, for I have been awake for an hour past. Rosette's chemise has a neck-trimming of Mechlin lace which is all torn, and her hair is escaping in confusion from her little cap. She is as pretty as a woman can be when you do not love her, although she is by your side.

"ROSETTE (seeing that I am no longer asleep)—'O the nasty sleeper!'

"MYSELF (yawning)—'A—a—ah!'

"ROSETTE—'Do not yawn like that, or I will not kiss you for a week.'

"MYSELF—'Oh!'

"ROSETTE—'It seems, sir, that you do not think it very important that I should kiss you?'

"MYSELF—'Yes, I do.'

"ROSETTE—'How carelessly you say that! Very well; you may expect that for the next week I shall not touch you with the tip of my lips. To-day is Tuesday—so till next Tuesday.'

"MYSELF—'Pshaw!'

"ROSETTE—'How, pshaw!'

"MYSELF—'Yes, pshaw! You will kiss me before this evening, or I die.'

"ROSETTE—'You will die! What a coxcomb! I have spoiled you, sir.'

"MYSELF—'I will live. I am not a coxcomb, and you have not spoiled me—quite the contrary. First of all, I request the suppression of the *Sir;* you are well enough acquainted with me to call me by my name, and to say *thou* to me.'

"ROSETTE—'I have spoiled thee, D'Albert.'

"MYSELF—'Good. Now bring your lips near.'

"ROSETTE—'No, next Tuesday.'

"MYSELF—'Nonsense. Are we not to pet each other for the future except with a calendar in our hands? We are both a little too young for that. Now, your lips, my infanta, or I shall get a crick in my neck.'

"ROSETTE—'No.'

"MYSELF—'Ah! you wish to be ravished, my pet; by heavens! you shall be. The thing is feasible, though perhaps it has not been done yet.'

"ROSETTE—'Impertinent man!'

"MYSELF—'Observe, most fair one, that I have paid you the compliment of a *perhaps;* it is very polite on my part. But we are wandering from the subject. Bend your head. Come: what is this, my favourite sultana? and what a cross face. We wish to kiss a smile and not a pout.'

"ROSETTE (stooping down to kiss me)—'How would you have me laugh? You say such harsh things to me!'

"MYSELF—'My intention is to say very tender ones.—Why do do you think that I say harsh things to you?'

"ROSETTE—'I don't know—but you do.'

"MYSELF—'You take jokes of no consequence for harshness.'

"ROSETTE—'Of no consequence! You call that of no consequence? Everything is of consequence in love. Listen, I would rather have you beat me than laugh as you are doing.'

"MYSELF—'You would like to see me weep, then?'

"ROSETTE—'You always go from one extreme to the other. You are not asked to weep, but to speak reasonably, and to give up this quizzing manner, which suits you very badly.'

"MYSELF—'It is impossible for me to speak reasonably and not to quiz; so I am going to beat you, since it is to your liking.'

"ROSETTE—'Do.'

"MYSELF (giving her a few little slaps on her shoulders)—'I would rather cut off my own head than spoil your adorable little body, and marble the whiteness of this charming back with blue. My goddess, whatever pleasure a woman may have in being beaten, you shall certainly not have it.'

"ROSETTE—'You love me no longer.'

"MYSELF—'That does not follow very directly from what precedes; it is about as logical as to say: It is raining, so do not give me my umbrella; or: It is cold, open the window.'

"ROSETTE—'You do not love me, you have never loved me.'

"MYSELF—'Ah! the matter is becoming complicated: you love me no longer, and you have never loved me. This is tolerably contradictory: how can I leave off doing a thing which I have never begun? You see, little queen, that you do not know what you are saying, and that you are perfectly absurd.'

"ROSETTE—'I wished so much to be loved by you that I assisted in deluding myself. People easily believe what they desire; but now I can quite see that I am deceived. You were deceived yourself; you took a liking for love, and desire for passion. The thing happens every day. I bear you no ill-will for it: it did not depend upon yourself to be in love; I must lay the blame on my own lack of charms. I should have been more beautiful, more playful, more coquettish; I should have tried to mount up to you, O my poet! instead of wishing you to come down to me: I was afraid of losing you in the clouds, and I dreaded lest your head should steal away your heart from me. I imprisoned you in my love, and I believed when giving up myself wholly to you that you would keep something——'

"MYSELF—'Rosette, move back a little, you are like a hot coal.'

"ROSETTE—'If I am in your way, I will get up. Ah! heart of rock, drops of water pierce the stone, and my tears cannot penetrate you.' (She weeps.)

"MYSELF—'If you weep like that, you will certainly turn our bed into a bath. A bath? I should say into an ocean. Can you swim, Rosette?'

"ROSETTE—'Villain!'

"MYSELF—'Well! all at once I am a villain! You flatter me, Rosette, I have not the honour: I am a gentle citizen, alas; and have never committed the smallest crime; I have done a foolish thing, perhaps, which was to love you to distraction: that is all. Would you absolutely make me repent of it? I have loved you, and I love you as much as I can. Since I have been your lover, I have always walked in your shadow: I have given up all my time to you, my days and my nights. I have not used lofty phrases with you, because I do not like them except in writing; but I have given you a thousand proofs of my fondness. I will say nothing to you of the most scrupulous fidelity, for that is of course; I have become seven quarters of a pound thinner since you have been my adoration. What more would you have? Here I am by your side; do people behave in this way with those whom they do not love? I do everything that you wish. You say "Go," and I go; "Stay," and I stay. I am the most admirable lover in the world, it seems to me.'

"ROSETTE—'That is just what I complain about—the most perfect lover in the world, in fact.'

"MYSELF—'What have you to reproach me with?'

"ROSETTE—'Nothing, and I would rather have some cause of complaint against you.'

"MYSELF—'This is a strange quarrel.'

"ROSETTE—'It is much worse. You do not love me. I cannot help it nor can you. What would you have done in such a case? Unquestionably I should prefer to have some fault to pardon in you. I would scold you; you would excuse yourself well or ill, and we should make it up.'

"MYSELF—'It would be all to your advantage. The greater the crime the more splendid would the reparation be.'

"ROSETTE—'You are quite aware, sir, that I am not yet reduced to employ that expedient, and that if I pleased presently, although you do not love me, and we are quarrelling——'

"MYSELF—'Yes, I acknowledge it as purely an effect of your clemency. Do please a little; it would be better than syllogising at random as we are doing.'

"ROSETTE—'You wish to cut short a conversation which is inconvenient to you; but, if you please, my fine friend, we shall content ourselves with speaking!'

"MYSELF—'It is an entertainment that does not cost much. I assure you that you are wrong; for you are wonderfully pretty, and I feel towards you——'

"ROSETTE—'What you will express to me another time.'

"MYSELF—'Oh come, adorable one, are you a little Hyrcanian tigress? You are incomparably cruel to-day! Are you eager to become a vestal? It would be an original caprice.'

"ROSETTE—'Why not? There have been stranger ones than that; but I shall certainly be a vestal for you. Learn, sir, that I am partial only to people who love me, or by whom I believe myself loved. You do not come under either of these two denominations. Allow me to rise!'

"MYSELF—'If you get up, I shall get up as well. You will have the trouble of getting into bed again: that is all.'

"ROSETTE—'Let me alone!'

"MYSELF—'By heavens, no!'

"ROSETTE (struggling)—'Oh! you will let me go!'

"MYSELF—'I venture, madame, to assure you of the contrary.'

"ROSETTE (seeing that she is not the stronger)—'Well! I will stay; you are squeezing my arm with such force!—What do you want with me?'

"MYSELF—'To remain where you are. I think you might have divined this much without asking any such superfluous question.'

"ROSETTE (already finding it impossible to defend herself)—'On condition that you will love me a great deal—I surrender.'

"MYSELF—'It is rather late to capitulate when the enemy is already in the fortress.'

"ROSETTE (throwing her arms around my neck)—'Then I surrender unconditionally—I trust to your generosity.'

"MYSELF—'You do well.'

"Here, my dear friend, I think it would not be amiss to put a line of asterisks, for the rest of the dialogue could scarcely be translated except by onomatopœia."

*   *   *   *   *   *

"The ray of sunshine has had time to make the circuit of the room since the beginning of this scene. An odour of lime-trees comes in from the garden, sweet and penetrating. The weather is the finest that could be seen; the sky is as blue as an Englishwoman's eye. We get up, and after breakfasting with great appetite, go for a long rural walk. The transparency of the air, the splendour of the country, and the joyous aspect of nature inspired my soul with enough sentimentality and tenderness to make Rosette acknowledge that after all I had a sort of heart like other people.

"Have you never remarked how the shade of woods, the murmuring of fountains, the singing of birds, smiling prospects, fragrance of foliage and flowers, all the baggage of eclogue and description which we have agreed to laugh at, none the less preserves over us, however depraved we may be, an occult power which it is impossible to resist? I will confide to you, under the seal of the greatest secret, that quite recently I surprised myself in a state of most countrified emotion towards a nightingale that was singing.

"It was in ——'s garden; although it was night, the sky had a clearness nearly equal to that of the finest day; it was so deep and so transparent that the gaze easily penetrated to God. It seemed to me that I could see the last folds of angels' robes floating over the pale windings of the Milky Way. The moon had risen, but a large tree hid her completely; she riddled its dark foliage with a million little luminous holes, and hung more spangles upon it than had ever the fan of a marchioness. Silence, filled with sounds and stifled sighs, was heard throughout the garden (this perhaps resembles pathos, but it is not my fault); although I saw nothing but the blue glimmering of the moon I seemed to be surrounded by a population of unknown and worshipped phantoms, and I did not feel alone, although there was only myself on the terrace.

"I was not thinking, I was not dreaming, I was blended with the nature that surrounded me; I felt myself quiver with the foliage, glisten with the water, shine with the ray, expand with the flower; I was not myself more than the trees, the water, and the great nightshade. I was all of these, and I do not believe that it would be possible to be more absent from one's self than I was at that moment. All at once, as though something extraordinary were going to happen, the leaf was stilled at the end of the branch, the water-drop in the fountain remained suspended in air, and did not complete its fall; the silver thread which had set out from the edge of the moon stopped on its way —only my heart beat so sonorously that it seemed to fill all that great space with sound. It ceased to beat, and there fell such a silence that you might have heard the grass grow, and a word whispered at a distance of two hundred leagues. Then from the little throat of the nightingale, which probably was only waiting for this moment to begin its song, there burst a note so shrill and piercing that I heard it with my heart as much as with my ears. The sound spread suddenly through the crystalline sky, which was void of noise, and formed a harmonious atmosphere, wherein, beating their wings, hovered the other notes which followed.

"I understood perfectly what it said, as though I had had the secret of the language of the birds. It was the history of the loves which had not been mine that this nightingale sang. Never was a history more accurate and true. It did not omit the smallest detail or the most imperceptible tint. It told me what I had been unable to tell myself, and explained to me what I had been unable to understand; it gave a voice to my dreaming, and caused the phantom, mute until then, to reply. I knew that I was loved, and the most languishing trilling taught me that I should be happy soon. I thought that through the quivering song, and beneath the rain of notes, I could see the white arms of my beloved stretched out towards me in a ray from the moon. She came up slowly with the perfume from the heart of a large hundred-leaved rose.

"I shall not try to describe her beauty. It was one of those things to which words are denied. How speak the unspeakable? how paint that which has neither form nor colour? how mark a voice which is without tone and speech? Never had I had so much love in my heart; I would have pressed nature to my bosom. I clasped the void in my arms as though I had closed them on a maiden's form; I gave kisses to the air that passed across my lips; I swam in effluence from my own radiant body. Ah! if Rosette had been there! What adorable nonsense would I have uttered to her! But women never know when to arrive opportunely. The nightingale ceased to sing; the moon, worn out with sleep, drew her cloud-cap over her eyes; and I—I left the garden, for the coldness of the night began to overtake me.

"As I was cold, I very naturally thought I should be warmer in Rosette's bed than in my own, and I went to share her couch. I entered with my pass-key, for every one in the house was slumbering. Rosette herself had fallen asleep, and I had the satisfaction of seeing that it was over an uncut volume of my latest poems. She had both her arms above her head, her mouth smiling and partly open, one leg stretched out and the other slightly bent in a posture of grace and ease; she looked so well that I felt mortal regret at not being more in love with her.

"While gazing upon her, I bethought me that I was as stupid as an ostrich. I had what I had desired so long, a mistress of my own like my horse and my sword, young, pretty, amorous, and intellectual—with no high-principled mother, decorous father, intractable aunt, or fighting brother; with the unspeakable charm of a husband duly sealed and nailed in a fine oak coffin lined with lead, and the whole covered over with a big block of freestone—a circumstance not to be despised, for it is, after all, but slight entertainment to be caught in the midst of amorous enjoyment, and to go and complete the sensation of the pavement, after describing an arc of form 40 to 50 degrees, according to the storey on which you happen to be—a mistress as free as mountain air, rich enough to indulge in the most exquisite refinements and elegancies, and devoid, moreover, of all moral ideas, never speaking to you of her virtue while trying a new position, nor of her reputation any more than if she had never had one; never intimate with women, and scorning them all nearly as much as if she were a man, making very light of Platonism without any concealment, and yet always bringing the heart into play: —a woman who, had she been placed in a different sphere, would undoubtedly have become the most notorious courtesan in the world, and made the glory of the Aspasias and Imperias grow pale!

"Then this woman so constituted was mine. I did what I would with her; I had the key of her room and her drawer; I opened her letters; I had taken her own name from her and given her another. She was my thing, my property. Her youth, beauty, love all belonged to me, and I used and abused them. I made her go to bed during the day and sit up at night, if I took a fancy to do so, and she obeyed me simply, without appearing to make a sacrifice, and without assuming the little airs of a resigned victim. She was attentive, caressing, and, monstrous circumstance, scrupulously faithful; that is to say, that if six months ago, when I was complaining of being without a mistress, I had been given even a distant glimpse of such happiness, I should have gone mad with joy, and sent my hat knocking against the sky in token of my rejoicing. Well! now that I have her, this happiness seems cold to me; I scarcely feel, I do not feel it, and the situation in which I am affects me so little, that I am often doubtful whether I have made a change. Were I to leave Rosette, I have an intimate conviction, that at the end of a month, perhaps before, I should have so completely and carefully forgotten her, that I should no longer be able to tell whether I had known her or not! Would she do as much on her part? I think not.

"I was reflecting, then, upon all these things, and, feeling a sort of repentance, I laid on the fair sleeper's forehead the chastest and most melancholy kiss that ever a young man gave a young woman on the stroke of midnight. She moved a little, and the smile on her lips became somewhat more decided, but she did not awake. I leant over her and stretching out my arms I coiled them around her in snake-like fashion. The contact of my body seemed to rouse her; she opened her eyes, raised herself, and, without speaking to me, she fastened her mouth to mine, and clung so tightly to me as to set my blood coursing rapidly, and I was warmed in less than no time. All the lyricism of the evening was turned into prose; but it was at least poetical prose. That night was one of the fairest sleepless nights that I have even spent: I can hope for such no longer.

"We still have agreeable moments, but it is necessary that they should have been led up to, and prepared for, by some external circumstance such as I have related, and at the beginning I had no need to excite my imagination by looking at the moon and listening to the nightingale's song, in order to have all the pleasure that is possible to a man who is not really in love. There are no broken threads as yet in our weft, but there are knots here and there, and the warp is not nearly so smooth.

"Rosette, who is still in love, does what she can to obviate these inconveniences. Unfortunately, there are two things in the world which cannot be commanded—love and weariness. On my part, I make superhuman efforts to overcome the somnolence which overtakes me in spite of myself, and, like country people who fall asleep at ten o'clock in town drawing-rooms, I keep my eyes as wide open as possible, and lift up my eyelids with my fingers! It is of no use, and I assume a conjugal freedom from restraint which is most unpleasing.

"The dear child, who the other day found herself the better for the rural system, brought me yesterday into the country.

"It might be to the purpose, perhaps, to give you a little description of the said country, which is rather pretty; it might enliven our metaphysics somewhat, and, besides, the characters must have a background; the figures cannot stand out against a blank, or against that vague brown tint with which painters fill the field of their canvas.

"The approaches to it are very picturesque. You arrive, by a highway bordered with old trees, at a star, the middle of which is marked by a stone obelisk surmounted by a ball of gilt copper. Five roads form the rays; then the ground becomes suddenly hollow. The road dips into a rather narrow valley, crosses the little stream, that occupies the bottom, by a one-arched bridge, and then with great strides reascends the opposite side, where stands the little village, the slated steeple of which can be seen peeping from among the thatched roofs and round-headed apple-trees. The horizon is not very vast, for it is bounded on both sides by the crest of the hill, but it is cheerful and rests the eye. Besides the bridge there is a mill, and a structure of red stones in the shape of a tower; the nearly perpetual barking, and the sight of some brachs and young bandy-legged turnspits warming themselves in the sun before the door, would tell you that it is there that the gamekeeper dwells, if the buzzards and martins nailed to the shutters could leave you in doubt about it for a moment.

"At this spot there begins an avenue of sorbs, the scarlet fruit of which attracts clouds of birds. As people do not pass there very often, there is only a white band along the middle; all the rest is covered over with a short fine moss, and in the double rut traced by the wheels of vehicles, little frogs, green as chrysoprase, croak and hop. After proceeding for some time you find yourself before a gilded and painted iron grating, its sides adorned with spiked fences and *chevaux-de-frise.* Then the road turns towards the mansion—which, being buried in the verdure like a bird's nest, cannot as yet be seen—without hastening too much, however, and not infrequently turning aside to visit an elegant kiosk or a fine prospect, crossing and recrossing the stream by Chinese or rustic bridges.

"Owing to the unevenness of the ground, and the dams erected for the service of the mill, the stream has, in several places, a fall of from four to five feet, and nothing can be more pleasant than to hear all these cascades prattling close at hand, most frequently without seeing them, for the osiers and elders which line the bank form an almost impenetrable curtain. But all this portion of the park is in a measure only the ante-chamber of the other part. A high road passing across this property unfortunately cuts it in two, an inconvenience which has been remedied in a very ingenious manner. Two great embattled walls full of barbicans and loop-holes, in imitation of a ruined fortress, stand on either side of the road; a tower on which hangs gigantic ivy, and which flanks the mansion, lets fall on the opposite bastion a veritable drawbridge with iron chains, which are lowered every morning.

"You pass through a pointed archway into the interior of the donjon, and thence into the second enclosure, where the trees, which have not been cut for more than a century, are of extraordinary height, with knotty trunks swaddled in parasitical plants, and are the finest and most singular that I have ever seen. Some have no leaves except at the top, where they terminate in broad parasols; others taper into plumes. Others, on the contrary, have near the body a large tuft, out of which the stripped stem shoots up to heaven like a second tree planted in the first; you would think that they formed the foreground of an artificial landscape, or the side-scenes of a theatrical decoration, so curiously deformed are they; while ivy passing from one to the other and suffocating them in its embrace, mingles its dark hearts with the green leaves and looks like their shadows. Nothing in the world could be more picturesque. The stream widens at this spot so as to form a little lake, and its shallowness allows the beautiful aquatic plants, which carpet its bed, to be seen beneath the transparent water. These are nymphaceæ and lotuses floating carelessly in the purest crystal, with the reflections of the clouds and of the weeping-willows that lean over on the bank. The mansion is on the other side, and this little skiff, painted apple-green and light red, will save you going rather a long round to reach the bridge.

"It is a collection of buildings, constructed at different epochs, with uneven gables, and a crowd of little bell-turrets. This pavilion is of brick, with corners of stone; this main building is of a rustic order, full of embossments and vermiculations. This other pavilion is quite modern; it has a flat roof, after the Italian fashion, with vases and a balustrade of tiles, and a vestibule of ticking in the shape of a tent. The windows are all of different sizes, and do not correspond; they are of all kinds. We find even trefoils and ogives, for the chapel is Gothic. Certain portions are latticed, like Chinese houses, with trellis-work planted in different colours, whereon climb woodbines, jessamines, nasturtiums, and virginian creepers, the long sprays of which enter the room familiarly, and seem to stretch out a hand to you and bid you good morning.

"In spite of this want of regularity, or rather by reason of it, the appearance of the building is charming. It has at least not all been seen at once, you can make a choice, and you are always bethinking yourself of something that had not been noticed. This dwelling, which I did not know of, as it is at a distance of twenty leagues, pleased me at the very first, and I was most grateful to Rosette for having had the triumphant idea of choosing such a nest for our loves.

"We arrived there at the close of day; and being fatigued, had nothing more urgent, after supping with great appetite, than to go to bed —separately, be it understood—for we intended to sleep seriously.

"I was dreaming some rose-coloured dream, full of flowers, perfumes, and birds, when I felt a warm breath on my forehead, and a kiss descending upon it with throbbing wings. A delicate noise of lips, and a soft moisture on the place that was touched, made me think that I was not dreaming. I opened my eyes, and the first thing that I saw was the fresh white neck of Rosette, who was bending down over the bed to kiss me. I threw my arms around her form, and returned her kiss more amorously than I had done for a long time.

"She went away to draw the curtain and open the window, then came back and sat down on the edge of my bed, holding my hand between both of hers and playing with my rings. Her attire was most coquettishly simple. She was without corset or petticoat, and had absolutely nothing on her but a large dressing-gown of cambric, as white as milk, very ample and with broad folds; her hair was drawn up on the top of her head with a little white rose, of the kind that has only three or four leaves; her ivory feet played in slippers worked in brilliant and variegated colours, as delicate as possible, though still too large, and with no quarter like those of the young Roman ladies. As I looked at her I regretted that I was her lover, and had not to become so.

"The dream that I had at the moment when she came to awake me in so agreeable a manner was not very remote from the reality. My room looked upon the little lake that I have just described. My window was framed with jessamine, which was shaking its stars in silver rain upon the floor. Large foreign flowers were poising their urns beneath my balcony as though to cense me; a sweet and undecided odour, formed of a thousand different perfumes, penetrated to my bed, whence I could see the water gleaming and scaling into millions of spangles; the birds were jargoning, warbling, chirping, and piping. It was a harmonious noise, and confused like the hum of a festival. Opposite, on a sunlit hill, stretched a lawn of golden green, on which some large oxen, scattered here and there, were feeding under the care of a little boy. Quite alone, and further away, might be seen immense squares of forest of a darker green, from which the bluish smoke of the charcoal kilns curled spirally upwards.

"Everything in this picture was calm, fresh, and smiling, and in whatever direction I turned my eyes, I saw nothing that was not fair and young. My room was hung in chintz, with mats on the floor; blue Japanese pots, with round bodies and tapering necks, and filled with singular flowers, were artistically arranged on the whatnots and on the dark-blue marble chimneypiece which was also filled with flowers; there were frieze-panels of gay colour and delicate design, representing scenes from rural or pastoral nature, and sofas and divans in every corner, and then—a beautiful and youthful woman all in white, her flesh giving a tender rose tint to her transparent dress where it touched it. It would be impossible to imagine anything better ordered for the gratification alike of soul and eye.

"Thus my contented and careless glance would pass with equal pleasure from a magnificent pot strewn with dragons and mandarins to Rosette's slipper, and from that to the corner of her shoulder which shone beneath the cambric; it would pause at the trembling stars of the jessamine and the white tresses of the willows on the bank, cross the water and wander on the hill, and then come back into the room, to be fixed on the rose-coloured bows on the corset of some shepherdess.

"Through the slashes in the foliage the sky was opening thousands of blue eyes; the water prattled softly, and I, plunged into tranquil ecstasy, without speaking, and with my hand still between Rosette's two little ones, gave myself up to all this joy.

"Do what we may, happiness is pink and white; it can scarcely be represented otherwise. Delicate colours suit it as a matter of course. On its palette it has only water-green, sky-blue, and straw-yellow. Its pictures are all bright like those of the Chinese painters. Flowers, light, perfumes, a soft and silken skin which touches yours, a veiled harmony coming you know not whence, with these there is perfect happiness, and there is no means of living happy in a different way. For myself, I, who have a horror of the common-place, who dream but of strange adventures, strong passions, delirious ecstasies, and odd and difficult situations, I must be foolishly happy in the manner I have indicated, and, for all my efforts, I have never been able to discover any other method of being so.

"I would have you know that I made none of these reflections then; it was after the event and when writing to you that they occurred to me; at the moment in question I was occupied only in enjoying—the sole occupation of a reasonable man.

"I will not describe to you the life that we are leading here; it may easily be imagined. There are walks in the great woods, violets and strawberries, kisses and little blue flowers, luncheons on the grass, readings and books forgotten beneath the trees; parties on the water with the end of a scarf or a white hand dipping in the current, long songs and long laughter repeated by the echo on the bank; the most Arcadian life that could be imagined!

"Rosette overwhelms me with caresses and attentions; cooing more than a dove in the month of May, she rolls herself about me and encircles me in her folds; she strives that I may have no other atmosphere than her breath, and no other horizon than her eyes; she invests me very carefully, and suffers nothing whatever to enter or come forth without permission; she has built a little guard-house beside my heart, whence she keeps watch over it night and day. She says charming things to me; she makes me the kindest madrigals; she sits at my feet and behaves before me quite like a humble slave before her lord and master—behaviour which suits me well enough, for I like these little submissive ways, and I have an inclination towards oriental despotism. She never does the smallest thing without taking my advice, and she seems completely to have renounced whim and wish; she tries to divine my thought and to anticipate it; she is wearisome with wit, tenderness, and kindness; she is perfect enough to be thrown out of the window. How the devil can I give up so adorable a woman without seeming a monster? It would be enough to discredit my heart for ever.

"Oh! how I long to find her in fault, and to discover something wrong against her! how impatiently I wait for an opportunity for a quarrel! but there is no danger that the rogue will furnish me with one! When I speak abruptly, and in a harsh tone to her, in order to bring about an altercation, she gives me such soft answers, in such silvery tones, with such moist eyes, and with such a sad and loving mien that I seem to myself something worse than a tiger, or else a crocodile at the very least, and, in spite of my rage, am obliged to ask her pardon.

"She literally murders me with love; she puts me to the torture, and every day brings the planks, between which I am caught, a notch closer. She probably wants to drive me into telling her that I detest her, that she wearies me to death, and that, if she does not leave me at peace, I will cut her face with a horsewhip. By heavens! she will succeed, and, if she continues to be so amiable, the devil take me but it will be before long.

"In spite of all these fair appearances, Rosette has had enough of me as I of her; but as she has committed glaring follies on my account, she will not, by a rupture, put herself in the wrong in the eyes of the worthy corporation of womankind. Every great passion pretends to be eternal, and it is very convenient to avail one's self of its advantages without being subjected to its drawbacks. Rosette reasons in this manner: 'Here is a young man who has only a remnant of liking for me, and being artless and gentle, he does not dare to show it openly, and is at his wit's end; it is clear that I weary him, but he will die with the trouble of it rather than take it upon himself to leave me. As he is a sort of poet, he has his head full of fine phrases about love and passion, and believes himself obliged, as a matter of conscience, to play the part of a Tristan or an Amadis. Hence, as nothing in the world is more intolerable than the caresses of one whom you are beginning to love no longer (and to love a woman no longer means to hate her violently), I am going to lavish them on him sufficiently to give him a fit of indigestion, and he will be obliged at any rate to send me to all the devils, or else begin to love me again as he did the first day, which he will carefully abstain from doing.'

"Nothing could be better conceived. Is it not charming to act the deserted Ariadne? People pity you and admire you, and cannot find sufficient imprecations for the wretch who has been monstrous enough to forsake so adorable a creature. You assume a resigned and mournful air, you rest your chin on your hand and your elbow on your knee in such a way as to bring out the pretty blue veins of your wrist. You wear more streaming hair, and for some time adopt dresses of a darker hue. You avoid uttering the name of the ungrateful one, but you make indirect allusions to it, heaving little admirably modulated sighs.

"A woman so good, so beautiful, so impassioned, who has made such great sacrifices, who is absolutely free from reproach, a chosen vessel, a pearl of love, a spotless mirror, a drop of milk, a white rose, an ideal essence for the perfume of a life—a woman who should have been worshipped on bended knees, and who, after her death, ought to be cut in small pieces for the purpose of relics—to abandon her iniquitously, fraudulently, villainously! Why, a corsair would not do worse! To give her her death-blow!—for she will assuredly die of it! A man must have a paving-stone in his body instead of a heart to behave in such a way.

"O men! men!

"I say this to myself; but perhaps it is not true.

"Excellent hypocrites as women naturally are, I can scarcely believe that they could go so far as this; are not Rosette's demonstrations after all only the accurate expression of her feelings towards me? However this may be, the continuation of the *tête-à-tête* is no longer possible, and the fair chatelaine has at last just sent off invitations to her acquaintances in the neighbourhood. We are busy making preparations to receive these worthy country people. Good-bye, dear friend."

V

"**I was wrong.** My wicked heart, being incapable of love, had given itself this reason that it might deliver itself from a weight of gratitude which it could not support. I had joyfully seized this idea in order to excuse myself in my own eyes. I had clung to it, but nothing in the world could have been more untrue. Rosette was not playing a part, and if ever a woman was true, it is she. Well! I almost bear her ill-will for the sincerity of her passion, which is one tie the more, and makes a rupture more difficult and less excusable; I would rather have her false and fickle. What a singular position is this! You wish to go away and you remain; you wish to say, 'I hate you,' and you say, 'I love you;' your past impels you onward and prevents you from returning or stopping. You are faithful, and you regret it. An indefinable kind of shame prevents you from giving yourself up entirely to other acquaintances, and makes you compound with yourself. You give to one all that you can take from the other without sacrificing appearances; times and opportunities for seeing each other, which once presented themselves so naturally, are now to be discovered only with difficulty. You begin to remember that you have business of importance.

"Such a situation full of twitchings is most painful, but it is not so much so as mine. When it is a new friendship that takes you away from the old it is easier to get free. Hope smiles sweetly on you from the threshold of the house that contains your young loves. A fairer and rosier illusion hovers white-winged over the newly closed tomb of its sister lately dead; another blossom more mature and more balmy, on which there trembles a heavenly tear, has sprung up suddenly from among the withered flower-cups of the old banquet; fair azure-tinted vistas open up before you; avenues of yoke-elms, discreet and humid, extend to the horizon; there are gardens with a few pale statues, or some bank supported by an ivy-clad wall, laws starred with daisies, narrow balconies where leaning on your elbow you gaze at the moon, shadows intersected with furtive glimmerings, drawing-rooms with light subdued by ample curtains; all the obscurity and isolation sought by the love which dares not show itself.

"It is like a new youth that comes to you. You have, besides, change of place, habit, and people; you feel, perhaps, a species of remorse, but the desire that hovers and buzzes about your head like a bee in the spring-time prevents you from hearkening to its voice; the void in your heart is filled, and your memories fade beneath new impressions. But in this case it is different. I love nobody, and it is only from lassitude and weariness of myself rather than of her that I wish that I could break with Rosette.

"My old notions, which had slumbered for a little while, awake more foolish than ever. I am tormented as before with the desire of having a mistress, and as before, in Rosette's very arms, I doubt whether I have ever had one. I see again the fair lady at her window in her park of the time of Louis XIII, and the huntress on her white horse gallops across the avenue in the forest. My ideal beauty smiles at me from the height of her hammock of clouds. I imagine that if I were to post off on the spot and go somewhere, far away and quickly, I should reach a spot where things that concern me are taking place and where my destinies are being decided.

"I feel that I am being waited for impatiently in some corner of the earth, I know not which. A suffering soul that cannot come to me calls eagerly for me and dreams of me; it is this that causes my disquietude, and renders me incapable of remaining where I am; I am drawn violently out of my element. My nature is not one of those that is the centre of others, one of these fixed stars around which other lights gravitate; I must wander over the plains of the sky like an unruly meteor, until I have met with the planet whose satellite I am to be, the Saturn on whom I am to place my ring. Oh! when will this marriage be accomplished? Until then I cannot hope to be in my proper position and at rest, and I shall be like the distracted and vacillating compass-needle when seeking for its pole.

"I have suffered my wings to be caught in this treacherous bird-lime, hoping that I should leave only a feather behind, and believing myself able to fly away when I should think fit to do so. Nothing could be more difficult; I find that I am covered with an imperceptible net more difficult to break than that forged by Vulcan, and the texture of the meshes is so fine and close that there is no aperture admitting of escape. The net, moreover, is large, and it is possible to move about inside it with an appearance of freedom; it can scarcely be perceived, save when an attempt is made to break it, but then it resists and becomes as solid as a wall of brass.

"How much time have I lost, O my ideal! without making the slightest effort to realise thee! How have I slothfully abandoned myself to the voluptuousness of a night! and how little do I deserve to find thee!

"Sometimes I think of forming another connection; but I have no one in view. More frequently I propose, if I succeed in breaking these bonds, never to enter into similar ones again; and yet there is nothing to justify such a resolution, for this affair has been apparently a very happy one, and I have not the least complaint to make against Rosette. She has always been good to me; her conduct could not have been better. Her fidelity to me has been exemplary; she has not occasioned the slightest suspicion. The most vigilant and restless jealousy would have found nothing to say against her, and would have been obliged to fall asleep. A man could have been jealous only for things that were past; although it is true that in that case he would have had abundant reason to be so. But jealousy of this description is a nicety which happily is rather rare; the present is quite enough without going back to search beneath the rubbish of old passion for phials of poison and cups of gall.

"What woman could you love if you thought of all this? You know, in a confused way, that a woman has had several lovers before you; but you say to yourself—so full of tortuous turnings and windings is the pride of man!—that you are the first that she has truly loved, and that it was owing to a concurrence of fatal circumstances that she found herself united to people unworthy of her, or perhaps that it was the vague longing of a heart which was seeking for its own satisfaction, and which changed because it had not found.

"Perhaps it is impossible really to love any one but a virgin—a virgin in body and mind—a frail bud which no zephyr has as yet caressed, and the closed bosom of which has received neither raindrop nor pearly dew, a chaste flower which unfolds its white robe for you alone, a fair lily with silver urn wherein no desire has been quenched, and which has been gilded only by your sun, rocked only by your breath, watered only by your hand. The radiance of noon is not worth the divine paleness of dawn, and all the fervour of a soul that has experience and knowledge of life yields to the heavenly ignorance of a young heart that is waking up to love. Ah! what a bitter and shameful thought is it that you are wiping away the kisses of another, that there is not, perhaps, a single spot on this brow, these lips, this throat, these shoulders, on this whole body which is yours now, that has not been reddened and marked by strange lips; that these divine murmurs coming to the assistance of the tongue, whose words have failed, have been heard before; that these senses, which are so greatly moved, have not learned their ecstasy and their delirium from you, and that deep down, far away in the retirement of one of these recesses of the soul that are never visited, there watches an inexorable recollection which compares the pleasures of former times with the pleasures of to-day!

"Although my natural supineness leads me to prefer high roads to unbeaten paths, and a public drinking-fountain to a mountain spring, I must absolutely try to love some virginal creature as pure as snow, as trembling as the sensitive plant, who can only blush, and cast down her eyes. Perhaps beneath this limpid flood, into which no diver has yet gone down, I may fish up a pearl of the purest water and fit to be the fellow of Cleopatra's; but to do this I should loose the bond that ties me to Rosette,—for it is not probable that I shall realise my wish with her,—and I do not in truth feel the power to do so.

"And then, if I must confess it, I have at bottom a secret and shameful motive which dares not come forth into the light, and which I must nevertheless mention to you, seeing that I have promised to hide nothing from you, and that a confession to be meritorious must be complete—a motive which counts for much amid all this uncertainty. If I break with Rosette, some time must necessarily elapse before she can be replaced, however compliant may be the kind of woman in whom I shall seek for her successor, and with her I have made pleasure a habit which I should find it painful to interrupt. It is, of course, possible to fall back upon courtesans—I liked them well enough once, and did not spare them in a like emergency—but now they disgust me horribly, and give me nausea. Having tasted of a more refined though still impure passion, such creatures are not again to be thought of. On the other hand, I cannot endure the idea of being one or two months without a woman for my companion. This is egoism, and of a depraved description; but I believe that the most virtuous, if they would be frank, might make somewhat analogous confessions.

"It is in this respect that I am most surely caught, and were it not for this reason, Rosette and I would have quarrelled irreparably long ago. And then in truth it is so mortally wearisome to pay court to a woman that I have no heart for it. To begin again to say all the charming fooleries that I have said so many times already, to re-enact the adorable, to write notes and to reply to them; to escort beauties in the evening two leagues from your own house; to catch cold in your feet and your head before a window while watching for a beloved shadow; to calculate on a sofa how many superposed tissues separate you from your goddess; to carry bouquets and frequent balls only to arrive at my present position—it is well worth the trouble!

"It was as good to remain in one's rut. Why come out of it only to fall again into one precisely similar, after disquieting one's-self greatly and doing one's-self much harm? If I were in love, matters would take

their own course, and all this would seem delightful to me; but I am not, although I have the greatest wish to be so, for after all there is only love in the world; and if pleasure, which is merely its shadow, has such allurements for us, what must the reality be? In what a flood of unspeakable ecstasy, in what lakes of pure delight must those swim whose hearts have been reached by one of its gold-tipped arrows, and who burn with the kindly ardour of a mutual flame!

"By Rosette's side I experience that dull calm, and that kind of lazy comfort which results from the gratification of the senses, but nothing more; and this is not enough. Often this voluptuous enervation turns to torpor, and this tranquillity to weariness; and I then fall into purposeless absence of mind, and into a kind of dull dreaming which fatigues me and wears me out. It is a condition that I must get out of at all costs.

"Oh! if I could be like certain of my friends who kiss an old glove with intoxication, who are rendered completely happy by the pressure of the hand, who would not exchange a few paltry flowers, half withered by the perspiration of the ball, for a Sultana's jewel-box, who cover with their tears and sew into their shirts, just over their hearts, a note written in wretched style, and stupid enough to have been copied from the 'Complete Letter Writer,' who worship women with big feet, and excuse themselves for doing so on the ground that they have a beautiful soul!

"If I could follow with trembling the last folds of a dress, and wait for the opening of a door that I might see a dear, white apparition pass into a flood of light; if a whispered word made me change colour; if I possessed the virtue to forego dining that I might arrive the sooner at a trysting-place; if I were capable of stabbing a rival or fighting a duel with a husband; if, by the special favour of heaven, it were given to me to find wit in ugly women, and goodness in those who are both ugly and foolish; if I could make up my mind to dance a minuet and to listen to sonatas played by young persons on harpsichord or harp; if my capacity could reach to the height of understanding ombre and reversis; if, in short, I were a man and not a poet, I should certainly be much happier than I am; I should be less wearied and less wearisome.

"Only one thing have I ever asked of women—beauty; I am very willing to dispense with wit and soul. For me a woman who is beautiful has always wit; she has the wit to be beautiful, and I know of none that is equal to this. It would take many brilliant phrases and sparkling flashes to make up the worth of the lightning from a beautiful eye. I prefer a pretty mouth to a pretty word, and a well-modelled shoulder to a virtue, even a theological one; I would give fifty souls for a delicate foot, and all our poetry and poets for the hand of Jeanne d'Aragon or the brow of the Virgin of Foligno. I worship beauty of form above all things; beauty is to me visible divinity, palpable happiness, heaven come down upon earth. There are certain undulating outlines, delicate lips, curved eyelids, inclinations of the head, and extended ovals which ravish me beyond all expression, and engage me for whole hours at a time.

"Beauty, the only thing that cannot be acquired, inaccessible for ever to those who are without it at first; ephemeral and fragile flower which grows without being sown, pure gift of heaven! O beauty! the most radiant diadem wherewith chance could crown a brow—thou art admirable and precious like all that is beyond the reach of man, like the azure of the firmament, like the gold of the star, like the perfume of the seraphic lily! We may exchange a stool for a throne; we may conquer the world, and many have done so; but who could refrain from kneeling before thee, pure personification of the thought of God?

"I ask for nothing but beauty, it is true; but I must have it so perfect that I shall probably never find it. Here and there I have seen, in a few women, portions that were admirable accompanied by what was commonplace, and I have loved them for the choice parts that they had, without taking the rest into account; it is, however, a rather painful task and sorrowful operation to suppress half of one's mistress in this way, and mentally to amputate whatever is ugly or ordinary in her by confining one's gaze to whatever goodness she may possess. Beauty is harmony, and a person who is equally ugly throughout is often less disagreeable to look at than a woman who is unequally beautiful. No sight gives me so much pain as that of an unfinished masterpiece, or of beauty which is wanting in something; a spot of oil offends less on a coarse drugget than on a rich material.

"Rosette is not bad; she might pass for being beautiful, but she is far from realising my dream; she is a statue, several portions of which have been finished to a nicety. The rest has not been wrought so clearly out of the block; there are some parts indicated with much delicacy and charm, and others in a more slovenly and negligent fashion. In the eyes of the vulgar the statue appears entirely finished, and its beauty complete; but a more attentive observer discovers many places where the work is not close enough, and outlines which, to attain to the purity that they ought to possess, would need the nail of the workman to pass and re-pass many more times over them; it is for love to polish this marble and complete it, which is as much as to say that it will not be I who will finish it.

"For the rest I do not limit beauty to any particular sinuosity of lines. Mien, gesture, walk, breath, colour, tone, perfume, all that life is enters into the composition of my ideal; everything that has fragrance that sings, or that is radiant belongs to it as a matter of course.

I love rich brocades, splendid stuffs with their ample and powerful folds; I love large flowers and scent-boxes, the transparency of spring water, the reflecting splendour of fine armour, thoroughbred horses and large white dogs such as we see in the pictures of Paul Veronese. I am a true pagan in this respect, and I in no wise adore gods that are badly made. Although I am not at bottom exactly what is called irreligious, no one is in fact a worse Christian than I.

"I do not understand the mortification of matter which is the essence of Christianity, I think it a sacrilegious act to strike God's handiwork, and I cannot believe that the flesh is bad, since He has Himself formed it with His own fingers and in His own image. I do not approve much of long dark-coloured smock-frocks with only a head and two hands emerging from them, and pictures in which everything is drowned in shadow except a radiant countenance. My wish is that the sun should enter everywhere, that there should be as much light and as little shadow as possible, that there should be sparkling colour and curving lines, that nudity should be displayed proudly, and that matter should be concealed from none, seeing that, equally with mind, it is an everlasting hymn to the praise of God.

"I can perfectly understand the mad enthusiasm of the Greeks for beauty; and for my part I see nothing absurd in the law which compelled the judges to hear the pleadings of the lawyers in a dark place, lest their good looks and the gracefulness of their gestures and attitude should prepossess them favourably and incline the scale.

"I would buy nothing of an ugly shopwoman; I would be more willing to give to beggars whose rags and leanness were picturesque. There is a little feverish Italian as green as a citron, with large black and white eyes which are half his face—you would think it was an unframed Murillo or Espagnolet exposed for sale by a second-hand dealer on the pavement; he always has a penny more than the others. I would never beat a handsome horse or dog, and I should not like to have a friend or a servant who had not an agreeable exterior.

"It is a real torture to me to see ugly things or ugly persons. Architecture in bad taste, a piece of furniture of bad shape, prevent me from taking pleasure in a house, however comfortable and attractive it may otherwise be. The best wine seems almost sour to me in an ill-turned glass, and I confess that I would rather have the most Lacedæmonian broth on an enamel by Bernard de Palissy than the most delicate game in an earthenware plate. Externals have always taken a violent hold on me, and that is the reason why I avoid the company of old people; it grieves me, and affects me disagreeably, because they are wrinkled and deformed, though some indeed have a beauty of their own; and a good deal of disgust is mingled with the pity that I feel for them. Of all the ruins in the world the ruin of a man is assuredly the saddest to contemplate.

"If I were a painter (and I have always regretted that I am not), I would people my canvases only with goddesses, nymphs, madonnas, cherubs, and cupids. To devote one's brush to the making of portraits, unless they be those of beautiful persons, appears to me high treason against the art; and, far from wishing to double ugly or ignoble faces, and insignificant and vulgar heads, I should be more inclined to have them cut off the originals. Caligula's ferocity turned in this direction would seem to me almost laudable.

"The only thing in the world that I have ever wished for with any consistency is to be handsome. By handsome, I mean as handsome as Paris or Apollo. To be free from deformity, and to have tolerably regular features, *i.e.*, to have one's nose in the middle of one's face, and neither snub nor hooked, eyes neither red nor blood-shot, and a mouth bcomingly cut, is not to be handsome. At this rate I should be so, and I am so remote from the idea that I have formed of manly beauty as if I were one of the clock-jacks that strike the hour on the bells; I might have a mountain on each shoulder, legs as crooked as those of a turnspit, and the nose and muzzle of an ape, and yet have as close a resemblance to it.

"I often look at myself in the glass for whole hours, with unimaginable fixity and attention to see whether some improvement has not taken place in my face; I wait for the lines to make a movement and become straighter or rounder with more delicacy and purity, for my eye to light up and swim in a more vivacious fluid, for the sinuosity that separates my forehead from my nose to be filled up, and for my profile thus to assume the stillness and simplicity of the Greek profile, and I am always very much surprised that this does not happen. I am always hoping that some spring or other I shall lay aside the form that I have, as a serpent sheds his old skin.

"To think that I want so little to be handsome, and that I shall never be so! What! half a line, a hundredth or a thousandth part of a line more or less in one place or another, a little less flesh on this bone, a little more on that—a painter or a statuary would have settled the affair in half an hour. What mattered it to the atoms composing me to crystallise in such or such a way? How did it concern this outline to come out here and to go in there, and where was the necessity that I should be as I am and not different? In truth if I had Chance by the throat I think I should strangle it. Because it has pleased a wretched particle of I know not what to fall I know not where, and to coagulate foolishly into the clumsy countenance that I display, I am to be unhappy for ever! Is it not the most foolish and miserable thing in the world? How is it that my soul, with her eager longing for it, cannot let the poor carrion that she keeps upright fall prostrate, and go and animate one of those statues whose exquisite beauty saddens and ravishes her?

"There are two or three persons whom I would assassinate with delight, being careful, however, not to bruise or spoil them, if I were in possession of the word that would effect the transmigration of souls from one body to the other. It has always seemed to me that to do what I wish (and what that is I do not know), I had need of very great and perfect beauty, and I imagine to myself that, if I had it, my life, which is so fettered and tormented, would have been left in peace.

"We see so many beautiful faces in pictures!—why is none of them mine?—so many charming heads hidden beneath the dust and smoke of time in the depths of the old galleries! Would it not be better if they left their frames and came and expanded on my shoulders? Would Raphaël's reputation suffer very much if one of the angels that he makes to fly in swarms in the ultramarine of his canvases, were to give up his mask to me for thirty years? So many of the most beautiful parts of his frescoes have peeled off and fallen away from old age! No one would heed it! What are their silent beauties, upon which common men bestow scarce a heedless glance, doing around these walls? and why has God or chance not wit enough to do what a man has accomplished with a few hairs fitted on a stick as a handle, and a few pastes of different colours tempered on a board?

"My first sensation before one of these marvellous heads, whose painted gaze seems to pass through you and extend to the infinite, is a shock, and a feeling of admiration which is not devoid of terror. My eyes grow moist, my heart beats; then, when I become a little more accustomed to it, and have penetrated further into the secret of its beauty, I make a tacit comparison between it and myself; jealousy twists itself at the bottom of my soul in more tangled knots than a viper, and I have all the trouble in the world to refrain from throwing myself upon the canvas and tearing it to pieces.

"To be handsome means to have in one's-self so great a charm that every one smiles on you and welcomes you, that before you have spoken everybody is already prepossessed in your favour and disposed to be of your opinion; that you have only to pass through a street or show yourself on a balcony to create friends or mistresses for you in the crowd. To have no need of being amiable in order to be loved, to be exempt from all the expenditure of wit and complaisance to which ugliness compels you, and from the thousand moral qualities which are necessary to make up for the absence of personal beauty;— what a splendid and magnificent gift!

"And if one could unite supreme beauty with supreme strength, and have the muscles of Hercules beneath the skin of Antinoüs, what more could he wish for? I am sure that with these two things and the soul that I have, I should in less than three years be emperor of the world! Another thing that I have desired almost as much as beauty and strength is the gift of transporting myself with the swiftness of thought from one place to another. With the beauty of an angel, the strength of a tiger and the wings of an eagle, I might begin to find that the world is not so badly organised as I at first believed. A beautiful mask to allure and fascinate its prey, wings to swoop down upon it and carry it off, and claws to rend it;—so long as I have not these I shall be unhappy.

"All the passions and tastes that I have had have been merely these three longings disguised. I like weapons, horses, and women: weapons to take the place of the sinews that I lacked; horses to serve me instead of wings; women that I might at least possess in somebody the beauty that was wanting in myself. I sought in preference the most ingeniously murderous weapons, and those which inflicted incurable wounds. I never had an opportunity of making us of a kris or yataghan: nevertheless I like to have them about me; I draw them from the sheath with a feeling of unspeakable security and strength, I fence with them at random with great energy, and if I chance to see the reflection of my face in a glass, I am astonished at its ferocious expression.

"As to horses, I so override them that they must die or tell the reason why. If I had not given up riding Ferragus he would have been dead long ago, and that would have been a pity, for he is a good animal. What Arab horse could have legs so ready and so slender as my desire? In women I have sought nothing but the exterior, and as those that I have seen up to the present are far from answering to the idea that I have formed of beauty, I have fallen back on pictures and statues;— a resource which is after all pitiful enough when one has senses so inflamed as mine. However, there is something grand and beautiful in loving a statue, in that the love is perfectly disinterested, and that you have not to dread the satiety or disgust of victory, and that you cannot reasonably hope for a second wonder similar to the story of Pygmalion. The impossible has always pleased me.

"Is it not singular that I who am still in the fairest months of adolescence, and who, so far from abusing everything, have not even made use of the simplest things, have become surfeited to such a degree that I am no longer tickled by what is whimsical or difficult? That satiety follows pleasure is a natural law and easy to be understood. That a man who has eaten largely of every dish at a banquet should be no longer hungry, and should seek to rouse his sluggish palate with the thousand arrows of spices or irritant wines may be most readily explained; but that a man who has just sat down to table and has scarcely tasted the first viands should be seized with such superb disgust, be unable to touch without vomiting any dishes but those possessing extreme relish and care only for high-flavoured meats, cheeses marbled with blue, truffles and wines with the taste of flint, is a phenomenon which can only result from a peculiar organisation; it is as though an infant six months old were to find its nurse's milk insipid and refuse to suck anything but brandy.

"I am as weary as if I had gone through all the prodigalities of Sardanapalus, and yet my life has been, in appearance, tranquil and chaste. It is a mistake to think that possession is the only road which leads to satiety. It can also be reached by desire, and abstinence is more wearing than excess. Desire such as mine fatigues differently from possession. Its glance traverses and penetrates the object which it fain would have, and which is radiant above it, more quickly and deeply than if it touched it. What more can it be taught by use? What experience can be equal to such constant and impassioned contemplation?

"I have passed through so many things, though I have made the circuit of very few, that only the steepest heights any longer tempt me. I am attacked by the malady which seizes nations and powerful men in their old age—the impossible. All that I can do has not the least attraction for me. Tiberius, Caligula, Nero, great Romans of the Empire, O you who have been so misunderstood, and are pursued by the baying of the rhetors' pack, I suffer from your disease and I pity you with all the pity that remains to me! I, too, would build a bridge across the sea and pave the waves; I have dreamed of burning towns to illuminate my festivals; I have wished to be a woman, that I might become acquainted with fresh voluptuousness.

"Thy gilded house, O Nero! is but a miry stable beside the palace that I have raised; my wardrobe is better equipped than thine, Heliogabalus, and of very different splendour. My circuses are more roaring and more bloody than yours, my perfumes more keen and penetrating, my slaves more numerous and better made; I, too, have yoked naked courtesans to my chariot, and I have trodden upon men with a heel as disdainful as yours. Colossuses of the ancient world, there beats beneath my feeble sides a heart as great as yours, and in your place I would have done what you did and perhaps more. How many Babels have I piled up one upon another to reach the sky, slap the stars and spit thence upon creation! Why am I not God, since I cannot be man?

"Oh! I think that a hundred thousand centuries of nothingness will be needed to rest me after these twenty years of life. God of Heaven, what stone will you roll upon me? into what shadow will you plunge me? of what Lethe will you cause me to drink? beneath what mountain will you bury the Titan? Am I destined to breathe a volcano from my mouth and make earthquakes when turning over?

"When I think that I was born of a mother so sweet and so resigned, whose tastes and habits were so simple, I am quite surprised that I did not burst through her womb when she was carrying me. How is it that none of her calm, pure thoughts passed into my body with the blood that she transmitted to me? and why must I be the son of her flesh only and not of her spirit? The dove has produced a tiger which would fain have all creation a prey to his claws.

"I lived among the calmest and chastest surroundings. It is difficult to dream of an existence so purely enshrined as mine. My years glided away beneath the shadows of my mother's arm-chair, with my little sisters and the house-dog. Around me I saw only the worthy, gentle, tranquil heads of old servants who had grown grey in our service and were in a fashion hereditary, and of grave and sententious relatives or friends, clad in black, who would place their gloves the one after the other on the brim of their hats; some aunts of a certain age, plump, tidy, discreet, with dazzling linen, grey skirts, thread mittens, and their hands on their girdles like religious persons; furniture severe even to sadness, bare oak wainscoting, leather hangings, the whole forming an interior of sober and subdued colour, such as is represented by certain Flemish masters.

"The garden was damp and dark; the box which marked out the beds, the ivy which covered the walls and a few fir-trees with peeled arms were charged with the representation of verdure and succeeded rather badly in their task; the brick house, with a very lofty roof, though roomy and in good condition, had something gloomy and drowsy about it. Surely nothing could have been more adapted for a separate, austere, and melancholy life than such an abode. It seemed impossible that children brought up in such a house should not end by becoming priests or nuns. Well! in this atmosphere of purity and repose, in this shadow and contemplation, I became rotten by degrees, and, without showing any signs of it, like a medlar upon straw. In the bosom of this worthy, pious, holy family I arrived at a horrible degree of depravity. It was not contact with the world, for I had not seen it; nor the fire of passions, for I was chilled by the icy sweat that oozed from those excellent walls. The worm had not crawled from the heart of another fruit into mine. It had been hatched of itself entirely within my own pulp which it had preyed upon and furrowed in every direction; without, there was no appearance and warning that I was spoiled. I had neither spot nor worm-hole; but I was completely hollow within, and there was left to me only a slight, brilliantly-coloured pellicle which would have been burst by the slightest shock.

"Is it not an inexplicable thing that a child, born of virtuous parents, brought up with care and discretion, and kept away from everything bad, should be perverted of himself to such a degree, and come to be what I am now? I am sure that if you went back as far as the sixth generation you would not find a single atom among my ancestors similar to those of which I am formed. I do not belong to my family; I am not a branch of that noble trunk, but a poisonous toadstool sprung up amid its moss-grown roots some heavy, stormy night; and yet no one has ever had more aspirations and soarings after the beautiful than I, no one has ever tried more stubbornly to spread his wings; but each attempt has made my fall the greater, and I have been lost through what ought to have saved me.

"Solitude is worse for me than society, although I wish for the first more than for the second. Everything that takes me out of myself is wholesome for me; companionship wearies me, but it snatches me away perforce from the vain dreaming, whose spiral I ascend and descend with bended brow and folded arms. Thus, since the *tête-à-tête* has been broken off, and there have been people here with whom I am obliged to put some constraint upon myself, I have been less liable to give myself up to my gloomy moods, and have been less tormented by the inordinate desires which swoop upon my heart like a cloud of vultures as soon as I am unoccupied for a moment.

"There are some rather pretty women, and one or two young fellows who are amiable enough and very gay; but in all this country swarm I am most charmed by a young cavalier who arrived two or three days ago. He pleased me from the very first, and I took a fancy to him, merely on seeing him dismount from his horse. It would be impossible to be more graceful; he is not very tall, but he is slender and has a good figure; there is something soft and undulating in his walk and gestures which is most agreeable; many women might envy him his hands and feet. The only fault that he has is that he is too beautiful, and has too delicate features for a man. He is provided with a pair of the finest and darkest eyes in the world, which have an indefinable expression, and whose gaze it is difficult to sustain; but as he is very young and has no appearance of a beard, the softness and perfection of the lower part of his face tempers somewhat the vivacity of his eagle eyes; his brown and lustrous hair flows over his neck in great ringlets, and gives a peculiar character to his head.

"Here, then, is at last one of the types of beauty that I dreamed of realised and walking before me! What a pity it is that he is a man, or rather that I am not a woman! This Adonis, who to his beautiful face unites a very lively and far-reaching wit, enjoys the further privilege of being able to utter his jests and pleasantries in silvery and thrilling tones which it is difficult to hear without emotion. He is truly perfect.

"He appears to share my taste for beautiful things, for his clothes are very rich and refined, his horse very frisky and thorough-bred; and, that everything might be complete and harmonious, he had a page fourteen or fifteen years old mounted on a pony behind him, fair, rosy, as pretty as a seraph, half asleep, and so fatigued with his ride, that his master was obliged to lift him off the saddle and carry him in his arms to his room. Rosette received him very kindly, and I think that she intends to make use of him to rouse my jealousy and in this way bring out the little flame that sleeps beneath the ashes of my extinguished passion. Nevertheless, formidable as such a rival may be, I am little disposed to be jealous of him, and I feel so drawn towards him that I would willingly enough abandon my love to have his friendship."

VI

wwwwwwwwwwww

At this point, if the gentle reader will permit us, we shall for a time leave to his dreams the worthy personage who, up to the present, has monopolised the stage and spoken for himself alone, and go back to the ordinary form of romance, without, however, prohibiting ourselves from taking up the dramatic form, if necessary, later on, and reserving to ourselves the right of drawing further on the species of epistolary confession addressed by the said young man to his friend, being persuaded that, however penetrating and full of sagacity we may be, we must know far less in this matter than he does himself.

... The little page was so worn out that he slept in his master's arms, his little head all dishevelled, swaying to and fro as though he were dead. It was some distance from the flight of steps to the room which had been assigned to the new arrival, and the servant who showed him the way offered to carry the child in his turn; but the young cavalier, to whom, moreover, the burden seemed but a feather, thanked him and would not relinquish it. He laid him down very gently on the couch, taking a thousand precautions not to awake him; a mother could not have done better. When the servant had retired and the door was shut, he knelt down in front of him and tried to draw off his boots; but the little feet, which were swelled and painful, rendered this operation somewhat difficult, and the pretty sleeper from time to time heaved vague and inarticulate sighs like one about to wake; then the young cavalier would stop and wait until sleep had again overpowered him. The boots yielded at last, this was the most important; the stockings offered only a slight resistance.

This operation accomplished, the master took both the child's feet and laid them beside each other on the velvet of the sofa; they were quite the most adorable pair of feet in the world, as small as could be, as white as new ivory and a little rosy from the pressure of the boots in which they had been imprisoned for seventeen hours—feet too

96

small for a woman, and which looked as though they had never walked; what was seen of the leg was round, plump, smooth, transparent, veiny, and most exquisitely delicate; a leg worthy of the foot.

The young man, who was still on his knees, regarded these two little feet with loving and admiring attention; he bent down, took the left one and kissed it, then the right and kissed it also; and then with kisses after kisses he went back along the leg as far as the place where the cloth began. The page raised his long eyelash a little, and cast upon his master a kind and drowsy look in which no surprise was apparent. "My belt is uncomfortable," he said, passing his finger beneath the ribbon, and fell asleep again. The master unfastened the belt, raised the page's head with a cushion, and touching his feet which, burning as they were before, had become rather cold, wrapped them up carefully in his cloak, took an easy-chair and sat down as close as possible to the sofa. Two hours passed in this way, the young man looking at the sleeping child and following the shadows of his dreams upon his brow. The only noise that was heard in the room was his regular breathing and the tick-tack of the clock.

It was certainly a very graceful picture. There was a means for effect in the contrast of these two kinds of beauty that a skilful painter would have turned to good account. The master was as beautiful as a woman, the page as beautiful as a young girl. The round and rosy head, set thus in its hair, looked like a peach beneath its leaves; it was as fresh and as velvety, though the fatigue of the journey had robbed it of its usual brilliance; the half-opened mouth showed little teeth of milky whiteness, and beneath his full and glossy temples a network of azure veins crossed one another; his eyelashes, which were like the golden threads that are spread round the heads of virgins in the missals, reached nearly to the middle of his cheeks; his long and silky hair resembled both gold and silver—gold in the shade and silver in the light; his neck was at once fat and frail, and had nothing of the sex that was indicated by his dress: two or three buttons, unfastened to facilitate respiration, allowed a lozenge of plump and rounded flesh of wonderful whiteness to be seen through the hiatus in a shirt of fine Holland linen, as well as the beginning of a certain curving line difficult of explanation on the bosom of a young boy; looking carefully at him it might also have been found that his hips were a little too much developed.

The reader may draw his own conclusions; we are offering him mere conjectures. We know as little of the matter as he does but we hope to know more after a time and we promise faithfully to keep him aware of our discoveries. If the reader's sight is better than ours, let his glance penetrate beneath the lace on that shirt and decide conscientiously whether the outline is too prominent or not prominent enough; but we warn him that the curtains are drawn, and that a twilight scarcely favourable for investigations of the kind reigns in the room.

The cavalier was pale, but of a golden paleness full of vigour and life; his pupils swam in a blue, crystalline humour; his straight and delicate nose imparted wonderful pride and energy to his profile, and its flesh was so fine that at the edge of the outline it suffered the light to pierce through; his mouth had, at certain moments, the sweetest of smiles, but usually it was arched at the corners, inwards rather than outwards, like some of the heads that we see in the pictures of the old Italian masters; and this gave him a little look of adorable disdain, a most piquant *smorfia*, an air of childish pouting and ill-humour, which was very singular and very charming.

What were the ties uniting master to page and page to master? There was assuredly something more between them than the affection which may exist between master and servant. Were they two friends or two brothers? If so, why this disguise? It would at all events have been difficult for any one who had witnessed the scene that we have just described, to believe that these two personages were in reality only what they appeared to be.

"The dear angel, how he sleeps!" said the young man in a low voice; "I don't think that he has ever travelled so far in his life. Twenty leagues on horseback, he who is so delicate! I am afraid that he will be ill from fatigue. But no, it will be nothing; there will be no sign of it to-morrow; he will have recovered his beautiful colour, and be fresher than a rose after rain. How beautiful he is so! If I were not

afraid of awaking him, I would eat him up with caresses. What an adorable dimple he has on his chin! what delicacy and whiteness of skin! Sleep well, dear treasure. Ah! I am truly jealous of your mother and I wish that I had made you. He is not ill? No; his breathing is regular, and he does not stir. But I think some one knocked——"

And indeed two little taps had been given as softly as possible on the panel of the door.

The young man rose, and, fearing that he was mistaken, delayed opening until there should be another knock. Two other taps, a little more accentuated, were heard again, and a woman's soft voice said in a very low tone; "It is I, Théodore."

Théodore opened the door, but with less eagerness than is usual with a young man opening to a young woman with a gentle voice who comes scratching mysteriously at his door towards nightfall. The folding door, being half-opened, gave passage to whom, think you?—to the mistress of the perplexed D'Albert, the princess Rosette in person, rosier than her name, and her bosom as moved as was ever that of a woman entering at evening the room of a handsome cavalier.

"Théodore!" said Rosette.

Théodore raised his finger and laid it on his lips, so that he looked like a statue of silence, and, showing her the sleeping child, conducted her into the next room.

"Théodore," resumed Rosette, who seemed to find singular pleasure in repeating the name, and to be seeking at the same time to collect her ideas. "Théodore," she continued, without releasing the hand which the young man had offered to her to lead her to an easy-chair, "so you have at last come back to us? What have you been doing all this time? where have you been? Do you know that I have not seen you for six months? Ah, Théodore, that is not well; some consideration and some pity is due to those who love us, even though we do not love them."

THÉODORE—"What have I been doing? I do not know. I have come and gone, slept and waked, wept and sung, I have been hungry and thirsty, too hot and too cold, I have been weary, I have less money, and am six months older, I have been living and that is all. And you, what have you been doing?"

ROSETTE—"I have been loving you."

THÉODORE—"You have done nothing else?"

ROSETTE—"Absolutely nothing else. I have been employing my time badly, have I not?"

THÉODORE—"You might have employed it better, my poor Rosette; for instance in loving some one who could return your love."

ROSETTE—"I am disinterested in love, as I am in everything. I do not lend love on usury; I give it as a pure gift."

THÉODORE—"That is a very rare virtue, and one which can only spring up in a chosen soul. I have often wished to be able to love you, at least in the way that you would like; but there is an insurmountable obstacle between us which I cannot explain to you. Have you had another lover since I left you?"

ROSETTE—"I have had one whom I have still."

THÉODORE—"What sort of man is he?"

ROSETTE—"A poet."

THÉODORE—"The devil! what kind of poet, and what has he written?"

ROSETTE—"I do not quite know; a sort of volume that nobody is acquainted with, and that I tried to read one evening."

THÉODORE—"So you have an unknown poet for your lover. That must be curious. Has he holes at his elbows, dirty linen, and stockings like the screw of a press?"

ROSETTE—"No; he dresses pretty well, washes his hands, and has no inkspots on the tip of his nose. He is a friend of C——'s; I met him at Madame de Thémines's house; you know, a big woman who acts the child and puts on little innocent airs."

THÉODORE—"And might one know the name of this glorious personage?"

ROSETTE—"Oh, dear, yes! He is called the Chevalier d'Albert."

THÉODORE—"The Chevalier d'Albert! It seems to me that he is the young man who was on the balcony when I was dismounting."

ROSETTE—"Exactly."

THÉODORE—"And who looked at me with such attention."

ROSETTE—"Himself."

THÉODORE—"He is well enough.—And he has not caused me to be forgotten?"

ROSETTE—"No. You are unfortunately not one of those who can be forgotten."

THÉODORE—"He is very fond of you, no doubt?"

ROSETTE—"I am not quite sure. There are times when you would think that he loved me very much; but in reality he does not love me, and he is not far from hating me, for he bears me ill-will because of his inability to love me. He has acted like many others more experienced than he; he mistook a keen liking for passion, and was quite surprised and disappointed when his desire was satisfied. It is a mistake to think that people must continue worshipping each other after they have become thoroughly satiated."

THÉODORE—"And what do you intend to do with this said lover, who is not in love?"

ROSETTE—"What is done with the old quarters of the moon, or with the last year's fashions? He is not strong enough to leave me the first, and, although he does not love me in the true sense of the word, he is attached to me by a habit of pleasure, and such habits are the most difficult to break. If I do not assist him he is capable of wearying himself conscientiously with me until the day of the last judgment, and even beyond it; for he has the germ of every noble quality in him; and the flowers of his soul seek only to blossom in the sunshine of everlasting love. Really, I am sorry that I was not the ray for him. Of all my lovers that I did not love, I love him the most; and if I were not so good as I am I should not give him back his liberty, and should keep him still. I shall not do so; I am at this moment finishing with him."

THÉODORE—"How long will that last?"

ROSETTE—"A fortnight or three weeks, but certainly a shorter time than it would have lasted had you not come. I know that I shall never be your mistress. For this, you say, there is a secret reason to which I would submit if you were permitted to reveal it to me. All hope must therefore be forbidden me in this respect, and yet I cannot make up my mind to be the mistress of another when you are present: it seems to me that it is a profanation, and that I have no longer any right to love you."

THÉODORE—"Keep him for the love of me."

ROSETTE—"If it gives you pleasure I will do so. Ah! if you could have been mine, how different would my life have been from what it has been! The world has a very false idea of me, and I shall pass away without any one suspecting what I was—except you, Théodore, who alone have understood me, and have been cruel to me. I have never desired anyone but you for my lover, and I have not had you. If you had loved me, Théodore! I should have been virtuous and chaste, I should have been worthy of you. Instead of that I shall leave behind me (if any one remembers me) the reputation of a gay woman, a sort of courtesan who differed from the one of the gutter only in rank and fortune. I was born with the loftiest inclination; but nothing corrupts like not being loved. Many despise me without knowing what I must have suffered in order to come to be what I am. Being sure that I should never belong to him whom I preferred above all others, I abandoned myself to the stream, I did not take the trouble to protect a body that could not be yours. As to my heart nobody has had it, or ever will have it. It is yours, though you have broken it; and unlike most of the women who think themselves virtuous, provided that they have not passed from the arms of one man to those of another, I have always been faithful in soul and heart to the thought of you.

"I have at least made some persons happy, I have sent fair illusions dancing round some pillows, I have innocently deceived more than one noble heart; I was so wretched at being repulsed by you that I was always terrified at the idea of subjecting anyone to similar torture. That was the only motive for many adventures which have been attributed to a pure spirit of libertinism! I! libertinism!! O world! If you knew, Théodore, how profoundly painful it is to feel that you have missed your life, and passed your happiness by, to see that everyone is mistaken concerning you and that it is impossible to change the opinion that people have of you, that your finest qualities are turned into faults, your purest essences into black poisons, and that what is bad in you has alone transpired; to find the doors always open to your vices and always closed to your virtues, and to be unable to bring a single lily or rose to good amid so much hemlock and aconite!—you do not know this, Théodore."

THÉODORE—"Alas! alas! what you say, Rosette, is the history of everyone; the best part of us is that which remains within us, and which we cannot bring forth. It is so with poets. Their finest poem is one that they have not written; they carry away more poems in their coffins than they leave in their libraries."

ROSETTE—"I shall carry my poem away with me."

THÉODORE—"And I, mine. Who has not made one in his lifetime? who is so happy or so unhappy that he has not composed one of his own in his head or his heart? Executioners perhaps have made some that are moist with the tears of the tenderest sensibility; and poets perhaps have made some which would have been suitable for executioners, so red and monstrous are they."

ROSETTE—"Yes. They might put white roses on my tomb. I have had ten lovers—but I am a virgin, and shall die one. Many virgins, upon whose tombs there falls a perpetual snow of jessamine and orange blossom, were veritable Messalinas."

THÉODORE—"I know your worth, Rosette."

ROSETTE—"You are the only one in the world who has seen what I am; for you have seen me under the blow of a very true and deep love, since it is without hope; and one who has not seen a woman in love cannot tell what she is; it is this that comforts me in my bitterness."

THÉODORE—"And what does this young man think of you who, in the eyes of the world, is at present your lover?"

ROSETTE—"A lover's thought is a deeper gulf than the Bay of Portugal, and it is very difficult to say what there is at bottom in a man; you might fasten the sounding-lead to a cord a hundred thousand fathoms long, and reel it off to the end, and it would still run without meeting anything to stop it. Yet in his case I have occasionally touched the bottom at places, and the lead has brought back sometimes mud and sometimes beautiful shells, but oftenest mud with fragments of coral mingled together. As to his opinion of me it has greatly varied; he began at first where others end, he despised me; young people who possess a lively imagination are liable to do this. There is always a tremendous downfall in the first step that they take, and the passage of their chimera into reality cannot be accomplished without a shock. He despised me, and I amused him: now he esteems me, and I weary him.

"In the first days of our union he saw only my vulgar side, and I think that the certainty of meeting with no resistance counted for much in his determination. He appeared extremely eager to have an affair, and I thought at first that it was one of those plenitudes of heart which seek but to overflow, one of those vague loves which people have in the May-month of youth, and which lead them, in the absence of women, to encircle the trunks of trees with their arms, and kiss the flowers and grass in the meadows. But it was not that; he was only passing through me to arrive at something else. I was a road for him, and not an end. Beneath the fresh appearance of his twenty years, beneath the first dawn of adolescence, he concealed profound corruption. He was worm-eaten at the core; he was a fruit that contained nothing but ashes. In that young and vigorous body there struggled a soul as old as Saturn's,—a soul as incurably unhappy as ever there existed.

"I confess to you, Théodore, that I was frightened and was almost seized with giddiness as I leaned over the dark depths of that life. Your griefs and mine are nothing in comparison with his. Had I loved him more I should have killed him. Something that is not of this world nor in this world attracts him, and calls him, and will take no denial; he cannot rest by night or by day; and, like a heliotrope in a cellar, he twists himself that he may turn towards the sun that he does not see. He is one of those men whose soul was not dipped completely enough in the waters of Lethe before being united to his body; from the heaven whence it comes it preserves recollections of eternal beauty which harass and torment it, and it remembers that it once had wings, and now has only feet. If I were God, the angel guilty of such negligence should be deprived of poetry for two eternities. Instead of having to build a castle of brilliantly coloured cards to shelter a fair young fantasy for a single spring, a tower should have been built more lofty than the eight superposed temples of Belus. I was not strong enough, I appeared not to have understood him, I let him creep on his pinions and seek for a summit whence he might spring into the immensity of space.

"He believes that I have seen nothing of all this because I have lent myself to all his caprices without seeming to suspect their aim. Being unable to cure him, I wished, and I hope that this will be taken into account some day before God, to give him at least the happiness of believing that he had been passionately loved. He inspired me with sufficient pity and interest to enable me to assume with him tones and manners tender enough to delude him. I played my part like a consummate actress; I was sportive and melancholy, sensitive and voluptuous; I feigned disquiet and jealousy; I shed false tears, and called to my lips swarms of affected smiles. I attired this puppet of love in the richest stuffs; I made it walk in the avenues of my parks; I invited all my birds to sing as it passed, and all my dahlias and daturas to salute it by bending their heads; I had to cross my lake on the silvery back of my darling swan; I concealed myself within, and lent it my voice, my wit, my beauty, my youth, and gave it so seductive an appearance that the reality was not so good as my falsehood.

"When the time comes to shiver this hollow statue I shall do it in such a way that he will believe all the wrong to be on my side, and will be spared remorse. I shall myself give the prick of the pin through which the air that fills this balloon will escape. Is this not meritorious and honourable deception? I have a crystal urn containing a few tears which I collected at the moment when they were about to fall. They are my jewel-box and diamonds, and I shall present them to the angel who comes to take me away to God."

THÉODORE—"They are the most beautiful that could shine on a woman's neck. The ornaments of a queen have less value. For my part I think that the liquid poured by Magdalene upon the feet of Christ was made up of the former tears of those whom she had comforted, and I think, too, that it is with such tears as these that the Milky Way is strewn, and not, as was pretended, with Juno's milk. Who will do for you what you have done for him?"

ROSETTE—"No one, alas! since you cannot."

THÉODORE—"Ah! dear soul! to think that I cannot! But do not lose hope. You are still beautiful, and very young. You have many avenues of flowering limes and acacias to traverse before you reach the damp road bordered with box and leafless trees, which leads from the porphyry tomb where your beautiful dead years will be buried, to the tomb of rough and moss-covered stone into which they will hastily thrust the remains of what was once you, and the wrinkled, tottering spectres of the days of your old age. Much of the mountain of life is still left for you to climb, and it will be long ere you come to the zone of snow. You have only arrived at the region of aromatic plants, of limpid cascades wherein the iris hangs her tri-coloured arch, of beautiful green oaks and scented larches. Mount a little higher, and from there, on the wider horizon which will be displayed at your feet, you shall perhaps see the bluish smoke rising from the roof where sleeps the man who is to love you. Life must not be despaired of at the very beginning; vistas of what we had ceased to look for are opened up thus in our destiny.

"Man in his life has often reminded me of a pilgrim following the snail-like staircase in a Gothic tower. The long granite serpent winds its coils in the darkness, each scale being a step. After a few circumvolutions the little light that came from the door is extinguished. The shadow of the houses that are not passed as yet, prevents the air-holes from letting in the sun. The walls are black and oozy; it is more like going down into a dungeon never to come forth again than ascending to the turret which from below appeared to you so slender and fine, and covered with laces and embroideries as though it were setting out for a ball.

"You hesitate as to whether you ought to go higher, this damp darkness weighs so heavily on your brow. The staircase makes some further turns and more frequent lutherns cut out their golden trefoils on the opposite wall. You begin to see the indented gables of the houses, the sculptures in the entablatures, and the whimsical shapes of the chimneys; a few steps more and the eye looks down upon the entire town; it is a forest of spires, steeples and towers which bristle up in every direction, indented, slashed, hollowed, punched and allowing the light to appear through their thousand cuttings. The domes and cupolas are rounded like the breasts of some giantess or the skulls of Titans. The islets of houses and palaces stand out in shaded or luminous slices. A few steps more and you will be on the platform; and then, beyond the town walls, you will see the verdant cultivation, the blue hills and the white sails on the clouded ribbon of the river.

"You are flooded with dazzling light, and the swallows pass and repass near you, uttering little joyous cries. The distant sound of the city reaches you like a friendly murmur, or the buzzing of a hive of bees; all the bells strip their necklaces of sonorous pearls in the air; the winds waft to you the scents from the neighbouring forest and from the mountain flowers; there is nothing but light, harmony and perfume. If your feet had become weary, or if you had been seized with discouragement and had remained seated on a lower step, or if you had gone down again altogether, this sight would have been lost to you.

"Sometimes, however, the tower has only a single opening in the middle or above. The tower of your life is constructed in this way; then there is need of more obstinate courage, of perseverance armed with nails that are more hooked, so as to cling in the shadow to the projections of the stones and reach the resplendent trefoil through which the sight may escape over the country; or perhaps the loopholes have been filled up, or the making of them has been forgotten, and then it is necssary to ascend to the summit; but the higher you mount without seeing, the more immense seems the horizon, and the greater is the pleasure and the surprise."

ROSETTE—"O Théodore, God grant that I may soon come to the place where the window is! I have been following the spiral for a long time through the profoundest night; but I am afraid that the opening has been built up and that I must climb to the summit; and what if this staircase with its countless steps were only to lead to a walled-up door or a vault of freestone?"

THÉODORE—"Do not say that, Rosette; do not think it. What architect would construct a staircase that should lead to nothing? Why suppose the gentle architect of the world more stupid and improvident than an ordinary architect? God does not mistake, and He forgets nothing. It is incredible that He should amuse Himself by shutting you up in a long stone tube without outlet or opening, in order to play you a trick. Why do you think that He should grudge poor ants such as we are their wretched happiness of a minute, and the imperceptible grain of millet that falls to them in this broad creation? To do that He should have the ferocity of a tiger or a judge; and, if we were so displeasing to Him, He would only have to tell a comet to turn a little from its path and strangle us with a hair of its tail. Why the deuce do you think that God would divert Himself by threading us one by one on a golden pin, as the Emperor Domitian used to treat flies? God is not a portress, nor a churchwarden, and although He is old He has not yet fallen into childishness. All such petty viciousness is beneath Him, and He is not silly enough to try to be witty with us and play pranks with us. Courage, Rosette, courage! If you are out of breath, stop a little to recover it, and then continue your ascent: you have, perhaps, only twenty steps to climb in order to reach the embrasure whence you will see your happiness."

ROSETTE—"Never! oh, never! and if I come to the summit of the tower, it will be only to cast myself from it."

THÉODORE—"Drive away, poor afflicted one, these gloomy thoughts which hover like bats about you, and shed the opaque shadow of their wings upon your brow. If you wish me to love you, be happy, and do not weep." (He draws her gently to him and kisses her on the eyes.)

ROSETTE—"What a misfortune it is to me to have known you! and yet, were it to be done over again, I should still wish to have known you. Your severity has been sweeter to me than the passion of others; and, although you have caused me much suffering, all the pleasure that I have had has come to me from you; through you I have had a glimpse of what I might have been. You have been a lightning-flash in my night, and you have lit up many of the dark places of my soul; you have opened up vistas in my life that are quite new. To you I owe the knowledge of love, unhappy love, it is true; but there is a deep and melancholy charm in loving without being loved, and it is good to remember those who forget us. It is a happiness to be able to love even when you are the only one who loves, and many die without having experienced it, and often the most to be pitied are not those who love."

THÉODORE—"They suffer and feel their wounds, but at least they live. They hold to something; they have a star around which they gravitate, a pole to which they eagerly tend. They have something to wish for; they can say to themselves: 'If I arrive there, if I have that, I shall be happy.' They have frightful agonies, but when dying, they can at least say to themselves: 'I die for him.' To die thus is to be born again. The really, the only irreparably unhappy ones are those

109

whose foolish embrace takes in the entire universe, those who wish for everything and wish for nothing, and who, if angel or fairy were to descend and say suddenly to them: 'Wish for something and you shall have it,' would be embarrassed and mute."

ROSETTE—"If the fairy came, I know what I should ask her."

THÉODORE—"You do, Rosette, and in that respect you are more fortunate than I, for I do not. Vague desires stir within me which blend together, and give birth to others which afterwards devour them. My desires are a cloud of birds whirling and hovering aimlessly; your desire is an eagle who has his eyes on the sun, and who is prevented by the lack of air from rising on his outstretched wings. Ah! if I could know what I want; if the idea which pursues me would extricate itself clear and precise from the fog that envelops it; if the fortunate or fatal star would appear in the depths of my sky; if the light which I am to follow, whether perfidious will-o'-the-wisp or hospitable beacon, would come and be radiant in the night; if my pillar of fire would go before me, even though it were across a desert without manna and without springs; if I knew whither I am going, though I were only to come to a precipice!—I would rather have the mad riding of accursed huntsmen through quagmires and thickets than this absurd and monotonous movement of the feet. To live in this way is to follow a calling like that of those horses which turn the wheel of some well with bandaged eyes, and travel thousands of leagues without seeing anything or changing their situation. I have been turning for a long time, and the bucket should have quite come up."

ROSETTE—"You have many points of resemblance with D'Albert, and when you speak it seems to me sometimes as though he were the speaker. I have no doubt that when you are further acquainted with him you will become much attached to him; you cannot fail to suit each other. He is harassed as you are by these aimless flights; he loves immensely without knowing what; he would ascend to heaven, for the earth appears to him a stool scarcely good enough for one of his feet, and he has more pride than Lucifer before his fall."

THÉODORE—"I was at first afraid that he was one of those numerous poets who have driven poetry from the earth, one of those string-

ers of sham pearls who can see nothing in the world but the last syllables of words, and who when they have rhymed *glade* with *shade*, *flame* with *name*, and *God* with *trod*, conscientiously cross their legs and arms and suffer the spheres to complete their revolution."

ROSETTE—"He is not one of those. His verses are inferior to him and do not contain him. What he has written would give you a very false idea of his own person; his true poem is himself, and I do not know whether he will ever compose another. In the recesses of his soul he has a seraglio of beautiful ideas which he surrounds with a triple wall, and of which he is more jealous than was ever sultan of his odalisques. He only puts those into his verses which he does not care about or which have repulsed him; it is the door through which he drives them away, and the world has only those which he will keep no longer."

THÉODORE—"I can understand this jealousy and shame. In the same way many people do not acknowledge the love they had until they have it no longer, nor their mistresses until they are dead."

ROSETTE—"It is so difficult to possess a thing alone in this world! every torch attracts so many butterflies, and every treasure so many thieves! I like those silent ones who carry their idea into their grave, and will not surrender it to the foul kisses and shameless touches of the crowd. I am delighted with the lovers who do not write their mistress's name on any bark, nor confide it to any echo, and who, when sleeping, are pursued by the dread lest they should utter it in a dream. I am one of the number; I have never spoken my thought, and none shall know my love—but see, it is nearly eleven o'clock, my dear Théodore, and I am preventing you from taking the rest that you must need. When I am obliged to leave you, I always feel a heaviness of heart, and it seems to me the last time that I shall see you. I delay the parting as much as possible; but one must part at last. Well, good-bye, for I am afraid that D'Albert will be looking for me; dear friend, good-bye."

Théodore put his arm about her waist, and led her thus to the door; there he stopped, following her for a long time with his gaze; the corridor was pierced at wide intervals with little narrow-paned windows, which were lit up by the moon, and made a very fantastic alternation of light and shade. At each window Rosette's white, pure form shone like a silver phantom; then it would vanish to reappear with greater brilliance a little further off; at last it disappeared altogether.

Théodore, seemingly lost in deep thought, remained motionless for a few minutes with folded arms; then he passed his hand over his forehead and threw back his hair with a movement of his head, reentered the room, and went to bed after kissing the brow of the page who was still asleep.

VII

~~~~~~~~~~~~~

As soon as it was light at Rosette's, D'Albert had himself announced with a promptness that was not usual with him.

"Here you are," said Rosette, "and I should say you are early, if you could ever come early. And so, to reward you for your gallantry, I grant you my hand to kiss."

And from beneath the lace-trimmed sheet of Flanders linen, she drew the prettiest little hand that was ever seen at the end of a round, plump arm.

D'Albert kissed it with compunction.

"And the other one, its little sister, are we not to kiss it as well?"

"Oh, dear, yes! nothing more feasible. I am in my Sunday humour to-day; here." And, bringing her other hand out of the bed, she tapped him lightly on the mouth. "Am I not the most accommodating woman in the world?"

"You are grace itself, and should have white marble temples raised to you in myrtle groves. Indeed I am much afraid that there will happen to you what happened to Psyche, and that Venus will become jealous of you," said D'Albert, joining both the hands of the fair one and carrying them together to his lips.

"How you deliver all that in a breath! One would say that it was a phrase you had learnt by heart," said Rosette with a delicious little pout.

"Not at all: you are quite worthy of having a phrase turned expressly for you, and you are made to pluck the virginity of madrigals," retorted D'Albert.

"Oh, indeed! really—what makes you so lively to-day? Are you ill that you are so polite? I fear that you will die. Do you know that it is a bad sign when anyone changes his character all at once with no apparent reason? Now, it is an established fact, in the eyes of all the women who have taken the trouble to love you, that you are usually as cross as you can be, and it is no less certain that at this moment you are as charming as one can be, and are displaying most inexplicable amiability. There, I do think that you are looking pale, my poor D'Albert; give me your arm, that I may feel your pulse." And she drew up his sleeve and counted the beats with comical gravity. "No, you are as well as possible, without the slightest symptom of fever. Then I must be furiously pretty this morning! Just get me my mirror, and let me see how far your gallantry is right or wrong."

D'Albert took up a little mirror that was on the toilet-table and laid it on the bed.

"In point of fact," said Rosette, "you are not altogether wrong. Why do you not make a sonnet on my eyes, sir poet? You have no reason for not doing so. Just see how unfortunate I am! to have eyes like that and a poet like this, and yet to be in want of sonnets, as though I were one-eyed with a water carrier for my lover! You do not love me, sir; you have not even written me an acrostic sonnet. And what do you think of my mouth? Yet I have kissed you with that mouth, and shall, perhaps, do so again, my handsome gloomy one; and, indeed, it is a favour that you scarcely deserve (this is not meant for to-day, for you deserve everything); but not to be always talking about myself, you have unparalleled beauty and freshness this morning, you look like a brother of Aurora; and although it is scarcely light you are already dressed and got up as though you were going to a ball. Perchance you have designs upon me? would you deal a treacherous blow at my virtue? do you wish to make a conquest of me? But I forgot that that was done already, and is now ancient history."

"Rosette, do not jest in that way; you know very well that I love you."

"Why, that depends. I don't know it very well; and you?"

"Perfectly; and so true is it that if you were so kind as to forbid your door to everybody, I should endeavour to prove it to you, and, I venture to flatter myself, in a victorious fashion."

"As for that, no; however much I may wish to be convinced, my door shall remain open; I am too pretty to have closed doors; the sun shines for everybody, and my beauty shall be like the sun to-day, if you have no objection."

"But I have, on my honour; however, act as though I thought it excellent. I am your very humble slave, and I lay my wishes at your feet."

"That is quite right; continue to have sentiments of the kind, and leave the key in your door this evening."

"The Chevalier Théodore de Sérannes," said a big negro's head, smiling and chubby-faced, appearing between the leaves of the folding-door, "wishes to pay his respects to you and entreats you to condescend to receive him."

"Ask the chevalier to come in," said Rosette, drawing up the sheet to her chin.

Théodore first went up to Rosette's bed and made her a most profound and graceful bow, to which she returned a friendly nod, and then turned towards D'Albert, and saluted him also with a free and courteous air.

"Where were you?" said Théodore. "I have perhaps interrupted an interesting conversation. Pray continue, and acquaint me with the subject of it in a few words."

114

"Oh, no!" replied Rosette with a mischievous smile; "we were talking of business."

Théodore sat down at the foot of Rosette's bed, for D'Albert had placed himself beside the pillow, as being the first arrival; the conversation wandered for some time from subject to subject, and was very witty, very gay and very lively, which is the reason why we shall not give any account of it; we should be afraid that it would lose too much if transcribed. Mien, accent, fire in speech and gesture, the thousand ways of pronouncing a word, all the spirit of it, like the foam of champagne which sparkles and evaporates immediately, are things that it is impossible to fix and reproduce. It is a lacuna which we leave to be filled up by the reader, and with which he will assuredly deal better than we; let him here imagine five or six pages filled with everything of the most delicate, most capricious, most curiously fantastical, most elegant and most glittering description.

We are aware that we are here employing an artifice which tends to recall that of Timanthes who, despairing of his ability to adequately represent Agamemnon's face, threw a drapery over his head; but we would rather be timid than imprudent.

It might perhaps be to the purpose to inquire into the motives which had prompted D'Albert to get up so early in the morning, and the incentive which had induced him to visit Rosette as early as if he had been still in love with her. It looked as though it were a slight impulse of secret and unacknowledged jealousy. He was certainly not much attached to Rosette, and he would even have been very glad to get rid of her, but he wished at least to give her up himself and not to be given up by her, a thing which never fails to wound a man's pride deeply, however well extinguished his first flame may otherwise be.

Théodore was such a handsome cavalier that it was difficult to see him appearing in a connection without being apprehensive of what had, in fact, often happened already, apprehensive, that is, lest all eyes should be turned upon him and all hearts follow the eyes; and it was a singular thing that, although he had carried off many women, no lover had ever maintained towards him the lasting resentment which is usually entertained towards those who have supplanted you. In all his ways there was such a conquering charm, such natural grace, and something so sweet and proud, that even men were sensible of it. D'Albert, who had come to see Rosette with the intention of speaking to Théodore with tartness, should he meet him there, was quite surprised to find himself free from the slightest impulse of anger in his presence, and so ready to receive the advances that were made to him.

At the end of half an hour you would have thought them friends from childhood, and yet D'Albert had an intimate conviction that if Rosette was ever to love, it would be this man, and he had every reason to be jealous at least for the future, for as to the present, he had as yet no suspicion; what would it have been had he seen the fair one in a white dressing-gown gliding like a moth on a moon-ray into the handsome youth's room, and not coming out until three or four hours afterwards with mysterious precautions? He might truly have thought himself more unfortunate than he was, for one of the things that we scarcely ever see is a pretty, amorous woman coming out of the chamber of an equally pretty cavalier exactly as she went in.

Rosette listened to Théodore with great attention, and in the way that people listen to someone whom they love; but what he said was so amusing and varied, that this attention seemed only natural and was easy of explanation. Accordingly D'Albert did not take umbrage at it. Théodore's manner towards Rosette was polished and friendly, but nothing more.

"What shall we do to-day, Théodore?" said Rosette; "suppose we take a sail? what do you think? or we might go hunting?"

"Let us go hunting, it is less melancholy than gliding over the water side by side with some languid swan, and bending the leaves of the water-lilies right and left,—is that not your opinion, D'Albert?"

"I might perhaps prefer to flow along in the boat with the current of the stream to galloping desperately in pursuit of a poor beast; but I will go where you go. We have now only to let Madame Rosette get up, and assume a suitable costume."

Rosette gave a sign of assent, and rang to have herself dressed. The two young men went off arm-in-arm, and it was easy to guess, seeing them so friendly together, that one was the formal lover and the other the beloved lover of the same person.

Everyone was soon ready. D'Albert and Théodore were already mounted in the first court when Rosette appeared in a riding-habit, on the top of the flight of steps. She had a little sprightly and easy air in this costume which became her very well. She leaped upon the saddle with her usual agility, and gave a switch to her horse which started off like an arrow. D'Albert struck in both his spurs and soon rejoined her. Théodore allowed them to get some way ahead, being sure of catching them up as soon as he wished to do so. He seemed to be waiting for something, and often looked round towards the mansion.

"Théodore, Théodore, come on! are you riding a wooden horse?" cried Rosette.

Théodore gave his animal a gallop, and diminished the distance separating him from Rosette, without, however, causing it to disappear.

He again looked towards the mansion of which they were beginning to lose sight; a little whirlwind of dust, in which something that could not yet be discerned was in very hasty motion, appeared at the end of the road. In a few moments it was at Théodore's side, and opening up, like the classic clouds in the Iliad, displayed the fresh and rosy face of the mysterious page.

"Théodore, come along!" cried Rosette a second time, "give your tortoise the spur and come up beside us."

Théodore gave the rein to his horse which was pawing and rearing with impatience, and in a few seconds he was several heads in advance of D'Albert and Rosette.

"Whoever loves me will follow me," said Théodore, leaping a fence four feet high. "Well, sir poet," he said, when he was on the other side, "you do not jump? Yet your mount has wings, so people say."

"Faith! I would rather go round; I have only one head to break after all; if I had several I should try," replied D'Albert, smiling.

"Nobody loves me then, since nobody follows me," said Théodore, drawing down the arched corners of his mouth even more than usual. The little page raised his large blue eyes towards him with a look of reproach, and brought his heels against his horse's sides.

The horse gave a prodigious bound.

"Yes! somebody," he said to him on the other side of the fence.

Rosette cast a singular look upon the child and blushed up to her eyes; then, giving a furious stroke with her whip on the neck of her mare, she crossed the bar of apple-green wood which fenced the avenue.

"And I, Théodore, do you think that I do not love you?"

The child cast a sly side-glance at her, and drew close to Théodore.

D'Albert was already in the middle of the avenue, and saw nothing of all this; for, from time immemorial, fathers, husbands, and lovers have been possessed of the privilege of seeing nothing.

"Isnabel," said Théodore, "you are mad, and so are you, Rosette! Isnabel, you did not take sufficient room for the leap, and you, Rosette, nearly caught your dress in the posts. You might have killed yourself."

"What matter?" replied Rosette with an accent so sad and melancholy, that Isnabel forgave her for having leaped the fence as well.

They went on for some time and reached the cross-roads where they were to find huntsmen and pack. Six arches cut in the thickness of the forest led to a little stone tower with six sides, on each of which was engraved the name of the road that terminated there. The trees rose to such a height that it seemed as if they wished to card the fleecy, flaky clouds sailing over their heads before a somewhat strong breeze; close, high grass and impenetrable bushes afforded retreats and fortresses to the game, and the hunt promised to be a success. It was a genuine old-world forest, with ancient oaks more than a century old, such as are to be seen no longer now that we plant no more trees, and have not patience enough to wait until those that are planted have grown up; a hereditary forest planted by great-grandfathers for the fathers, and by the fathers for the grandsons, with avenues of prodigious breadth, an obelisk surmounted by a ball, a rock-worn fountain, the indispensable pond, and white-powdered keepers in yellow leather breeches and sky-blue coats; one of those dark, bushy forests wherein stand out in admirable relief the white satiny cruppers of the great horses of Wouvermans, and the broad flags on the Dampierre horns, which Parrocelli loves to display radiant on the huntsmen's backs.

A multitude of dog's tails, like pruning knives or hedge-bills were curled friskily in a dusty cloud. The signal was given, the dogs, which were straining hard enough at the leash to strangle themselves were uncoupled, and the hunt began. We shall not describe very minutely the turnings and windings of the stag through the forest; we do not even know with exactitude whether it was a full grown stag, and in spite of all our researches we have not been able to ascertain, which is really distressing. Nevertheless we think that only full grown stags could have been found in such a forest, so ancient, so shady, and so lordly, and we see no reason why the animal after which the four principal characters of this illustrious romance were galloping on horses of different colours and *non passibus aequis,* should not have been one.

The stag ran like the true stag that he was, and the fifty dogs at his heels were no ordinary spur to his natural swiftness. The run was so quick that only a few rare bays were to be heard.

Théodore, being the best mounted and the best horseman, followed hard on the pack with incredible eagerness. D'Albert was close behind him. Rosette and the little page Isnabel came after, separated by an interval which was increasing every minute.

The interval was soon so great as to take away all hopes of restoring an equilibrium.

"Suppose we stop for a little," said Rosette, "to give our horses breath? The hunt is going in the direction of the pond, and I know a cross-road which will take us there as soon as they."

Isnabel drew the bridle of his little mountain horse which, shaking the hanging locks of his mane over his eyes, bent his head, and began to scrape the sand with his hoofs.

This little horse formed the most perfect contrast with Rosette's: he was as black as night, the other as white as satin; he was quite

shaggy and dishevelled, the other had its mane plaited with blue, and its tail curled and crisped. The second looked like a unicorn, and the first like a barbet.

The same antithetical difference was to be remarked in the masters as in the steeds. Rosette's hair was as dark as Isnabel's was fair; her eyebrows were very neatly traced and in a very apparent manner; the page's were scarcely more vigorous than his skin and resembled the down on a peach. The colour of the one was brilliant and strong like the light of noon; the complexion of the other had the transparencies and blushings of the dawn of day.

120

"Suppose we try to catch up the hunt now?" said Isnabel to Rosette; "the horses have had time to take breath."

"Come along!" replied the pretty amazon, and they started off at a gallop down a rather narrow, transverse avenue which led to the pond; the two animals were abreast and took up nearly the whole breadth.

On Isnabel's side a great branch projected like an arm from a twisted and knotted tree, which seemed to be shaking its fist at the riders. The child did not see it.

"Take care!" cried Rosette, "bend down on your saddle! you will be unhorsed!"

The warning had been given too late; the branch struck Isnabel in the middle of the body. The violence of the blow made him lose his stirrups, and, as his horse continued to gallop and the branch was too strong to bend, he found himself lifted out of the saddle and fell heavily behind.

The child lay senseless from the blow. Rosette, greatly frightened, threw herself from her horse, and hastened to the page who showed no signs of life.

His cap had fallen off, and his beautiful fair hair streamed on all sides in disorder on the sand. His little open hands looked like hands of wax, so pale were they. Rosette knelt down beside him and tried to restore him. She had neither salts nor flask about her, and her perplexity was great. At last she noticed a tolerably deep rut in which the rain-water had collected and become clear; she dipped her finger into it, to the great terror of a little frog who was the naïad of this sea, and shook a few drops upon the bluish temples of the young page. He did not appear to feel them, and the water-pearls rolled along his white cheeks like a sylphid's tears along the leaf of a lily. Rosette, thinking that his clothes might distress him, unfastened his belt, undid the buttons of his tightly-fitting coat and opened his shirt that his breast might have freer play.

Rosette there saw something which to a man would have been one of the most agreeable surprises in the world, but which seemed to be very far from giving her pleasure—for her eyebrows drew close together, and her upper lip trembled slightly—namely, a very white bosom, scarcely formed as yet, but which gave admirable promise, and was already fulfilling much of it; a round, polished ivory bosom—to speak like the Ronsardizers—delicious to see, and more delicious to kiss.

"A woman!" she said, "a woman! ah! Théodore!"

Isnabel—for we shall continue to give him this name, although it was not his—began to breathe a little, and languidly raised his long eyelashes; he had not been wounded in any way, but only stunned. He soon sat up, and with Rosette's assistance was able to stand up on his feet and remount his horse, which had stopped as soon as he had felt that his rider was gone.

They proceeded at a slow pace as far as the pond, where they did in fact meet again with the rest of the hunt. Rosette, in a few words, related to Théodore what had taken place. The latter changed colour several times during Rosette's narration, and kept his horse beside Isnabel's for the remainder of the way.

They came back very early to the mansion; the day which had commenced so joyously ended rather sadly.

Rosette was pensive, and D'Albert seemed also to be plunged in deep thought. The reader will soon know what had occasioned this.

VIII

"No, my dear Silvio, no, I have not forgotten you; I am not one of those who pass through life without ever throwing a look behind; my past follows me and invades my present, and almost my future; your friendship is one of the sun-lit spots which stand out most clearly on the horizon quite blue as it already is of my later years; often do I turn to contemplate it, from the summit I have reached, with a feeling of unspeakable melancholy.

"Oh! what a glorious time was that, when we were pure as angels! Our feet scarcely touched the ground; we had as it were wings upon our shoulders, our desires swept us away, and in the breeze of spring-time there trembled about our brows the golden glory of adolescence.

"Do you remember the little island planted with poplars at that part where the river branches off? To reach it, it was necessary to cross a somewhat long and very narrow plank which used to bend strangely in the middle; a real bridge for goats, and one, indeed, which was scarcely used but by them: it was delicious. Short, thick grass wherein the forget-me-not blinkingly opened its pretty little blue eyes, a path as yellow as nankeen which formed a girdle for the island's green robe and clasped its waist, while an ever moving shade of aspens and poplars were not the least of the delights of this paradise. There were great pieces of linen which the women would come to spread out to bleach in the dew; you would have thought them squares of snow;—and that little girl so brown and sunburnt whose large wild eyes shone with such brilliant splendour beneath the long locks of her hair, and who used to run after the goats threatening them and shaking her osier rod when they made as though they would walk over the linens that were under her care—do you remember her?

"And the sulphur-coloured butterflies with unequal and quivering flight, and the king-fisher which we so often tried to catch and which had its nest in that alder thicket? and those paths down to the river, with their rudely hewn steps and their posts and stakes all green below, which were nearly always shut in by screens of plants and boughs? How limpid and mirror-like was the water! how clearly could we see the bed of golden gravel! and what a pleasure it was, seated on the bank, to let the tips of our feet dangle in it! The golden-flowered water-lilies spreading gracefully upon it looked like green hair flowing over the agate back of some bathing nymph. The sky looked at itself in this mirror with azure smiles and most exquisite transparencies of pearl-gray, and at all hours of the day there were turquoises, spangles,

123

wools and moires in exhaustless variety. How I loved those squadrons of little ducks with the emerald necks which used to sail incessantly from one bank to the other making wrinkles across the pure glass!

"How well were we suited to be the figures in that landscape! how well adapted were we to that sweet calm nature, and how readily did we harmonise with it! Spring without, youth within, sun on the grass, smiles on our lips, flakes of blossoms on all the bushes, fair illusions full-blown in our souls, modest blushes on our cheeks and on the eglantine, poetry singing in our heart, unseen birds warbling in the trees, light, cooings, perfumes, a thousand confused murmurs, the heart beating, the water stirring a pebble, a grass-blade or a thought upspringing, a drop of water flowing along a flower-cup, a tear overflowing along an eyelash, a sigh of love, a rustling of leaves . . . what evenings we spent there walking slowly, and so close to the edge that we had often one foot in the water and the other on the ground!

"Alas! this lasted but a short time, with me, at least, for you have been able, while acquiring the knowledge of the man, to preserve the purity of the child. The germ of corruption that was in me has developed very quickly, and the gangrene has pitilessly devoured all of me that was pure and holy. Nothing good is left to me but my friendship for you.

"I am accustomed to conceal nothing from you, neither actions nor thoughts. The most secret fibres of my heart I have laid bare before you; however whimsical, ridiculous, and eccentric the impulses of my soul may be, I must describe them to you; but, in truth, what I have experienced for some time is so strange, that I can scarcely dare to acknowledge it to myself. I told you somewhere that I feared lest, from seeking the beautiful and disquieting myself to attain it, I should at last fall into the impossible or monstrous. I have almost come to this; oh, when shall I emerge from all these currents which conflict and draw me to left and right; when will the deck of my vessel cease to tremble beneath my feet and be swept by the waves of all these storms? where shall I find a harbour where I may cast anchor, and a rock immovable and beyond the reach of the billows where I may dry myself and wring the foam from my hair?

"You know the eagerness with which I have sought for physical beauty, the importance that I attach to external form, and the love of the visible world that possesses me. I cannot be otherwise; I am too corrupted and surfeited to believe in moral beauty, and to pursue it with any consistency. I have completely lost the knowledge of good and evil, and from sheer depravity have almost returned to the ignorance of the savage or the child. In truth, nothing appears to me worthy of praise or blame, and the strangest actions astonish me but little. My conscience is deaf and dumb. Adultery appears to me the most innocent thing in the world; I deem it quite a simple matter that a young girl should prostitute herself; it seems to me that I would betray my friends without the least remorse, and that I should not have the slightest scruple about kicking people who annoyed me down a precipice if I were walking with them along the edge. I would look with coolness on the most atrocious sights, and there is something in the sufferings and misfortunes of humanity which is not displeasing to me. I experience at the sight of some calamity falling upon the world the same feeling of acrid and bitter voluptuousness that is experienced by a man who at last avenges an old affront.

"O world, what hast thou done to me that I should hate thee thus? Who has filled me so with gall against thee? what was I expecting from thee that I should preserve such rancour against thee for having deceived me? to what lofty hope hast thou been false? what eaglet wings hast thou shorn? What doors wast thou to open which have remained closed, and which of us has failed in respect of the other?

"Nothing touches me, nothing moves me; I no longer feel, on hearing the recital of heroic deeds, those sublime quiverings which at one time would run through me from head to foot. All this even appears to me to be somewhat silly. No accent is deep enough to bite the slackened fibres of my heart and cause them to vibrate: I see the tears of my fellow-creatures flow with as indifferent an eye as the rain, unless indeed they be of a fine water, and the light be reflected in them in picturesque fashion and they flow over a beautiful cheek. For animals, and for them almost alone, I have a feeble residue of pity. I would suffer a peasant or a servant to be beaten without mercy, and could not patiently endure to have the same treatment given in my presence to a horse or a dog; yet I am not wicked—I have never done, and probably shall never do, any harm to anybody in the world; but this is rather a result of my indifference and the sovereign contempt which I have for all persons who do not please me, and which does not allow me to be occupied with them even to do them an injury.

"I abhor the whole world in a body, and in the whole collection I scarcely deem one or two worthy of a special hatred. To hate anyone is to disquiet yourself as much about him as though you loved him; to distinguish him, isolate him from the crowd; to be in a violent condition on account of him; to think of him by day and dream of him by night; to bite your pillow and grind your teeth at the thought that he exists; what more could you do for one you loved? Would you bestow the same trouble and activity on pleasing a mistress as on ruining an enemy? I doubt it—in order really to hate anybody, we must love another. Every great hatred serves as a counterweight to a great love: and whom could I hate, I who love nobody?

"My hate, like my love, is a confused and general feeling, which seeks to fasten upon something and cannot; I have a treasure of hate and love within me which I cannot turn to account, and which weighs horribly upon me. If I can find no means of pouring forth one or other of them, or both, I shall burst, and break asunder like bags crammed too full of money which rupture themselves and rip their seams. Oh! if I could abhor somebody, if one of the stupid people with whom I live could insult me in such a way as to make my old viper blood boil in my icy veins and rouse me from the dull somnolence wherein I stagnate; if thou couldst bite me on the cheek with thy rat-like teeth and communicate thy venom and thy rage to me, old sorceress with palsied head; if someone's death could be my life; if the last heart's throb of an enemy writhing beneath my foot could impart delicious quiverings to my hair, and the odour of his blood become sweeter to my parched nostrils than the aroma of flowers, oh! how readily would I abandon love, and how happy would I esteem myself!

"Mortal embraces, tiger-like bitings, boa entwinings, elephant feet pressed on a cracking and flattening breast, steeled tail of the scorpion, milky juice of the euphorbia, curling kris of Java, blades that glitter in the night and are extinguished in blood, you it is that, with me, shall take the place of leafless roses, humid kisses and the entwinings of love!

"I have said that I love nothing; alas! I am now afraid of loving something. It were ten thousand times better to hate than so to love! I have found the type of beauty that I dreamed of so long. I have discovered the body of my phantom; I have seen it, it has spoken to me, I have touched its hand, it exists; it is not a chimera. I well knew that I could not be mistaken, and that my presentiments never lied. Yes, Silvio, I am by the side of my life's dream; its room is there and mine is here. I can see the trembling of the curtain at its window and the light of its lamp. Its shadow has just passed across the curtain. In an hour we shall sup together.

"The beautiful Turkish eyelashes, the deep and limpid gaze, the warm colour of pale amber, the long and lustrous black hair, the nose finely cut and proud, the joints and slender delicate extremities after the manner of Parmeginiano, the dainty curves, the purity of oval, which give so much elegance and aristocracy to a face, all that I wished for, and that I should have been happy to find disseminated in five or six persons, I have found united in one!

"What I most adore of all things in the world is a pretty hand. If you saw this one! what perfection! what vivacious whiteness! what softness of skin! what penetrating moisture! how admirably tapering the extremity of the fingers! how clear the oval markings on the nails! what polish and what splendour! you would compare them to the inner leaves of a rose,—the hands of Anne of Austria, so vaunted and celebrated, are in comparison but those of a turkey-herd or of a scullery-maid. And then what grace is there and what art in the slightest movements of this hand! how gracefully does this little finger curve and keep itself a little apart from its tall brothers! The thought of this hand maddens me, and causes my lips to quiver and burn. I close my eyes that I may see it no longer; but with the tips of its delicate fingers it takes my eyelashes and opens the lids, and causes a thousand visions of ivory and snow to pass before me.

"Ah! it is Satan's claw, no doubt, that is gloved beneath this satin skin;—it is some jesting demon who is befooling me;—there is some sorcery here. It is too monstrously impossible.

"This hand—I shall set out for Italy to see the pictures of the great masters, to study, compare, draw, and in short become a painter that I may represent it as it is, as I see it, as I feel it; it will perhaps be a means of ridding myself of this species of possession.

"I wished for beauty; I knew not what I asked. It is to be desirous of looking without eyelids at the sun, to be desirous of touching fire. I suffer horribly. To be unable to assimilate this perfection, to be unable to pass into it and have it pass into me, to have no means of representing it and making it felt! When I see something beautiful I wish to touch it with the whole of myself, everywhere and at the same time. I wish to sing it, and paint it, to sculpture it and write it, to be loved by it as I love it; I wish what is, and ever will be, impossible.

"Your letter has done me harm, much harm—forgive me for saying so. All the calm, pure happiness that you enjoy, the walks in the reddening woods, the long talks so tender and intimate which end with a chaste kiss upon the brow; the separate and serene life; the days so quickly spent that the night seems to advance, make me find the internal perturbations in which I live more tempestuous still. So you are to be married in two months; all the obstacles are removed, and you are now sure of belonging to each other for ever. Your present felicity is increased by all your future felicity. You are happy and you have the certainty of being still happier soon. What a lot is yours! Your loved one is beautiful, but what you love in her is not lifeless and palpable beauty, material beauty, but the beauty that is invisible and eternal, the beauty that never grows old, the beauty of the soul. She is full of grace and purity; she loves you as such souls know how to love. You did not seek to know whether the gold of her hair approached in tone the tresses of Rubens and Giorgione; but it pleased you because it was *hers*. And I will wager, happy lover that you are, that you do not even know whether your mistress's type is

Greek or Asiatic, English or Italian. O Silvio! how rare are the hearts that are satisfied with love pure and simple and desire neither a hermitage in the forests, nor a garden on an island in Lake Maggiore.

"If I had the courage to tear myself from here, I would go and spend a month with you; it might be that I should be purified in the air that you breathe, and that the shadows of your avenues would shed a little freshness on my burning brow; but no, it is a paradise wherein I must not set my foot. Scarcely should I be permitted to gaze from a distance over the wall at the two beautiful angels walking in it, hand in hand and eye to eye. The demon cannot enter into Eden save in the form of a serpent, and, dear Adam, for all the happiness in heaven, I would not be the serpent to your Eve.

"What fearful work has been wrought in my soul of late? who has turned my blood and changed it into venom? Monstrous thought, spreading thy pale green branches and thy hemlock umbels in the icy shadow of my heart, what poisoned wind has lodged there the germ whence thou art sprung? It was this then that was reserved for me, it was to this that all the paths, so desperately essayed, were to lead me! O fate, how thou dost mock us! All the eagle-flights towards the sun, the pure flames aspiring to heaven, the divine melancholy, the love deep and restrained, the religion of beauty, the fancy so curious and graceful, the exhaustless and ever-mounting flood from the internal spring, the ecstasy ever open-winged, the dreaming that bore more blossoms than the hawthorn in May, all the poetry of my youth, all these gifts so beautiful and rare, were only to succeed in placing me beneath the lowest of mankind!

"I wished to love. I went like a madman calling and invoking love; I writhed with rage beneath the feeling of my impotence; I fired my blood, and dragged my body to the sloughs of pleasure; I clasped to suffocation against my arid heart a fair young woman who loved me; I pursued the passion that fled from me. I degraded myself, and acted like a virgin going to an evil place in hope of finding a lover among those brought thither by impure motives, instead of waiting patiently in discreet and silent shadow until the angel reserved for me by God should appear to me with radiant penumbra, a flower from heaven ready to my hand. All the years that I have wasted in childish disquietude, hastening hither and thither, and trying to force nature and time, I ought to have spent in solitude and meditation, in striving to render myself worthy of being loved; that would have been wisely done; but I had scales before my eyes and I walked straight to the precipice. Already I have one foot suspended over the void, and I believe that I shall soon raise the other. My resistance is in vain, I feel it, I must roll to the bottom of the new abyss which has just opened up within me.

"Yes, it was indeed thus that I had imagined love. I now feel that of which I had dreamed. Yes, here is the charming and terrible sleeplessness in which the roses are thistles and the thistles roses; here is the sweet grief and the wretched happiness, the unspeakable trouble which surrounds you with a golden cloud and, like drunkenness, causes the shape of objects to waver before you, the buzzings in the ear wherein there ever rings the last syllable of the well-beloved's name, the paleness, the flushings, the sudden quiverings, the burning and icy sweat: it is indeed thus; the poets do not lie.

"When I am about to enter the drawing-room in which we usually meet, my heart beats with such violence that it might be seen through my dress, and I am obliged to restrain it with both my hands lest it should escape. If I perceive this form at the end of an avenue or in the park, distance is straightway effaced, and the road passes away I know not where: the devil must carry it off or I must have wings. Nothing can divert my attention from it: I read, and the same image comes between the book and my eyes; I ride, I gallop, and I still believe that I can feel in the whirlwind its long hair mingling with mine, and hear its hurried respiration and its warm breath passing lightly over my cheek. This image possesses and pursues me everywhere, and I never see it more than when I see it not.

"You pitied me for not loving, pity me now for loving, and above all for loving whom I love. What a misfortune, what a hatchet-stroke upon my life that was already so mutilated! what senseless, guilty, odious passion has laid hold upon me! It is a shame whose blush will never fade from my brow. It is the most lamentable of all my aberrations, I cannot understand it, I cannot comprehend it at all, everything is confused and upset within me; I can no longer tell who I am or what others are, I doubt whether I am a man or a woman, I have a horror of myself, I experience strange and inexplicable emotions, and there are moments when it seems to me as if my reason were departing, and when the feeling of my existence forsakes me altogether. For a long time I could not believe what was; I listened to myself and watched myself attentively. I strove to unravel the confused skein that was entangled in my soul. At last, through all the veils which enveloped it, I discovered the frightful truth. Silvio, I love—Oh! no, I can never tell you—I love a man."

IX

"*It is so.* I love a man, Silvio. I long sought to delude myself; I gave a different name to the feeling that I experienced; I clothed it in the garment of pure and disinterested friendship; I believed that it was merely the admiration which I entertain for all beautiful persons and things; for several days I walked in the treacherous, pleasant paths that wander about every waking passion; but I now recognise the profound and terrible road to which I am pledged. There is no means of concealment: I have examined myself thoroughly, and coldly weighed all the circumstances; I have accounted to myself for the smallest detail; I have explored my soul in every direction with the certainty which results from the habit of self-investigation; I blush to think and write about it; but the fact, alas! is only too certain, I love this young man not from friendship but from love;—yes, from love.

"You whom I have loved so much, Silvio, my good, my only comrade, you have never inspired me with a similar feeling, and yet, if ever there was under heaven a close and lively friendship, if ever two souls, though different, understood each other perfectly, it was our friendship and our two souls. What winged hours have we spent together! what talks without end and always too soon terminated! how many things have we said to each other which people have never said to themselves! We had towards each other in our hearts the window which Momus would have liked to open in man's bosom. How proud I was of being your friend, I who was younger than you, I so insane and you so full of reason!

"What I feel towards this young man is truly incredible; no woman has ever troubled me so singularly. The sound of his clear, silvery voice affects my nerves and agitates me in a strange manner; my soul hangs on his lips, like a bee on a flower, to drink in the honey of his words. I cannot brush him as I pass without quivering from head to foot, and when, in the evening, as we are separating, he gives me his soft, satin-like, adorable hand, all my life rushes to the spot that he has touched, and an hour afterwards I still feel the pressure of his fingers.

"This morning I gazed at him for a long time without his seeing me. I was concealed behind my curtain. He was at his window which is exactly opposite to mine. This part of the mansion was built at the end of Henri IV's reign; it is half brick, half ashlar, according to the custom of the time; the window is long and narrow, with a lintel and balcony of stone. Théodore—for you have no doubt already guessed that it is he who is in question—was resting his elbow on the parapet with a melancholy air, and appeared to be in a profound reverie. A drapery of red, large-flowered damask, which was half caught up, fell in broad folds behind him and served as a background. How handsome he was, and how marvellously his dark and pale head was set off by the purple tint! Two great clusters of black, lustrous hair, like the grape-bunches of the ancient Erigone, hung gracefully down his cheeks, and framed in a most charming manner the correct delicate oval of his beautiful face. His round, plump neck was entirely bare, and he had on a dressing-gown with broad sleeves which was tolerably like a woman's dress. In his hand he held a yellow tulip, picking it pitilessly to pieces in his reverie and throwing the fragments to the wind.

"One of the luminous angles traced by the sun on the wall chanced to be projected against the window, and the picture was gilded with a warm, transparent tone which would have made Giorgione's most brilliant canvas envious.

"With his long hair stirred softly by the breeze, his marble neck thus uncovered, his ample robe clasped around his waist, and his beautiful hands issuing from their ruffles like the pistils of a flower from the midst of their petals, he looked not the handsomest of men but the most beautiful of women, and I said in my heart—'It is a woman, oh! it is a woman!' Then I suddenly remembered the nonsense which, as you know, I wrote to you a long time ago, respecting my ideal and the manner in which I should assuredly meet with it: the beautiful lady in the Louis XIII park, the red and white mansion, the large terrace, the avenues of old chestnut trees, and the interview at the window; I once gave you all these details. It was just so,—what I saw was the exact realisation of my dream. It was just the style of architecture, the effect of light, the description of beauty, the colour and the character that I had desired;—nothing was wanting, only the lady was a man;—but I confess to you that for the moment I had completely forgotten this.

"Théodore must be a woman disguised; the thing is impossible otherwise. Such beauty, even for a woman, is not the beauty of a man, were he Antinoüs, the friend of Adrian; were he Alexis, the friend of Virgil. It is a woman, by heaven, and I was very foolish to torment myself in such a manner. In this way everything is explained in the most natural fashion in the world, and I am not such a monster as I believed.

"Would God put those long, dark, silken fringes on the coarse eyelids of a man? Would he dye our ugly blobber-lipped and hairbristling mouths with carmine so delicate and bright? Our bones, hewn into shape as with blows of a hedge-bill and coarsely fitted together, are not worthy of being swaddled in such white and tender flesh; our indented skulls are not made to be bathed in floods of such wonderful hair.

"O beauty! we were created only to love thee and worship thee on our knees, if we have found thee, and to seek thee eternally through the world, if this happiness has not been given to us; but to possess thee, to be thyself, is possible only to angels and to women. Lovers, poets, painters and sculptors, we all seek to raise an altar to thee, the lover in his mistress, the poet in his song, the painter in his canvas, the sculptor in his marble; but it is everlasting despair to be unable to give palpability to the beauty that you feel, and to be enshrouded in a body which in no way realises the body which you know to be yours.

"I once saw a young man who had robbed me of the form that I ought to have had. The rascal was just such as I should have wished to be. He had the beauty of my ugliness, and beside him I looked like a rough sketch of him. He was of my height, but more slender and vigorous; his figure resembled mine, but had an elegance and nobility that I do not possess. His eyes were not of a different colour than my own, but they had a look and a brilliancy that mine will never have. His nose had been cast in the same mould as mine, but it seemed to have been retouched by the chisel of a skilful statuary; the nostrils were more open and more impassioned, the flat parts more cleanly cut, and there was something heroic in it which is altogether wanting to that respectable portion of my individuality: you would have said that nature had first tried in my person to make this perfected self of mine.

"I looked like the erased and shapeless draught of the thought whereof he was the copy in fair, moulded writing. When I saw him walk, stop, salute the ladies, sit and lie down with the perfect grace which results from beauty of proportion, I was seized with sadness and frightful jealousy, such as must be felt by the clay model drying and splitting obscurely in a corner of the studio, while the haughty marble statue, which would not have existed without it, stands proudly on its sculptured socle, and attracts the attention and praises of the visitors. For the rogue is, after all, only my own self which has succeeded a little better, and been cast with less rebellious bronze, that has made its way more exactly into the hollows of the mould. I think that he has great hardihood to strut in this way with my form and to display as much insolence as though he were an original type: he is, when all is said, only a plagiarism from me, for I was born before him, and without me nature would not have conceived the idea of making him as he is.

"When women praised his good manners and personal charms, I had every inclination in the world to rise and say to them—'Fools that you are, just praise me directly, for this gentleman is myself and it is uselessly circuitous to transmit to him what is destined to come back to me.' At other times I itched horribly to strangle him to turn his soul out of the body which belonged to me, and I would prowl about him with compressed lips and clenched fists like a lord prowling around his palace in which a family of ragamuffins has established itself in his absence, and not knowing how to cast them out. For the rest, this young man is stupid, and succeeds all the better for it. And sometimes I envy him his stupidity more than his beauty.

"The Gospel saying about the poor in spirit is not complete: 'They shall have the kingdom of Heaven;' I know nothing about that, and it is a matter of indifference to me; but they most certainly have the kingdom of the earth,—they have the money and the beautiful women, in other words the only two desirable things in the world. Do you know a sensible man who is rich, or a fellow with heart and some merit who has a passable mistress? Although Théodore is very handsome, I nevertheless have not wished for his beauty, and I would rather he had it than I.

"Those strange loves of which the elegies of the ancient poets are full, which surprised us so much and which we could not understand, are probable, therefore, and possible. In the translations that we used to make of them we substituted the names of women for those which were actually there. Juventius was made to terminate as Juventia, Alexis was changed into Ianthe. The beautiful boys became beautiful girls, we thus reconstructed the monstrous seraglio of Catullus, Tibullus, Martial, and the gentle Virgil. It was a very gallant occupation which only proved how little we had comprehended the ancient genius.

"I am a man of the Homeric times; the world in which I live is not mine, and I have no comprehension of the society which surrounds me. Christ has not come for me; I am as much a pagan as were Alcibiades and Phidias. I have never gone to pluck passion flowers upon Golgotha, and the deep river which flows from the side of the Crucified One and forms a red girdle round the world has not bathed me in its flood. My rebellious body will not recognise the supremacy of the soul, and my flesh does not admit that it should be mortified. I deem the earth as fair as heaven, and I think that correctness of form is virtue. Spirituality does not suit me, I prefer a statue to a phantom, and noon to twilight. Three things please me: gold, marble and purple, splendour, solidity and colour. My dreams are composed of them, and all my chimerical palaces are constructed of these materials.

"Sometimes I have other dreams,—of long cavalcades of perfectly white horses, without harness or bridle, ridden by beautiful naked youths who defile across a band of dark blue colour as on the friezes of the Parthenon, or of theories of young girls crowned with bandelets, with straight-folded tunics and ivory sistra, who seem to wind around an immense vase. Never mist or vapour, never anything uncertain or wavering. My sky has no clouds, or, if there be any, they are solid chisel-carved clouds, formed with the marble fragments fallen from the statue of Jupiter. Mountains with sharp-cut ridges indent it abruptly on the borders, and the sun, leaning on one of the loftiest summits, opens wide his lion-yellow eye with its golden lashes. The grasshopper cries and sings, the corn-ear cracks; the shadow, vanquished and exhausted by the heat, rolls itself up and collects itself at the foot of the trees: everything is radiant, shining, resplendent. The smallest detail becomes firm and is boldly accentuated; every object assumes a robust form and colour. There is no room for the softness and dreaming of Christian art.

"Such a world is mine. The streams in my landscapes fall in a sculptured tide from a sculptured urn; through the tall green reeds, sonorous as those of the Eurotas, may be seen glistening the round, silvery hip of some nymph with glaucous hair. Here is Diana passing through this dark oak forest with her quiver at her back, her flying scarf, and her buskins with intertwining bands. She is followed by her pack and her nymphs with harmonious names. My pictures are painted with four tints, like the pictures of the primitive painters, and often they are only coloured basso-relievos; for I love to touch what I have seen with my finger and to pursue the roundness of the outlines into its most fugitive windings; I view each thing from every side and go around it with a light in my hand.

"I have looked upon love in the light of antiquity and as a more or less perfect piece of sculpture. How is this arm? Pretty well. The hands are not wanting in delicacy. What do you think of this foot? I think that the ankle is without nobility, and that the heel is commonplace. But the breast is well placed and of good shape, the serpentine line is sufficiently undulating, the shoulders are fat and of a handsome character. This woman would be a passable model, and it would be possible to cast several portions of her. Let us love her.

"I have always been thus. I look upon women with the eyes of a sculptor and not of a lover. I have all my life been troubled about the shape of the flagon, never about the quality of its contents. I might have had Pandora's box in my hand, and I believe that I should not have opened it. Just now I said that Christ had not come for me; Mary, star of the modern Heaven, sweet mother of the glorious babe, has not come either.

"For a long time and very often I have stopped beneath the stone foliage in cathedrals, in the trembling brightness from the windows, at an hour when the organ was moaning of itself, when an invisible finger touched the keys and the wind breathed in the pipes, and I have plunged my eyes deep into the pale azure of the long eyes of the Madonna. I have followed piously the wasted oval of her face, and the scarcely indicated arch of her eyebrows; I have admired her smooth and luminous brow, her chastely transparent temples, her cheek-bones shaded with a sober virginal colour, tenderer than the blossom of the peach; I have counted one by one the beautiful golden lashes casting their palpitating shadow; through the half-tint which bathes her I have distinguished the fleeting lines of her frail and modestly bended neck; I have even, with rash hand, raised the folds of her tunic and contemplated unveiled the virgin, milk-distended bosom which was never pressed but by lips divine; I have pursued its delicate blue veins into their most imperceptible ramifications, I have laid my finger upon it that I might cause the celestial drink to spring forth in white streams; I have touched with my mouth the bud of the mystic rose.

"Well! I confess that all this immaterial beauty, so winged and vaporous that one feels that it is about to take its flight, has affected me very moderately. I prefer the Venus Anadyomene a thousand times. The antique eyes turned up at the corners, the lips so pure and so firmly cut, so amorous and so inviting for a kiss, the low full brow, the hair undulating like the sea and knotted carelessly behind the head, the firm and lustrous shoulders, the back with its thousand charming curves, the small and gently swelling bosom, all the well-rounded shapes, the breadth of hips, the delicate strength, the expression of superhuman vigour in a body so adorably feminine, ravish and enchant me to a degree of which you can form no idea, you who are a Christian and discreet.

"Mary, in spite of the humble air which she affects, is far too proud for me; scarcely does even the tip of her foot, in its encircling white bandelets, touch the surface of the globe which is already growing blue and on which the old serpent is writhing. Her eyes are the most beautiful in the world, but they are always turned towards heaven or cast down; they never look you in the face and have never reflected a human form. And then, I do not like the nimbuses of smiling cherubs which circle her head in a golden vapour. I am jealous of the tall pubescent angels with floating robes and hair who are so amorously eager in her assumptions; the hands entwined to support her, the wings in motion to fan her, displease and annoy me. These heavenly coxcombs, so coquettish and triumphant, with their tunics of light, their perukes of golden thread, and their handsome blue and green feathers, seem too gallant to me, and if I were God I should take care not to give such pages to my mistress.

"Venus emerges from the sea to land upon the world—as is fitting in a divinity that loves men—quite naked and quite alone. She prefers the earth to Olympus, and has more men than gods for her lovers; she does not enwrap herself in the languorous veils of mysticism; she stands erect, her dolphin behind her, her foot on her conch of mother of pearl, the sun strikes upon her polished body, and with her white hand she holds up in the air the flood of her beautiful hair on which old Father Ocean has strewn his most perfect pearls. You may look at her: she conceals nothing, for modesty was made for the ugly alone, and is a modern invention, daughter of the Christian contempt for form and matter.

"O ancient world! so all that thou hast revered is scorned; so thy idols are overthrown in the dust; wasted anchorites, clad in rags that are full of holes, and blood-covered martyrs, with shoulders torn by the tigers in thy circuses, have perched themselves upon the pedestals of thy beautiful, charming gods: Christ has wrapped the world in his shroud. Beauty must blush at itself and assume a winding sheet. Beautiful youths with oil-rubbed limbs who wrestle in lyceum or gymnasium, beneath the brilliant sky, in the full sight of the Attic sun, before the astonished crowd; young Spartan girls who dance the bibasis, and run naked to the summit of Taygetus, resume your tunics and your chlamydes: your reign is past. And you, shapers of marble, Prometheuses of bronze, break your chisels: there are to be no more sculptors. The palpable world is dead. A dark and lugubrious thought alone fills the immensity of the void. Cleomene goes to the weavers to see what folds are made by cloth or linen.

"Virginity, bitter plant, born on a soil steeped with blood, whose etiolated and sickly flower opens painfully in the dark shade of cloisters, beneath a cold lustral rain;—scentless rose all bristling with thorns, thou hast taken the place, with us, of the beautiful, joyous roses bathed in spikenard and Falernian of the dancing women of Sybaris!

"The ancient world did not know thee, fruitless flower; never didst thou enter into its wreaths of intoxicating fragrance; in that vigorous and healthy society thou wouldst have been trampled scornfully underfoot. Virginity, mysticism, melancholy,—three unknown words,—three new maladies brought in by Christ. Pale spectres who flood our world with your icy tears and who, with your elbow on a cloud and your hand in your bosom, can only say—'O death! O death!' you could not have set foot in that world so well peopled with indulgent and wanton gods!

"I consider woman, after the manner of the ancients, as a beautiful slave designed for our pleasure. Christianity has not rehabilitated her in my eyes. To me she is still something dissimilar and inferior that we worship and play with, a toy which is more intelligent than if it were of ivory or gold, and which gets up of itself if we let it fall. I have been told, in consequence of this, that I think badly of women; I consider, on the contrary, that it is thinking very well of them.

"I do not know, in truth, why women are so anxious to be regarded as men. I can understand a person wishing to be a boa, a lion or an elephant; but that anyone should wish to be a man is something quite beyond my comprehension. If I had been at the Council of Trent when they discussed the important question of whether a woman is a man, I should certainly have given my opinion in the negative.

"I have written some love-verses during my lifetime, or, at least, some which assumed to pass for such. I have just read a portion of them again. They are altogether wanting in the sentiment of modern love. If they were written in Latin distichs instead of in French rhymes, they might be taken for the work of a bad poet of the time of Augustus. And I am astonished that the women, for whom they were written, were not seriously angry, instead of being quite charmed with them. It is true that women know as little about poetry as cabbages and roses, which is quite natural and plain, being themselves poetry, or, at least, the best instruments for poetry: the flute does not hear nor understand the air that is played upon it.

"In these verses nothing is spoken of but golden or ebony hair, marvellous delicacy of skin, roundness of arm, smallness of foot, and shapely daintiness of hand, and the whole terminates with a humble supplication to the divinity to grant the enjoyment of all these beautiful things as speedily as possible. In the triumphant passages there is nothing but garlands hung upon the threshold, torrents of flowers, burning perfumes, Catullian addition of kisses, sleepless and charming nights, quarrels with Aurora, and injunctions to the same Aurora to return and hide herself behind the saffron curtains of old Tithonus;— brightness without heat, sonorousness without vibration. They are accurate, polished, written with consistent elaboration; but through all the refinements and veils of expression you may divine the short, stern voice of the master trying to be mild while speaking to the slave. There is no soul, as in the erotic poetry writen since the Christian era, asking another soul to love it because it loves; there is no azure-tinted, smiling lake inviting a brook to pour itself into its bosom that they may reflect the stars of heaven together; there is no pair of doves spreading their wings at the same time to fly to the same nest.

"Cynthia, you are beautiful; make haste. Who knows whether you will be alive to-morrow? Your hair is blacker than the lustrous skin of an Ethiopian virgin. Make haste; a few years hence, slender silver threads will creep into its thick clusters; these roses smell sweet to-day, but to-morrow they will have the odour of death, and be but the corpses of roses. Let us inhale thy roses while they resemble thy cheeks; let us kiss thy cheeks while they resemble thy roses. When you are old, Cynthia, no one will have anything more to do with you,— not even the lictor's servants when you would pay them,—and you will run after me whom now you repulse. Wait until Saturn with his nail has scratched this pure and shining brow, and you will see how your threshold, so besieged, so entreated, so warm with tears and so decked with flowers, will be shunned, and cursed, and covered with weeds and briars. Make haste, Cynthia; the smallest wrinkle may serve as a grave for the greatest love.

"Such is the brutal and imperious formula in which all ancient elegy is contained: it always comes back to it; it is its greatest, its strongest reason, the Achilles of its arguments. After this it has scarcely anything to say, and, when it has promised a robe of twice-dyed byssus and a union of equal-sized pearls, it has reached the end of its tether. And it is also nearly the whole of what I find most conclusive in a similar emergency.

"Nevertheless I do not always abide by so scanty a programme, but embroider my barren canvas with a few differently coloured silken threads picked up here and there. But these pieces are short or are twenty times renewed, and do not keep their places well on the ground-work of the woof. I speak of love with tolerable elegance because I have read many fine things about it. It only needs the talent of an actor to do so. With many women this appearance is enough; my habitual writing and imagination prevent me from being short of such materials, and every mind that is at all practised may easily arrive at the same result by application; but I do not feel a word of what I say, and I repeat in a whisper like the ancient poet: Cynthia, make haste.

"I have often been accused of deceit and dissimulation. Nobody in the world would be so pleased as myself to speak freely and pour forth his heart! but, as I have not an idea or a feeling similar to those of the people who surround me,—as, at the first true word that I let fall, there would be a hurrah and a general outcry, I have preferred to keep silence, or, if speaking, to discharge only such follies as are admitted and have rights of citizenship. I should be welcome if I said to the ladies what I have just written to you! I do not think that they would have any great liking for my manner of seeing and ways of looking upon love.

"As for men, I am equally unable to tell them to their face that they are wrong not to go on all fours; and that is in truth the most favour-able thought that I have with respect to them. I do not wish to have a quarrel at every word. What does it matter, after all, what I think or do not think; or if I am sad when I seem gay, and joyous when I have an air of melancholy? I cannot be blamed for not going naked: may I not clothe my countenance as I do my body? Why should a mask be more reprehensible than a pair of breeches, or a lie than a corset?

"Alas! the earth turns round the sun, roasted on one side and frozen on the other. A battle takes place in which six hundred thousand men cut each other to pieces; the weather is as fine as possible; the flowers display unparalleled coquetry, and impudently open their luxuriant bosoms beneath the very feet of the horses. To-day a fabulous number of good deeds have been performed; it is pouring fast, there is snow and thunder, lightning and hail; you would think that the world was coming to an end. The benefactors of humanity are muddy to the waist and as dirty as dogs, unless they have carriages. Creation mocks pitilessly at the creature, and shouts keen sarcasms at it every minute. Everything is indifferent to everything, and each lives or vegetates in virtue of its own law. What difference does it make to the sun, to the beetroots, or even to men, whether I do this or that, live or die, suffer or rejoice, dissemble or be sincere?

"A straw falls upon an ant and breaks its third leg at the second articulation; a rock falls upon a village and crushes it: I do not believe that one of these misfortunes draws more tears than the other from the golden eyes of the stars. You are my best friend, if the expression is not as hollow as a bell; but were I to die, it is very evident that, mourn as you might, you would not abstain from dining for even two days, and would, in spite of such a terrible catastrophe, continue to play trick-track very pleasantly. Which of my friends or mistresses will know my name and Christian names twenty years hence, or would recognise me in the street if I were to appear with a coat out at elbows? Forgetfulness and nothingness are the whole of man.

"I feel myself as perfectly alone as is possible, and all the threads passing from me to things and from things to me have been broken one by one. There are few examples of a man who, preserving a knowledge of the movements that take place within him, has arrived at such a degree of brutishness. I am like a flagon of liqueur which has been left uncorked and whose spirit has completely evaporated. The beverage has the same appearance and colour; but taste it, and you will find in it nothing but the insipidity of water.

"When I think of it, I am frightened at the rapidity of this decomposition; if it continues I shall be obliged to salt myself, or I shall inevitably grow rotten, and the worms will come after me, seeing that I have no longer a soul, and that the latter alone constitutes the difference between a body and a corpse. One year ago, not more, I had still something human in me; I was disquieted, I was seeking. I had a thought cherished above all others, a sort of aim, an ideal; I wanted to be loved and I had the dreams that come at that age,—less vaporous, less chaste, it is true, than those of ordinary youths, but yet contained within just limits.

"Little by little the incorporeal part was withdrawn and dissipated, and there was left at bottom of me only a thick bed of coarse slime. The dream became a nightmare, and the chimera a succubus; the world of the soul closed its ivory gates against me: I now understand only what I touch with my hands; my dreams are of stone; everything condenses and hardens about me, nothing floats, nothing wavers, there is neither air nor breath; matter presses upon me, encroaches upon me and crushes me; I am like a pilgrim who, having fallen asleep with his feet in the water on a summer's day, has awakened in winter with his feet locked fast in the ice. I no longer wish for anybody's love or friendship; glory itself, that brilliant aureola which I had so desired for my brow, no longer inspires me with the slightest longing. Only one thing, alas! now palpitates within me, and that is the horrible desire which draws me towards Théodore. You see to what all my moral notions are reduced. What is physically beautiful is good, all that is ugly is evil. I might see a beautiful woman who, to my own knowledge, had the most villainous soul in the world, and was an adulteress and a poisoner, and I confess that this would be a matter of indifference to me and would in no way prevent me from taking delight in her, if the shape of her nose suited me.

"This is the way in which I picture to myself supreme happiness; there is a large square building, without any windows looking outward; a large court surrounded by a white marble colonnade, a crystal fountain in the centre with a jet of quicksilver after the Arabian fashion, and boxes of orange and pomegranate trees placed alternately; overhead, a very blue sky and a very yellow sun; large greyhounds with pike-like noses should be sleeping here and there; from time to time barefooted negroes with rings of gold on their legs, and beautiful white, slender serving-women, clothed in rich and capricious garments, should pass through the hollow arcades, baskets on their

arms or amphoras on their heads. For myself, I should be there, motionless and silent, beneath a magnificent canopy, surrounded with piles of cushions, having a huge tame lion supporting my elbow and the naked breast of a young slave like a stool beneath my foot, and smoking opium in a large jade pipe.

"I cannot imagine paradise differently; and, if God really wishes me to go there after my death, he will build me a little kiosk on this plan in the corner of some star. Paradise, as it is commonly described, appears to me much too musical, and I confess, with all humility that I am perfectly incapable of enduring a sonata which would last for merely ten thousand years.

"You see the nature of my Eldorado, of my promised land: it is a dream like any other; but it has this special feature: that I never introduce any known countenance into it; that none of my friends has crossed the threshold of this imaginary palace; and that none of the women that I have possessed has sat down beside me on the velvet of the cushions: I am there alone in the midst of phantoms. I have never conceived the idea of loving all the women's faces, and graceful shadows of young girls with whom I people it; I have never supposed one of them in love with me. In this fantastic seraglio I have created no favourite sultana. There are negresses, mulattoes, Jewesses with blue skin and red hair, Greeks and Circassians, Spaniards and Englishwomen; but they are to me only symbols of colour and feature, and I have them just as a man has all kinds of wines in his cellar, and every species of humming-bird in his collection. They are objects to be admired, pictures which have no need of a frame, statues which come to you when you call them and wish to look at them closely. A woman possesses this unquestionable advantage over a statue, that she turns of herself in the direction that you wish, whereas you are obliged to walk round the statue and place yourself at the point of sight;—which is fatiguing.

"You must see that with such ideas I cannot remain in these times nor in this world of ours; for it is impossible to exist thus by the side of time and space. I must find something else.

"Such thoughts lead simply and logically to this conclusion. As only satisfaction of the eye, polish of form, and purity of feature are sought for, they are accepted wherever they are found. This is the explanation of the singular aberrations in the love of the ancients.

"Since the time of Christ there has not been a single human statue in which adolescent beauty has been idealised and represented with the care that characterises the ancient sculptors. Woman has become the symbol of moral and physical beauty: man has really fallen from the day that the infant was born at Bethlehem. Woman is the queen of creation; the stars unite in a crown upon her head, the crescent of the moon glories in waxing beneath her foot, the sun yields his purest gold to make her jewels, painters who wish to flatter the angels give them women's faces, and, certes, I shall not be the one to blame them.

"Previous to the gentle and worthy narrator of parables, it was quite the opposite; gods or heroes were not made feminine when it was wished to make them charming; they had their own type, at once vigorous and delicate, but always male, however amorous their outlines might be, and however smooth and destitute of muscles and veins the workman might have made their divine legs and arms. He was more ready to bring the special beauty of women into accordance with this type. He enlarged the shoulders, attenuated the hips, gave more prominence to the throat, and accentuated the joints of the arms and thighs more strongly. There is scarcely any difference between Paris and Helen. And so the hermaphrodite was one of the most eagerly cherished chimeras of idolatrous antiquity.

"This son of Hermes and Aphrodite is, in fact, one of the sweetest creations of Pagan genius. Nothing in the world can be imagined more ravishing than these two bodies, harmoniously blended together and both perfect, these two beauties so equal and so different, forming but one superior to both, because they are reciprocally tempered and improved. To an exclusive worshipper of form, can there be a more delightful uncertainty than that into which you are thrown by the sight of the back, the ambiguous loins, and the strong, delicate legs, which you are doubtful whether to attribute to Mercury ready to take his flight or to Diana coming forth from the bath? The torso is a compound of the most charming monstrosities: on the bosom, which is plump and quite pubescent, swells with strange grace the breast of a young maiden; beneath the sides, which are well covered and quite feminine in their softness, you may divine the muscles and the ribs, as in the sides of a young lad; the belly is rather flat for a woman, and rather round for a man, and in the whole habit of the body there is something cloudy and undecided which it is impossible to describe, and which possesses quite a peculiar attraction. Théodore would certainly be an excellent model for this kind of beauty; nevertheless I think, that the feminine portion prevails with him, and that he has preserved more of Salmacis than did the Hermaphrodite of the Metamorphoses.

"It is a singular thing that I have nearly ceased to think about his sex, and that I love him in perfect indifference to it. Sometimes I seek to persuade myself that such love is ridiculous, and I tell myself so as severely as possible; but it only comes from my lips—it is a piece of reasoning which I go through but do not feel: it really seems to me as if it were the simplest thing in the world and as if any one else would do the same in my place.

"I see him, I listen to him speaking or singing—for he sings admirably—and take an unspeakable pleasure in doing so. He produces the impression of a woman upon me to such an extent that one day, in the heat of conversation, I inadvertently called him *Madame,* which made him laugh in what appeared to me to be a somewhat constrained manner.

"Yet, if it were a woman, what motives could there be for this disguise? I cannot account for them in any way. It is comprehensible for a very young, very handsome and perfectly beardless cavalier to disguise himself as a woman; he can thus open a thousand doors which would have remained obstinately shut against him, and the *quid pro quo* may involve him in quite a labyrinthine and jovial complication of adventures. You may, in this manner, reach a woman who is strictly guarded, or realise a piece of good fortune under favour of the surprise.

"But I am not very clear as to the advantages to be derived by a young and beautiful woman from rambling about in man's clothes.

147

A woman ought not to give up in this way the pleasure of being courted, madrigalised and worshipped; she should rather give up her life, and she would be right, for what is a woman's life without all this? Nothing, or something worse than death. And I am always astonished that women who are thirty years old, or have the small-pox, do not throw themselves down from the top of a steeple.

"In spite of all this, something stranger than any reasoning cries to me that it is a woman, and that it is she of whom I have dreamed, she whom alone I am to love, and by whom I alone am to be loved. Yes, it was she, the goddess with eagle glance and beautiful royal hands, who used to smile with condescension upon me from the height of her throne of clouds. She has presented herself to me in this disguise to prove me, to see whether I should recognise her, whether my amorous gaze would penetrate the veils which enwrap her, as in those wondrous tales where the fairies appear at first in the forms of beggars, and then suddenly stand out resplendent with gold and precious stones.

"I have recognised thee, O my love! At the sight of thee my heart leaped within my bosom as did St. John in the womb of St. Elisabeth, when she was visited by the Virgin; a blazing light was shed through the air; I perceived, as it were, an odour of divine ambrosia; I saw the trail of fire at thy feet, and I straightway understood that thou wert not a mere mortal.

"The melodious sounds of St. Cecilia's viol, to which the angels listen with rapture, are harsh and discordant in comparison with the pearly cadences which escape from thy ruby lips: the Graces, young and smiling, dance a ceaseless roundel about thee; the birds, warbling, bend their little variegated heads to see thee better as thou passest through the woods, and pipe to thee their prettiest refrains; the amorous moon rises earlier to kiss thee with her pale silver lips, for she has forsaken her shepherd for thee; the wind is careful not to efface the delicate print of thy charming foot upon the sand; the fountain becomes smoother than crystal when thou bendest over it, fearing to wrinkle and distort the reflection of thy celestial countenance; the modest violets themselves open up their little hearts to thee and display a thousand coquetries before thee; the jealous strawberry is piqued to emulation and strives to equal the divine carnation of thy mouth; the imperceptible gnat hums joyously and applauds thee with the beating of its wings: all nature loves and admires thee, who art her fairest work!

"Ah! now I live;—until this moment I was but a dead man: now I am freed from the shroud, and stretch both my wasted hands out of the grave towards the sun; my blue, ghastly colour has left me: my blood circulates swiftly through my veins. The frightful silence which reigned around me is broken at last. The black, opaque vault which weighed heavy on my brow is illumined. A thousand mysterious voices whisper in my ear; charming stars sparkle above me, and sand the windings of my path with their spangles of gold; the daisies laugh sweetly to me, and the bell-flowers murmur my name with their little restless tongues. I understand a multitude of things which I used not to understand, I discover affinities and marvellous sympathies, I know the language of the roses and nightingales and I read with fluency the book which once I could not even spell.

"I have recognised that I had a friend in the respectable old oak all covered with mistletoe and parasitic plants, and that the frail and languid periwinkle, whose large blue eye is ever running over with tears, had long cherished a discreet and restrained passion for me. It is love, it is love that has opened my eyes and given me the answer to the enigma. Love has come down to the bottom of the vault where my soul cowered numb and somnolent; he has taken it by the finger-tips and has brought it up the steep and narrow staircase leading without. All the locks of the prison were picked, and for the first time this poor Psyche came forth from me in whom she had been shut up.

"Another life has become mine. I breathe with the breast of another, and a blow wounding him would kill me. Before this happy day I was like those gloomy Japanese idols which look down perpetually at their own bellies. I was a spectator of myself, the audience of the comedy that I was playing; I looked at myself living, and I listened to the oscillations of my heart as to the throbbing of a pendulum. That was all. Images were portrayed on my heedless eyes, sounds struck my inattentive ear, but nothing from the external world reached my soul. The existence of any one else was not necessary to me; I even doubted any existence other than my own, concerning which again I was scarcely sure. It seemed to me that I was alone in the midst of the universe, and that all the rest was but vapours, images, vain illusions, fleeting appearances destined to people this nothingness. What a difference!

"And yet what if my presentiment is deceiving me, and Théodore is really a man, as every one believes him to be! Such marvellous beauties have sometimes been seen, and great youth assists such an illusion. It is something that I will not think of and that would drive me mad; the seed fallen yesterday into the sterile rock of my heart has already pierced it in every direction with its thousand filaments; it has clung vigorously to it, and to pluck it up would be impossible. It is already a blossoming and green-growing tree with twisting muscular roots. If I came to know with certainty that Théodore is not a woman, I do not know, alas! whether I should not still love him."

X

"*My fair friend*, you were quite right in dissuading me from the plan that I had formed of seeing men and studying them thoroughly before giving my heart to any among them. I have for ever extinguished love within me, and even the possibility of love.

"Poor young girls that we are, brought up with so much care, surrounded in such maidenly fashion with a triple wall of reticence and precaution, who are allowed to understand nothing, to suspect nothing, and whose principal knowledge is to know nothing, in what strange errors do we live, and what treacherous chimeras cradle us in their arms!

"Ah! Graciosa, thrice cursed be the minute when the idea of this disguise occurred to me; what horrors, infamies, brutalities have I been forced to witness or to hear! what a treasure of chaste and precious ignorance have I dissipated in but a short time!

"It was in a fair moonlight, do you remember? we were walking together, at the very bottom of the garden, in that dull, little-frequented alley, terminated at one end by a statue of a flute-playing Faun which has lost its nose, and whose whole body is covered with a thick leprosy of blackish moss, and at the other by a counterfeit view painted on the wall, and half-effaced by the rain.

"Through the yet spare foliage of the yoke-elm we could here and there see the twinkling of the stars and the curved crescent of the moon. A fragrance of young shoots and fresh plants reached us from the parterre with the languid breath of a gentle breeze; a hidden bird was piping a languorous and whimsical tune; we, like true young girls, were talking of love, wooers, marriage, and the handsome cavalier that we had seen at mass; we were exchanging our few ideas of the world and things; we were turning over an expression that we had chanced to hear and whose meaning seemed obscure and singular to us, in a hundred different ways; we were asking a thousand of those absurd questions which only the most perfect innocence can imagine. What primitive poetry and what adorable foolishness were there in those furtive conversations between two little simpletons who had but just left a boarding-school!

"You wished to have for your lover a bold, proud young fellow, with black moustache and hair, large spurs, large feathers, and a large sword—a sort of bully in love, and you indulged to the full in the heroic and triumphant: you dreamed of nothing but duels and escalades, and miraculous devotion, and you would have been ready to throw your glove into the lions' den that your Esplandian might follow to fetch it. It was very comical to see you, a little girl as you were then, blonde, blushing, and yielding to the faintest blast, delivering yourself of such generous tirades all in a breath, and with the most martial air in the world.

"For myself, although I was only six months older than you, I was six years less romantic: one thing chiefly disquieted me, and this was to know what men said among themselves and what they did after leaving drawing-rooms and theatres; I felt that there were many faulty and obscure sides to their lives, which were carefully veiled from our gaze, and which it was very important that we should know. Sometimes hidden behind a curtain, I would watch from a distance the gentlemen who came to the house, and it seemed to me then as if I could distinguish something base and cynical in their manner, a coarse carelessness or a wild preoccupied look, which I could no longer discern in them as soon as they had come in, and which they seemed to lay aside, as by enchantment, on the threshold of the room. All, young as well as old, appeared to me to have uniformly adopted conventional masks, conventional opinions and conventional modes of speech when in the presence of women.

"From the corner of the drawing-room, where I used to sit as straight as a doll, without leaning back in my easy-chair, I would listen and look as I rolled my bouquet between my fingers; although my eyes were cast down I could see to right and to left, before me and behind me: like the fabulous eyes of the lynx, my eyes could pierce through walls, and I could have told what was going on in the adjoining room.

"I had also perceived a noteworthy difference in the way in which they spoke to married women; they no longer used discreet, polished, and childishly embellished phrases such as were addressed to myself and my companions, but displayed bolder sprightliness, less sober and more disembarrassed manner, open reticence, and the ambiguity that quickly comes from a corruption which knows that it has similar corruption before it: I was quite sensible that there existed an element in common between them which did not exist between us, and I would have given anything to know what this element was.

"With what anxiety and furious curiosity I would follow with eye and ear the laughing, buzzing groups of young men, who, after making a halt at some points in the circle, would resume their walk, talking and casting ambiguous glances as they passed. On their scornfully puffed-up lips hovered incredulous sneers; they looked as though they were scoffing at what they had just said, and were retracting the compliments and adoration with which they had overwhelmed us. I could not hear their words; but I knew from the movements of their lips that they were uttering expressions in a language with which I was unacquainted, and of which no one had ever made use in my presence.

"Even those who had the most humble and submissive air would raise their heads with a very perceptible shade of revolt and weariness; a sigh of breathlessness, like that of an actor who has reached the end of a long couplet, would escape from their bosoms in spite of themselves, and when leaving us they would make a half-turn of their heels in an eager, hurried manner which denoted a sort of internal satisfaction at their release from the hard task of being polite and gallant.

"I would have given a year of my life to listen, without being seen, to an hour of their conversation. I could often understand, by certain attitudes, indirect gestures and side-glances, that I was the subject of their conversation, and that they were speaking of my age or my face. Then I would be on burning coals; the few subdued words and partial scraps of sentences reaching me at intervals would excite my curiosity to the highest degree, without being capable of satisfying it, and I would indulge in strange perplexities and doubts.

"Generally, what was said seemed to be favourable to me, and it was not this that disquieted me: I did not care very much about being thought beautiful; it was the slight observations dropped into the hollow of the ear, and nearly always followed by long sneers and singular winkings of the eye, that is what I should have liked to hear; and I would have cheerfully abandoned the most flowery and perfumed conversation in the world to hear one of such expressions as are whispered behind a curtain or in the corner of a doorway.

"If I had had a lover I should have greatly liked to know the way

153

in which he spoke of me to another man, and the terms in which, with a little wine in his head and both elbows on the table-cloth, he would boast of his good fortune to the companions of his orgie.

"I know this now, and in truth I am sorry that I know it. It is always so.

"My idea was a mad one, but what is done is done, and what is learned cannot be unlearned. I did not listen to you, my dear Graciosa, and I am sorry for it; but we do not always listen to reason, especially when it comes from such pretty lips as yours, for, from some reason or other, we can never imagine advice to be wise unless it is given by some old head that is hoary and grey, as though sixty years of stupidity could make one intelligent.

"But all this was too much torment, and I could not stand it; I was broiling in my little skin like a chestnut on the pan. The fatal apple swelled in the foliage above my head, and I was obliged to end by giving it a bite, being free to throw it away afterwards, if the flavour seemed bitter to me.

"I acted like fair Eve, my very dear great-grandmother, and bit it.

"The death of my uncle, the only relation left to me, giving me freedom of action, I put into practice what I had dreamed of for so long. My precautions were taken with the greatest care to prevent any one from suspecting my sex. I had learned how to handle a sword and fire a pistol; I rode perfectly, and with a hardihood of which few horsemen would have been capable; I carefully studied the way to wear my cloak and make my riding-whip clack, and in a few months I succeeded in transforming a girl who was thought rather pretty into a far more pretty cavalier, who lacked scarcely anything but a moustache. I realised my property, and left the town, determined not to return without the most complete experience.

"It was the only means of clearing up my doubts; to have had lovers would have taught me nothing, or would at least have afforded me but incomplete glimpses, and I wished to study man thoroughly, to anatomise him with inexorable scalpel fibre by fibre, and to have him alive and palpitating on my dissecting table; to do this it would be necessary to see him at home, alone and undressed, and to follow him when he went out walking, and visited the tavern or other places. With my disguise I could go everywhere without being remarked; there would be no concealment before me, all reserve and constraint would be thrown aside, I would receive confidences, and would give false ones to provoke others that were true. Alas! women have read only man's romance and never his history.

"It is a frightful thing to think of, and one which is not thought of, how profoundly ignorant we are of the life and conduct of those who appear to love us, and whom we are going to marry. Their real existence is as completely unknown to us as if they were inhabitants of Saturn or of some other planet a hundred million leagues from our sublunary ball: one would think that they were of a different species, and that there is not the slightest intellectual link between the two sexes; the virtues of the one are the vices of the other, and what excites admiration for a man brings disgrace upon a woman.

"As for us, our life is clear and may be pierced at a glance. It is easy to follow us from our home to the boarding-school, and from the boarding-school to our home; what we do is no mystery to anybody; every one may see our bad stump-drawings, our water-colour bouquets composed of a pansy and a rose as large as a cabbage, and with the stalk tastefully tied with a bright-coloured ribbon: the slippers which we embroider for our father's or grandfather's birthday have nothing very occult and disquieting in them. Our sonatas and ballads are gone through with the most desirable coldness. We are well and duly tied to our mother's apron strings, and at nine or ten o'clock at the latest we retire into our little white beds at the end of our discreet and tidy cells, wherein we are virtuously bolted and padlocked until next morning. The most watchful and jealous susceptibility could find nothing to complain of.

"The most limpid crystal does not possess the transparency of such a life.

"The man who takes us knows what we have done from the minute we were weaned, and even before it if he likes to pursue his researches so far. Our life is not a life, it is a species of vegetation like that of mosses and flowers; the icy shadow of the maternal stem hovers over us, poor, stifled rosebuds who dare not bloom. Our chief business is to keep ourselves very straight, well laced, and well brushed, with our eyes becomingly cast down, and for immobility and stiffness to surpass manikins and puppets on springs.

"We are forbidden to speak, or to mingle in the conversation, except to answer yes or no if we are asked a question. As soon as anybody is going to say something interesting we are sent away to practice the harp or harpsichord, and our music-masters are all at least sixty years old, and take snuff horribly. The models hung up in our rooms have a very vague and evasive anatomy. Before the gods of Greece can present themselves in a young ladies' boarding-school they must first purchase very ample box-coats at an old-clothes shop and get themselves engraved in stippling, after which they look like porters or cabmen, and are little calculated to inflame the imagination.

"In the anxiety to prevent us from being romantic we are made idiots. The period of our education is spent not in teaching us something, but in preventing us from learning something.

"We are really prisoners in body and mind; but how could a young man, who has freedom of action, who goes out in the morning not to return until the next morning, who has money, and who can make it and spend it as he pleases, how could he justify the employment of his time? what man would tell his sweetheart all that he did day and night? Not one, even of those who are reputed the most pure.

"I had sent my horse and my garments to a little grange of mine at some distance from the town. I dressed, mounted, and rode off, not without a singular heaviness of heart. I regretted nothing, for I was leaving nothing behind, neither relations nor friends, nor dog nor cat, and yet I was sad, and almost had tears in my eyes; the farm which I had visited only five or six times had no particular interest for me, and it was not the liking that we take for certain places and that affects us when leaving them which prompted me to turn round two or three times to see again from a distance its spiral of bluish smoke ascending amid the trees.

"There it was that I had left my title of woman with my dresses and petticoats; twenty years of my life were locked up in the room where I had made my toilet, years which were to be counted no longer, and which had ceased to concern me. 'Here lies Madelaine de Maupin' might have been written on the door, for I was, in fact, no longer Madelaine de Maupin but Théodore de Sérannes, and no one would call me any more by the sweet name of Madelaine.

"The drawer which held my henceforth useless dresses appeared to me like the coffin of my fair illusions; I was a man, or, at least, had the appearance of one: the young girl was dead.

"When I had completely lost sight of the chestnut trees which surround the grange, it seemed to me as if I were no longer myself but another, and I looked back to my former actions as to the actions of a stranger which I had witnessed, or the beginning of a romance which I had not read through to the end.

"I recalled complacently a thousand little details, the childish simplicity of which brought an indulgent, and sometimes a rather scornful smile to my lips, like that of a young libertine listening to the arcadian and pastoral confidences of a third-form schoolboy; and, just as I was separating myself from them for ever, all the puerilities of my childhood and girlhood ran along the side of the road making a thousand signs of friendship to me and blowing me kisses from the tips of their white tapering fingers.

"I spurred my horse to rid myself of these enervating emotions; the trees sped rapidly past me on either side; but the wanton swarm, buzzing more than a hive of bees, began to run on the sidewalks and call to me, 'Madelaine! Madelaine!'

"I struck my animal's neck smartly with my whip, which made him redouble his speed. So rapidly was I riding, that my hair was nearly straight behind my head, and my cloak was horizontal, as though its folds were sculptured in stone; once I looked behind, and I saw the dust raised by my horse's hoofs like a little white cloud far away on the horizon.

"I stopped for a while.

"I perceived something white moving in a bush of eglantine at the side of the road, and a little clear voice as sweet as silver fell upon my ear: 'Madelaine, Madelaine, where are you going so far away, Madelaine? I am your virginity, dear child; that is why I have a white dress, a white crown, and a white skin. But why are you wearing boots, Madelaine? Methought you had a very pretty foot. Boots and hose, and a large plumed hat like a cavalier going to the wars! Wherefore, pray, this long sword beating and bruising your thigh? You have a strange equipment, Madelaine, and I am not sure whether I should go with you.'

" 'If you are afraid, my dear, return home, go water my flowers and care for my doves. But, in truth, you are wrong; you would be safer in these garments of good cloth than in your gauze and flax. My boots prevent it being seen whether I have a pretty foot; this sword is for my defence, and the feather waving in my hat is to frighten away all the nightingales who would come and sing false love-songs in my ear.'

"I continued my journey: in the sighs of the wind I thought I could recognise the last phrase of the sonata which I had learned for my uncle's birthday, and in a large rose lifting its full-blown head above a little wall, the model of the big rose from which I had made so many water-colour drawings; passing before a house I saw the phantom of my curtains moving at a window. All my past seemed to be clinging to me to prevent me from advancing and attaining to a new future.

"I hesitated two or three times and turned my horse's head in the opposite direction.

"But the little blue snake of curiosity hissed softly to me insidious words, and said: 'Go on, go on, Théodore; the opportunity for instruction is a good one; if you do not learn to-day, you will never know. Will you give your noble heart to chance, to the first appearance of honesty and passion? Men hide many extraordinary secrets from us, Théodore!'

"I resumed my gallop.

"The hose was on my body, but not in my disposition; I felt a sort of uneasiness, and, as it were, a shudder of fear, to give it its proper name, at a dark part of the forest; the report of a poacher's gun nearly made me faint. If it had been a robber, the pistols in my holsters and my formidable sword would certainly have been of little assistance to me. But by degrees I became hardened, and paid no more attention to it.

"The sun was sinking slowly beneath the horizon, like the lustre in a theatre which is turned down when the performance is over. Rabbits and pheasants crossed the road from time to time; the shadows became longer, and the distance was tinted with red. Some portions of the sky were of a very sweet and softened lilac colour, others resembled the citron and orange; the night-birds began to sing, and a crowd of strange sounds issued from the wood: the little light that remained died away, and the darkness became complete, increased, as it was, by the shade cast by the trees.

"I, who had never gone out alone at night, in a large forest at eight o'clock in the evening! Can you imagine such a thing, Graciosa, I who used to be dying of fear at the end of the garden? Terror seized me more than ever, and my heart beat terribly: I confess that it was with great satisfaction that I saw the lights of the town to which I was going, peeping and sparkling at the back of a hill. As soon as I saw those brilliant specks, like little terrestrial stars, my fright completely left me. It seemed to me as if these indifferent gleams were the open eyes of so many friends who were watching for me.

"My horse was no less pleased than I was myself, and, inhaling a sweet stable odour more agreeable to him than the scents of the daisies and strawberries in the woods, he hastened straight to the Red Lion Hotel.

"A golden gleam shone through the leaden casements of the inn, the tin signboard of which was swinging right and left, and moaning like an old woman, for the north wind was beginning to freshen. I intrusted my horse to a groom, and entered the kitchen.

"An enormous fire-place opened its red and black jaws in the background, swallowing up a faggot at each mouthful, while at either side of the andirons two dogs, seated on their haunches and nearly as high as a man, were toasting themselves with all the phlegm in the world, contenting themselves with lifting their paws a little and heaving a sort of sigh when the heat became too intense; but they would certainly have let themselves be reduced to cinders rather than have retired a step.

"My arrival did not appear to please them; and it was in vain that I tried to become acquainted with them, by stroking their heads now and then; they cast stealthy looks at me which imported nothing good. This surprised me, for animals come readily to me.

"The inn-keeper came up and asked me what I wished for supper.

"He was a paunch-bellied man, with a red nose, wall eyes, and a smile that went round his head. At every word he uttered he displayed a double row of teeth, which were pointed and separated like an ogre's. The large kitchen-knife which hung by his side had a dubious appearance, and looked as if it might serve several purposes. When I had told him what I wanted he went up to one of the dogs and gave him a kick somewhere. The dog rose, and proceeded towards a sort of wheel which he entered with a cross and pitiful look, casting a glance of reproach at me. At last, seeing that no mercy was to be hoped for, he began to turn his wheel, and with it the spit on which the chicken for my supper was broached. I inwardly promised to throw him the remains of it for his trouble, and began to look round the kitchen until it should be ready.

"The ceiling was crossed by broad oaken joists, all blistered and blackened by the smoke from the hearth and candles. Pewter dishes brighter than silver, and white crockery-ware, with blue nosegays on it, shone in the shade on the dressers. Along the walls were numerous files of well-scoured pans, not unlike the ancient bucklers which were hung up in a row along the Grecian or Roman triremes (forgive me, Graciosa, for the epic magnificence of this comparison). One or two big servant-girls were busy about a large table moving plates and dishes and forks, the most agreeable of all music when you are hungry, for then the hearing of the stomach becomes keener than that of the ear.

"In short, notwithstanding the money-box mouth and sawlike teeth of the inn-keeper, the inn had quite an honest and jovial look; and if the inn-keeper's smile had been a fathom longer, and his teeth three times as long and as white, still the rain was beginning to patter on the panes, and the wind to howl in such a fashion as to take away all inclination to leave, for I know nothing more lugubrious than such wailings on a dark and rainy night.

"An idea occurred to me and made me smile, and it was this,—that nobody in the world would come to look for me where I was.

"Who, indeed, would have thought that little Madelaine, instead of being in her warm bed with her alabaster night-lamp beside her, a novel under her pillow, and her maid in the adjoining room ready to hasten to her at the slightest nocturnal alarm, would be balancing herself on a rush-bottom chair at a country inn twenty leagues from her home, her booted feet resting on the andirons, and her hands swaggeringly thrust into her pockets?

"Yes, Madelinette did not remain like her companions, idly resting her elbow on the edge of the balcony among the bind-weed and jessamine at the window, and watching the violet fringes on the horizon at the end of the plain, or some little rose-coloured cloud rounded by the May breeze. She did not strew lily leaves through mother-of-pearl palaces wherein to house her chimeras; she did not, like you, fair dreamers, clothe some hollow phantom with all imaginable perfections; she wished to be acquainted with men before giving herself to a man; she forsook everything, her beautiful brilliant robes of velvet and silk, her necklaces, bracelets, birds and flowers; she voluntarily gave up adoration, prostrate politeness, bouquets and madrigals, the pleasure of being considered more beautiful and better dressed than you, her sweet woman's name and all that she was, and departed, quite alone, like a brave girl, to learn the great science of life throughout the world.

"If this were known, people would say that Madelaine is mad. You have said it yourself, my dear Graciosa; but the truly mad are those who fling their souls to the wind, and sow their love at random on stone and rock, not knowing whether a single seed will germinate.

"O Graciosa! there is a thought that I have never had without terror; the thought of loving some one unworthy of being loved! of laying your soul bare before impure eyes and letting profanity penetrate into the sanctuary of your heart! of rolling your limpid tide for a time with a miry wave! However perfect the separation may be, something of the slime always remains, and the stream cannot recover its former transparency.

"To think that a man has kissed you and touched you; that he has seen your person; that he can say: She is like this or that; she has such a mark in such a place; she has such a shade in her soul; she laughs at this and weeps at that; her dream is of this description; here is a feather from her chimera's wing in my portfolio; this ring is plaited with her hair; a piece of her heart is folded up in this letter; she used to caress me after such a fashion, and this was her usual expression of fondness!

"Ah! Cleopatra, I can now understand why in the morning you had killed the lover with whom you had spent the night. Sublime cruelty, for which formerly I could not find sufficient imprecations! Great voluptuary, how well you knew human nature, and what penetration was shown in this barbarity! You would not suffer any living being to divulge the mysteries of your bed; the words of love which had escaped your lips should not be repeated. Thus you preserved your pure delusion. Experience came not to strip piecemeal the charming phantom that you had cradled in your arms. You preferred to be separated from him by sudden blow of axe rather than by slow distaste.

"What torture, in fact, it is to see the man whom you have chosen false every minute to the idea you had formed of him; to discover a thousand littlenesses in his character which you had not suspected; to perceive that what had appeared so beautiful to you through the prism of love is really very ugly, and that he whom you took for a true hero of romance is, after all, only a prosaic citizen who wears dressing gown and slippers!

"I have not Cleopatra's power, and if I had, I should assuredly not possess the energy to make use of it. Hence, being unable or unwilling to cut off the heads of my lovers as they leave my couch, and being, further, indisposed to endure what other women endure, I must look twice before taking one; I shall do so three times rather than twice if I feel any inclination in that direction, which is doubtful enough after

what I have seen and heard; unless, in some happy unknown land, I meet with a heart like my own, as the romances say—a virgin heart and pure, which has never loved, and which is capable of doing so in the true sense of the word,—by no means an easy matter.

"Several gentlemen entered the inn; the storm and darkness had prevented them from continuing their journey. They were all young, and the eldest was certainly not more than thirty. Their dress showed that they belonged to the upper classes, and without their dress the insolent ease of their manners would have readily made this understood. One or two of them had interesting faces; the others all displayed, to a greater or less degree, that species of brutal joviality and careless good-nature which men have among themselves, and which they lay aside completely when in our presence.

"If they could have suspected that the frail young man, half asleep in his chair at the corner of the fireplace, was anything but what he appeared to be, and was really a young girl, and fit for a king, as they say, they would certainly have quickly changed their tone, and you would immediately have seen them bridling up and making a display. They would have approached with many bows, their legs cambered, their elbows turned out, and a smile in their eyes, on their lips, in their nose, in their hair, and in their whole bodily appearance; they would have boned the words they made use of, and spoken to me only in velvet and satin phrases; at the least movement, on my part, they would have looked like stretching themselves over the floor after the manner of a carpet, lest the delicacy of my feet should be offended by its unevenness; all their hands would have been advanced to support me; the softest seat would have been prepared in the best place—but I looked like a pretty boy, and not like a pretty girl.

"I confess that I was almost ready to regret my petticoats when I saw what little attention they paid to me. For a minute I was quite mortified; for, from time to time, I forgot that I was wearing man's clothes, and had to think of the fact in order to prevent myself from growing cross.

"There I was, not speaking a word, my arms folded, looking apparently with great attention at the chicken, which was assuming a more and more rosy-tinted complexion, and the unfortunate dog which I had so unluckily disturbed, and which was striving in its wheel like several devils in the same holy-water basin.

"The youngest of the set came up, and, giving me a clap on the shoulder, which, upon my word, hurt me a good deal, and drew a little involuntary cry from me, asked me whether I would not rather sup with them than quite by myself, seeing that the drinking would go on all the better for plenty of company. I replied that this was a pleasure I should not have dared to hope for, and that I should be very happy to do so. Our covers were then laid together, and we sat down to table.

"The panting dog, after snapping up an enormous porringerful of water with three laps of his tongue, went back to his post opposite the other dog, which had not stirred any more than if he had been made of porcelain, the newcomers, by Heaven's special grace, not having asked for a chicken.

"From some words which they let drop, I learned that they were repairing to the court, which was then at——, where they were to join other friends of theirs. I told them that I was a gentleman's son who was leaving the university and going to some relations in the country by the regular pupil's road, namely, the longest he could find. This made them laugh, and after some remarks about my innocent and candid looks they asked me whether I had a mistress. I replied that I did not know, and they laughed still more. The bottles followed one another with rapidity; although I was careful to leave my glass nearly always full, my head was somewhat heated, and not losing sight of my purpose, I brought the conversation round to women. This was not difficult; for, next to theology and æsthetics, they are the subject on which men are the readiest to talk when drunk.

"My companions were not precisely drunk,—they carried their wine too well for that,—but they began to enter into moral discussions at random, and to put their elbows unceremoniously on the table. One of them had even passed his arm around the thick waist of one of the serving-women, and was nodding his head in very amorous fashion. Another swore that he would instantly burst, like a toad that had been given snuff, if Jeannette would not let him take a kiss on each of the big red apples which served her for cheeks; and Jeannette, not wishing him to burst like a toad, presented them to him with a very good grace, and did not even arrest a hand that audaciously found its way through the folds of her neckerchief into the moist valley of her bosom, which was very imperfectly guarded by a little golden cross, and it was only after a short whispered parley that he let her go and take away the dish.

"Yet they belonged to the court, and had elegant manners, and unless I had seen it, I should certainly never have thought of accusing them of such familiarities with the servants of an inn. Probably they had just left charming mistresses to whom they had sworn the finest oaths in the world. In truth, I should never have dreamed of charging my lover not to sully the lips on which I had laid my own along the cheeks of a trollop.

"The rogue appeared to take great pleasure in this kiss, neither more nor less than if he had embraced Phyllis or Ariadne. It was a big kiss, solidly and frankly applied, which left two little white marks on the wench's flaming cheek, and the trace of which she wiped away with the back of the hand that had just washed the plates and dishes. I do not believe that he ever gave so naturally tender a one to his heart's pure deity. This was apparently his own thought, for he said in an undertone, with quite a scornful movement of his elbow—

" 'To the devil with lean women and lofty sentiments!'

"This moral appeared to suit the company, and they all wagged their heads in token of assent.

" 'Upon my word,' said the other, following out his idea, 'I am unfortunate in everything. Gentlemen, I must confide to you under the seal of the greatest secrecy, that I, I who am speaking to you, have at this moment a flame.'

" 'Oh! oh!' said the others, 'a flame! That is lugubrious to the last degree. And what do you do with a flame?'

" 'She is a virtuous woman, gentlemen; you must not laugh, gentlemen; for, after all, why should I not have a virtuous woman? Have I said anything ridiculous. Here! you over there! I will throw the house at your head if you are not quiet.'

" 'Well! what next?'

" 'She is mad about me. She has the most beautiful soul in the world; in point of souls, I understand them,—I understand them at least as well as I do horses, and I assure you that it is a soul of the first quality. There are elevations, ecstasies, devotions, sacrifices, refinements of tenderness, everything you can think of that is most transcendent; but she has scarcely any bosom, she has none at all, even, like a little girl of fifteen at most. She is otherwise pretty enough; her hand is delicate, and her foot small; she has too much mind and not enough flesh, and I often think of leaving her in the lurch. The devil! One can't be content with minds. I am very unfortunate; pity me, my dear friends.' And, affected by the wine that he had drunk, he began to weep bitterly.

" 'Jeannette will console you for the misfortune of going to bed with sylphids,' said his neighbour, pouring him out a bumper; 'her soul is so thick that you might make bodies of it for other people, and she has flesh enough to clothe the carcasses of three elephants.'

"O pure and noble woman! didst thou but know what is said at random of thee, in a tavern, and in the presence of strangers, by the man whom thou lovest best in the world, and to whom thou hast sacrificed everything! how he strips thee without shame, and impudently surrenders thee in thy nakedness to the drunken gaze of his comrades, whilst thou art mournful yonder, thy chin in thy hand, and thine eyes turned towards the road by which he is to return!

"Had some one come and told thee that thy lover, twenty-four hours perhaps after leaving thee, was courting a base servant-girl, and had arranged to pass the night with her, thou wouldst have maintained that it was impossible, and wouldst have refused to believe it; scarcely wouldst thou have trusted thine eyes and ears. Yet it was so.

"The conversation lasted some time longer, and was the maddest and most shameless in the world; but through all the facetious exaggeration and the often filthy jests, there was apparent a deep and genuine feeling of perfect contempt for women, and I learned more during that evening than by reading twenty cart-loads of moralists.

"The monstrous and unheard-of things that I was listening to imparted a tinge of sadness and severity to my face, which the rest of the guests perceived, and about which they teased me good-naturedly; but my gaiety could not return. I had, indeed, suspected that men were not such as they appear to us, but yet I did not think that they were so different from their masks, and my disgust was not greater than my surprise.

"It should require only half an hour of such conversation to cure a romantic young girl for ever; it would do her more good than any maternal remonstrances.

"Some boasted of gaining as many women as they pleased, and that to do so cost them only a word; others communicated recipes for procuring mistresses, or enlarged upon the tactics to be pursued when laying siege to virtue; others again ridiculed the women whose lovers they were, and proclaimed themselves the most arrant fools on earth to be attached, in this way, to such trulls. They all made light of love.

"These, then, are the thoughts which they conceal from us beneath all their fair appearances! Who would ever think it, to see them so humble, so cringing, so ready to do anything? Ah! how hardily they raise their heads after their conquest, and insolently set the heel of their boot on the brow which they used to worship at a distance on their knees! what vengeance they take for their passing abasement! how dearly must their politeness be paid for! and through what many insults they repose after the madrigals they made! What mad brutality of language and thought! what inelegance of manners and deportment! It is a complete change, and one which certainly is not to their advantage. However far my previsions might reach, they fell far short of the reality.

"Ideal, blue flower with heart of gold, blooming all pearly with dew beneath the sky of spring, in the scented breath of soft dreamings, whose fibrous roots, a thousand times more slender than fairies' silken tresses, sink into the depths of our souls with their thousand hair-covered heads to drink in thence the purest substance; flower so sweet and so bitter, we cannot pluck thee forth without causing the heart to bleed in all its recesses; from the broken stem ooze red drops, which, falling one by one into the lake of our tears, serve to measure for us the limping hours of our death-watch by the bedside of expiring Love.

"Ah! cursed flower, how thou hadst sprung up in my soul! thy branches had multiplied more than nettles in a ruin. The young nightingales came to drink from thy cup and sing beneath thy shade; diamond butterflies, with emerald wings and ruby eyes, hovered and danced about thy frail gold-powdered pistils; swarms of flaxen bees sucked thy poisonous honey without mistrust; chimeras folded their swan-like wings and crossed their lion claws beneath their beauteous throats to rest beside thee. The tree of the Hesperides was not better guarded; sylphids gathered the tears of the stars in the urns of the lilies, and watered thee each night with their magic watering-vessels.

"Plant of the ideal, more venomous than the manchineel or the upas tree, what it costs me, despite thy treacherous blossoms and the poison inhaled with thy perfume, to uproot thee from my soul! Neither the cedar of Lebanon, nor the gigantic baobab, nor the palm a hundred cubits high, could together fill the place which thou didst occupy quite alone, little blue flower with heart of gold!

"Supper came to an end at last, and we contemplated going to bed; but, as the number of sleepers was double that of the beds, it naturally followed that we must go to bed in turn or else two together. It was a very simple matter for the rest of the company, but not so by any means for me, taking into account certain protuberances which were disguised conveniently enough beneath vest and doublet, but which a simple shirt would have betrayed in all their damnable roundness; and I was certainly little disposed to disclose my incognito in favour of any of these gentlemen who at that moment appeared to me veritable and ingenuous monsters, though I afterwards found them very decent fellows, and worth at least as much as any of their species.

"He with whom I was to share a bed was fairly drunk. He threw himself on the mattress, with one leg and arm hanging to the ground, and at once went to sleep, not the sleep of the just, but a sleep so profound that if the angel of the last judgment had come and blown his clarion in his ear he would have failed to wake him. Such a sleep greatly simplified the difficulty; I took off nothing but my doublet and boots, strode over the sleeper's body, and stretched myself on the sheets at the edge of the bed.

"I was careful to keep my distance. It was not a bad beginning! I confess that, in spite of my assurance, I was singularly troubled. The situation was so strange, so novel, that I could scarcely admit that it was not a dream. The other slept his best, but I could not close an eye the whole night.

"He was a young man, about twenty-four years of age, with rather a handsome face, dark eyelashes, and a nearly blonde moustache; his long hair rolled around his head like the waves from the inverted urn of a river-god, a light blush passed beneath his pale cheeks like a cloud beneath the water, his lips were half open and smiling with a vague and languid smile.

"I raised myself upon my elbow, and remained a long time watching him by the flickering light of a candle, of which the tallow had nearly all run down in broad sheets, and the wick was laden with black wasters.

"We were separated by a considerable interval. He occupied one extreme edge of the bed, while I, as an additional precaution, had thrown myself quite on the other.

"What I had heard was assuredly not of a nature to predispose me to tenderness and voluptuousness: I held men in abomination. Nevertheless I was more disquieted and agitated than I ought to have been: my body did not share in the repugnance of my mind so completely as it should have done. My heart was beating violently, I was hot, and on whatever side I turned I could not find repose.

"The most profound silence reigned in the inn; you could only hear at wide intervals the dull noise caused by the hoof of some horse striking the stone-floor in the stable, or the sound of a drop of water falling upon the ashes through the shaft of the chimney. The candle, reaching the end of the wick, went out in smoke.

"The densest darkness fell like a curtain between us. You cannot conceive the effect which the sudden disappearance of the light had upon me. It seemed to me as if all were ended, and I were never more to see clearly in my life. For a moment I wished to get up; but what could I have done? It was only two o'clock in the morning, all the lights were out, and I could not wander about like a phantom in a strange house. I was obliged to remain where I was and wait for daylight.

"There I was on my back, with both hands crossed, striving to think of something, and always coming back to this: that a man was lying near me. At one moment I went so far as to wish that he would awake and perceive that I was a woman. No doubt the wine that I had drunk, though sparingly, had something to do with this extraordinary idea, but I could not help recurring to it. I was on the point of stretching out my hands towards him, to wake him up, but a fold in the bedclothes which checked my arm prevented me from going through with it. Time was thus given me for reflection, and while I was freeing my arm, my senses, which I had altogether lost, came back to me, not entirely, perhaps, but sufficiently to restrain me.

"How curious it would have been, if I, scornful beauty as I was, I who wished to be acquainted with ten years of a man's life before giving him my hand to kiss, had surrendered myself on a pallet in an inn to the first comer! and upon my word such a thing might have happened.

"Can a sudden effervescence, a boiling of the blood, so completely subdue the most superb resolves? Does the voice of the body speak in higher tones than the voice of the mind? Whenever my pride sends too many puffs heavenwards, I bring the recollection of that night before its eyes to recall it to earth. I am beginning to be of man's opinion: what a poor thing is woman's virtue! on what, good heavens, does it depend!

"Ah! it is vain to seek to spread one's wings, they are laden with too much clay; the body is an anchor which holds back the soul to earth: fruitlessly does she open her sails to the wind of the loftiest ideas, the vessel remains motionless, as though all the remoras of the ocean were clinging to the keel. Nature takes pleasure in such sarcasms at our expense. When she sees a thought standing on its pride as on a lofty column, and nearly touching heaven with its head, she whispers to the red fluid to quicken its pace and crowd at the gates of the arteries; she commands the temples to sing and the ears to tingle, and, behold, giddiness seizes the proud idea. All images are blended and confused, the earth seems to undulate like the deck of a bark in a storm, the heavens turn round, and the stars dance a saraband; the lips which used to utter only austere maxims are wrinkled and put forward as though for kisses; the arms so firm to repel grow soft, and become more supple and entwining than scarves. Add to this contact with an epidermis and a breath across your hair, and all is lost.

"Often even less is sufficient. A fragrance of foliage coming to you from the fields through your half-opened window, the sight of two birds billing each other, an opening daisy, an old love-song which re-

turns to you in your own despite and which you repeat without understanding its meaning, a warm wind which troubles and intoxicates
you, the softness of your bed or divan—one of these circumstances is
sufficient; even the solitude of your room makes you think that it
would be comfortable for two, and that no more charming nest could
be found for a brood of pleasures. The drawn curtains, the twilight,
the silence, all bring back to you the fatal idea which brushes you with
its dove-like wings and coos so sweetly about you. The tissues which
touch you seem to caress you, and cling with amorous folds along your
body. Then the young girl opens her arms to the first wooer with
whom she finds herself alone: the philosopher leaves his page unfinished, and, with his head in his mantle, runs in all haste to assuage
his passion.

"I certainly did not love the man who was causing me such strange
perturbations. He had no other charm than that he was not a woman,
and, in the condition in which I found myself, this was enough! A man!
that mysterious thing which is concealed from us with so much care,
that strange animal, of whose history we know so little, that demon
or god who alone can realise all the dreams of vague voluptuousness
wherewith the spring-time flatters our sleep, the sole thought that we
have from fifteen years of age!

"A man! The confused notion of pleasure floated through my
dulled head. The little that I knew of it kindled my desire still more. A
burning curiosity urged me to clear up once for all the doubts which
perplexed me, and were for ever recurring to my mind. The solution of
the problem was over the leaf: it was only necessary to turn it, the
book was beside me. A handsome cavalier, a narrow bed, a dark night!
—a young girl with a few glasses of champagne in her head! what a
suspicious combination! Well! the result of it all was but a very
virtuous nothingness.

"On the wall, upon which I kept my eyes fixed, I began, in the
diminishing darkness, to distinguish the position of the window, the
panes less opaque, and the grey light of dawn, glancing behind them,
restored their transparency; the sky brightened by degrees: it was
day. You cannot imagine the pleasure given me by that pale ray of

light on the green dye of the Aumale serge which surrounded the glorious battlefield whereon my virtue had triumphed over my desires! It seemed to me as though it were my crown of victory.

"As to my companion, he had fallen out on to the ground.

"I got up, adjusted my dress as quickly as possible, and ran to the window; I opened it, and the morning breeze did me good. I placed myself before the looking-glass in order to comb my hair, and was astonished at the paleness of my countenance, which I had believed to be purple.

"The others came in to see whether we were still asleep, and pushed their friend with their feet, who did not appear much surprised at finding himself where he was.

"The horses were saddled, and we set out again.

"But this is enough for to-day. My pen will not write any more, and I do not want to mend it; another time I will tell you the rest of my adventures; meanwhile, love me as I love you, well-named Graciosa, and do not, from what I have just told you, form too bad an opinion of my virtue."

XI

Many things are tiresome. It is tiresome to pay back the money you have borrowed and become accustomed to look on as your own; it is tiresome to fondle to-day the woman you loved yesterday; it is tiresome to go to a house at the dinner-hour and find that the owners left for the country a month ago; it is tiresome to write a novel, and more tiresome to read one; it is tiresome to have a pimple on your nose and cracked lips on the day that you visit the idol of your heart; it is tire-

some to wear facetious boots which smile on the pavement from every seam, and, above all, to harbour a vacuum behind the cobwebs in your pocket; it is tiresome to be a door-porter; it is tiresome to be an emperor; it is tiresome to be yourself, and even to be some one else; it is tiresome to go on foot because it hurts your corns, on horseback because it skins the antithesis of the front, in a coach because a big man infallibly makes a pillow of your shoulder, on the packet because you are sea-sick and vomit your entire self; it is tiresome to have winter because you shiver, and summer because you perspire; but the most tiresome thing on earth, in hell, or in heaven is assuredly a tragedy, unless it be a drama or a comedy.

"It really makes my heart ache. What could be more silly and stupid? Are not the great tyrants with voices like bulls, who stride across the stage from one wing to the other, making their hairy arms go like the wings of a windmill, and imprisoned in flesh-coloured stockings, but sorry counterfeits of Bluebeard or Bogey! Their rodomontades might make any one who could keep awake burst out laughing.

"Women who are unfortunate in love are no less ridiculous. It is diverting to see them advance, clad in black or white, with their hair weeping on their shoulders, sleeves weeping on their hands, and their bodies ready to leap from the corset like a fruit-stone pressed between the fingers; looking as if they were dragging the floor by the sole of their satin slippers, and, in their great impulses of passion, spurning their trains backward with a little kick from their heel. The dialogue, composed exclusively of Oh! and Ah! which they cluck as they display their feathers, is truly agreeable food and easy of digestion. Their princes are also very charming; they are only somewhat dark and melancholy, which does not, however, prevent them from being the best companions in the world or elsewhere.

"As to comedy which is to correct manners, and which fortunately acquits itself badly enough of its task, the sermons of fathers and iterations of uncles are, to my mind, as wearisome on the stage as in real life. I am not of opinion that the number of fools should be doubled by the representation of them; there are quite enough of them as it is, thank heaven, and the race is not likely to come to an end.

Where is the necessity of portraying somebody who has a pig's snout or ox's muzzle, and of gathering together the trash of a clown whom you would throw out of the window if he came into your house? The image of a pedant is no more interesting than the pedant himself, and his reflection in a mirror does not make him the less a pedant. An actor who succeeded in imitating the attitudes and manners of cobblers to perfection would not amuse me more than a real cobbler.

"But there is a theatre which I love, a fantastic, extravagant, impossible theatre, in which the worthy public would pitilessly hiss from the first scene, for want of understanding a single word.

"It is a singular theatre. Glow-worms take the place of Argand lamps, and a scarabæus, beating time with his antennæ, is placed at the desk. The cricket takes his part; the nightingale is first flute; little sylphs issuing from the peas-blossom hold basses of citron-peel between their pretty legs which are whiter than ivory, and with mighty power of arm move their bows, made with a hair from Titania's eyelash, over strings of spiders' thread; the little wig with its three hammers, which the scarabæus conductor wears, quivers with pleasure and diffuses about it a luminous dust, so sweet is the harmony and so well executed the overture!

"A curtain of butterflies' wings, more delicate than the interior pellicle of an egg, rises slowly after the three indispensable raps. The house is full of the souls of poets seated in stalls of mother-of-pearl, and watching the performance through dewdrops set on the golden pistils of lilies. These are their opera-glasses.

"The scenery is not like any known scenery; the country which it represents is as strange as was America before its discovery. The palette of the richest painter has not half the tones with which it is diapered. All is painted in odd and singular colours. The verditer, the blue-ash, the ultramarine, and the red and yellow lake are in profusion.

"The sky, which is of a greenish-blue, is striped zebra-wise with broad flaxen and tawny bands; in the middle distance spare and slender trees wave their scanty foliage the colour of dried roses; the distance, instead of being drowned in its azure-tinted vapour, is of the most beautiful apple-green, and here and there escape spirals of golden smoke. A wandering ray hangs on the portal of a ruined temple or the spire of a tower. Towns full of bell-turrets, pyramids, domes, arcades, and ramps, are seated on the hills and reflected in crystal lakes; large trees with broad leaves, deeply carved by the chisels of the fairies, inextricably entwine their trunks and branches to form the wings. Over their heads the clouds of heaven collect like snow-flakes, through their interstices the eyes of dwarfs and gnomes are seen to sparkle, and their tortuous roots sink into the soil like the finger of a giant-hand. The woodpecker keeps time as he taps them with his horny beak, and emerald lizards bask in the sun on the moss at their foot.

"The mushroom looks on at the comedy with his hat on his head, like the insolent fellow that he is. The dainty violet stands up on her little tiptoes between two blades of grass, and opens her blue eyes wide to see the hero pass.

"The bullfinch and the linnet lean down at the end of the boughs to prompt the actors in their parts.

"Through the tall grasses, the lofty purple thistles and the velvet-leaved burdocks, wind, like silver snakes, brooks that are formed with the tears of stags at bay. At wide intervals anemones are seen shining on the turf like drops of blood, and daisies, like veritable duchesses, carrying high their heads laden with crowns of pearls.

"The characters are of no time or country; they come and go without our knowing why or how; they neither eat nor drink, they dwell nowhere and have no occupation; they possess neither lands, nor incomes, nor houses; only sometimes they carry under their arm a little box full of diamonds as big as pigeons' eggs; as they walk they do not shake a single drop of rain from the heads of the flowers nor raise a single grain of the dust on the roads.

"Their dress is the most extravagant and fantastical in the world. Pointed steeple-shaped hats with brims as broad as a Chinese parasol and immoderate plumes plucked from the tails of the bird of paradise and the phœnix; cloaks striped with brilliant colours, doublets of velvet and brocade, letting the satin or silver-cloth lining be seen through their gold-laced slashings; hose puffed and swollen like balloons; scarlet stockings, with embroidered clocks, shoes with high heels and large rosettes; little slender swords, with the point in the air and the hilt depressed, covered with cords and ribbons—so for the men.

"The women are no less curiously accoutred.

"The drawings of Della Bella and Romain de Hooge might serve to represent the character of their attire. There are stuffed, undulating robes with great folds, whose colours play like those on the necks of turtle-doves, and reflect all the changing tints of the iris, large sleeves whence other sleeves emerge, ruffs of open-slashed lace rising higher than the head which they serve to frame, corsets laden with knots and embroideries, aiglets, strange jewels, crests of heron plumes, necklaces of big pearls, fans formed from the peacock's tail with mirrors in the centre, little slippers and pattens, garlands of artificial flowers, spangles, wire-worked gauzes, paint, patches, and everything that can add flavour and piquancy to a theatrical toilette.

"It is a style which is not precisely English, nor German, nor French, nor Turkish, nor Spanish, nor Tartar, though it partakes somewhat of all these, and is one which has adopted what is most graceful and characteristic from every country. Actors dressed in this manner may say what they will without doing violence to probability. Fancy may rove in all directions, style may at its ease unroll its diapered rings like a snake basking in the sun; the most exotic conceits may fearlessly spread their singular flower-cups and diffuse around them their perfume of amber and musk. Nothing hinders it,—neither places, nor names, nor costume.

"How amusing and charming are their utterances! They are not such actors as contort their mouths and make their eyes start out of their heads in order to despatch their tirade with effect like our dramatic howlers; they, at least, have not the appearance of workmen at their task, or of oxen yoked to the action and hastening to get done with it; they are not plastered with chalk and rouge half an inch thick; they do not carry tin daggers nor keep a pig's bladder filled with chicken's blood in reserve beneath their cloaks; they do not trail the same oil-stained rags through entire acts.

"They speak without hurry or clamour, like well-bred people who

177

attach no great importance to what they are doing: the lover makes his declaration with the easiest air in the world; he taps his thigh with the tip of his white glove, or adjusts the leg of his trousers while he is speaking; the lady carelessly shakes the dew from her bouquet and exchanges witticisms with her attendant; the lover takes very little trouble to soften his cruel fair: his principal business is to drop clusters of pearls and bunches of roses from his lips, and to scatter poetic gems like a true spendthrift; often he effaces himself entirely, and lets the author court his mistress in his stead. Jealousy is no fault of his, and he is of the most accommodating disposition. With his eyes raised to the flies and friezes of the theatre, he complacently waits until the poet has finished saying what has taken his fancy, to resume his part and place himself again upon his knees.

"All is woven and unwoven with admirable carelessness: effects have no causes, and causes no effects; the most witty character is he who says most absurdities; the most foolish says the wittiest things; young girls talk in a way that would make courtesans blush, and courtesans utter maxims of morality. The most unheard-of adventures follow one after another without any explanation; the noble father arrives from China in a bamboo junk expressly to recognise a little girl who has been carried off; gods and fairies do nothing but ascend and descend in their machines. The action plunges into the sea beneath the topaz dome of the waves, traversing the bottom of the ocean through forests of coral and madrepore, or rises to heaven on the wings of lark and griffin.

"The dialogue is most universal: the lion contributes a vigorously uttered oh! oh!—the wall speaks through its chinks, and provided that he has a witticism, rebus, or pun to interpose, any one is free to interrupt the most interesting scene: the ass's head of Bottom is as welcome as the golden head of Ariel; the author's mind may be discerned beneath every form, and all these contradictions are like so many facets which reflect its different aspects while imparting to it the colours of the prism.

"This apparent pell-mell and disorder succeeds after all in representing real life with more exactness in its fantastic presentations than the most minutely studied drama of manners. Every man comprises the whole of humanity within himself, and by writing what comes into his head, he succeeds better than by copying through a magnifying glass objects which are external to him.

"What a glorious family! young romantic lovers, roaming damsels, serviceable attendants, caustic buffoons, artless valets and peasants, gracious kings, whose names and kingdoms are unknown to historian and geographer; motley graciosos, clowns with sharp repartees and miraculous capers; O you who give utterance to free caprice through your smiling lips, I love you and adore you among and above all others: Perdita, Rosalind, Celia, Pandarus, Parolles, Silvio, Leander, and the rest, all those charming types, so false and so true, who, in the checkered wings of folly soar above gross reality, and in whom the poet personifies his joy, his melancholy, his love, and his most intimate dream beneath the most frivolous and flippant appearances.

"Among these plays which were written for the fairies, and should be performed by the light of the moon, there is one piece which principally delights me—a piece so wondering, so vagrant, with so vaporous a plot and such singular characters, that the author himself, not knowing what title to give it, has called it 'As You Like It,' an elastic name which satisfies every requirement.

"When reading this strange piece, you feel that you are transported into an unknown world, of which, however, you have some vague recollection: you can no longer tell whether you are dead or alive, dreaming or awake; pleasant faces smile sweetly on you, and give as they pass you a kindly good-day; you feel moved and troubled at the sight of them, as though at the turn of a road you had suddenly met with your ideal, or the forgotten phantom of your first mistress had suddenly stood before you. Springs flow murmuring half-subdued complaints; the wind stirs the old trees of the ancient forest over the head of the aged exiled duke with compassionate sighs; and, when the melancholy Jacques gives his philosophic griefs to the stream with the leaves of the willow, it seems to you as though you were yourself the speaker, and the most obscure and secret thoughts of your heart were illumined and revealed.

"O young son of the brave knight Roland de Bois, so ill-used by fate! I cannot but be jealous of thee; thou hast still a faithful servant, the good Adam, whose old age is so green beneath the snow of his hair. Thou art banished, but not at least until thou hast wrestled and triumphed; thy wicked brother robs thee of all thine estate, but Rosalind gives thee the chain from her neck; thou art poor, but thou art loved; thou leavest thy country, but the daughter of thy persecutor follows thee beyond the seas.

"The dark Ardennes open their great arms of foliage to receive thee and conceal thee; the good forest, in the depths of its grottos, heaps its most silky moss to form thy couch; it stoops its arches above thy brow to protect thee from rain and sun; it pities thee with the tears of its springs and the sighs of its belling fawns and deer; it makes of its rocks kindly desks for thy amorous epistles; it lends thee thorns from its bushes wherewith to hang them, and commands the satin bark of its aspen trees to yield to the point of thy stiletto when thou wouldst grave thereon the character of Rosalind.

"If only it were possible, young Orlando, to have like thee a great and shady forest that one might retire and be alone in his pain, and, at the turning of a walk meet the sought for she, recognisable though disguised! But alas! the world of the soul has no verdant Ardennes, and only in the garden of poetry bloom the wild, capricious little flowers whose perfume gives complete forgetfulness. In vain do we shed tears; they form not those fair silvery cascades; in vain do we sigh: no kindly echo troubles to return us our complaints graced with assonances and conceits. Vainly do we hang sonnets on the prickles of every bramble: Rosalind never gathers them, and it is for nothing that we gash the bark of the trees with amorous characters.

"Birds of the sky lend me each a feather, swallow no less than eagle, and humming bird than roc, that I may make me a pair of wings to fly high and fast through regions unknown, where I may find nothing to bring back to my recollection the city of the living, where I may forget that I am myself, and live a life strange and new, farther than America, than Africa, than Asia, than the last island of the world, through the ocean of ice, beyond the pole where trembles the aurora borealis, in the impalpable kingdom whither the divine creations of the poets and the types of supreme beauty take their flight.

"How is it possible to sustain ordinary conversations in clubs and drawing-rooms after hearing thee speak, sparkling Mercutio, whose every phrase bursts in gold and silver rain like a firework shell beneath a star-strewn sky? Pale Desdemona, what pleasure wouldst thou have us take in any terrestrial music after the romance of the Willow? What women seem not ugly beside your Venuses, ancient sculptors, poets in marble strophes?

"Ah! despite the furious embrace with which I wished to clasp the material world for lack of the other, I feel that I have an evil nature, that life was not made for me, and that it repulses me; I cannot concern myself with anything: whatever road I follow I go astray; the smooth alley and the stony path alike lead me to the abyss. If I wish to take my flight the air condenses about me, and I am caught with my wings spread and unable to close them. I can neither walk nor fly; the sky attracts me when I am on earth, and the earth when I am in the sky; above, the north wind tears away my plumes; below, the pebbles wound my feet. My soles are too tender to walk upon the broken glass of reality; my wings of too short a span to soar above things, and rise from circle to circle into the azure depths of mysticism, even to the inaccessible summits of eternal love; I am the most unfortunate hippogriff, the most wretched heap of heterogeneous pieces that ever existed, since ocean first loved the moon and man was deceived by woman: the monstrous Chimæra slain by Bellerophon, with its maiden's head, lion's paws, goat's body, and dragon's tail, was an animal of simple composition in comparison with me.

"In my frail breast dwell together the violet-strewn dreamings of the chaste young girl and the mad burnings of revelling courtesans: my desires go, like lions, sharpening their claws in the shade and seeking for something to devour; my thoughts, more feverish and restless than goats, cling to the most menacing crests; my hatred, poison-puffed, twists its scaly folds in inextricable knots, and drags itself at length through ruts and ravines.

"A strange land is my soul, a land flourishing and splendid in appearance, but more saturated with putrid and deleterious nuisances than the land of Batavia: the least ray of sunshine on the slime causes reptiles to hatch and mosquitoes to swarm; the large yellow tulips, the nagassaris and the angsoka flowers pompously veil unclean carrion. The amorous rose opens her scarlet lips, and smiling shows her little dewdrop teeth to the wooing nightingales who repeat madrigals and sonnets to her: nothing could be more charming; but the odds are a hundred to one that there is a dropsical toad in the grass beneath the bushes, crawling on limping feet and silvering his path with his slime.

"There are springs more limpid and clear than the purest diamond; but it would be better for you to draw the stagnant water of the marsh beneath its cloak of rotten rushes and drowned dogs than to dip your cup in such a wave. A serpent is hidden at the bottom, and wheels round with frightful quickness as he discharges his venom.

"You planted wheat, and there springs up asphodel, henbane, darnel, and pale hemlock with verdigris branches. Instead of the root which you had buried, you are astonished to see emerging from the earth the hairy, twisted limbs of the dark mandragora.

"If you leave a souvenir, and should come to take it again some time afterwards, you will find it greener with moss and more abounding with woodlice and disgusting insects than a stone placed on the dank floor of a cave.

"Seek not to cross its dark forests; they are more impracticable than the virgin forests of America or the jungles of Java. Creepers, strong as cables, run from one tree to another; plants bristling and pointed like spear-heads obstruct every passage; the grass itself is covered with a scorching down like that of a nettle. To the arches of foliage gigantic bats of the vampire kind cling by their claws; scarabees of enormous size shake their threatening horns and lash the air with their quadruple wings; monstrous and fantastic animals, such as are seen passing in nightmares, advance painfully breaking the reeds before them. There are troops of elephants crushing the flies between the wrinkles of their dried skin or rubbing their flanks along the stones and walls, rhinoceroses with rugose carapace, hippopotami with

182

swollen muzzle and bristling hair, which, as they go, knead the mud and detritus of the forest with their broad feet.

"In the glades, yonder where the sun thrusts in a luminous ray like a wedge of gold, across the dank humidity, at the place where you would have wished to seat yourself, you will always find some family of tigers carelessly couched, breathing the air through their nostrils, winking their sea-green eyes and glossing their velvety fur with their blood-red, papillæ-covered tongues; or, it may be, a knot of boa serpents half asleep and digesting the bull they swallowed last.

"Dread everything—grass, fruit, water, air, shadow, sun, everything is mortal.

"Close your ear to the chatter of the little paroquets, with golden beak and emerald neck, which descend from the trees and come and perch on your finger with throbbing wings; for the little emerald-necked paroquets will finish by prettily putting out your eyes with their golden beaks at the moment that you are bending down to kiss them. So it is!

"The world will have none of me; it repulses me as a spectre escaped from the tombs, and I am nearly as pale as one. My blood refuses to believe that I am alive, and will not colour my skin; it creeps slowly through my veins like stagnant water in obstructed canals. My heart beats for nothing which causes the heart of man to beat. My griefs and joys are not those of my fellow-creatures. I have vehemently desired what nobody desires; I have scorned things which are madly longed for. I have loved women when they did not love me, and I have been loved when I would fain have been hated. Always too soon or too late, more or less, on this side or on that; never what ought to have been; either I have not arrived, or I have been too far. I have flung my life through the windows, or concentrated it upon a single point, and from the restless activity of the ardelio I have come to the dull somnolence of the teriaki and the stylite on his column.

"What I do has always the appearance of a dream; my actions seem to be the result rather of somnambulism than of a free-will; there is something within me which I feel vaguely at a great depth, and which causes me to act without my own participation and always independently of general laws; the simple and natural side of things is never revealed to me until after all the others, and at first I always fasten upon what is eccentric and odd. However slightly the line may slant I soon make it into a spiral more twisted than a serpent; outlines, if they are not fixed in the most precise manner, become confused and distorted. Faces assume a supernatural air, and look at you with frightful eyes.

"Thus, by a species of instinctive reaction, I have always clung desperately to matter, to the external silhouette of things, and in art have always given a very important place to the plastic. I understand a statue perfectly, while I cannot understand a man; where life begins, I stop and shrink back affrighted, as though I had seen Medusa's head. The phenomenon of life causes me an astonishment which I cannot overcome. No doubt I shall make an excellent dead man, for I am a very poor living one, and the sense of my existence completely escapes me. The sound of my voice surprises me to an unimaginable degree, and I might be tempted sometimes to take it for the voice of another. When I wish to stretch forth my arm, and my arm obeys me, the fact seems quite a prodigious one to me, and I sink into the profoundest stupefaction.

"On the other hand, Silvio, I have a perfect comprehension of the unintelligible; the most extravagant notions seem quite natural to me, and I enter into them with singular facility. I can find with ease the connection of the most capricious and disordered nightmare. This is the reason why the kind of pieces I was just speaking to you about pleases me beyond all others.

"We have great discussions on this subject with Théodore and Rosette. Rosette has little liking for my system, she is for the *true* truth; Théodore gives more latitude to the poet, and admits a conventional and optical truth; for my part, I maintain that the author must have a clear stage and that fancy should reign supreme.

"Many of the company grounded their arguments chiefly on the fact that such pieces were, as a general rule, independent of theatrical conditions and could not be performed; I replied that this was true in one sense and false in another, like nearly everything that is said, and that the ideas entertained respecting scenic possibilities and impossibilities appeared to me to be wanting in exactness, and to be the result rather of prejudices than of reason. Among other things, I said that the piece 'As You Like It' was assuredly most presentable, especially for people in society who were not practiced in other parts.

"This suggested the idea of performing it. The season is advancing, and we have exhausted every description of amusement; we are tired of hunting, and of parties on horseback, or on the water; the chances of boston, varied as they are, have not piquancy enough to fill up an evening, and the proposal was received with universal enthusiasm.

"A young man who knew how to paint volunteered to make the scenery; he is working at it now with much ardour, and in a few days it will be finished. The stage is erected in the orangery, which is the largest hall in the mansion, and I think that everything will turn out well. I am taking the part of Orlando, and Rosette was to have played Rosalind,—which was a most proper arrangement. As my mistress, and the mistress of the house, the part fell to her of right; but owing to a caprice singular enough in her, prudery not being one of her faults, she would not disguise herself as a man. Had I not been sure of the contrary, I should have believed that her legs were badly shaped. Actually none of the ladies of the party would show herself less scrupulous than Rosette, and this nearly caused the failure of the piece; but Théodore, who had taken the part of the melancholy Jaques, offered to replace her, seeing that Rosalind is a cavalier nearly the whole time, except in the first act where she is a woman, and that with paint, corset, and dress, he will be able to effect the illusion sufficiently well, having as yet no beard, and being of a very slight figure.

"We are engaged in learning our parts, and it is something curious to see us. In every solitary nook in the park you are sure to find some one, paper in hand, muttering phrases in a whisper, raising his eyes to heaven, suddenly casting them down, and repeating the same gesture seven or eight times. If it were not known that we are to perform a comedy, we should assuredly be taken for a houseful of lunatics or poets (which is almost a pleonasm).

"I think that we shall soon know enough to have a rehearsal. I am expecting something very singular. Perhaps I am wrong. I was afraid for a moment that instead of playing by inspiration our actors would endeavour to reproduce the attitudes and voice-inflections of some fashionable performer; but fortunately they have not watched the stage with sufficient accuracy to fall into this inconvenience, and it is to be expected that, through the awkwardness of people who have never trod the boards, they will display precious flashes of nature and that charming ingenuousness which the most consummate talent cannot reproduce.

"Our young painter has truly wrought wonders. It would be impossible to give a stranger shape to the old trunks of trees and the ivy which entwines them; he has taken pattern by those in the park, accentuating and exaggerating them as necessary for the stage. Everything is expressed with admirable boldness and caprice; stones, rocks, clouds, are of a mysteriously grimacing form; mirror-like reflections play on the trembling waters which are less stable than quicksilver, and the ordinary coldness of the foliage is marvellously relieved by saffron tints dashed in by the brush of autumn; the forest varies from emerald green to cornelian purple; the warmest and the freshest tones show harmoniously together, and the sky itself passes from the softest blue to the most burning colours.

"He has designed all the costumes after my instructions, and they are of the handsomest description. At first the performers cried that they could not be produced in silk or velvet nor in any known material, and I nearly saw the moment when troubadour costume was to be generally adopted. The ladies said that such glaring colours would eclipse their eyes. To which we replied that their eyes were stars which were perfectly inextinguishable, and that on the contrary it was their eyes that would eclipse the colours, and even, if need were, the Argand lamps, the lustre, and the sun. They had no reply to this; but there were other objections which kept springing up in a bristling crowd like the Lernean hydra; no sooner was the head of one cut off than another more obstinate and more stupid would arise.

" 'How do you think this will keep together?'—'It is all very well on paper, but it is another matter when on one's back; I shall never

be able to get into that!'—'My petticoat is at least four finger-lengths too short; I shall never dare to show myself in that disguise!'—'This ruff is too high; I look as if I were a hunchback and had no neck.'—'This headdress makes me look intolerably old.'

" 'With starch, pins, and good-will, everything will hold.'—'You are joking! a waist like yours, more frail than a wasp's, and one which would go through the ring of my little finger! I will wager twenty-five louis to a kiss that it will be necessary to take in this bodice!'—'Your petticoat is very far from being too short, and if you knew what an adorable leg you have, you would most certainly be of my opinion.'—'On the contrary, your neck stands out and is admirably set off by its aureola of lace.'—'This headdress does not make you look old in the least, and, even if you appeared to be a few years older, you are so extremely young that this ought to be a matter of perfect indifference to you; indeed, you would give us grounds for strange suspicions if we did not know where the pieces of your last doll are'—etc.

"You cannot imagine what a prodigious quantity of madrigals we were obliged to dispense in order to compel our ladies to put on charming costumes which were most becoming to them.

"We found it equally troublesome to induce them to place their patches in an appropriate manner. What a devil of a taste women have! and what Titanic obstinacy possesses a vapourish, foppish woman who believes that glazed straw-yellow suits her better than jonquil or bright rose-colour. I am sure that if I had devoted to public affairs half the artifices and intrigues that I have employed in order to have a red feather placed on the left and not on the right, I should be a minister of state or emperor at the least.

"What a pandemonium! what an enormous and inextricable rout must a real theatre be!

"From the time that the performance of a comedy was first spoken of, everything here has been in the most complete disorder. All the drawers are opened, all the wardrobes emptied; it is genuine pillage. Tables, easy-chairs, consoles, everything is littered, and a person does not know where to set his foot. Trailing about the house are prodigious quantities of dresses, mantelets, veils, petticoats, cloaks, caps, and hats; and when you think that all these are to be arranged on the bodies of seven or eight persons, you involuntarily think of those mountebanks at the fair who wear eight or ten coats one over another, and you find it impossible to conceive that the whole of this heap will only furnish one costume for each.

"The servants are constantly coming and going; there are always two or three on the road from the mansion to the town, and if this continues all the horses will become broken-winded.

"A theatrical manager has no time to be melancholy, and I have seldom been so for some time past. I am so deafened and overwhelmed that I am beginning to lose all understanding of the piece. As I support the character of impresario as well as that of Orlando, my task is a twofold one. When any difficulty arises recourse is had to me, and as my decisions are not always listened to as oracles, they degenerate into interminable discussions.

"If what is called living is to be always on one's legs, to be equal to twenty persons, to go up and down stairs and not to think for a minute during the day, I have never lived so much as during this week. Nevertheless, I have a smaller share in this animation than might be believed. The agitation is very shallow, and the stagnant, unflowing water might be found a few fathoms below; life does not penetrate me so readily as that, and my vitality is even the smallest when I seem to be working and engaging in what is going on. Action dulls and fatigues me to an extent which is inconceivable; where I am not employed actively, I think or at least dream, and this is a sort of existence, but I lose it as soon as I emerge from my porcelain-image repose.

"Up to the present I have done nothing, and I do not know whether I shall ever do anything. I cannot check my brain, which is all the difference between a man of talent and a man of genius; it is an endless boiling, wave urging wave; I cannot master this species of internal jet which rises from my heart to my head, and, for want of outlets, drowns all my thoughts. I can produce nothing, owing not to sterility, but to superabundance; my ideas spring up so thick-set and close that they are stifled and cannot ripen. Never will execution, however rapid and impetuous it may be, attain to such velocity. When I write a phrase, the thought which it represents is already as far distant from me as though a century had elapsed instead of a second, and it often happens that in spite of myself I mingle with it something of the thought which has taken its place in my head.

"This is why I cannot live, whether as a poet or as a lover. I can only give out the ideas which have left me; I have women only when I have forgotten them, and am loving others;—a man, how can I bring forth my wish to the light since, hasten as I may, I lose the consciousness of what I do, and act only in accordance with a feeble reminiscence?

"To come upon a thought in a vein of your brain, to take it out rude at first like a block of marble as it is got from the quarry, to set it before you and, with a chisel in one hand and a hammer in the other, to knock, cut, and scrape from morning till evening, and then carry off at night a pinch of dust to throw upon your writing—that is what I shall never be able to do.

"In idea I can separate the slender form from the coarse block very well, and have a very clear vision of it; but there are so many angles to knock away, so many splinters to make fly, so many strokes of rasp and hammer to be given in order to come near to the shape and lay hold on the just sinuosity of the contour, that my hands become blistered, and I let my chisel fall to the ground.

"If I persevere, the fatigue reaches such a degree of intensity that my inmost sight is totally darkened, and I can no longer distinguish through the cloud of marble the fair divinity which is concealed within its thickness. Then I pursue her at random and in groping fashion; I bite too deeply into one place, and do not go far enough into another; I take away what ought to have been a leg or an arm, and leave a compact mass where there ought to have been a void; instead of a goddess I make a grotesque, and sometimes even less, and the magnificent block drawn at so great expense and with so much toil from the entrails of the earth, hammered, cut, and hollowed out in all directions, looks more as if it had been gnawed and perforated by polyps to make a hive than fashioned by a statuary after a settled design.

"How dost thou contrive, Michael Angelo, to cut the marble in

slices as a child carves a chestnut? of what steel were thine uncon-
quered chisels formed? and what sturdy sides sustained you, all ye
fertile artists and workers, whom no matter can resist, and who can
cause your dream to flow entire into colour and bronze?

"It is in a fashion an innocent and permissible vanity, after the cruel
things that I have just told you of myself, and you will not be one
to blame me for it, O Silvio!—but, though the universe be destined to
know nothing of it, and my name be beforehand devoted to oblivion,
I am a poet and a painter! I have had as beautiful ideas as any poet
in the world; I have created types as pure and as divine as those that
are most admired in the masters. I see them there before me as clear
and distinct as though they were really depicted, and were I able to
open up a hole in my head, and place a glass in it to be looked through,
there would be the most marvellous picture gallery that was ever
seen. No earthly king can boast the possession of such a one. There
are Rubenses as flaming and bright as the purest at Antwerp; my
Raphaëls are in the best state of preservation, and his Madonnas
have no more gracious smiles; Buonarotti cannot contort a muscle
in bolder and more terrible fashion; the sun of Venice shines upon
this canvas as though it were signed 'Paulus Cagliari;' the shadows of
Rembrandt himself are heaped in the background of that frame where
in the distance there trembles a pale star of light; the pictures wrought
in the manner peculiar to myself would assuredly be scorned by none.

"I am quite aware that it looks strange for me to say this, and that
I shall appear giddy with the coarse intoxication of the most foolish
pride; but it is so, and nothing will shake my conviction of it. No one
doubtless will share it; what then? Every one is born marked with a
black or a white seal. Mine apparently is black.

"Sometimes, even, I have difficulty in covering up my thought
sufficiently in this respect; it often happens that I speak too familiarly
of these lofty geniuses whose footsteps should be adored, and whose
statues should be contemplated from afar and on the knees. Once I
forgot myself so far as to say 'We.' Happily it was before a person
who did not notice it, else I should infallibly have been taken for the
most enormous coxcomb that ever lived.

"I *am* a poet and a painter, Silvio; am I not?

"It is a mistake to believe that all those who have passed for having genius were really greater men than others. It is unknown how much was contributed to Raphaël's reputation by the pupils and obscure painters whom he employed in his works; he gave his signature to the soul and talents of many—that is all.

"A great painter or a great writer occupies and fills by himself a whole century; his only care is to invade all styles at once, so that if a rival should start up he may accuse him at the very outset of plagiarism and check him at the first step in his career. These are well-known tactics, and though not new, succeed none the less every day.

"It may happen that a man who is already celebrated has precisely the same sort of talent that you would have had. Under penalty of being thought to copy him, you are obliged to turn aside your natural inspiration and cause it to take a different direction. You were born to blow full-mouthed on the heroic clarion or to evoke the wan phantoms of times that are no more, and you are obliged to play your fingers on the seven-holed flute or to make knots on a sofa in the recesses of some boudoir, simply because your father did not take the trouble to cast you in a mould eight or ten years sooner, and the world does not understand that two men may cultivate the same field.

"It is in this way that many noble intellects have been forced to take wittingly a path which is not theirs, and to keep for ever along the borders of their own domain from which they have been banished, happy still to cast a glance by stealth over the hedge, and to see on the other side blooming in the sun the beautiful variegated flowers which they possess as seeds but cannot sow for lack of soil.

"As regards myself, I do not know whether,—apart from the greater or less opportuneness of circumstances, the greater or less amount of air and sun, the door which has remained closed and which ought to have been opened, the meeting lost, the somebody whom I ought to have known and whom I have not known,—I should have ever attained to anything.

"I have not the necessary degree of stupidity to become what is absolutely called a *genius*, nor the enormous obstinacy which is afterwards deified under the fine name of 'will,' when the great man has arrived at the radiant mountain-top, and which is indispensable for reaching the latter; I am too well acquainted with the hollowness of all things and the rottenness that is in them, to cling for very long to any one of them and pursue it eagerly and solely through thick and thin.

"Men of genius are very narrow-minded, and it is on this account that they are men of genius. The want of intelligence prevents them from perceiving the obstacles which separate them from the object which they desire to reach; they go, and in two or three strides devour the intermediate spaces. As their minds are obstinately closed to certain courses, and they notice only such things as are the most immediately connected with their projects, they make a much smaller outlay of thought and action. Nothing distracts them, nothing turns them aside, they act rather by instinct than otherwise, and many when taken out of their special groove are mere ciphers in a way that it is difficult to understand.

"The making of good verses is assuredly a rare and charming gift; few people take more pleasure than I do in matters of poetry; but yet I cannot limit and circumscribe my life within the twelve feet of an Alexandrine; there are a thousand things which disquiet me as much as a hemistitch. It is not the condition of society and the reforms that should be made; I care little enough whether the peasants know how to read or not, and whether men eat bread or browse on grass; but a hundred thousand visions pass through my head in an hour which have not the least connection with cæsura or rhyme, and it is this which causes me to execute so little, although I have more ideas than certain poets who might be burnt with their own works.

"I worship beauty and feel it; I can express it as well as the most amorous statuaries can comprehend it, and yet I sculpture nothing. The ugliness and imperfection of the rough sketch revolt me; I cannot wait until, by dint of polishing and repolishing, the work finally succeeds; if I could make up my mind to leave certain things in my work alone, whether in verse or in painting, I might perhaps in the end produce a poem or a picture that would make me famous, and those who love me (if there is anyone in the world who takes the trouble to do so) would not be obliged to believe in me on trust, and would have a triumphant reply to the sardonic sneerings of the detractors of that great but unknown genius—myself.

"I see many men who will take palette and pencils and cover their canvas without any great anxiety concerning what caprice is producing at the extremity of their brush, and others who will write a hundred verses one after another without making an erasure or once raising their eyes to the ceiling. I always admire themselves, even if I sometimes fail to admire their productions; from my heart I envy the charming intrepidity and happy blindness which prevent them from seeing even their most palpable faults. As soon as I have drawn anything wrong I see it at once, and am pre-occupied with it beyond measure; and as I am far more accomplished in theory than in practice, it very often happens that I am unable to correct a mistake of which I am conscious. In that event I turn the canvas with its face to the wall and never go back to it again.

"The idea of perfection is so present with me, that I am instantly seized with distaste for my work and prevented from carrying it on.

"Ah! when I compare its ugly pout on canvas or paper with the soft smiles of my thought, when I see a frightful bat passing in place of the beautiful dream that spread its long wings of light upon the bosom of my nights, when I see a thistle springing up from the idea of a rose, and hear an ass's bray where I looked for the sweetest melodies of the nightingale, I am so horribly disappointed, so angry with myself, so furious at my own impotence that I resolve never again to write or speak a single word of my life rather than thus commit crimes of high treason against my thoughts.

"I cannot even succeed in writing such a letter as I should wish. I often say something quite different; some portions are excessively developed, others dwindle away so as to become imperceptible, while frequently the idea which I intended to express is absent, or present only in a postscript.

"When commencing to write to you I had certainly no intention of telling you one-half of what I have said. I was merely going to inform you that we were about to act a play; but a word leads to a phrase; parentheses are big with other little parentheses which again contain others ready to be brought forth. There is no reason why such writing should come to an end, and should not extend to two hundred folio volumes,—which would assuredly be too much.

"As soon as I take up my pen a buzzing and a rustling of wings begin in my brain as though multitudes of cockchafers were set free within it. There is a knocking against the sides of my skull, a turning, ascending and descending with horrible noise; it is my thoughts which are fain to fly away, and are seeking for an outlet; they all endeavour to come forth at once; more than one breaks its legs and tears the crape of its wing in the attempt: sometimes the door is so blocked up that not one can cross the threshold and reach the paper.

"Such is my nature. Not an excellent one doubtless, but what can I do? The fault rests with the gods and not with me, poor helpless devil that I am. I have no need to entreat your indulgence, my dear Silvio; I have it beforehand, and you are so kind as to read my illegible scrawlings, my headless and tailless dreamings, through to the end. However unconnected and absurd they may be they have always interest for you because they come from me, and anything that is myself, even if it be not good, is not altogether without value in your eyes.

"I may let you see what is most revolting to the generality of men—sincere pride. But a truce for a while to all these fine things, and since I am writing to you about the piece that we are to perform, let us return to it and say something about it.

"The rehearsal took place to-day. I was never so confused in my life, not owing to the embarrassment inseparable from reciting anything before so many people, but from another cause. We were in costume and ready to begin; Théodore alone had not yet arrived. A message was sent to his room to know what was keeping him; he replied that he was just ready and was coming down.

"He came in fact. I heard his step in the corridor long before he appeared, and yet no one in the world has a lighter step than Théodore; but the sympathy which I feel with him is so powerful that I can in a measure divine his movements through the walls, and, when I knew that he was about to lay his hand on the handle of the door, I was seized with a kind of trembling, and my heart beat with horrible violence. It seemed to me that something of importance in my life was about to be decided, and that I had reached a solemn and long-expected moment.

"The door opened slowly and closed in the same way.

"There was a general cry of admiration. The men applauded, and the women grew scarlet. Rosette alone became extremely pale and leaned against the wall, as though a sudden revelation were passing through her brain. She made in a contrary direction, the same movement as I did. I always suspected her of loving Théodore.

"No doubt she at that moment believed as I did that the pretended Rosalind was really nothing less than a young and beautiful woman, and the frail card-castle of her hope all at once gave way, while mine rose upon its ruins; at least this is what I thought: I may, perhaps, be mistaken, for I was scarcely in a condition to make accurate observations.

"There were three or four pretty women present, without counting Rosette; they appeared to be revoltingly ugly. By the side of this sun the star of their beauty was suddenly eclipsed, and everyone was asking how it had been possible to think them even passable. Men who previously would have esteemed themselves most fortunate to have them as mistresses, would scarcely have been willing to take them as servants.

"The image which, till then, had shown itself only feebly and with vague outlines, the phantom that I had worshipped and vainly pursued was there before my eyes, living, palpable, no longer in twilight and vapour, but bathed in floods of white light; not in a vain disguise, but in its real costume; no longer in the derisive form of a young man, but with the features of the most charming woman.

"I experienced a sensation of enormous comfort, as though a mountain or two had been lifted off my breast. I felt my self-horror vanishing, and was released from the pain of regarding myself as a monster. I came again to conceive quite a pastoral opinion of myself, and all the violets of spring bloomed once more in my heart.

"He, or rather she (for I wish henceforth to forget that I had the

195

stupidity to take her for a man) remained motionless for a minute on the threshold of the room, as though to give the gathering time to utter its first exclamation. A bright ray lit her up from head to foot, and on the dark back-ground of the corridor which receded far into the distance behind, the carved door case serving her as a frame, she shone as though the light had emanated from her instead of being merely reflected, and she might rather have been taken for a marvellous production of the brush than for a human creature made of flesh and bone.

"Her long, brown hair, intermingled with strings of great pearls, fell in natural ringlets along her lovely cheeks! her shoulders and breast were uncovered, and I had never seen any in the world so beautiful; the sublimest marble cannot come near to such exquisite perfection. To see the life coursing beneath the clouded transparency! how white and yet so ruddy the flesh! how happily the harmonious golden tints effect the transition from skin to hair! what entrancing poems in the soft undulations of these outlines, more supple and velvety than the neck of a swan! Were there words to express what I feel I would give you a description fifty pages long; but languages were made by some scoundrels or other who had never gazed attentively on a woman's back or bosom, and we do not possess half of the most indispensable terms.

"I decidedly believe that I must become a sculptor, for to see such beauty and to be unable to express it in one way or another is sufficient to make a man furious and mad. I have made twenty sonnets to these shoulders but that is not enough: I should like something which I could touch with my finger and which would be exactly like; verses express only the phantom of beauty and not beauty itself. The painter attains to a more accurate semblance, but it is only a semblance. Sculpture has all the reality that anything completely false can possess; it has a multiple aspect, casts a shadow and may be touched. Your sculptured differs from your veritable mistress only in this that she is a little harder and does not speak—two very trifling defects!

"Her dress was made of a stuff of varying colour, azure in the light, and golden in the shade; a well and close fitting boot was on a foot which, apart from this, was excessively small, and stockings of scarlet silk wound amorously round a most shapely and enticing leg; her arms which were bare to the elbows and emerged from a cluster of lace, were round, plump, and white, as splendid as polished silver, and with unimaginably delicate lineaments; her hands, which were laden with jewellery, were softly swaying a large fan of singularly variegated feathers, which looked like a little pocket rainbow.

"She advanced into the room, her cheeks slightly kindled with a red which was not paint, and everyone was in raptures, crying out and asking whether it was really possible that it could be he, Théodore de Sérannes, the daring rider, the demon duellist, the determined hunter, and whether he was perfectly sure that it was not his twin sister.

197

"But you would think that he had never worn any other costume in his life! His movements are not in the least embarrassed; he walks very well, and does not get entangled in his train; he ogles and flirts with his fan in a ravishing manner! and his waist is so slender! you might enclose it with your fingers! It is extraordinary, inconceivable! the illusion is as complete as it can be: you would almost think that he had a bosom, his breast is so developed and well filled, and then not a hair on his face, not a single one; and his voice so sweet! Oh! the beautiful Rosalind! and who would not wish to be her Orlando?

"Yes, who would not wish to be the Orlando of such a Rosalind, even at the cost of the torments I have suffered? To love as I did with a monstrous love which could not be confessed and yet which could not be uprooted from your heart; to be condemned to keep the profoundest silence, and to shrink from indulging in what the most discreet and respectful lover might fearlessly say to the most prudish and severe of women; to feel yourself devoured by insane longings without excuse even in the eyes of the most abandoned libertines; what are ordinary passions to such a one as that, a passion ashamed of itself and hopeless, whose improbable success would be a crime and would cause you to die of shame? To be reduced to wish for failure, to dread favourable chances and opportunities, and to avoid them as another would seek them—such was my fate.

"The deepest discouragement had taken possession of me; I looked upon myself with horror, mingled with surprise and curiosity. What was most revolting to me was the thought that I had never loved before, and that this was my first effervescence of youth, the first Easter-daisy in the springtide of my love.

"This monstrosity took the place with me of the fresh and chaste illusions of early years; my fondly cherished dreams of tenderness at evening on the skirts of the woods, down the little reddening paths, or along the white marble terraces, near the sheet of water in the park, were then to be metamorphosed into this perfidious sphinx with doubtful smile and ambiguous voice, and before which I stood without venturing to undertake the solution of the enigma! To interpret it wrongly would have caused my death; for, alas! it is the only tie which unites me to the world; when it is broken, all will be over. Take from me this spark and I shall be more gloomy and inanimate than the band-swathed mummy of the most ancient Pharaoh.

"On the occasions when I felt myself most forcibly drawn toward Théodore, I would throw myself back with dismay into the arms of Rosette, although she was infinitely displeasing to me; I tried to interpose her like a barrier and shield between myself and him, and I felt secret satisfaction when lying beside her in thinking that she had been proved to be a woman, and that although I had ceased to love, I was still loved by her sufficiently well to prevent our union from degenerating into intrigue and debauch.

"Nevertheless, at the bottom of my heart, I felt through all this a kind of regret at being thus faithless to the idea of my impossible passion; I felt resentful against myself for, as it were, an act of treason, and, though I well knew that I should never possess the object of my love, I was discontented with myself, and resumed my coldness towards Rosette.

"The rehearsal was much better than I had hoped for; Théodore especially proved admirable; it was also considered that I acted uncommonly well. This, however, was not because I possess the qualities necessary to make a good actor, and it would be a great mistake to suppose me capable of taking other parts in the same fashion; but, through rather a singular chance, the words which I had to utter agreed with my situation so well, that they seemed to me to have been invented by myself rather than learnt by heart from a book. Had my memory failed me at certain passages, I should certainly not have hesitated for a minute before supplying the void with an improvised phrase. Orlando was I, at least, as much as I was Orlando; it would be impossible to meet with a more wonderful coincidence.

"In the wrestling scene, when Théodore unfastened the chain from his neck and presented it to me, in accordance with his part, he cast upon me so sweetly languorous and promising a look, and uttered the sentence:

>*'Gentleman,*
>*Wear this for me, one out of suits with fortune*
>*That could give more but that her hand lacks means.'*

with such grace and nobility, that I was really troubled by it and could scarcely go on:

>*'What passion hangs these weights upon my tongue?*
>*I cannot speak to her, yet she urged conference.*
>*O poor Orlando!'*

"In the third act Rosalind, dressed like a man and under the name of Ganymede, reappears with her cousin, Celia, who has changed her name to Aliena.

"This made a disagreeable impression upon me. I had already become so well accustomed to the feminine costume which indulged my desires with some hopes, and kept me in a perfidious but seducing error! We very soon come to look upon our wishes as realities on the testimony of the most fleeting appearances, and I became quite gloomy when Théodore reappeared in his man's dress, more gloomy than I had been before; for joy only serves to make us feel grief more keenly; the sun strives only to give us a better understanding of the horror of darkness, and the gaiety of white is only intended to give relief to all the sadness of black.

"His coat was the most gallant and coquettish in the world, of an elegant and capricious cut, all adorned with trimmings and ribbons, nearly in the style of the wits of the court of Louis XIII; a pointed felt hat with a long curled feather shaded the ringlets of his beautiful hair, and the lower part of his travelling cloak was raised by a long damaskeened sword.

"Yet he was dressed in such a way as to give one a presentiment that these manly clothes had a feminine lining; a breadth of hip, a fullness of bosom, and a sort of undulation never seen in cloth on the body of a man, left but slight doubts respecting the person's sex.

"He had a half deliberate, half timid manner which was most diverting, and, with infinite art, he assumed as embarrassed an appearance in a costume which was his usual one, as he had seemed to be at ease in garments which were not his own.

"My serenity returned to some extent, and I persuaded myself afresh that it was really a woman. I recovered sufficient composure to play my part in a fitting manner.

"Do you know this piece? Perhaps not. For the last fortnight I have done nothing but read it and declaim it, I know it entirely by heart, and I cannot imagine that everybody is not as conversant with its knot and plot as I am myself. I fall commonly enough into the error of believing that when I am drunk all creation is fuddled and incapable, and if I knew Hebrew I would to a certainty ask my servant in Hebrew for my dressing-gown and slippers, and be very much astonished that he did not understand me. You will read it if you wish; I shall assume that you have read it and only touch upon such passages as have some bearing upon my situation.

"Rosalind, when walking in the forest with her cousin, is greatly astonished to find that instead of blackberries and sloes the bushes bear madrigals in her praise: strange fruits which fortunately do not grow on brambles as a rule; for when you are thirsty it is better to find good blackberries on the branches than bad sonnets. She is very anxious to know who has spoiled the bark of the young trees in this way by cutting the letters of her name upon it. Celia, who has already encountered Orlando, tells her, after many entreaties, that the rhymer is none other than the young man who vanquished the Duke's athlete Charles, in the wrestling match.

"Soon Orlando himself appears, and Rosalind enters into conversation with him by asking him what o'clock it is. Certes, this opening is simple in the extreme; nothing in the world could be more homely. But be not afraid: from this commonplace and vulgar phrase you will see gathered in a harvest of unexpected conceits, full of flowers and whimsical comparisons as from the most vigorous and best manured soil.

"After some lines of sparkling dialogue, whose every word, falling on the phrase, causes millions of sportive spangles to fly right and left like a hammer on a red-hot iron bar, Rosalind asks Orlando whether peradventure he may know the man who hangs odes on hawthorns and elegies on brambles, and who seems to have the quotidian of love upon him, an ill which she is quite able to cure. Orlando confesses that it is he that is so tormented by love, and asks her to do him the favour of showing him a remedy for this sickness, seeing that she has boasted of having several infallible ones for its cure. 'You in love?' replies Rosalind; 'you have none of the marks whereby a lover may be known; you have neither a lean cheek nor a blue and sunken eye; your hose is not ungartered, nor your sleeve unbuttoned, and your shoe is most gracefully tied; if you are in love with anyone it is assuredly with yourself, and you need not my remedies.'

"It was not without genuine emotion that I replied textually as follows:

" 'Fair youth, I would I could make thee believe I love.'

"This answer so unexpected and strange, which is led up to by nothing, and had seemingly been written expressly for me as though by a species of provision on the part of the poet, greatly affected me as I uttered it standing before Théodore, whose divine lips were still slightly swelled with the ironic expression of the phrase that he had just spoken, while his eyes smiled with inexpressible sweetness, and a bright ray of kindness gilded all the loftiness of his young and beautiful countenance.

" 'Me believe it! You may as soon make her that you love believe it; which I warrant she is apter to do, than to confess she does; that is one of the points in the which women still give the lie to their consciences. But, in good sooth, are you he that hangs these fair praises of Rosalind on the trees, and have you truly need of a remedy for your madness?'

"When she is quite satisfied that it is he, Orlando, and none other, who has rhymed these admirable verses going on so many feet, beautiful Rosalind consents to tell him her recipe. Its composition was as follows:—She pretended to be the beloved of the love-sick suitor, who was obliged to woo her as though she had been his very mistress, and to cure him of his passion she indulged in the most extravagant caprices; would now weep and then smile; one day entertain him, another forswear him; would scratch him and spit in his face, and not for a single moment be like herself: fantastical, inconstant, prudish, and languishing, she was all these in turns and the poor wretch had to endure or execute all the unruly fancies engendered by weariness, vapours, and the blues in the hollow head of a frivolous woman. A goblin, an ape, and an attorney all in one had not devised more maliciousness. This miraculous treatment had not failed to produce its effect; the sick one was driven from his mad humour of love into a living humour of madness—which was to forswear the full stream of the world and to live in a nook truly monastic; a most satisfactory result, and one, too, which might easily be expected.

"Orlando, as may well be believed, is not very anxious to recover his health by such means; but Rosalind insists and is desirous of undertaking the cure. She uttered the sentence: 'I would cure you if you would but call me Rosalind, and come every day to my cote and woo me,' with so marked and visible an intention, and casting on me so strange a look, that I found it impossible not to give it a wider meaning than belongs to the words, nor see in it an indirect admonition to declare my true feelings. And when Orlando replies: 'With all my heart, good youth,' it was in a still more significant manner, and with a sort of spite at failing to make herself understood, that she uttered the reply: 'Nay, you must call me Rosalind.'

"Perhaps I was mistaken and thought I saw what had really no existence, but it seemed to me that Théodore had perceived my love, though I had most certainly never spoken a word of it to him, and that he was alluding, through the veil of these borrowed expressions, beneath this theatrical mask and in these hermaphrodite words to his real sex and to our mutual situation. It is quite impossible that so spiritual and refined a woman as she is should not have distinguished, from the very beginning, what was passing in my soul. In the absence of my words, my eyes and troubled air spoke plainly enough, and the veil of ardent friendship which I had cast over my love, was not so impenetrable that it could not be easily pierced by an attentive and interested observer. The most innocent and inexperienced girl would not have been checked by it for a moment.

"Some important reason, and one that I cannot discover, doubtless compels the fair one to this cursed disguise, which has been the cause of all my torments and was nearly making a strange lover of me: but for this, everything would have gone evenly and easily like a carriage with well-greased wheels on a level and finely sanded road; I might have abandoned myself with sweet security to the most amorously vagrant dreamings, and taken in my hands the little white silky hand of my divinity without shuddering with horror, or shrinking twenty paces back as though I had touched a red-hot iron, or felt the claws of Beelzebub in person.

"Instead of being in despair and as agitated as a real maniac, of doing my utmost to feel remorse and of grieving because I failed, I should have said to myself every morning, stretching my arms with a sense of duty done and conscience at rest: 'I am in love,' a sentence as agreeable to say to yourself in the morning with your head on a soft pillow, and warm bed-clothes covering you, as any other imaginable sentence of four words,—always excepting this one: 'I have money.'

"After rising I should have placed myself before my glass, and there, looking at myself with a sort of respect, have waxed tender, as I combed my hair, over my poetic paleness, resolving at the same time to turn it to good account and duly make the most of it, for nothing can be viler than to make love with a scarlet phiz; and when you are so unfortunate as to be ruddy and in love, circumstances which may come together, I am of opinion that you should flour your physiognomy daily or renounce refinement and stick to the Margots and Toinons.

"I should then have breakfasted with compunction and gravity in order to nourish this dear body, this precious box of passion, to compose sound, amorous chyle and quick, hot blood for it from the juice of meat and game, and keep it in a condition to afford pleasure to charitable souls.

"Breakfast finished, and while picking my teeth, I should have woven a few heteroclite rhymes after the manner of a sonnet, and all in honour of my mistress; I should have found out a thousand little comparisons, each more unusual than another, and infinitely gallant. In the first quatrain there would have been a dance of suns, and in the

second a minuet of theological virtues; the two tercets would not have been of an inferior style; Helen would have been treated like an inn-servant, and Paris like an idiot; the East would have had nothing to be envied for in the magnificence of metaphor; the last line, especially, would have been particularly admirable and would have contained at least two conceits in a syllable; for a scorpion's venom is in its tail, and the merit of a sonnet is in the last line.

"The sonnet completed and well and duly transcribed on glazed and perfumed paper, I should have left the house a hundred cubits tall, bending my head lest I should knock against the sky and be caught in the clouds (a wise precaution), and should have gone and recited my new production to all my friends and enemies, then to

205

infants at the breast of their nurses, then to the horses and donkeys, then to the walls and trees, just to know the opinion of creation respecting the last product of my vein.

"In social circles I should have spoken with women in a doctoral manner, and maintained sentimental theses in a grave and measured tone of voice, like a man who knows much more than he cares to say concerning the subject in hand, and has not acquired his knowledge from books;—a style which never fails to produce a prodigious effect, and causes all the women in the company who have ceased to mention their age, and the few little girls not invited to dance to turn up the whites of their eyes.

"I might have led the happiest life in the world, treading on the pug-dog's tail without its mistress making too great an outcry, upsetting tables laden with china, and eating the choicest morsel at table without leaving any for the rest of the party. All this would have been excused out of consideration for the well-known absentmindedness of lovers; and as they saw me swallowing up everything with a wild look, everyone would have clasped his hands and said, 'Poor fellow!'

"And then the dreamy, doleful air, the dishevelled hair, the untidy stockings, the slack cravat, the great hanging arms that I should have had! how I should have hastened through the avenues in the park, now swiftly, now slowly, after the fashion of a man whose reason is completely gone! How I should have stared at the moon and made rings in the water with profound tranquillity!

"But the gods have ordained it otherwise.

"I am smitten with a beauty in doublet and boots, with a proud Bradamant who scorns the garments of her sex, and leaves you at times wavering amid the most disquieting perplexities; her features and body are indeed the features and body of a woman, but her mind is unquestionably that of a man.

"My mistress is most proficient with the sword, and might teach the most experienced fencing master's assistant; she has had I do not know how many duels, and has killed or wounded three or four persons; she clears ditches ten feet wide on horseback, and hunts like an old country squire—singular qualities for a mistress! such things never happen except with me.

"I laugh, but I have certainly no cause for doing so, for I never suffered so much, and the last two months seemed to me like two years or rather two centuries. There was an ebb and flow of uncertainties in my head sufficient to stupefy the strongest brain; I was so violently agitated and pulled in all directions, I had such furious transports, such dull atonies, such extravagant hopes and such deep despairs, that I really do not know how it was that I did not die from the pain of it. This idea so occupied and possessed me that I was astonished that it was not seen clearly through my body like a candle in a lantern, and I was in mortal terror lest someone should chance to discover the object of my insane love.

"However, Rosette, being the person most interested in watching the movements of my heart, appeared to perceive nothing; I believe that she was too much engaged in loving Théodore to pay attention to my cooling towards her; otherwise I must be a master of the art of dissimulation, and I am not so conceited as to have this belief. Théodore himself up to that day never showed that he had the faintest suspicion of the condition of my soul, and always spoke to me in a familiar and friendly fashion, as a well-bred young fellow speaks to another of his own age—nothing more. His conversation with me used to turn on all sorts of subjects, arts, poetry, and other similar matters, but never on anything of an intimate and exact nature having reference to himself or to me.

"It may be that the motives compelling him to this disguise have ceased to exist, and that he will soon resume the dress that is suitable for him. This I do not know; the fact remains that Rosalind uttered certain words with peculiar inflexions, and in a very marked manner emphasized all the passages in her part which had an ambiguous meaning and might point in a particular direction.

"In the trysting scene, from the moment when she reproaches Orlando for not coming two hours too soon as would befit a genuine lover instead of two hours too late, until the sorrowful sigh which, fearful at the extent of her passion, she heaves as she throws herself into

Aliena's arms: 'O coz, coz, my pretty little coz, that thou didst know how many fathoms deep I am in love!' she displayed miraculous talent. It was an irresistible blending of tenderness, melancholy, and love; there was a trembling and agitation in her voice, and behind the laugh might be felt the most violent love ready to burst forth; add to this all the piquancy and singularity of the transposition and the novelty of seeing a young man woo a mistress whom he takes for a man, and who has all the appearance of one.

"Expressions which in other situations would have appeared ordinary and common-place, were in ours thrown into peculiar relief, and all the small change of amorous comparisons and protestations in vogue on the stage seemed struck with quite a new stamp; besides, had the thoughts, instead of being rare and charming as they are, been more worn than a judge's robe or the crupper of a hired donkey, the style in which they were delivered would have caused them to be apparently characterized by the most marvellous refinement and best taste in the world.

"I forgot to tell you that Rosette, after declining the part of Rosalind, compliantly undertook the secondary part of Phœbe. Phœbe is a shepherdess in the forest of Arden, loved to distraction by the shepherd Silvius, whom she cannot endure, and whom she overwhelms with constant harshness. Phœbe is as cold as the moon whose name she bears; she has a heart of snow which is not to be melted by the fire of the most burning sighs, but whose icy crust constantly thickens and hardens like diamond; but scarcely had she seen Rosalind in the dress of the handsome page Ganymede, than all this ice dissolves to tears, and the diamond becomes softer than wax.

"The haughty Phœbe who laughed at love, is herself in love, and now suffers the torments which she formerly made others endure. Her pride is humbled so far as to make every advance; she sends poor Silvius to Rosalind with an ardent letter containing the avowal of her passion in most humble and supplicating terms. Rosalind, touched with pity for Silvius, and having, moreover, most excellent reasons for not responding to Phœbe's love, subjects her to the harshest treatment, and mocks her with unparalleled cruelty and animosity.

Nevertheless, Phœbe prefers these outrages to the most delicate and impassioned madrigals from her hapless shepherd; she follows the handsome stranger everywhere, and, by dint of her importunities, extracts the promise,—the most favourable she can obtain,—that if ever he marries a woman, he will most certainly marry her; meanwhile he binds her to treat Silvius well, and not to nurse too flattering a hope.

"Rosette acquitted herself of her part with a sad, fond grace and a tone of mournful resignation which went to the heart; and when Rosalind said to her, 'I would love you if I could,' the tears were on the point of overflowing her eyes, and she found it difficult to restrain them, for Phœbe's history is hers, just as Orlando's is mine, with the difference that everything turns out happily for Orlando, while Phœbe, deceived in her love, is reduced to marrying Silvius, instead of the charming ideal she would fain embrace. Life is ordered thus: that which makes the happiness of one, makes of necessity the misfortune of another. It is very fortunate for me that Théodore is a woman; it is very unfortunate for Rosette that he is not a man; and she now finds herself amid the amorous impossibilities in which I was lately lost.

"At the end of the piece Rosalind lays aside the doublet of the page Ganymede for the garments of her sex, and makes herself known to the duke as his daughter, and to Orlando as his mistress. The god Hymen then arrives with his saffron livery and lawful torches. Three marriages take place—Orlando weds Rosalind, Phœbe Silvius, and the facetious Touchstone the artless Audrey. Then comes the salutation of the epilogue, and the curtain falls.

"We have been very greatly interested and occupied with all this. It was in some measure a play within a play, an invisible drama unknown to the audience, which we acted for ourselves alone, and which, in symbolical words, summed up our entire life, and expressed our most hidden desires. Without Rosalind's singular recipe, I should have become more sick than ever, without even the hope of a distant cure, and should have continued to wander sadly through the crooked paths of the dark forest.

"Nevertheless, I have only a moral certainty; I am without proofs, and I cannot remain any longer in this state of uncertainty; I really must speak to Théodore in a more definite manner. I have gone up to him twenty times with a sentence prepared, and could not manage to utter it. I dare not; I have many opportunities of speaking to him alone, either in the park or in my room, or in his own, for he visits me, and I him, but I let them slip without availing myself of them, although the next moment I feel mortal regret, and fall into horrible passions with myself. I open my mouth, and, in spite of myself, other words take the place of those that I would utter; instead of declaring my love, I enlarge upon the rain or the fine weather, or some other similar stupidity. Yet the season is drawing to a close, and we shall soon return to town; the facilities which here are opened up favourably to my desires will never be met with again. We shall perhaps lose sight of each other, and opposite currents will no doubt carry us away.

"Country freedom is so charming and convenient a thing, the trees, even when they have lost some of their leaves in autumn, afford such delicious shades to the dreamings of incipient love! it is difficult to resist amid the surroundings of beautiful nature! the birds have such languorous songs, the flowers such intoxicating scents, the backs of the hills such golden and silky turf! Solitude inspires you with a thousand voluptuous thoughts, which the whirlwind of the world would have scattered or have caused to fly hither and thither, and the instinctive movement of two beings listening to the beating of their hearts in the silence of the deserted country is to entwine the arms more closely and enfold each other, as though they were indeed the only living creatures in the world.

"I was out walking this morning; the weather was mild and damp, and though the sky gave no glimpse of the smallest lozenge of azure, it was neither dark nor lowering. Two or three tones of pearl-grey, harmoniously blended, bathed it from end to end, and across this vapourous background cottony clouds, like large pieces of wool, passed slowly along; they were being driven by the dying breath of a little breeze, scarcely strong enough to shake the summits of the most restless aspens; flakes of mist were rising among the tall chestnut-trees and marking the course of the river in the distance. When the breeze took breath again, parched and reddened leaves would scatter in agitation and hasten along the path before me like swarms of timid sparrows; then the breath ceasing, they would sink down a few paces' further on—a true image of those natures which seem to be birds flying freely with their wings, but which after all are only leaves withered by the morning frost, the toy and sport of the slighest passing breeze.

"The distance was stumped with vapour and the fringes of the horizon ravelled on the border in such a manner that it was scarcely possible to determine the exact point at which the earth ended and the sky began: a grey which was somewhat more opaque, and a mist which was somewhat more dense, vaguely indicating the separation and the difference of the planes. Through this curtain the willows, with their ashen tops, looked like spectral rather than real trees, and the curves of the hills had a greater resemblance to the undulations of an accumulation of clouds than to the bearings of solid ground. The outlines of objects wavered to the eye, and a species of grey weft of unspeakable fineness, like a spider's web, stretched between the foreground of the landscape and the retreating depths behind; in shaded places the hatchings were much more clearly drawn, displaying the meshes of the network; in the brighter parts this misty thread was imperceptible, and became lost in a diffused light. In the air there was something drowsy, damply warm, and sweetly dull, which strangely predisposed to melancholy.

"As I went along I thought that with me too autumn was come and the radiant summer vanished never to return; the tree of my soul was perhaps stripped even barer than the trees of the forests; only, on the loftiest bough a single green little leaf remained, swaying, and quivering, and full of sadness to see its sisters leave it one by one.

"Remain on the tree, O little leaf the colour of hope, cling to the bough with all the strength of thy ribs and fibres; let not thyself be dismayed by the whistlings of the wind, O good little leaf! for, when thou art gone, who will mark whether I will be a dead or a living tree, and who will restrain the woodman that he cut not my foot with blows of his axe nor make faggots of my boughs? It is not yet the time when trees are bare of leaves, and the sun may yet rid himself of the misty swaddling-clothes which are about him.

"This sight of the dying season impressed me greatly. I thought that time was flying fast, and that I might die without clasping my ideal to my heart.

"As I returned home I formed a resolution. Since I could not make up my mind to speak, I wrote all my destiny on a sheet of paper. Perhaps it is ridiculous to write to some one living in the same house with you, and whom you may see any day at any hour; but I am no longer one to consider what is ridiculous or not.

"I sealed my letter not without trembling and changing colour; then, choosing a time when Théodore was out, I placed it on the middle of his table, and fled with as much agitation as though I had performed the most abominable action in the world."

XII

"I promised you the continuation of my adventures; but I am so lazy about writing, that I really must love you as the apple of my eye, and know that you are more inquisitive than Eve or Psyche, to be able to sit down before a table with a large sheet of white paper which is to be turned quite black, and an ink-bottle deeper than the sea, whose every drop must turn into thoughts, or something like them, without coming to the sudden resolution of mounting on horse-back and going at full speed over the eighty enormous leagues which separate us, to tell you *viva-voce* what I am going to scrawl to you

in imperceptible lines, so that I may not be frightened myself at the prodigious volume of my Picaresque odyssey.

"Eighty leagues! to think that there is all this space between me and the person whom I love best in the world! I have a great mind to tear up my letter and have my horse saddled. But I forgot; in the dress that I am wearing I could not approach you and resume the familiar life which we used to lead together when we were very ingenuous and innocent little girls. If I ever go back to petticoats, it will certainly be from this motive.

"I left you, I think, at the departure from the inn where I had passed such a comical night, and where my virtue was nearly making shipwreck as it was leaving the harbour. We all set out together, going in the same direction. My companions were in the greatest raptures over the beauty of my horse, which is, in fact, a thoroughbred, and one of the best coursers in existence; this raised me at last half a cubit in their estimation, and they added all my mount's deserts to my own. Nevertheless, they seemed to fear that it was too frisky and spirited for me. I bade them calm their fears, and to show them that there was no danger, made it curvet several times; then I cleared rather a high fence, and set off at a gallop.

"The band tried in vain to follow me; I turned bridle when I was far enough away, and returned at full speed to meet them; when I was close to them I checked my horse as he was launched out on his four feet and stopped him short, which, as you know, or, as you do not know, is a genuine feat of strength.

"From esteem they passed at a bound to the profoundest respect. They had not suspected that a young scholar, who had only just left the university, was so good a horseman as all that. This discovery that they made was of greater service to me than if they had recognised in me every theological and cardinal virtue;—instead of treating me as a youngster they spoke to me with a tone of obsequious familiarity which was very gratifying to me.

"I had not laid aside my pride with my clothes: being no longer a woman, I wished to be in every respect a man, and not to be satisfied with having merely the external appearance of one. I had made up my mind to have as a gentleman the success to which, in the character of a woman, I could no longer pretend. What I was most anxious about was to know how I should proceed in order to possess courage; for courage and skill in bodily exercises are the means by which men find it easiest to establish their reputation. It is not that I am timid for a woman, and I am devoid of the idiotic pusillanimity to be seen in many; but from this to the fierce and heedless brutality which is the glory of men there still remains a wide interval, and my intention was to become a little fire-eater, a hector like men of fashion, so that I might be on a good footing in society and enjoy all the advantages of my metamorphosis.

"But the course of events showed me that nothing was easier, and that the recipe for it was very simple.

"I will not relate to you, after the custom of travellers, that I did so many leagues on such a day, and went from such a place to such another, that the roast at the White Horse or the Iron Cross was raw or burnt, the wine sour, and the bed in which I slept hung with figured or flowered curtains: such details are very important and fitting to be preserved for posterity; but posterity must do without them for once, and you must submit to be ignorant of the number of dishes composing my dinner, and whether I slept well or ill during the course of my travels.

"Nor shall I give you an exact description of the different landscapes, the corn-fields and forests, the various modes of cultivation and the hamlet-laden hills which passed in succession before my eyes: it is easy to imagine them; take a little earth, plant a few trees and some blades of grass in it, daub on a bit of greyish or pale blue sky behind, and you will have a very sufficient idea of the moving background against which our little caravan was to be seen. If, in my first letter, I entered into some details of the kind, pray excuse me, I will not relapse into the same fault again: as I had never gone out before, the least thing seemed to me of enormous importance.

"One of the gentlemen, the sharer of my bed, he whom I had nearly pulled by the sleeve in that memorable night the agonies of which I have described to you at length, conceived a great passion for me, and kept his horse by the side of mine the whole time.

"Except that I would not have accepted him for a lover though he brought me the fairest crown in the world, he was not at all displeasing; he was well-informed, and was not without wit and good-humour: only, when he spoke of women, he did so with an air of contempt and irony, for which I would most willingly have torn both his eyes out of his head, and this the more because, for all its exaggeration, there was a great deal in what he said that was cruelly true, and the justice of which my man's attire compelled me to admit.

"He invited me so pressingly and so often to go with him on a visit to one of his sisters, whose widowhood was nearly over, and who was then living at an old mansion with one of his aunts, that I could not refuse him. I made a few objections for form's sake, for in reality I was as ready to go there as anywhere else, and I could attain my end as well in this fashion as in another; and, as he assured me that he would feel quite offended if I did not give him at least a fortnight, I replied that I was willing, and that the matter was settled.

"At a branching of the road, my companion, pointing to the right stroke of this natural Y, said to me: 'It is down there!' The rest gave us a grasp of the hand and departed in the other direction.

"After a few hours' travelling we reached our destination.

"A moat, which was rather broad, but which was filled with abundant and bushy vegetation instead of with water, separated the park from the high-road; it was lined with freestone, and the angles bristled with gigantic spikes, which looked as if they had grown like natural plants between the disjointed blocks of the wall. A little one-arched bridge crossed this dry channel and gave access to the gateway.

"An avenue of lofty elms, arched like an arbour and cut in the old style, appeared before you first of all; and, after following it for some time, you arrived at a kind of cross-roads.

"The trees looked superannuated rather than old; they appeared to be wearing wigs and white powder; only a little tuft of foliage had been spared to them quite at the top; all the remainder was carefully pruned, so that they might have been taken for huge plumes planted at intervals in the ground.

"After leaving the cross-way, which was covered with fine, carefully-rolled grass, you had then to pass beneath a curious piece of foliage architecture ornamented with fire-pots, pyramids and rustic columns, all wrought with the assistance of shears and hedgebills in an enormous clump of box. In different perspectives to right and left might be seen now a half-ruined rock-work castle, now the moss-eaten staircase of a dried-up waterfall, or perhaps a vase, or a statue of a nymph and shepherd with nose and fingers broken and some pigeons perched on their shoulders and head.

"A large flower-garden, laid out in the French style, stretched before the mansion; all the divisions were traced with box and holly in the most rigorously symmetrical manner; it had quite as much the appearance of a carpet as of a garden: large flowers in ball-dress, with majestic bearing and serene air, like duchesses preparing to dance a minuet, bent their heads slightly to you as you passed; others, apparently less polished, remained stiff and motionless, like dowagers working tapestry. Shrubs of every possible shape, always excepting the natural one, round, square, pointed and triangular, in green and grey boxes, seemed to walk in procession along the great avenue, and lead you by the hand to the foot of the steps.

"A few turrets, half entangled in more recent constructions, rose above the line of the building by the whole height of their slate extinguishers, and their dove-tailed vanes of iron-plate bore witness to a sufficiently honourable antiquity. The windows of the pavilion in the centre all opened upon a common balcony ornamented with a very rich and highly-wrought iron balustrade, and the rest were surrounded with stone facings sculptured in figures and knots.

"Four or five large dogs ran up with open-mouthed barkings and prodigious gambols. They frisked about the horses, jumping up to their noses, and gave a special welcome to my comrade's horse, which probably they often visited in the stable or followed out-of-doors.

"A kind of servant, looking half labourer and half groom, at last appeared at all this noise, and taking our beasts by the bridle led them away. I had not as yet seen a living soul, with the exception of a little peasant-girl, as timid and wild as a deer, who had fled at the sight of us and crouched down in a furrow behind some hemp, although we had called to her over and over again, and done all we could to reassure her.

"No one was to be seen at the windows; you would have thought that the mansion was not inhabited at all, or only by spirits, for not the slightest sound could be heard from without.

"We were beginning to ascend the steps, jingling our spurs, for our legs were rather numb, when we heard a noise inside like the opening and shutting of doors, as if some one were hastening to meet us.

"In fact, a young woman appeared at the top of the steps, cleared the space separating her from my companion at a single bound, and threw herself on his neck. He embraced her most affectionately, and putting his arm round her waist, and almost lifting her up, carried her in this way to the top.

" 'Do you know that you are very amiable and polite for a brother, my dear Alcibiades? It is not at all unnecessary, sir, is it, to apprise you that he is my brother, for he certainly has scarcely the ways of one?' said the young and fair one turning towards me.

"To which I replied that a mistake might possibly be made about it, and that it was in some measure a misfortune to be her brother and be thus excluded from the list of her adorers; and that were this my case, I should become at once the happiest and most miserable cavalier on the earth. This made her smile gently.

"Talking thus we entered a parlour, the walls of which were decorated with high-warped Flanders tapestry. There were large trees, with sharp-pointed leaves, supporting swarms of fantastic birds; the colours, altered by time, showed strange transpositions of tints; the sky was green, the trees royal blue with yellow lights, and in the drapery of the figures the shadow was often of an opposite colour to the ground formed by the material; the flesh resembled wood, and the nymphs walking beneath the faded shades of the forest looked like unswathed mummies; their mouths alone, the purple of which had preserved its primitive tint, smiled with an appearance of life. In the foreground bristled tall plants of singular green, with broad-striped flowers, the pistils of which resembled peacocks' crests. Herons with serious and thoughtful air, their heads sunk between their shoulders, and their long beaks resting on their plump crops, stood philosophically on one of their thin legs in black and stagnant water streaked with tarnished silver threads; through the foliage there were distant glimpses of little mansions with turrets like pepper-boxes and balconies filled with beautiful ladies in grand attire watching processions or hunts pass by.

"Capriciously indented rockeries, with torrents of white wool falling from them, mingled with dappled clouds on the edge of the horizon.

"One of the things that struck me most was a huntress shooting a bird. Her open fingers had just released the string and the arrow was gone; but, as this part of the tapestry happened to be at a corner, the arrow was on the other side of the wall and had described a sharp curve, while the bird was flying on motionless wings, and apparently desirous of gaining a neighbouring branch.

"This arrow, feathered and gold-tipped, always in the air and never reaching the mark, had a most singular effect; it was like a sad and mournful symbol of human destiny, and the more I looked at it, the more I discovered in it mysterious and sinister meanings. There stood the huntress with her foot advanced, her knee bent, and her eye, with its silken lashes, wide open, and no longer able to see the arrow which had deviated from its path. She seemed to be looking anxiously for the mottled-plumed phenicopter which she was desirous of bringing down and expecting to see fall before her pierced through and through. I do not know whether it was a mistake of my imagination, but I thought that the face had as dull and despairing an expression as that of a poet dying without having written the work which he expected to establish his reputation, and seized by the pitiless death-rattle while endeavouring to dictate it.

"I am talking to you at length about this tapestry, certainly at a greater length than the importance of the subject demands; but that fantastic world created by the workers in high warp is a thing which has always strangely preoccupied me.

"I am passionately fond of its imaginary vegetation, the flowers and plants which have no existence in reality, the forests of unknown trees wherein wander unicorns and snowy caprimules and stags with golden crucifixes between their antlers, and commonly pursued by red-bearded hunters in Saracen costume.

"When I was a child, I scarcely ever entered a tapestried chamber without experiencing a kind of shiver, and when there I hardly dared to stir.

"All the figures standing upright against the wall, and deriving a sort of fantastic life from the undulation of the material and the play of light, seemed to me so many spies engaged in watching my actions in order to give an account of them at a proper time and place, and I would not have eaten a stolen apple or cake in their presence.

"How many things would these grave personages have to tell could they open their lips of red thread, and could sounds penetrate into the concha of their embroidered ears! Of how many murders, treasons, infamous adulteries and monstrosities of all kinds are they not silent and impassible witnesses!

"But let us leave the tapestry and return to our story.

" 'Alcibiades, I will have my aunt informed of your arrival.'

" 'Oh! there is no great hurry about that, my dear sister; let us sit down first and talk a little. I have to introduce to you a gentleman, Théodore de Sérannes, who will spend some time here. I have no need to recommend you to give him a hearty welcome; he is himself a sufficient recommendation.' (I am telling you what he said; do not accuse me unreasonably of conceit.)

"The fair one slightly bent her head as though to give assent, and we spoke of something else.

"While conversing, I looked at her minutely, and examined her with more attention than I had found possible until then.

"She was perhaps twenty-three or twenty-four years of age, and her mourning was most becoming to her; truth to tell, she had not a very lugubrious or disconsolate appearance, and I suspect that she would have eaten the ashes of her Mausolus in her soup like rhubarb. I do not know whether she had wept plenteously for her deceased spouse; if so, there was, at all events, little appearance of it, and the pretty cambric handkerchief which she held in her hand was as perfectly dry as it was possible to be.

"Her eyes were not red, but, on the contrary, were the brightest and most brilliant in the world, and you would have sought in vain on her cheeks for the furrow where her tears had flowed; there were in fact only two little dimples hollowed by an habitual smile, and it is right to say that, for a widow, her teeth were very frequently to be seen—certainly not a disagreeable sight, for they were small and very regular. I esteemed her at the very first for not having believed that, because a husband had died, she was obliged to discolour her eyes and give herself a violet nose. I was also grateful to her for not assuming a doleful little air, and for speaking naturally, with her sonorous and silvery voice, without drawling her words and breaking her phrases with virtuous sighs.

"This appeared to me in very good taste; I judged her from the first to be a woman of sense, as indeed she is.

"She was well made, with a very becoming hand and foot; her black costume was arranged with all possible coquettishness, and so gaily that the lugubriousness of the colour completely disappeared, and she might have gone to a ball dressed as she was without any one considering it strange. If ever I marry and become a widow, I shall ask for a pattern of her dress, for it becomes her angelically.

"After some conversation we went up to see the old aunt.

"We found her seated in a large, easy-backed arm-chair, with a little stool under her foot, and beside her an old dog, bleared and sullen, which raised its black muzzle at our arrival, and greeted us with a very unfriendly growl.

"I have never looked at an old woman without horror. My mother died when quite young; no doubt, if I had seen her slowly growing old and seen her features becoming distorted in an imperceptible progression, I should have quietly come to be used to it. In my childhood I was surrounded only by young and smiling faces, so that I have preserved an insurmountable antipathy towards old people. Hence I shuddered when the beautiful widow touched the dowager's yellow forehead with her pure, vermilion lips. It is what I could not undertake to do. I know that I shall be like her when I am sixty years old; but it is all the same, I cannot help it, and I pray God that He may make me die young like my mother.

"Nevertheless, this old woman had retained some simple and

majestic traces of her former beauty which prevented her from falling into that roast-apple ugliness which is the portion of women who have been only pretty or simply fresh; her eyes, though terminating at their corners in claws of wrinkles, and covered with large, soft eyelids, still possessed a few sparks of their early fire, and you could see that in the last reign they must have darted dazzling lightnings of passion. Her thin and delicate nose, somewhat curved like the beak of a bird of prey, gave to her profile a sort of serious grandeur, which was tempered by the indulgent smile of her Austrian lip, painted with carmine, after the fashion of the last century.

"Her costume was old-fashioned without being ridiculous, and was in perfect harmony with her face; for head-dress she had a simple mob-cap, with small lace; her long, thin hands, which you could see had been very beautiful, trembled in mittens without either fingers or thumb; a dress of dead-leaf colour, figured with flowerings of deeper hue, a black mantle and an apron of pigeon's neck paduasoy, completed her attire.

"Old women should always dress in this way, and have sufficient respect for their approaching death not to harness themselves with feathers, garlands of flowers, bright-coloured ribbons, and a thousand baubles which are becoming only to extreme youth. It is vain for them to make advances to life, life will have no more of them; with the expenses to which they put themselves, they are like superannuated courtesans who plaster themselves with red and white, and are spurned on the pavement by drunken muleteers with kicks and insults.

"The old lady received us with that exquisite ease and politeness which is the gift of those who belonged to the old court, and the secret of which seemingly is being lost from day to day, like so many other excellent secrets, and with a voice which, broken and tremulous as it was, still possessed great sweetness.

"I appeared to please her greatly, and she looked at me for a very long time with much attention and with apparently deep emotion. A tear formed in the corner of her eye and crept slowly down one of her great wrinkles, wherein it was lost and dried. She begged me to excuse

her and told me that I was very like a son of hers who had been killed in the army.

"Owing to this real or imaginary likeness, the whole time that I stayed at the mansion, I was treated by the worthy dame with extraordinary and quite maternal kindness. I discovered more charms in her than I should have at first believed possible, for the greatest pleasure that elderly people can give me is never to speak to me, and to go away when I arrive.

"I shall not give you a detailed account of my daily doings at R——. If I have been somewhat diffused through all this commencement, and have sketched you these two or three physiognomies of persons or places with some care, it is because some very singular though very natural things befell me there, things which I ought to have foreseen when assuming the dress of a man.

"My natural levity caused me to be guilty of an indiscretion of which I cruelly repent, for it has filled a good and beautiful soul with a perturbation which I cannot allay without discovering what I am and compromising myself seriously.

"In order to appear perfectly like a man, and to divert myself a little, I thought that I could not do better than woo my friend's sister. It appeared very funny to me to throw myself on all fours when she dropped her glove and restore it to her with profound obeisances, to bend over the back of her easy-chair with an adorably languorous little air, and to drop a thousand and one of the most charming madrigals into the hollow of her ear. As soon as she wished to pass from one room to another I would gracefully offer her my hand; if she mounted on horseback I held the stirrup, and when walking I was always by her side; in the evening I read to her and sang with her; in brief, I performed all the duties of a 'cavaliere servente' with scrupulous exactness.

"I pretended everything that I had seen lovers do, which amused me and made me laugh like the true madcap that I am, when I was alone in my room, and reflected on all the impertinent things I had just uttered in the most serious tone in the world.

"Alcibiades and the old marchioness appeared to view this intimacy with pleasure and very often left us together. I sometimes regretted that I was not really a man, that I might have profited better by it; had I been one, the matter would have been in my own hands, for our charming widow seemed to have totally forgotten the deceased, or, if she did remember him, she would willingly have been faithless to his memory.

"After beginning in this fashion I could not honourably draw back again, and it was very difficult to effect a retreat with arms and baggage; yet I could not go beyond a certain limit, nor had I much knowledge of how to be amiable except in words: I hoped to be able to reach in this way the end of the month which I was to spend at R—— and then to retire, promising to return, but without the intention of doing so. I thought that at my departure the fair one would console herself, and seeing me no more would soon forget me.

"But in my sport I had aroused a serious passion, and things turned out differently—an illustration of a long well-drawn truth, namely, that you should never play either with fire or with love.

"Before seeing me, Rosette knew nothing of love. Married very young to a man much older than herself, she had been unable to feel for him anything more than a sort of filial friendship; no doubt she had been courted, but, extraordinary as it may appear, she had not had a lover: either the gallants who had paid her attention were sorry seducers, or, what is more likely, her hour had not yet struck. Country squires and lordlings, always talking of fumets and leashes, hog-steers and antlers, morts and stags of ten, and mingling the whole with almanac charades and madrigals mouldy with age, were certainly little adapted to suit her, and her virtue had not to struggle much to resist them.

"Besides, the natural gaiety and liveliness of her disposition were a sufficient defence to her against love, that soft passion which has such a hold upon the pensive and melancholy; the idea which her old Tithonus had been able to give her of voluptuousness must have been a very indifferent one not to cause her to be greatly tempted to make still further trials, and she was placidly enjoying the pleasure of being a widow so soon and having still so many years in which to be beautiful.

"But on my arrival everything was quite changed. I at first believed that if I had kept within the narrow limits of cold and scrupulous politeness towards her, she would not have taken much notice of me; but, in truth, the sequel obliged me to admit that it would have been just the same, neither more nor less, and that though my supposition was a very modest, it was a purely gratuitous one. Alas! nothing can turn aside the fatal ascendant, and no one can escape the good or evil influence of his star.

"Rosette's destiny was to love only once in her lifetime, and with an impossible love; she must fulfil it, and she will fulfil it.

"I have been loved, O Graciosa! and it is a sweet thing, though it was only by a woman, and though there was an element of pain in such an irregular love which cannot belong to the other;—oh! a very sweet thing! When you awake in the night and rise upon your elbow and say to yourself: 'Some one is thinking or dreaming of me; some one is occupied with my life; a movement of my eyes or lips makes the joy or the sadness of another creature; a word that I have chanced to let fall is carefully gathered up and commented on and turned over for whole hours; I am the pole to which a restless magnet points, my eye is a heaven, my mouth a paradise more desired than the true one; were I to die, a warm rain of tears would revive my ashes, and my tomb would be more flowery than a marriage gift; were I in danger some one would rush between the sword's point and my breast; everything would be sacrificed for me!'—it is glorious; I do not know what more one can wish for in the world.

"This thought gave me pleasure for which I reproached myself, since I had nothing to give in return for it all, but was in the position of a poor person accepting presents from a rich and generous friend without the hope of ever being able to do the like for him in turn. It charmed me to be adored in this way, and at times I abandoned myself to it with singular complacency. From hearing every one call me 'Sir,' and seeing myself treated as though I were a man, I was insensibly forgetting that I was a woman; my disguise seemed to me my natural dress, and I was forgetting that I had ever worn another; I had ceased to remember that I was after all only a giddy girl who had made a sword of her needle, and cut one of her skirts into a pair of breeches.

"Many men are more womanish than I. I have little of the woman, except her breast, a few rounder lines, and more delicate hands; the skirt is on my hips, and not in my disposition. It often happens that the sex of the soul does not at all correspond with that of the body, and this is a contradiction which cannot fail to produce great disorder. For my own part, for instance, if I had not taken this resolution—mad in appearance, but in reality very wise—and renounced the garments of a sex which is mine only materially and accidentally, I should have been very unhappy: I like horses, fencing, and all violent exercises; I take pleasure in climbing and running about like a youth; it wearies me to remain sitting with my feet close together and my elbows glued to my sides, to cast my eyes modestly down, to speak in a little, soft, honeyed voice, and to pass a bit of wool ten million times through the holes in a canvas; I have not the least liking for obedience, and the expression that I most frequently employ is: 'I will.' Beneath my smooth forehead and silken hair move strong and manly thoughts; all the affected nonsense which chiefly beguiles women has never stirred me to any great degree, and, like Achilles disguised as a young girl, I should be ready to relinquish the mirror for a sword. The only thing that pleases me in women is their beauty; in spite of the inconveniences resulting from it, I would not willingly renounce my form, however ill-assorted it may be with the mind which it contains.

"There was an element of novelty and piquancy in such an intrigue, and I should have been greatly amused by it had it not been taken seriously by poor Rosette. She began to love me most ingenuously and conscientiously, with all the power of her good and beautiful soul—with the love that men do not understand and of which they could not form even a remote conception, tenderly and ardently, as I would wish to be loved, and as I should love, could I meet with the reality of my dream. What a splendid treasure lost, what white transparent pearls, such as divers will never find in the casket of the sea! what sweet breaths, what soft sighs dispersed in air, which might have been gathered by pure and amorous lips!

"Such a passion might have rendered a young man so happy! so many luckless ones, handsome, charming, gifted, full of intellect and heart, have vainly supplicated on their knees insensible and gloomy idols! so many good and tender souls have in despair flung themselves into the arms of courtesans, or have silently died away like lamps in tombs, who might have been rescued from debauchery and death by a sincere love!

"What whimsicality is there in human destiny! and what a jester is chance!

"What so many others had eagerly longed for came to me, to me who did not and could not desire it. A capricious young girl takes a fancy to ramble about the country in man's dress in order to obtain some knowledge as to what she may depend upon in the matter of her future lovers; she goes to bed at an inn with a worthy brother who conducts her with the tip of his finger to his sister, who finds noth-

ing better to do than fall in love with her like a puss, like a dove, like all that is most amorous and languorous in the world. It is very evident that, if I had been a young man and this state of things might have been of some service to me, it would have been quite different, and the lady would have abhorred me. Fortune loves thus to give slippers to those who have wooden legs, and gloves to those who have no hands; the inheritance which might have enabled you to live at your ease usually comes to you on the day of your death.

"Sometimes, though not so often as she would have wished, I visited Rosette at her bedside; usually she received only when she was up, but this rule was overlooked in my favour. Many other things might have been overlooked, had I wished; but, as they say, the most beautiful girl can only give what she has, and what I had would not have been of much use to Rosette.

"She would stretch out her little hand for me to kiss—and I confess that I did not kiss it without pleasure, for it is very smooth, very white, exquisitely scented, and softly tender with incipient moisture; I could feel it quiver and contract beneath my lips, the pressure of which I would maliciously prolong. Then Rosette, quite moved and with a look of entreaty, would turn towards me her long eyes laden with voluptuousness and bathed in humid and transparent light, and let her pretty head, raised a little for my better reception, fall back again upon her pillow. Beneath the clothes I could see the undulations of her restless bosom and the sudden movements of her whole frame. Certainly any one in a condition to venture might have ventured much; he would surely have met with gratitude for his temerity, and thankfulness for having skipped some chapters of the romance.

"I used to remain an hour or two with her, without relinquishing the hand I had replaced on the coverlet; we had charming and interminable talks, for although Rosette was very much preoccupied with her love, she believed herself too sure of success to lose much of her freedom and playfulness of disposition. Only now and then would her passion cast a transparent veil of sweet melancholy upon her gaiety, and this rendered her still more pleasing.

"In fact, it would have been an unheard-of thing that a young beginner, such as I was to all appearance, should not have deemed himself very well off with such good fortune and have profited by it to the best of his ability. Rosette, indeed, was by no means one likely to encounter great cruelties, and not knowing more about me, she counted on her charms and on my youth in default of my love.

"Nevertheless, as the situation was beginning to be prolonged beyond its natural limits, she became uneasy about it, and scarcely could a redoubling of flattering phrases and fine protestations restore her to her former state of unconcern. Two things astonished her in me, and she noticed contradictions in my conduct which she was unable to reconcile: they were my warmth of speech and my coldness of action.

"You know better than any one, my dear Graciosa, that my friendship has all the characteristics of a passion; it is sudden, eager, keen, exclusive, with love even to jealousy, and my friendship for Rosette was almost exactly similar to the friendship I have for you. A mistake might have been caused by less. Rosette was the more completely mistaken about it, because the dress I wore scarcely allowed of her having a different idea.

"As I have never yet loved a man, the excess of my tenderness has, in a measure, found a vent in my friendships with young girls and young women; I have displayed the same transport and exultation in them as I do in everything else, for I find it impossible to be moderate in anything, and especially in what concerns the heart. In my eyes there are only two classes of people—those whom I worship, and those whom I execrate; the others are to me as though they did not exist, and I would urge my horse over them as I would over the highway: they are identical in my mind with pavements and milestones.

"I am naturally expansive, and have very caressing manners. When walking with Rosette, I would sometimes, forgetful of the import of such demonstrations, pass my arm about her person as I used to do when we walked together in the lonely alley at the end of my uncle's garden; or, perhaps, leaning on the back of her easy-chair while she was working embroidery, I would roll the fair down on the plump nape of her neck between my fingers, or with the back of my hand smooth her beautiful hair stretched by the comb and give it additional lustre,—or, perhaps, it would be some other of those endearments which, as you know, I habitually employ with my dear friends.

"She took very good care not to attribute these caresses to mere friendship. Friendship, as it is usually understood, does not go to such heights; but seeing that I went no further, she was inwardly astonished and scarcely knew what to think; she decided thus: that it was excessive timidity on my part, caused by my extreme youth and a lack of experience in love affairs, and that I must be encouraged by all kinds of advances and kindnesses.

"In consequence, she took pains to contrive for me a multitude of opportunities for private conversations in places calculated to embolden me by their solitude and remoteness from all noise and intrusion; she took me for several walks in the great woods, to try whether the voluptuous dreaming and amorous desires with which tender souls are inspired by the thick and kindly shade of the forests might not be turned to her advantage.

"One day, after having made me wander for a long time through a very picturesque park which extended for a great distance behind the mansion, and which was unknown to me with the exception of those parts which were in the neighbourhood of the buildings, she led me, by a little capriciously winding path bordered with elders and hazel trees, to a rustic cot, a kind of charcoal-burner's hut built of billets placed transversely, with a roof of reeds, and a door coarsely made of five or six pieces of roughly-planed wood, the interstices of which were stopped up with mosses and wild plants; quite close, among the green roots of tall ashes with silvery bark, dotted here and there with dark patches, gushed a vigorous spring, which, a few feet further on, fell over two marble steps into a basin filled with cress of more than emerald green.

"At places where there was no cress might be seen fine sand as white as snow; the water had the transparency of crystal and the coldness of ice; issuing suddenly from the ground, and never touched by the faintest sun-ray, beneath those impenetrable shades, it had no time to become warm or troubled. In spite of its crudity I love such spring water, and, seeing it there so limpid, I could not resist a desire to drink of it; I stooped down and took some several times in the hollow of my hand, having no other vessel at my disposal.

"Rosette intimated a wish to drink also of this water to quench her thirst, and requested me to bring her a few drops, for she dared not, she said, stoop down far enough to reach it herself. I plunged both my hands, which I had joined together as accurately as possible, into the clear fountain, then raised them like a cup to Rosette's lips, and kept them thus until she had drained the water contained in them—not a long time, for there was very little, and that little trickled through my fingers, however tightly I closed them; it made a very pretty group, and it is almost a pity that there was no sculptor to take a sketch of it.

"When she had almost finished and my hand was close to her lips, she could not refrain from kissing it, in such a way, however, as to make it look like an act of suction for the purpose of draining the last pearl of water gathered in my palm; but I was not deceived by it, and the charming blush which suddenly overspread her countenance betrayed her plainly enough.

"She took my arm again, and we proceeded towards the cot. The fair one walked as close to me as possible, and when speaking to me leaned over in such a way that her bosom rested entirely on my sleeve —a very cunning position, and one capable of disturbing any one else but me; I could feel its pure firm outline and soft warmth perfectly well—nay, I could even remark a hurried undulating motion which, whether affected or real, was none the less flattering and engaging.

"In this way we reached the door of the cot, which I opened with a kick, and I was certainly not prepared for the sight that met my eyes. I had thought that the hut was carpeted with rushes, with a mat on the floor and a few stools to rest on: not at all.

"It was a boudoir furnished with all imaginable elegance. The frieze panels represented the gallantest scenes in Ovid's Metamorphoses: Salmacis and Hermaphrodite, Venus and Adonis, Apollo and

Daphne, and other mythological loves in bright lilac camaieu; the piers were formed of pompon roses very delicately sculptured, and little daisies, which, with a refinement of luxury, had only their hearts gilded, their leaves being silvered. All the furniture was edged with silver cord which relieved a tapestry of the softest blue that could possibly be found, and one marvellously adapted to set off the whiteness and lustre of the skin; mantelpiece, consoles, and what-nots were laden with a thousand charming curiosities, and there was such a luxurious number of settees, couches and sofas, as pretty clearly showed that this nook was not designed for very austere occupations, and that certainly no maceration went on in it.

"A handsome rock-work clock, standing on a richly-inlaid pedestal, faced a large Venetian mirror, and was repeated in it with singular gleamings and reflections. It had stopped, moreover, as though it would have been something superfluous to mark the hours in a place intended to forget them.

"I told Rosette that this refinement of luxury pleased me, that I thought it in very good taste to conceal the greatest choiceness beneath an appearance of simplicity, and that I greatly approved of a woman having embroidered petticoats and lace-trimmed chemises with an outer covering of simple material; that to the lover whom she had or might have it was a delicate attention for which he could not be sufficiently grateful, and that it was unquestionably better to put a diamond into a nut, than a nut into a golden box.

"To prove to me that she was of my opinion, Rosette raised her dress a little and showed me the edge of a petticoat very richly embroidered with large flowers and leaves; it only rested with myself to be let into the secret of greater internal magnificence; but I did not ask to see whether the splendour of the chemise corresponded with that of the petticoat: it is probable that it was equally luxurious. Rosette let the fold of her dress fall again, vexed at not having shown more.

"Nevertheless, the exhibition had been sufficient to display the beginning of a perfectly turned calf, suggesting the most excellent ascensional ideas. The leg which she held out in order to show off her petticoat to better advantage was indeed miraculously delicate and graceful in its neat well-drawn stocking of pearl-grey silk, and the little heeled shoe, adorned with a tuft of ribbons in which it terminated, was like the glass slipper worn by Cinderella. I paid her very sincere compliments about it, and told her that I had never known a prettier leg or a smaller foot, and that I did not think they could possibly be of a better shape. To which she replied with charming and lively frankness and ingenuousness:

" ' 'Tis true.'

"Then she went to a panel contrived in the wall, took out one or two flagons of liqueurs and some plates of sweetmeats and cakes, placed the whole on a little round table, and came and sat down beside me in a somewhat narrow easy chair, so that, in order not to be very uncomfortable, I was obliged to pass my arm behind her waist. As she had both hands free, and I had just my left to make use of, she filled my glass herself, and put fruits and sweets upon my plate; and soon even, seeing that I was rather awkward, she said to me: 'Come, leave it alone; I am going to feed you, child, since you are not able to eat all by yourself.' Then she herself conveyed the morsels to my mouth, and forced me to swallow them more quickly than I wished, pushing them in with her pretty fingers, just as people do with birds that are being crammed, and laughing very much over it.

"I could scarcely dispense with paying her fingers back the kiss which she had lately given to the palms of my hands, and, as though to prevent me from doing so, but really to enable me to impart a greater pressure to my kiss, she struck my mouth two or three times with the back of her hand.

"She had drunk a few drops of Crème des Barbades, with a glass of Canary, and I about as much. It was certainly not a great deal; but it was sufficient to enliven a couple of women accustomed to drink scarcely anything stronger than water. Rosette leaned backwards, throwing herself across my arm in very amorous fashion. She had cast aside her mantle, and the upper part of her bosom, strained and stretched by this arched position, could be seen; it was enchantingly delicate and transparent in tone, while its shape was one of marvellous daintiness and solidity combined. I contemplated her for some time with indefinable emotion and pleasure, and the reflection occurred to me that men were more favoured in their loves than we, seeing that we gave them possession of the most charming treasures while they had nothing similar to offer us.

"What a pleasure it must be to let their lips wander over this smooth fine skin, and these rounded curves which seem to go out to meet the kiss and challenge it! this satin flesh, these undulating and mutually involving lines, this silky hair so soft to the touch; what exhaustless sources of delicate voluptuousness which we do not possess in common with men! Our caresses can scarcely be other than passive, and yet it is a greater pleasure to give than to receive.

"These are remarks which undoubtedly I should not have made last year, and I might have seen all the bosoms and shoulders in the world without caring whether their shape was good or bad; but, since I have laid aside the dress belonging to my sex and have lived with young men, a feeling which was unknown to me has developed within me: the feeling of beauty. Women are usually denied it, I know not why, for at first sight they would seem better able to judge of it than men; but as they are the possessors of beauty, and self-knowledge is more difficult than that of any other description, it is not surprising that they know nothing at all about it.

"Commonly, if one woman thinks another woman pretty, you may be sure that the latter is very ugly, and that no man will take any notice of her. On the other hand, all women whose beauty and grace are extolled by men are unanimously considered abominable and affected by the whole petticoated tribe; there are cries and clamours without end. If I were what I appear to be, I should be guided in my choice by nothing else, and the disapprobation of women would be a sufficient certificate of beauty for me.

"At present I love and know beauty; the dress I wear separates me from my sex, and takes away from me all species of rivalry; I am able to judge it better than another. I am no longer a woman, but I am not yet a man, and desire will not blind me so far as to make me take puppets for idols; I can see coldly without any prejudice for or against, and my position is as perfectly disinterested as it could possibly be.

"The length and delicacy of the eyelashes, the transparency of the temples, the limpidity of the crystalline, the curvings of the ear, the tone and quality of the hair, the aristocracy of foot and hand, the more or less slender joints of leg and wrist, a thousand things of which I used to take no heed, but which constitute real beauty and prove purity of race, guide me in my estimates, and scarcely admit of a mistake. I believe that if I had said of a woman: 'Indeed, she is not bad,' you might accept her with your eyes shut.

"By a very natural consequence I understand pictures better than I did before, and though I have but a very superficial tincture of the masters, it would be difficult to make me pass a bad work as a good one; I find a deep and singular charm in this study; for, like everything else in the world, beauty, moral or physical, requires to be studied, and cannot be penetrated all at once.

"But let us return to Rosette; the transition from this subject to her is not a difficult one, for they are two ideas which are bound up in each other.

"As I have said, the fair one had thrown herself back across my arm and her head was resting against my shoulder; emotion shaded her beautiful cheeks with a tender rose-colour which was admirably set off by the deep black of a very coquettishly placed little patch; her teeth gleamed through her smile like raindrops in the depths of a poppy, and the humid splendour of her large eyes was still further heightened by her half-drooping lashes; a ray of light caused a thousand metallic lustres to play on her silky clouded hair, some locks of which had escaped and were rolling in ringlets along her plump round neck, and relieving its warm whiteness; a few little downy hairs, more mutinous than the rest, had got loose from the mass, and were twisting themselves in capricious spirals, gilded with singular reflections, and, traversed by the light, assuming all the shades of the prism: you would have thought that they were such golden threads as surround the heads of the virgins in the old pictures. We both kept silence, and

I amused myself with tracing her little azure-blue veins through the nacreous transparency of her temples, and the soft insensible depression of the down at the extremities of her eyebrows.

"The fair one seemed to be inwardly meditating and to be lulling herself in dreams of infinite voluptuousness; her arms hung down along her body as undulating and as soft as loosened scarfs; her head bent back more and more as though the muscles supporting it had been cut or were too feeble for their task. She had gathered up her two little feet beneath her petticoat, and had succeeded in crouching down altogether in the corner of the lounge that I was occupying, in such a way that, although it was a very narrow piece of furniture, there was a large empty space on the other side.

"Her easy, supple body modelled itself on mine like wax, following its external outline with the greatest possible accuracy: water would not have crept into all the sinuosity of line with more exactness. Clinging thus to my side, she suggested the double stroke which painters give their drawings on the side of the shadow, in order to render them more free and full. Only with a woman in love can there be such undulations and entwinings. Ivy and willow are a long way behind.

"The soft warmth of her body penetrated through her garments and mine; a thousand magnetic currents streamed around her; her whole life seemed to have left her altogether and to have entered into me. Every minute she was more languishing, expiring, yielding; a light sweat stood in beads upon her lustrous brow; her eyes grew moist, and two or three times she made as though she would raise her hands to hide them; but half-way her wearied arms fell back upon her knees, and she could not succeed in doing so;—a big tear overflowed from her eyelid and rolled along her burning cheek where it was soon dried.

"My situation was becoming very embarrassing and tolerably ridiculous; I felt that I must look enormously stupid, and this provoked me extremely, although no alternative was in my power. Enterprising conduct was forbidden me, and such was the only kind that would have been suitable. I was too sure of meeting with no resistance to risk it, and I was, in fact, at my wits' end. To pay compliments and repeat madrigals would have been excellent at the beginning, but nothing would have appeared more insipid at the stage that we had reached; to get up and go out would have been unmannerly in the extreme; and besides I am not sure that Rosette would not have played the part of Potiphar's wife and held me by the corner of my cloak.

"I could not have assigned any virtuous motive for my resistance; and then, I confess it to my shame, the scene, equivocal as its nature was for me, was not without a charm which detained me more than it should have done; this ardent desire kindled me with its flame, and I was really sorry to be unable to satisfy it. I even wished to be, as I actually appeared to be, a man, that I might crown this love, and I greatly regretted that Rosette was deceived. My breathing became hurried, I felt blushes rising to my face, and I was little less troubled than my poor lover. The idea of our similitude in sex gradually faded away, leaving behind only a vague idea of pleasure; my gaze grew dim, my lips trembled, and, had Rosette been a man instead of what she was, she would assuredly have made a very easy conquest of me.

"At last, unable to bear it any longer, she got up abruptly with a sort of spasmodic movement, and began to walk about the room with great activity; then she stopped before the mirror and adjusted some locks of her hair which had lost their folds. During this promenade I cut a poor figure, and scarcely knew how to look.

"She stopped before me and appeared to reflect.

"She thought that it was only a desperate timidity that restrained me, and that I was more of a schoolboy than she had thought at first. Beside herself and excited to the last degree of amorous exasperation, she would try one supreme effort and stake all on the result at the risk of losing the game.

"She came up to me, sat down on my knees more quickly than lightning, passed her arms around my neck, crossed her hands behind my head, and clung with her lips to mine in a furious embrace; I felt her half-naked and rebellious bosom bounding against my breast, and her twined fingers twitching in my hair. A shiver ran through my whole body, and my heart beat violently.

"Rosette did not release my mouth; her lips enveloped mine, her teeth struck against my teeth, our breaths were mingled. I drew back for an instant, and turned my head aside two or three times to avoid this kiss; but a resistless attraction made me again advance, and I returned it with nearly as much ardour as she had given it. I scarcely know how it would all have ended had not a loud barking been heard outside the door, together with the sound of scratching feet. The door yielded, and a handsome white greyhound came yelping and gambolling into the cot.

"Rosette rose up suddenly, and with a bound sprang to the end of the room. The handsome white greyhound leaped gleefully and joyously about her, and tried to reach her hands in order to lick them; she was so much agitated that she found great difficulty in arranging her mantle upon her shoulders.

"This greyhound was her brother Alcibiades's favourite dog; it never left him, and whenever it appeared, its master to a certainty was not far off; this is what had so greatly frightened poor Rosette.

"In fact Alcibiades himself entered a minute later, booted and spurred, and whip in hand. 'Ah! there you are,' said he; 'I have been looking for you for an hour past, and I should certainly not have found you had not my good greyhound Snug unearthed you in your hiding place.' And he cast a half-serious, half-playful look upon his sister which made her blush up to the eyes. 'Apparently you must have had very knotty subjects to treat of, to retire into such profound solitude? You were no doubt talking about theology and the twofold nature of the soul?'

" 'Oh! dear no; our occupation was not nearly so sublime; we were eating cakes and talking about the fashions—that is all.'

" 'I don't believe a word of it; you appeared to me to be deep in some sentimental dissertation; but to divert you from your vaporish conversation, I think that it would be a good thing if you came and took a ride with me. I have a new mare that I want to try. You shall ride her as well, Théodore, and we will see what can be made of her.'

"We went out all three together, he giving me his arm, and I giving mine to Rosette. The expressions on our faces were singularly different. Alcibiades looked thoughtful, I quite at ease, and Rosette excessively annoyed.

"Alcibiades had arrived very opportunely for me, but very inopportunely for Rosette, who thus lost, or thought she lost, all the fruits of her skilful attacks and ingenious tactics. No progress had been made; a quarter of an hour later and the devil take me if I know what issue the adventure could have had—I cannot see one that would not have been impossible. Perhaps it might have been better if Alcibiades had not come in at the ticklish moment like a god in his machine: the thing must have ended in one way or another. During the scene I was two or three times on the point of acknowledging who I was to Rosette; but the dread of being thought an adventuress and of seeing my secret revealed kept back the words that were ready to escape from my lips.

"Such a state of things could not last. My departure was the only means of cutting short this bootless intrigue, and accordingly I announced officially at dinner that I should leave the very next day. Rosette, who was sitting beside me, nearly fainted on hearing this piece of news, and let her glass fall. A sudden paleness overspread her beautiful face: she cast on me a mournful and reproachful look which made me nearly as much affected and troubled as she was herself.

"The aunt raised her old wrinkled hands with a movement of painful surprise, and said in her shrill, trembling voice, which was even more tremulous than usual: 'My dear Monsieur Théodore, are you going to leave us in that fashion? That is not right; yesterday you did not seem in the least disposed to go. The post has not come, and so you have received no letters, and are without any motive. You had granted us a fortnight longer, and now you are taking it back; you have really no right to do so: what has been given cannot be taken away again. See how Rosette is looking at you, and how angry she is with you; I warn you that I shall be at least as angry as she is, and look quite as sternly at you, and a stern face at sixty-eight is a little more terrible than one at twenty-three. See to what you are voluntarily exposing yourself: the wrath both of aunt and niece, and all on account of some caprice which has suddenly entered your head at dessert.'

"Alcibiades, giving the table a great blow with his fist, swore that he would barricade the doors of the mansion and hamstring my horse sooner than let me go.

"Rosette cast another look upon me, and one so sad and supplicating that nothing short of the ferocity of a tiger that had been fasting for a week could have failed to be moved by it. I did not withstand it, and though it gave me singular annoyance, I made a solemn promise to stay. Dear Rosette would willingly have fallen on my neck and kissed me on the mouth for this kindness; Alcibiades enclosed my hand in his huge one and shook my arm so violently that he nearly dislocated my shoulder, made my rings oval instead of round, and cut three of my fingers somewhat deeply.

"The old lady, rejoicing, took an immense pinch of snuff.

"Rosette, however, did not completely recover her gaiety; the idea that I might go away and that I wished to do so, an idea which had never yet come clearly before her mind, plunged her deep in thought. The colour which had been chased from her cheeks by the announcement of my departure did not return to them with the same brilliance as before; there still was paleness on her cheek and disquiet in the depths of her soul. My conduct towards her surprised her more and more. After the marked advances which she had made, she could not understand the motives which induced me to put so much restraint into my relations with her; her object was to lead me up to a perfectly decisive engagement before my departure, not doubting that afterwards she would find it extremely easy to keep me as long as she liked.

"In this she was right, and, had I not been a woman, her calculation would have been correct; for, whatever may have been said about the satiety of pleasure and the distaste which commonly follows possession, every man whose heart is at all in the right place, and who is not miserably used up and without resource, feels his love increased by his good fortune, and frequently the best means of retaining a lover who is ready to leave you is to surrender yourself unreservedly to him.

239

"Rosette intended to bring me to something decisive before my departure. Knowing how difficult it is to subsequently take up a *liaison* just where it had been dropped, and being besides not at all sure of finding me again under such favourable circumstances, she neglected no opportunity that presented itself of placing me in a position to speak out clearly and abandon the evasive demeanour behind which I had entrenched myself. As on my part, I had the most formal intention of avoiding every species of meeting similar to that in the rustic pavilion, and yet could not, without being ridiculous, affect much coolness towards Rosette and assume girlish prudery in my relations with her, I scarcely knew how to behave, and tried always to have a third person with us.

"Rosette, on the contrary, did everything in her power to secure being alone with me, and, as the mansion was at a distance from town and seldom visited by the neighbouring nobility, she frequently succeeded in her design. My obtuse resistance saddened and surprised her; there were moments when she had doubts and hesitations about the power of her charms, and, seeing herself so little loved, she was sometimes not far from believing herself ugly. Then she would redouble her attention and coquetry, and although her mourning did not permit her to make use of all the resources of the toilet, she nevertheless knew how to give it grace and variety in such a manner as to be twice or thrice as charming every day—which is saying a great deal. She tried everything: she was playful, melancholy, tender, impassioned, kind, coquettish, and even affected; she put on in succession all those adorable masks which become women so well that it is impossible to say whether they are veritable masks or real faces;— she assumed eight or ten contrasted individualities one after another in order to see which pleased me, and to fix upon it. In herself alone she provided me with a complete seraglio wherein I had only to throw the handkerchief; but she had, of course, no success.

"The failure of all these stratagems threw her into a state of profound stupefaction. She would, indeed, have turned Nestor's brain, and melted the ice of the chaste Hippolytus himself,--and I appeared to be anything but Nestor or Hippolytus. I am young, and I had a lofty and determined air, boldness of speech, and everywhere except in solitary interviews, a resolute countenance.

"She might have thought that all the witches of Thrace and Thessaly had cast their spells upon my person, or that I was at least unmanned, and have formed a most detestable opinion of my virility, which is in fact poor enough. Apparently, however, the idea did not occur to her, and she attributed this singular reserve only to my lack of love for her.

"The days passed away without any advancement of her interests, and she was visibly affected by it: an expression of restless sadness had taken the place of the ever fresh-blooming smile on her lips; the corners of her mouth, so joyously arched, had become sensibly lower, and formed a firm and serious line; a few little veins appeared in a more marked fashion on her tender eyelids; her cheeks, lately so like the peach, had now nothing of it left save its imperceptible velvet down. I often saw her, from her window, crossing the garden in a morning gown; scarcely raising her feet, she would walk as though she were gliding along, both arms loosely crossed upon her breast, her head bent more than a willow-branch dipping into the water, and with something undulating and sinking about her like a drapery which is too long and the edge of which touches the ground. At such moments she looked like one of the amorous women of antiquity, victims to the wrath of Venus, and furiously assailed by the pitiless goddess; it is thus, to my fancy, that Psyche must have been when she had lost Cupid.

"On the days when she did not endeavour to vanquish my coldness and reluctance, her love had a simple and primitive manner which might have charmed me; it was a silent and confiding surrender, a chaste facility of caress, an exhaustless abundance and plenitude of heart, all the treasures of a fine nature poured forth without reserve. She had none of that bitterness and meanness to be seen in nearly all women, even in those that are the best endowed; she sought no disguise, and tranquilly suffered me to see the whole extent of her passion. Her self-love did not revolt for an instant at my failure to respond to so many advances, for pride leaves the heart on the day that love enters it; and if ever anyone was truly loved, I was loved by Rosette.

"She suffered, but without complaint or bitterness, and she attributed the failure of her attempts only to herself. Nevertheless her paleness increased every day; a mighty combat had been waged on the battle-field of her cheeks between the lilies and the roses, and the latter had been decisively routed; it distressed me, but in all truth I was less able than anyone to remedy it. The more gentle and affectionate my words and the more caressing my manner, the more deeply I plunged into her heart the barbed arrow of impossible love. To comfort her to-day I made ready a much greater despair for the future; my remedies poisoned her wound while appearing to soothe it. I repented in a measure of all the agreeable things I had ever said to her, and, owing to my extreme friendship for her, I would fain have discovered the means to make her hate me. Disinterestedness could not be carried further, for such a result would unquestionably have greatly grieved me;—but it would have been better.

"I made two or three attempts to speak harshly to her, but I soon returned to madrigals, for I dread her tears even more than her smile. On such occasions, although the honesty of my intention fully acquitted me in my conscience, I was more touched than I should have been, and felt something not far removed from remorse. A tear can scarcely be dried except by a kiss; the office cannot decently be left to a handkerchief, be it of the finest cambric in the world. I undid what I had done, the tear was quickly forgotten, more quickly than the kiss, and there always ensued an increase of embarrassment for me.

"Rosette, seeing that I am going to escape her, again fastens obstinately and miserably upon the remnants of her hope, and my position is growing more and more complicated. The strange sensation which I experienced in the little hermitage, and the inconceivable confusion into which I was thrown by the ardent caresses of my fair mistress, have been several times renewed though with less violence; and often when seated beside Rosette with her hand in mine, and listening to her speak to me in her soft cooing voice, I fancy that I am a man as she believes me to be, and that it is pure cruelty on my part not to respond to her love.

"One evening, by some chance or other, I happened to be alone with the old lady in the green room;—she had some tapestry work in her hand, for, in spite of her sixty-eight years, she never remained idle, wishing, as she said, to finish before she died a task which she had commenced and at which she had now wrought for a long time. Feeling somewhat fatigued, she laid her work aside and lay back in her large easy chair. She looked at me very attentively, and her grey eyes sparkled through her spectacles with strange vivacity; she passed her hand two or three times across her wrinkled forehead, and appeared to be reflecting deeply. The recollection of times that were no more and that she regretted imparted an expression of emotion to her face. I did not speak lest I should disturb her in her thoughts, and the silence lasted for some minutes. At last she broke it.

" 'They are Henri's—my dear Henri's very eyes; the same humid and brilliant gaze, the same carriage of the head, the same sweet and proud physiognomy; one would think it were he. You cannot imagine the extent of this likeness, Monsieur Théodore; when I see you I cannot believe that Henri is dead; I think that he has only been on a long journey, and has now at last come back. You have given me much pleasure and much pain, Théodore: pleasure by reminding me of my poor Henri, and pain by showing me how great has been my loss; sometimes I have taken you for his phantom. I cannot reconcile myself to the idea that you are going to leave us; it seems to me like losing my Henri once more.'

"I told her that if it were really possible for me to remain longer I should do so with pleasure, but that my stay had already been prolonged far beyond the limits it should have had; besides, I quite expected to return, and I should retain memories of the mansion far too agreeable to forget it so quickly.

" 'However sorry I may be at your departure, Monsieur Théodore,' she resumed, pursuing her own train of thought, 'there is some one here who will feel it more than I. You understand whom I mean without my telling you. I do not know what we shall do with Rosette when you are gone; but this old place is very dull. Alcibiades is always hunting, and for a young girl like her, the society of a poor infirm woman like me is not very diverting.'

" 'If anyone should have regrets, it is not you, madame, nor Rosette, but I; you are losing little, I much, you will easily discover society more charming than mine, but it is more than doubtful whether I shall ever be able to replace Rosette's and yours.'

" 'I do not wish to pick a quarrel with your modesty, my dear sir, but I know what I know, and what I say is fact. It will probably be a long time before we see Madame Rosette in a good humour again, for at present her smiles and tears depend only on you. Her mourning is about to end, and it would be a pity if she laid aside her gaiety with her last black dress; it would be a very bad example, and quite contrary to natural laws. This is a thing which you could prevent without much trouble, and which you will prevent, no doubt,' said the old lady, laying great emphasis on the last words.

" 'Unquestionably I will do all in my power that your dear niece may not lose her charming gaiety, since you suppose me to have such influence over her. Nevertheless, I scarcely see what method I can adopt.'

" 'Oh! really, you scarcely see! What are your handsome eyes for? I did not know that you were so short-sighted. Rosette is free; she has an income of eighty thousand livres wholly under her own control, and women twice as ugly as she is, are often considered pretty. You are young, handsome, and, as I imagine, unmarried; it appears to me to be the simplest thing in the world, unless you have an unsurmountable horror of Rosette, which it is difficult to believe——'

" 'Which is not and could not be the case, for her soul is as excellent as her person, and she is one of those who might be ugly without our noticing it or wishing them otherwise——'

" 'She might be ugly with impunity and she is charming. That is to be doubly in the right; I have no doubt of what you say, but she has taken the wisest course. So far as she is concerned I would willingly answer for it that there are a thousand whom she hates more than you, and that if she were asked several times she would perhaps end by confessing that you do not altogether displease her. You have a ring on your finger which would suit her perfectly, for your hand is nearly as small as hers, and I am almost sure that she would accept it with pleasure.'

"The good lady stopped for a few moments to see what effect her words would produce on me, and I do not know whether she had reason to be satisfied with the expression of my face. I was cruelly embarrassed and did not know what to reply. From the beginning of the conversation I had perceived the tendency of all her insinuations; and, although I almost expected what she had just said, I was quite surprised and confused by it; I could not but refuse; but what valid motives could I give for such a refusal? I had none, except that I was a woman: an excellent motive it is true, but precisely the only one that I was unwilling to state.

"I could hardly fall back upon stern and ridiculous parents; all the parents in the world would have accepted such a union with enthusiasm. Had Rosette not been what she was, good, fair, and well-born, the eighty thousand livres a year would have removed all difficulty. To say that I did not love her would have been neither true nor honourable, for I did really love her very much and more than any woman loves a woman. I was too young to pretend that I was engaged in another quarter. What I thought it best to do was to let it be understood that being a younger son the interests of my house required me to enter the Maltese Order, and did not permit me to think of matrimony, a circumstance which had caused me all the sorrow in the world since I had seen Rosette.

"This reply was not worth much, and I was perfectly sensible of the fact. The old lady was not deceived by it, and did not regard it as definite; she thought that I had spoken in this way to gain time for reflection and for consulting my parents. Indeed, such a union was so advantageous for me, and one so little to be expected, that it would not have been possible for me to refuse it even though I had felt little or no love for Rosette; it was a piece of good fortune that was not to be slighted.

"I do not know whether the aunt made this overture at the instance of her niece, but I am inclined to believe that Rosette had nothing to do with it: she loved me too simply and too eagerly to think of anything else but the immediate possession of me, and marriage would assuredly have been the last of the means that she would have employed. The dowager, who had not failed to remark our intimacy, and doubtless thought it much greater than it was, had contrived the whole of this plan in her head in order to keep me near her, and as far as possible replace her dear son Henri, who had been killed in the army, and to whom, as she considered, I bear so striking a likeness. She had been pleased by this idea and had taken advantage of the moment of solitude to come to an explanation with me. I saw by her mien that she did not look upon herself as beaten, and that she intended to return soon to the charge;—at which I felt extremely annoyed.

"That same night Rosette, on her part, made a last attempt which had such serious results that I must give you a separate account of it, and cannot relate it in this letter which is already swelled to an extravagant size. You will see to what singular adventures I was predestined, and how heaven had cut me out beforehand to be a heroine of romance; I am not quite sure, though, what moral could be drawn from it all,—but existences are not like fables, each chapter has not a rhymed sentence at the end. Very often the meaning of life is that it is not death. That is all. Good-bye, dear, I kiss you on your lovely eyes. You will shortly receive the continuation of my triumphant biography."

XIII

"Théodore,—Rosalind,—for I know not by what name to call you,—I have only just seen you and I am writing to you.—Would that I knew your woman's name! it must be pleasant as honey, and hover sweeter and more harmonious than poetry on the lips! Never could

I have dared to tell you this, and yet I should have died for lack of saying it. What I have suffered no one knows nor can know, nor could I myself give any but a faint idea of it; words will not express such anguish; I should appear to have turned my phrases carefully, to have striven to say new and singular things, and to be indulging in the most extravagant exaggeration when merely depicting what I have experienced with the help of unsatisfying images.

"O Rosalind! I love you, I worship you; why is there not a word more expressive than that! I have never loved, I have never worshipped any one save you; I prostrate myself, I humble myself before you, and I would fain compel all creation to bend the knee before my idol; you are more to me than the whole of nature, more than myself, more than God,—nay, it seems strange to me that God does not descend from heaven to become your slave. Where you are not all is desolate, all is dead, all is dark; you alone people the world for me; you are life, sunshine—you are everything. Your smile makes the day, and your sadness the night; the spheres follow the movements of your body, and the celestial harmonies are guided by you, O my cherished queen! O my glorious and real dream! You are clothed with splendour and swim ceaselessly in radiant effluence.

"I have known you scarcely three months, but I have long loved you. Before seeing you, I languished for love of you; I called you, sought for you, and despaired of ever meeting with you in my path, for I knew that I could never love any other woman. How many times have you appeared to me at the window of the mysterious mansion leaning in melancholy fashion on your elbow in the balcony and casting the petals of some flower to the wind, or else a petulant Amazon on your Turkish horse, whiter than snow, galloping through the dark avenues of the forest! It was indeed your proud and gentle eyes, your diaphanous hands, your beautiful waving hair, and your faint, adorably disdainful smile. Only you were less beautiful, for the most ardent and unbridled imagination, the imagination of a painter and a poet, could not attain to the sublime poetry of this reality.

"There is in you an exhaustless spring of graces, an ever-gushing fountain of irresistible seductions: you are an ever-open casket of most precious pearls, and, in your slightest movements, in your most forgetful gestures, in your most unstudied attitudes, you every moment throw away with royal profusion inestimable treasures of beauty. If the soft waving contour, if the fleeting lines of an attitude could be fixed and preserved in a mirror, the glasses before which you had passed would cause Raphaël's divinest canvases to be despised and be looked upon as tavern sign-boards.

"Every gesture, every pose of your head, every different aspect of your beauty, are graven with a diamond point upon the mirror of my soul, and nothing in the world could efface the deep impression; I know in what place the shadow was, and in what the light, the flat part glistening beneath the ray, and the spot where the wandering reflection was blended with the more softened tints of neck and cheek. I could draw you in your absence; the idea of you is ever placed before me.

"When quite a child I would remain whole hours standing before the old pictures of the masters, and eagerly explore their dark depths. I gazed upon those beautiful faces of saints and goddesses whose flesh, white as ivory or wax, stands out so marvellously against the obscure backgrounds that are carbonised by the decomposition of the colours; I admired the simplicity and magnificence of their shape, the strange grace of their hands and feet, the pride and fine expression of their features which are at once so delicate and firm, the grandeur of the draperies which flutter around their divine forms, and the purplish folds of which seem to extend like lips to kiss those beauteous bodies.

"From obstinately burying my eyes beneath the veil of smoke thickened by ages, my sight grew dim, the outlines of objects lost their precision, and a species of motionless and dead life animated all those pale phantoms of vanished beauties; I ended by finding that these faces had a vague resemblance to the fair unknown whom I worshipped at the bottom of my heart; I sighed as I thought that she whom I was to love was perhaps one of them, and had been dead for three hundred years. This idea often affected me so far as to make me shed tears, and I would indulge in great anger against myself for not having been born in the sixteenth century, when all these fair ones had lived. I thought it unpardonable awkwardness and clumsiness on my part.

"When I grew older the sweet phantom beset me still more closely. I continually saw it between me and the women whom I had for mistresses, smiling with an ironic air and deriding their human beauty with all the perfection of its own which was divine. It caused me to find ugliness in women who really were charming and capable of giving happiness to any one who had not become enamoured of this adorable shadow whose body I did not think existed and which was only the presentiment of your own beauty. O Rosalind! how unhappy have I been on your account, before I knew you! O Théodore! how unhappy I have been on your account, after I knew you! If you will, you can open to me the paradise of my dreams. You are standing on the threshold like a guardian angel wrapped in his wings, and you hold the golden key in your beautiful hands. Say, Rosalind, say, will you?

"I wait for but a word from you to live or to die—will you pronounce it?

"Are you Apollo driven from heaven, or the fair Aphrodite coming forth from the bosom of the sea? where have you left your chariot of gems yoked with its four flaming steeds? what have you done with your nacreous conch and your azure-tailed dolphins? what amorous nymph has blended her body with yours in the midst of a kiss, O handsome youth, more charming than Cyparissus and Adonis, more adorable than all women?

"But you are a woman, and we are no longer in the days of metamorphoses; Adonis and Hermaphrodite are dead, and such a degree of beauty can no longer be attained by man;—for, since heroes and gods have ceased to be, you alone preserve in your marble bodies, as in a Grecian temple, the precious gift of form anathematized by Christ, and show that the earth has no cause to envy heaven; you worthily represent the first divinity of the world, the purest symbolisation of the eternal essence,—beauty.

"As soon as I saw you something was rent within me, a veil fell, a door was opened, I felt myself inwardly flooded by waves of light; I understood that my life was before me, and that I had at last arrived at the decisive crossway. The dark and hidden portions of the half radiant figure which I was seeking to separate from the shadow were suddenly illuminated; the browner tints drowning the background of the picture were softly lighted; a tender roseate gleam crept over the greenish ultramarine of the distance; the trees which had formed only confused silhouettes began to be more clearly defined; the dew-laden flowers dotted with brilliant specks the dull verdure of the turf. I saw the bull-finch with his scarlet breast at the end of an elder bough, the little white pink-eyed straight-eared rabbit putting out his head between two sprays of wild thyme and passing his paw across his nose, and the fearful stag coming to drink at the spring and admire his antlers in the water.

"From the morning when the sun of love rose upon my life everything has been changed; there, where in the shadow used to wander ill-defined forms rendered terrible or monstrous by their uncertainty, groups of flowering trees show themselves with elegance, hills curve in graceful amphitheatres, and silver palaces, their terraces laden with vases and statues, bathe their feet in azure lakes and seem to float between two skies; what in the darkness I took for a gigantic dragon having two wings armed with claws and crawling over the night with its scaly feet, is nothing but a felucca with silken sail, and painted and gilded oars, filled with women and musicians, and that frightful crab which methought was shaking its fangs and claws above my head, is nothing but a fan-palm whose long and narrow leaves were stirred by the nocturnal breeze. My chimeras and my errors have vanished: — I love.

"Despairing of ever finding you I accused my dream of a lie and quarrelled furiously with fate: I told myself that I was altogether mad to seek for such a type, or that nature was very barren and the Creator very unskilful to be unable to realise the simple idea of my heart. Prometheus had the noble pride to desire to make a man and rival God; I had created a woman, and I believed that, as a punishment for my audacity, a never satisfied desire would gnaw my liver like a second vulture; I was expecting to be chained with diamond fetters on a hoary rock at the edge of the savage ocean,—but the fair marine nymphs with their long green hair, raising their white pointed breasts above the waves, and displaying to the sun their nacreous bodies all streaming with the tears of the sea, would not have come and leaned their elbows on the shore to converse with me and console me in my pain as in the play of old Æschylus.

"There has been nothing of all this.

"You came, and I had reason to reproach my imagination with its impotence. My torment was not what I dreaded, to be the perpetual prey of an idea on a sterile rock; but I suffered none the less. I had seen that you did in fact exist, that my presentiments had not been false to me on this point; but you manifested yourself to me with the ambiguous and terrible beauty of the sphinx. Like the mysterious goddess, Isis, you were wrapped in a veil which I dared not raise lest I should be stricken dead.

"If you knew with what panting and restless heed, beneath my apparent inattention, I watched you and followed you even in your slightest movements! Nothing escaped me; how eagerly I gazed upon the little flesh that appeared at your neck or wrist in my endeavour to determine your sex! your hands have been the subject of profound studies by me, and I am able to say that I know their smallest curves, their most imperceptible veins, and their slightest dimple; though you were to conceal yourself from head to foot in the most impenetrable domino, I should recognise you on seeing merely one of your fingers. I analysed the undulations in your walk, the manner in which you placed your feet, and dressed your hair; I sought to discover your secret in the habits of your body. I especially watched you in those hours of indolence when the bones seem to be withdrawn from the body and the limbs sink and bend as though they had lost their stiffness, to see whether the feminine line would be more boldly pronounced amid this forgetfulness and carelessness. Never was anyone eyed so eagerly as you.

"For whole hours I would forget myself in this contemplation. Apart in some corner of the drawing-room, with a book in my hand which I was not reading, or crouched behind the curtain in my room, when you were in yours and your window-blinds were raised, then, penetrated with the marvellous beauty which is diffused about you like a luminous atmosphere, I would say to myself, 'Surely it is a woman;'—then suddenly an abrupt bold movement, a manly accent or an off-hand manner would in a minute destroy my frail edifice of probabilities and throw me back again into my former irresolution.

"I would be voyaging with flowing sails over the limitless ocean of amorous dreaming, and you would come and ask me to fence or play tennis with you; the young girl, transformed into a young cavalier, would give me terrible blows and strike the foil from my hand as quickly and cleverly as the most experienced swashbuckler; at every moment of the day there was some such disappointment.

"I would be about to approach you and say to you, 'My dear fair one, 'tis you that I adore,' and I would see you bending down tenderly to a lady's ear and breathing puffs of madrigals and compliments through her hair. Judge of my situation. Or, perhaps, some woman whom, in my strange jealousy, I could have flayed alive with all the voluptuousness in the world, would hang on your arm, and draw you aside to confide some puerile secrets to you, and would keep you for hours together in an embrasure of the window.

"I was maddened to see women talking to you, for it made me believe that you were a man, and, had you been so, it would have cost me extreme pain to endure it. When men came up in a free and familiar fashion, I was still more jealous, because then I thought that you were a woman and that they had a suspicion of it like myself; I was a prey to the most contrary passions and did not know what conclusion to arrive at.

"I was angry with myself, and addressed the harshest reproaches to myself for being thus tormented by such a love and for not having the strength to uproot from my heart the venomous plant which had sprung up there in a night like a poisonous toad-stool; I cursed you, I called you my evil genius; I even believed for a moment that you were Beelzebub in person, for I could not explain the sensation which I experienced in your presence.

"When I was quite persuaded that you were in fact nothing else but a woman in disguise, the improbability of the motives with which

I sought to justify such a caprice plunged me again into my uncertainty, and I began again to lament that the form which I had dreamed of for the love of my soul belonged to one of the same sex as myself;—I accused chance which had clothed a man with such charming appearance, and, to my everlasting misfortune, had caused me to meet with him just when I had lost the hope of seeing realised the absolute idea of pure beauty which I had cherished in my heart for so long.

"Now, Rosalind, I have the profound certainty that you are the most beautiful of women; I have seen you in the costume of your sex, I have seen your pure and correctly rounded shoulders and arms. The beginning of your bosom, of which your gorget gave a glimpse, could belong only to a young girl: neither the beautiful hunter Meleager, nor the effeminate Bacchus, with their dubious forms, ever had such sweetness of line or such delicacy of skin, even though they be both of Paros marble and polished by the kisses of twenty centuries. I am tormented no longer in this respect. But this is not all: you are a woman, and my love is no longer reprehensible, I may give myself up to it without remorse and abandon myself to the billow which is bearing me towards you; great and unbridled as the passion that I feel may be, it is permitted and I may confess it; but you, Rosalind, for whom I was consumed in silence and who knew not the immensity of my love, you whom this tardy revelation will only, it may be, surprise, do you not hate me, do you love me, can you ever love me? I do not know,—and I tremble, and am yet more unhappy than before.

"There are moments when it seems to me that you do not hate me; when we acted 'As You Like It,' you gave a peculiar accent to certain passages in your part which strengthened their meaning, and, in a measure, invited me to declare myself. I believed that I could see in your eyes and smile gracious promises of indulgence, and could feel your hand respond to the pressure of mine. If I was deceived, O God! it is a thing on which I dare not reflect. Encouraged by all this and impelled by my love, I have written to you, for the dress you wear is ill-suited to such avowals, and my words have a thousand times been stayed upon my lips; even though I had the idea and firm conviction that I was speaking to a woman, that manly costume would startle all my tender loving thoughts and hinder them from taking their flight towards you.

"I beseech you, Rosalind, if you do not yet love me, strive to love me who have loved you in spite of everything, and beneath the veil in which you wrap yourself, no doubt out of pity for us; do not devote the remainder of my life to the most frightful despair and the most gloomy discouragement; think that I have worshipped you ever since the first ray of thought shone into my head, that you were revealed to me beforehand, and that, when I was quite little, you appeared to me in my dreams with a crown of dew-drops, two prismatic wings, and the little blue flower in your hand; that you are the end, the means, and the meaning of life; that without you I am but an empty shadow, and that, if you blow upon the flame that you have kindled, nothing will remain within me but a pinch of dust finer and more impalpable than that which besprinkles the very wings of death. Rosalind, you who have so many recipes to cure the sickness of love, cure me, for I am very sick; play your part to the end, cast aside the dress of the handsome page Ganymede, and stretch out your white hand to the younger son of the brave knight Rowland-de-Bois."

XIV

"*I was* at my window engaged in looking at the stars which were blooming joyously in the gardens of the sky, and inhaling the perfume of the Marvel of Peru wafted to me by an expiring breeze. The wind from the open casement had extinguished my lamp, the last remaining light in the mansion. My thoughts were degenerating into vague dreaming, and a sort of somnolence was beginning to overtake me; nevertheless, whether owing to fascination by the charm of the night, or to carelessness and forgetfulness, I still remained leaning with my elbow on the stone balustrade. Rosette, no longer seeing the light of my lamp and being unable to distinguish me owing to a great corner of shadow which fell just across the window, had no doubt concluded that I was in bed, and it was for this that she was waiting in order to risk a last desperate attempt. She pushed open the door so softly that I did not hear her enter, and was within two steps of me before I had perceived her. She was very much astonished to see me still up; but, soon recovering from her surprise, she came up to me and took hold of my arm calling me twice by my name:—'Théodore, Théodore!'

" 'What! you, Rosette, here, at this hour, quite alone, without a light and so completely undressed!'

"I must tell you that the fair one had nothing on her but a night-mantle of excessively fine cambric, and the triumphant lace-trimmed chemise which I was not willing to see on the day of the famous scene in the little kiosk in the park. Her arms, smooth and cold as marble, were entirely bare, and the linen covering her body was so supple and diaphanous that it allowed the nipples of her breasts to be seen, as in the statues of bathers covered with wet drapery.

" 'Is that a reproach, Théodore, that you are making against me? or is it only a simple, purely exclamatory phrase? Yes, I, Rosette, the fine lady here, in your very room and not in my own where I ought to be, at eleven or perhaps twelve o'clock at night, with neither duenna, chaperon, nor maid, scantily clad, in a mere night-wrapper;—that is very astonishing, is it not? I am as surprised at it as you are, and scarcely know what explanation to give you.'

"As she said this she passed one of her arms around my body, and let herself fall on the foot of my bed in such a way as to draw me along with her.

" 'Rosette,' I said, endeavouring to disengage myself, 'I am going to try to light the lamp again; there is nothing more melancholy than darkness in a room; and then, when you are here, it is really a sin not to see clearly and so lose the sight of your charms. Allow me by a piece of tinder and a match, to make myself a little portable sun to throw into relief all that the jealous night is effacing beneath its shades.'

" 'It's not worth while; I would as soon you did not see my blushes; I can feel my cheeks burning all over, for it is enough to make me die of shame.' She hid her face upon my breast, and for some minutes remained thus as if suffocated by her emotion.

"As for myself, during this interval, I passed my fingers mechanically through the long ringlets of her disordered hair, and searched my brain for some honourable evasion to relieve me of my embarrassment. I could find none, however, for I had been driven into my last entrenchment, and Rosette appeared perfectly determined not to leave the room as she had entered it. Her attire was of a formidable easy nature, which did not promise well. I myself was wearing only an open dressing-gown which would have been a poor protection for my incognito, so that I was extremely anxious about the result of the battle.

" 'Théodore, listen to me,' said Rosette, rising and throwing back her hair from both sides of her face, as far as I could see by the feeble light which the stars and a very slender crescent of the rising moon shed into the room through the still open window;—'the step which I am taking is a strange one;—everyone would blame me for having taken it. But you are leaving soon, and I love you! I cannot let you go in this way without coming to an explanation with you. Perhaps you will never return; perhaps it is the first and the last time that I am to see you. Who knows where you will go? But wherever you go you will carry away my soul and my life with you. If you had remained I should not have been reduced to this extremity. The happiness of looking at you, of listening to you, of living by your side would have been sufficient for me: I would not have asked for anything more. I would have shut up my love within my heart; you would have thought that you had in me only a good and sincere friend;— but that cannot be. You say that it is absolutely necessary that you should leave.

" 'It annoys you, Théodore, to see me clinging thus to your footsteps like a loving shadow which cannot but follow you and would fain blend itself with your body; it must displease you always to find behind you beseeching eyes and hands stretched forth to seize the edge of your cloak. I know it, but I cannot prevent myself from acting thus. Besides, you cannot complain; it is your own fault. I was calm, tranquil, almost happy before knowing you. You arrived handsome, young, smiling, like Phœbus the charming god. You paid me the most assiduous and delicate attentions; never was cavalier more sprightly and gallant. Your lips every moment let fall roses and rubies;—everything served you as an opportunity for a madrigal, and you know how to turn the most insignificant phrases so as to convert them into adorable compliments.

" 'A woman who had hated you mortally at first would have ended by loving you, and I, I loved you from the very moment when first I saw you. Why do you appear so surprised, then, after being so lovable and so well loved? Is it not quite a natural consequence? I am neither mad, nor thoughtless, nor yet a romantic little girl who becomes enamoured of the first sword that she sees. I am well-bred, and I know what life is. What I am doing, every woman, even the most virtuous or most prudish, would equally have done. What was your idea and your intention? to please me, I imagine, for I can suppose no other. How is it, then, that you look sorry, in a measure, for having succeeded so well? Have I, without knowing it, done anything to displease you? I ask your pardon for it. Have you ceased to think me beautiful, or have you discovered some defect in me which repels you?

" 'You have the right of being hard to please in beauty, but either you have strangely lied to me, or else I too am beautiful! I am as young as you, and I love you; why do you now disdain me? You used to be so eager about me, you supported my arm with such constant solicitude, you pressed the hand I surrendered to you so tenderly, you raised such languorous eyes towards me: if you did not love me, what was the use of all this intrigue? Could you perchance have had the cruelty to kindle love in a heart in order to have afterwards a subject for mirth? Ah! that would be horrible mockery, impiety, sacrilege! such could be the amusement only of a frightful soul, and I cannot believe it of you, quite inexplicable as is your behaviour towards me.

257

" 'What, then, is the cause of this sudden change? For my part, I can see none. What mystery is concealed behind such coldness? I cannot believe that you have a repugnance to me; your conduct proves the contrary, for no one woos a woman he dislikes with such eagerness were he the greatest impostor on earth. O Théodore, what have you against me? who has changed you thus? what have I done to you? If the love which you appeared to have for me has taken its flight, mine, alas! has remained, and I cannot uproot it from my heart. Have pity on me, Théodore, for I am very unhappy. At least pretend to love me a little, and say some gentle words to me; it will not cost you much, unless you have an insurmountable horror of me.'

"At this pathetic portion of her discourse, her sobs completely stifled her voice; she crossed both her hands upon my shoulder and laid her forehead upon them in quite a broken-hearted attitude. All that she said was perfectly correct, and I had no good reply to make. I could not assume a bantering tone. It would not have been suitable. Rosette was not one of those creatures who could be treated so lightly: —I was, moreover, too much affected to be able to do it. I felt myself guilty for having trifled in such a manner with the heart of a charming woman, and I experienced the keenest and sincerest remorse in the world.

"Seeing that I made no reply, the dear child heaved a long sigh and made a movement as though to rise, but she fell back again, weighed down by her emotion; then she encircled me in her arms, the freshness of which penetrated my doublet, laid her face upon mine, and began to weep silently.

"It had a singular effect upon me to feel this exhaustless flow of tears, which did not come from my own eyes, streaming in this way down my cheek. It was not long before they were mingled with mine, and there was a veritable bitter rain sufficient to cause a new deluge had it only lasted forty days.

"At that moment the moon happened to shine straight upon the window; a pale ray dipped into the room and illuminated our taciturn group with a bluish light.

"With her white wrapper, her bare arms, her uncovered breast and throat, of nearly the same colour as her linen, her dishevelled hair and her mournful look, Rosette had the appearance of an alabaster figure of Melancholy seated on a tomb. As to myself I scarcely know what appearance I had since I could not see myself, and there was no glass to reflect my image, but I think that I might very well have posed for a statue of Uncertainty personified.

"I was moved, and bestowed a few more tender caresses than usual upon Rosette; from her hair my hand had descended to her velvety neck, and thence to her smooth round shoulder, which I gently stroked, following its quivering line. The child vibrated beneath my touch like a keyboard beneath a musician's fingers; her flesh started and leaped abruptly, and amorous thrillings ran through her body.

"I myself felt a vague and confused species of desire, whose aim I could not discern, and I felt great voluptuousness in going over these pure delicate contours. I left her shoulder, and, profiting by the hiatus of a fold, suddenly closed my hand upon her little frightened breast, which palpitated distractedly like a turtle-dove surprised in its nest;— from the extreme outline of her cheek which I touched with an almost insensible kiss, I reached her half-parted lips, and we remained like this for some time. I do not know, though, whether it was two minutes, or a quarter of an hour, or an hour; for I had totally lost the notion of time, and I did not know whether I was in heaven or on earth, here or elsewhere, living or dead. The heady wine of voluptuousness had so intoxicated me at the first mouthful that I had drunk, that any reason I possessed had left me.

"Rosette clasped me more and more tightly in her arms and covered me with her body;—she leaned convulsively upon me and pressed me to her naked, panting breast; at every kiss her life seemed to rush wholly to the spot that was touched, and desert the rest of her person. Strange ideas passed through my head; had I not dreaded the betrayal of my incognito, I should have given play to Rosette's impassioned bursts, and should, perhaps, have made some vain and mad attempt to impart a semblance of reality to the shadow of pleasure so ardently embraced by my fair mistress; I had not yet had a lover; and these keen attacks, these reiterated caresses, the contact with this beautiful body, and these sweet names lost in kisses, agitated me to the highest degree, although they were those of a woman;—and then the nocturnal visit, the romantic passion, the moonlight, all had a freshness and novel charm for me which made me forget that after all I was not a man.

"Nevertheless, making a great effort over myself, I told Rosette that she was compromising herself horribly by coming into my room at such an hour and remaining in it so long, and that her women might notice her absence and see that she had not passed the night in her own apartment.

"I said this so gently that Rosette only replied by dropping her cambric mantle and her slippers, and by gliding into my bed like a snake into a bowl of milk; for she imagined that this proceeding on her part might lead to more precise demonstrations upon mine.

"She believed, poor child, that the happy hour which had been so laboriously contrived, was at last about to strike for her; but it only struck two in the morning. My situation was as critical as it well could be, when the door turned on its hinges and gave passage to the very Chevalier Alcibiades in person; he held a candlestick in one hand and his sword in the other.

"He went straight to the bed, threw back the curtains, and, in holding the light to the face of the confused Rosette, said to her in a jeering tone—'Good morning, sister.' Little Rosette was unable to find a word in reply.

" 'So it appears, my dearest and most virtuous sister, that having in your wisdom judged that the Seigneur Théodore's bed was softer than your own, you have come to share it? or perhaps it is on account of the ghosts in your room, and you thought that you would be in greater safety in this one under the protection of the said seigneur? 'Tis very well advised. Ah! Chevalier de Sérannes, so you have cast your amorous glance upon my sister, and you think that it will end there. I fancy that it would not be unwholesome to have a little cutting of each other's throats, and if you will be so kind I shall be infinitely obliged to you. Théodore, you have abused the friendship that I had for you, and you make me repent of the good opinion which at the very first I had formed of the integrity of your character: it is bad, very bad.'

"I could not offer any valid defence: appearances were against me. Who would have believed me if I had said, as was indeed the case, that Rosette had come into my room in spite of me, and that, far from seeking to please her, I was doing everything in my power to estrange her from me? I had only one thing to say, and I said it—'Seigneur Alcibiades, there shall be as much throat-cutting as you like.'

"During this colloquy, Rosette had not failed to faint according to the soundest rules of the pathetic;—I went to a crystal cup full of water in which the stem of a large white, half leafless rose was immersed, and threw a few drops over her face, which promptly brought her round again.

"Scarcely knowing what face to put on the matter, she crouched down at the bedside and buried her pretty head beneath the clothes, like a bird settling itself to sleep. She had so gathered the sheets and pillows about her that it would have been very difficult to make out what there was beneath the heap;—only by a few soft sighs issuing from time to time could it have been guessed that it was a young repentant sinner, or at least one extremely sorry at being a sinner in intention only and not in deed,—which was the case with the unfortunate Rosette.

"The brother, having no further anxiety about his sister, resumed the dialogue, and said in a somewhat gentler tone: 'It is not absolutely indispensable to cut each other's throats at once, that is an extreme measure which may be resorted to at any time. Listen:—we are not equally matched. You are in early youth and much less vigorous than I, if we were to fight I should certainly kill you or maim you—and I should not like either to kill or disfigure you—which would be a pity; Rosette, who is over there under the bed-clothes and does not utter a word, would bear me ill-will for it all her life; for she is as spiteful and wicked as a tigress when she sets about it, the dear little dove. You don't know this, you who are her Prince Galaor, and who receive only charming kindnesses from her; but it is no slight matter. Rosette is free and so are you; it appears that you are not irreconcilable enemies;

her widowhood is about to end, and things could not be better. Marry her; she will have no need to return to her own couch, while I shall in this way be freed from the necessity of taking you as a sheath for my sword, which would not be agreeable either for you or for me;—what do you think?'

"I had every reason for making a horrible grimace, for his proposal was of all things in the world the most impracticable for me: I could sooner have walked on all fours on the ceiling, like the flies, or taken down the sun without having a stool to stand on, than do what he asked of me, and yet the last proposition was unquestionably more agreeable than the first.

"He appeared surprised that I did not accept with ecstasy, and he repeated what he had said as if to give me time to reply.

" 'An alliance with you would be a most honourable one for me, and I should never have dared to pretend to it: I know that it would be an unprecedented piece of good fortune for a youth, who, as yet, has neither rank nor standing in the world, and one that the most illustrious would esteem themselves fortunate to obtain;—but yet I can only persist in my refusal, and, since I am free to choose between a duel and marriage, I prefer the duel. 'Tis a singular taste—and few people would have it—but it is mine.'

"Here Rosette gave the most mournful sob in the world, put forth her head from beneath the pillow, and seeing my impassible and determined countenance put it in again like a snail whose horns have been struck.

" 'It is not that I have no love for Madame Rosette, I love her infinitely; but I have reasons for not marrying which you would yourself consider excellent if it were possible for me to tell them to you. Moreover things have not gone so far as appearances might lead one to believe; except a few kisses which a lively friendship is sufficient to explain and to justify, nothing has passed between us that may not be acknowledged, and your sister's virtue is assuredly the most intact and blameless in the world. I owed her this testimony. Now, Seigneur Alcibiades, at what time do we fight, and where?'

" 'Here, at once,' cried Alcibiades, intoxicated with rage.

" 'Can you think of it? before Rosette!'

" 'Draw, villain, or I shall assassinate you,' he continued, brandishing his sword and whirling it around his head.

" 'Let us at least leave the room.'

" 'If you do not put yourself on guard I will pin you to the wall like a bat, my fine Celadon, and though you may flap your wings to eternity, you will not get free, I give you warning.' And he rushed upon me with his weapon raised.

"I drew my rapier,—for he would have done as he had said,—and at first contented myself with parrying his thrusts.

"Rosette made a superhuman effort to come and throw herself between our swords, for both combatants were equally dear to her; but her strength deserted her, and she rolled senseless on to the foot of the bed.

"Our blades gleamed and made a noise like that of an anvil, for want of space obliged us to engage our swords very closely.

"Two or three times Alcibiades nearly reached me, and had I not been an excellent master of fence my life would have been in the greatest danger; for his skill was astonishing and his strength prodigious. He exhausted all the tricks and feints in fencing to touch me. Enraged at his want of success, he exposed himself twice or thrice; I would not take advantage of it; but he returned to the attack with such desperate and savage fury, that I was forced to seize upon the opening that he gave me; moreover, the noise and whirling flashes of the steel intoxicated and dazzled me. I did not think of death and had not the least fear; the keen and mortal point which came before my eyes every second had no more effect upon me than if I were fighting with buttoned foils; only I was indignant at Alcibiades's brutality, and my indignation was still further heightened by the consciousness of my perfect innocence. I wished merely to prick him in the arm or shoulder and so make him drop his sword, for I had vainly tried to disarm him. He had a wrist of iron, and the devil could not have made him move it.

"At last he made a thrust so quick and so long that I could only partially parry it; my sleeve was pierced and I felt the chill of the iron on my arm; but I was not wounded. At sight of this I became angry, and instead of defending myself attacked in turn;—I forgot that he was Rosette's brother and I fell upon him as though he had been my mortal enemy. Taking advantage of a mistake in the position of his sword I made so close a flanconnade that I reached his side, and with an 'Oh!' he fell backwards.

"I thought that he was dead but he was really only wounded, and his fall was occasioned by a false step that he had made while trying to defend himself. I cannot express, Graciosa, the sensation that I experienced; certainly, it is not difficult to make the reflection that if you strike flesh with a fine, sharp point, a hole will be pierced and blood will gush out. Nevertheless I was profoundly stupefied on perceiving red streams trickling over Alcibiades's doublet. I, of course, had not thought sawdust would come out as from a burst doll; but I know that never in my life did I experience such great surprise, and it seemed to me that some unheard-of thing had just happened to me.

"The unheard-of thing was not, as it appeared to me, that blood should flow from a wound, but that the wound should have been given by me, and that a young girl of my age (I was going to write 'a young man,' so well have I entered into the spirit of my part) should have laid low a vigorous captain so well trained in the art of fence as Alcibiades:—and all this, what is more, for the crime of seducing and refusing to marry a very rich and charming woman!

"I was truly in a cruel embarrassment, with the sister in a swoon, the brother, as I believed, dead, and myself nearly swooning or dead like one or other of them. I hung to the bell-rope, chimed loud enough to wake the dead, and, leaving the task of explaining matters to the servants and the old aunt to be performed by the fainting Rosette and the embowelled Alcibiades, went straight to the stable. The air restored me at once; I took out my horse, and saddled and bridled him myself; I ascertained that the crupper was properly fastened and the curb in a right condition; I made the stirrups of equal length, drew the girth a notch tighter:—in a word, I harnessed him with an attention that was at least singular at such a moment, and with a calmness quite inconceivable after a combat terminated in such a way.

"I mounted my beast and crossed the park by a path that I knew.

The branches of the trees all laden with dew, lashed my face and wetted it: you would have thought that the old trees were stretching out their arms to stop me and keep me for the love of their mistress. Had I been in a different mood, or at all superstitious, I might have believed that they were so many phantoms who wished to seize me and were showing me their fists.

"But in reality I had not a single idea either of that kind or of any other; a leaden stupor, so great that I was scarcely conscious of it, weighed upon my brain like too tight a helmet; only it did seem to me that I had killed some one yonder and that it was for this that I was going away. I was, moreover, horribly inclined to sleep, whether owing to the lateness of the hour or to the fact that the emotions of the evening had had a physical reaction and had corporally fatigued me.

"I reached a little postern which opened upon the fields in a secret way which Rosette had shown me in our walks. I dismounted, touched the knob and pushed open the door: I regained my saddle after leading my horse through, and put him to the gallop until I reached the highroad to C——, at which place I arrived at early dawn.

"Such is the very faithful and circumstantial history of my first intrigue and my first duel."

XV

"It was five o'clock in the morning when I entered the town. The houses were beginning to look out of window; the worthy natives were showing their benign countenances surmounted by colossal nightcaps behind the panes. At the sound of my horse's iron-shod hoofs ringing upon the uneven flinty pavement there would emerge from every dormer window the big curiously red countenances and the matutinally uncovered breasts of the local Venuses who lost themselves in conjectures about the unwonted appearance of a traveller at C——, at such an hour and in such an equipment, for my attire was on a very small scale, and my appearance was, at the least, suspicious.

"I got a little rascal, who had his hair over his eyes, and lifted up his spaniel's muzzle in the air that he might consider me more comfortably, to point me out an inn; I gave him a few coppers for his trouble, and a conscientious cut with my riding-whip, which made him flee away screaming like a jay that had been plucked alive. I threw myself upon a bed and fell fast asleep. When I awoke it was three o'clock in the afternoon,—a length of time scarcely sufficient to rest me completely. In fact it was too much for a sleepless night, an intrigue, a duel, and a very rapid though quite victorious flight.

"I was very anxious about the wound that I had given Alcibiades; but some days afterwards I was completely reassured, for I learnt that it had not been attended by dangerous consequences, and that he was quite convalescent. This relieved me of a singular weight, for the idea of having killed a man tormented me strangely although it had been in lawful self-defence, and against my own wish. I had not yet arrived at that sublime indifference towards men's lives to which I afterwards attained.

"At C—— I again came across several of the young fellows with whom we had travelled. This pleased me; I formed a closer connection with them, and they introduced me into several agreeable houses. I had become completely used to my dress, and the ruder and more active life that I had led, and the violent exercises to which I had devoted myself, had made me twice as robust as I had been before. I followed these mad-caps everywhere; I rode, hunted, had orgies with them, for little by little I had come to drink; without attaining to the perfectly German capacity of some among them, I could empty two or three bottles for my share without getting very tipsy, which was very satisfactory progress. I made verses like a god with extreme copiousness, and kissed inn-servants with sufficient boldness.

"In short, I was an accomplished young cavalier in complete conformity with the last fashionable pattern. I got rid of certain countrified notions that I had had about virtue and other similar tarradiddles; on the other hand, I became so prodigiously delicate in point of honour that I fought a duel nearly every day: it even became a necessity with me to do so, a sort of indispensable exercise without which I should have felt out of sorts the whole day. Accordingly, when no one had looked at me or trodden on my foot and I had no motive for fighting, rather than remain idle and not exercise myself in fencing, I would act as second to my comrades or even to men whom I knew only by name.

"I had soon a colossal renown for bravery, and nothing short of it was necessary to check the pleasantries which would infallibly have been suggested by my beardless face and effeminate appearance. But two or three superfluous button-holes that I had opened in some doublets, and a few slices that I very delicately cut from some recalcitrant skins, caused my appearance to be generally considered more manly that that of Mars in person or of Priapus himself, and you might have met with people who would have sworn that they had held bastards of mine over the baptismal font.

"Through all this apparent dissipation, amid this riotous, extravagant life, I ceased not to pursue my original idea, that is to say the conscientious study of man and the solution of the great problem of a perfect lover, a problem somewhat more difficult to solve than that of the philosopher's stone.

"Certain ideas are like the horizon which most certainly exists since you see it in front of you in whatever direction you turn, but which flees obstinately before you, and, whether you go at a foot pace or at a gallop, keeps always at the same distance from you; for it cannot manifest itself except with a determined condition of remoteness; it is destroyed in proportion as you advance, to be formed further away with its fleeting imperceptible azure, and it is in vain that you try to detain it by the hem of its flowing mantle.

"The further I progressed in my knowledge of the animal, the more I saw how utterly impossible was the realisation of my desire, and how completely external to the conditions of its nature was that which I found indispensable to an auspicious love. I convinced myself that the man who would be the most sincerely in love with me would with the greatest readiness in the world find means to make me the most wretched of women, and yet I had already abandoned many of my girlish requirements. I had come down from the sublime clouds, not altogether into the street and the kennel, but upon a hill of medium height, accessible though somewhat steep.

"The ascent, it is true, was rude enough; but I was so proud as to believe that I was quite worth the trouble of the effort, and that I should be a sufficient compensation for the pains that had been taken. I could never have prevailed upon myself to take a step forward; I waited, perched patiently upon my summit.

"My plan was as follows:—In my male attire I should have made the acquaintance of some young man whose exterior pleased me; I should have lived on familiar terms with him; by means of skilful questions and false confidences which would have challenged true ones, I should soon have acquired a complete knowledge of his feelings and thoughts; and, if I found him such a one as I wished him to be, I should have alleged some journey, and kept away from him for three or four months to give him time to forget my features; then I should have returned in my woman's costume, and arranged a voluptuous little house, buried amid trees and flowers, in a retired suburb; then I should have so ordered matters that he would have met me and wooed me; and, if he showed a true and faithful love, I should have given myself to him without restriction or precaution:—the title of his mistress would have appeared honourable to me, and I should not have asked him for any other.

"But assuredly this plan will never be put into execution, for it is characteristic of plans never to be executed, wherein principally appear the frailty of the will and the mere nothingness of man. The proverb 'God wills what woman wills' has no more truth in it than any other proverb, that is to say, it has hardly any at all.

"So long as I had seen men only at a distance and through the medium of my desire, they had appeared comely to me, and my sight had deceived me. Now I consider them frightful in the highest degree, and do not understand how a woman can admit such a creature into her bed; for my part, it would turn my stomach, and I could never bring myself to it.

"How coarse and ignoble are their lineaments, and how devoid of delicacy and elegance! what unfinished and unpleasing lines! what hard, dark, and furrowed skin! Some are as swarthy as men that had been hanged for six months, emaciated, bony, hairy, with violin-strings on their hands, large drawbridge feet, dirty moustaches always full of food and twirled back to the ears, hair as rough as a broom's bristles, chins ending like boars' heads, lips cracked and dried by strong liquors, eyes surrounded by three or four dark orbs, necks full of twisted veins, big muscles and prominent cartilages. Others are stuffed with red meat, and push on before them a belly that their waist-belt can scarcely span; they blink as they open their little sea-green eyes inflamed with luxury, and resemble hippopotamuses in breeches rather than human creatures. They always smell either of wine or brandy, or tobacco, or else of their own natural odour, which is the very worst of all. As to those whose forms are somewhat less disgusting, they are like misshapen women. And that is all.

"I had not remarked all this. I had been in life as in a cloud, and my feet scarcely touched the earth. The odour of the roses and lilacs of spring went to my head like too strong a perfume. I dreamt only of accomplished heroes, faithful and respectful lovers, flames worthy of the altar, marvellous devotions and sacrifices, and I should have thought that I had found them all in the first blackguard that bade me good day. Yet this first, coarse intoxication had no long duration; strange suspicions seized me, and I could have no rest until I had cleared them up.

"At first my horror of men was pushed to the last degree of exaggeration, and I looked upon them as dreadful monstrosities. Their modes of thought, their manners and their carelessly cynical language, their brutality and their scorn of women shocked and revolted me extremely, so little did the idea that I had formed of them correspond with the reality. They are not monsters, if you will, but something, on my word, that is much worse! They are capital fellows of very jovial disposition, who eat and drink well, will do you all kinds of services, are good painters and musicians, and are suitable for a thousand things, with, however, the single exception of that one for which they were created, namely, to be the male of the animal called woman, with which they have not the slightest affinity, physical or moral.

"Originally, I could scarcely disguise the contempt with which they inspired me, but by degrees I became accustomed to their manner of life. I was as little annoyed by the jests that they launched against women as if I had myself belonged to their own sex. On the contrary, I made some very good ones, the success of which singularly flattered my pride; certainly none of my comrades went so far as I did in the matter of sarcasm and pleasantries on this subject. My perfect knowledge of the ground gave me a great advantage, and, besides any piquant turn that they might have, my epigrams shone in virtue of an accuracy that was often wanting in theirs. For although all the evil that is said of women has always some foundation, it is nevertheless difficult for men to preserve the composure requisite in order to jest about them well, and there is often a good deal of love in their invectives.

"I remarked that it was those that were most tender and had most feeling about women who treated them worse than the rest, and who returned to the subject with quite a peculiar bitterness as though they owed them a mortal grudge for not being what they wished them to be, and for falsifying the good opinion they had first formed about them.

"What I desired above all things was not physical beauty, it was beauty of the soul, love; but love, as I am sensible of it, is perhaps beyond human possibilities. And yet it seems to me that I should love in this way, and that I should give more than I require.

"What magnificent madness! what sublime extravagance!

"To surrender yourself entirely without any self-reservation, to renounce the possession of yourself and the freedom of your will, to place the latter in the hands of another, to see only with his eyes and hear only with his ears, to be but one in two bodies, to blend and mingle your souls so that you cannot tell whether you are yourself or the other, to absorb and radiate continually, to be now the moon and now the sun, to see the whole of the world and of creation in a single being, to displace the centre of life, to be ready, at any time, for the greatest sacrifices and the most absolute abnegation, to suffer in the bosom of the person loved as though it were your own; O wonder! to double yourself while giving yourself—such is love as I conceive it.

"Fidelity like that of the ivy, entwinings as of the young vine, and cooings as of the turtle-dove, these are matters of course, and are the first and simplest conditions.

"Had I remained at home, in the costume of my sex, turning my wheel with melancholy or making tapestry behind a pane in the embrasure of a window, what I have sought for through the world would perhaps have come and found me of itself. Love is like fortune, and dislikes to be pursued. It visits by preference those that are sleeping on the edge of wells, and the kisses of queens and gods often descend upon closed eyes. It is a lure and a deception to think that all adventures and all happiness exist only in those places where you are not, and it is a miscalculation to have your horse saddled and to post off in quest of your ideal. Many people make, and many others will again make this mistake. The horizon is always of the most charming azure, although when you reach it the hills composing it are usually but poor, cracked clay, or ochre washed by the rain.

"I had imagined that the world was full of adorable youths, and that populations of Esplandians, Amadises, and Lancelots of the Lake were to be met with on the roads in pursuit of their Dulcineas; and I was greatly astonished that the world took very little heed of this sublime search and was content to share the couch of the first prostitute that came in the way. I am well punished for my curiosity and distrust. I am surfeited in the most horrible manner possible without having enjoyed. With me knowledge has gone before use; nothing can be worse than such premature experiences which are not the fruit of action.

"The completest ignorance would be a thousand times better; it would at least make you do many foolish things which would serve to instruct and to rectify your ideas; for, beneath the disgust of which I have been speaking, there is always a lively and rebellious element which produces the strangest disorders: the mind is vanquished, but the body is not, and will not subscribe to this superb disdain. The young and robust body strives and kicks beneath the mind like a vigorous stallion ridden by a feeble old man, whom, however, he is unable to throw, for the cavesson holds his head and the bit tears his mouth.

"Since I have lived with men, I have seen so many women basely betrayed, so many secret connections imprudently divulged, the purest loves dragged carelessly through the mire, young fellows hastening to frightful courtesans on leaving the arms of the most charming mistresses, the most firmly established amours suddenly broken off without any plausible motive, that I now find it impossible to decide on taking a lover. It would be to throw oneself in broad daylight and with open eyes into a bottomless abyss. Nevertheless, the secret desire of my heart is still to have one. The voice of nature stifles the voice of reason. I am quite sensible that I shall never be happy if I cannot love and be loved:—but the misfortune is that only a man can be had as a lover, and if men are not altogether devils, they are very far from being angels. It would be vain for them to stick feathers on their shoulder-blades, and put a glory of gilt paper on their heads: I know them too well to be deceived. All the fine things that they could whisper to me would be of no avail. I know beforehand what they are going to say, and could say it for them.

"I have seen them studying their parts and rehearsing them before going on in front; I know the chief of the tirades that they intend to be effective and the passages on which they rely. Neither paleness of face nor alteration of feature would convince me. I know that these prove nothing. A night of orgie, a few bottles of wine, and two or three girls, are sufficient to wrinkle your face most becomingly. I have seen this trick practised by a young marquis, by nature very rosy and fresh-coloured, who found himself all the better for it, and owed the crowning of his passion only to this touching and well-gained paleness. I know also how the most languorous Celadons console them-

selves for the harshness of their Astraeas and find means for being
patient while waiting for the happy hour. I have seen sluts serving as
substitutes for chaste Ariadnes.

"Truly, after this, man tempts me but little; for he does not possess
beauty like woman, beauty, that splendid garment which so well
disguises the imperfections of the soul, that divine drapery cast by
God over the nakedness of the world, and which makes it in some
measure excusable to love the vilest courtesan of the kennel if she
owns this magnificent and royal gift.

"In default of the virtues of the soul, I should at least wish for
exquisite perfection of form, satinity of flesh, roundness of contour,
sweetness of line, delicacy of skin, all that makes the charm of women.
Since I cannot have love, I would have voluptuousness, and, well or
ill, replace the brother by the sister. But all the men that I have seen
seem to me frightfully ugly. My horse is a hundred times more handsome, and I should have less repugnance to kissing him than to
kissing sundry wonderful fellows who believe themselves very charming. Certainly a fop like those of my acquaintance would not be a
brilliant theme for me to embellish with variations of pleasure.

"A soldier would suit me nearly as little; military men have something mechanical in their walk and something bestial in their face
which makes me look upon them as scarcely human creatures; gentlemen of the long robe are not more delightful to me, they are dirty, oily,
shaggy, threadbare, with glaucous eyes and lipless mouths; they smell
immoderately rancid and mouldy, and I should feel no inclination to
lay my face against their lynx or badger-like muzzles. As to poets,
they think of nothing in the world but the endings of words and go
no further back than to the penultimate, and, in truth, are difficult
to make use of suitably; they are more wearisome than the others,
but they are as ugly and have not the least distinction or elegance in
their figure and dress, which is truly singular:—men who are occupied
the whole day with form and beauty do not perceive that their boots
are badly made and their hats ridiculous! They look like country
apothecaries or teachers of learned dogs out of work, and would give
you a distaste for poetry and verse for several eternities.

"As for painters, their stupidity also is enormous; they see nothing except the seven colours. One with whom I had spent a few days at R——, and who was asked what he thought of me, made this ingenious reply: 'He is rather warm in tone, and in the shadows pure Naples yellow should be employed instead of white, with a little Cassel ochre and reddish brown.' Such was his opinion, and, moreover, his nose was crooked and his eyes like his nose; which did not improve his chances. Whom shall I take?—a soldier with bulging crop, a limb of the law with convex shoulders, a poet or painter with a wild look, a lean little coxcomb without consistence? Which cage shall I choose in this menagerie? I am quite unable to say; I feel as little inclination in one direction as in another, for they are as perfectly equal in point of foolishness and ugliness as they can possibly be.

"Another alternative would still be open to me, which would be to take any one that I loved though he were a porter or a jockey; but I do not love even a porter. O unhappy heroine that I am! unmated turtle-dove condemned eternally to utter elegiac cooings!

"Oh! how many times have I wished to be really a man as I appear to be! How many women are there with whom I should have had a fellow-feeling, and whose hearts would have understood mine! how perfectly happy should I have been rendered by those delicacies of love, those noble flights of pure passion to which I could have replied! What sweetness, what delight! how would all the sensitive plants of my soul have bloomed freely without being obliged every minute to contract and close beneath some coarse touch! What charming efflorescence of invisible flowers which will never open, and whose mysterious perfume would have tenderly embalmed the fraternal soul! It seems to me that it would have been an enchanting life, an infinite ecstasy with ever outstretched wings; walks, with hands entwined never releasing their hold, beneath avenues of golden sand, through groves of eternally-smiling roses, in parks full of fish-ponds with gliding swans, and alabaster vases standing out against the foliage.

"Had I been a youth, how I should have loved Rosette! what worship it would have been! Our souls were truly made for each other, two pearls destined to blend together and make but one! How perfectly should I have realised the ideas that she had formed of love! Her character suits me completely, and her style of beauty pleases me. It is a pity that our love should be totally condemned to indispensable platonism!

"An adventure befell me lately.

"I used to visit a house in which there was a charming little girl, fifteen years old at the very most: I have never seen a more adorable miniature. She was fair, but so delicately and transparently fair that ordinary blondes would have appeared excessively brown and as dark as moles beside her; you would have thought that she had golden hair powdered with silver; her eyebrows were of so mild and soft a tint that they were scarcely apparent to the sight; her pale blue eyes had the most velvety look and the most silky lashes imaginable; her mouth, too small to put the tip of your finger into it, added still further to the childish and exquisite character of her beauty, and the gentle curves and dimples of her cheeks had an ingenuousness that was unspeakably charming. The whole of her dear little person delighted me beyond all expression; I loved her frail, white, little hands through which you could see the light, her bird-like foot which scarcely touched the ground, her figure which a breath would have broken, and her pearly shoulders, little developed as yet, which her scarf, placed awry, happily disclosed.

"Her prattle, in which artlessness imparted fresh piquancy to her natural wit, would engage me for whole hours, and I took singular pleasure in making her talk; she would utter a thousand delicious comicalities, now with extraordinary nicety of intention, and now without having apparently the slightest comprehension of their scope,—which made them a thousand times more attractive. I used to give her bon-bons and lozenges, kept expressly for her in a light tortoise-shell box, which pleased her greatly, for she is dainty like the true little puss that she is. As soon as I arrived she would run up to me and try my pockets to see whether the blissful bon-bon box was there; I would make her run from one hand to the other, and this would occasion a little battle in which she in the end infallibly got the upper hand and completely plundered me.

"One day, however, she contented herself with greeting me in a very grave manner, and did not come as usual to see whether the sweetmeat fountain was still flowing in my pocket; she remained haughtily on her chair, quite upright and with her elbows drawn back.

" 'Well! Ninon,' I said to her, 'have you become fond of salt now, or are you afraid that sweets will make your teeth drop out?' And as I spoke I tapped the box, which gave forth the most honeyed and sugary sound in the world from beneath my jacket.

"She put her little tongue half way out on the edge of her lips as though to taste the ideal sweetness of the absent bon-bon, but she did not stir.

"Then I drew the box from my pocket, opened it, and began religiously to swallow the burnt almonds of which she was especially fond: the greedy instinct was for a moment stronger than her resolution; she put out her hand to take some and drew it back again immediately, saying, 'I am too big to eat sweets!' And she heaved a sigh.

" 'It did not strike me that you had grown very much since last week; you must be like the mushrooms which spring up in a night. Come and let me measure you.'

" 'Laugh as much as you like,' she rejoined with a charming pout; 'I am no longer a little girl, and I want to grow very big.'

" 'Your resolutions are excellent, and should be adhered to; but might it be known, my dear young lady, what has caused these lofty ideas to come into your head? For, a week ago, you appeared quite content to be small, and craunched your burnt almonds without caring very much about compromising your dignity.'

"The little creature looked at me in a singular manner, glanced around her, and, when she had quite satisfied herself that no one could hear us, leaned over towards me in a mysterious fashion and said:

" 'I have a lover.'

" 'The deuce! I am no longer surprised that you have ceased to care for lozenges; you were wrong, however, not to take some, for you might have had a doll's dinner-party with him, or exchanged them for a shuttlecock.'

"The child made a scornful movement with her shoulders and appeared to look upon me with perfect contempt. As she continued to maintain her attitude of an offended queen, I continued:

" 'What is the name of this glorious personage? Arthur, I suppose, or else Henry.' These were two little boys with whom she used to play, and whom she called her husbands.

" 'No, neither Arthur nor Henry,' she said, fixing her clear, transparent eye upon me, 'a gentleman.' She raised her hand above her head to give me an idea of height.

" 'As tall as that? Why, this is getting serious. And who is this tall lover?'

" 'Monsieur Théodore, I will tell you, but you must not speak about it to any one, neither to mamma, or Polly (her governess), or your friends who think me a child and would make fun of me.'

"I promised the most inviolable secrecy, for I was very curious to know who the gallant personage was, and the child, seeing that I was making fun of the matter, hesitated to take me entirely into her confidence.

"Reassured by the word of honour that I gave her to be carefully silent about it, she left her easy-chair, came and leaned over the back of mine, and whispered the name of the beloved prince very softly in my ear.

"I was confounded: it was Chevalier de G——, a dirty, intractable animal, with the morals of a schoolmaster and the physique of a drum-major, the most intemperate debauchee of a man that could possibly be seen, a genuine satyr, minus the goat's feet and the pointed ears. This inspired me with grave apprehensions for dear Ninon, and I made up my mind to put the matter to rights.

"Some people came in, and the conversation dropped.

"I withdrew into a corner and searched my brain for the means of preventing things from going further, for it would have been quite a sin for so delicate a creature to fall to such an arrant scoundrel.

"The little one's mother was a kind of courtesan who kept gaming tables and had a literary *salon*. Bad verses were read at her house and good money lost, which was a compensation. She had not much love for her daughter, who was, to her, a sort of living baptismal certificate which prevented her falsifying her chronology. Besides, the child was growing up, and her budding charms gave rise to comparisons which were not to the advantage of the prototype, already somewhat worn by the action of years and men. The child was accordingly rather neglected, and was left defenceless to the enterprises of the black-guards who frequented the house. If her mother had taken any notice of her, it would probably have been only to profit by her youth and trade on her beauty and innocence. In one way or another the fate that awaited her was not in doubt. This pained me, for she was a charming little creature who was assuredly deserving of better things, a pearl of the finest water lost in that infectious slough; the thought of it affected me so far that I resolved to get her at all costs out of that frightful house.

"The first thing to be done was to prevent the chevalier from pursuing his design. I thought that the best and simplest way was to pick a quarrel with him and make him fight a duel, and I had all the trouble in the world to do so, for he is as cowardly as he can be and dreads blows more than any one. At last I said so many stinging things to him, that he was obliged to make up his mind to come on the ground, although it was greatly against the grain. I even threatened to have him cudgelled by my footman if he did not put a better face on it. Nevertheless he could handle his sword well enough, but he was so confused by fear that we had hardly crossed our weapons when I was able to administer a nice little thrust which sent him to bed for a fortnight. This satisfied me; I had no wish to kill him, and would as soon have let him live to be hanged later on—a touching attention for which he ought to have been more grateful to me! My rogue being stretched between a pair of sheets and duly trussed with bandelets, it only remained to induce the little one to leave the house, which was not extremely difficult.

"I told her a story about her lover's disappearance, which was giving her extraordinary anxiety. I informed her that he had gone off with an actress belonging to the company then at C——, which, as you may believe, made her very indignant. But I consoled her by speaking ill in every way of the chevalier, who was ugly, drunken, and already old, and I ended by asking her whether she would not rather have me for a wooer. She replied that she would, because I was handsomer, and my clothes were new. This artlessness, spoken with enormous seriousness, made me laugh till I cried. I turned the little one's head and succeeded in inducing her to leave the house. A few bouquets, about as many kisses, and a pearl necklace that I gave her, charmed her to an extent difficult to describe, and she assumed an important air in the presence of her little friends which was extremely laughable.

"I had a very rich and elegant page's costume of about her size made, for I could not take her away in her girl's dress, unless I myself resumed female attire, which I was unwilling to do. I bought a pony, which was gentle and easy to ride, and yet a sufficiently good courser to follow my barb when it was my pleasure to go quickly. Then I told the fair one to try to come down at dusk to the door, where I would call for her; and this she very punctually did. I found her mounting guard behind the half-opened door. I passed very close to the house; she came out, I stretched out my hand to her, she rested her foot on the tip of mine, and jumped very nimbly up behind me, for she possessed marvellous agility. I spurred my horse, and succeeded in returning home through seven or eight circuitous and deserted lanes without any one seeing us.

"I made her exchange her clothes for her disguise, and myself acted as her maid; at first she made a little fuss, and wished to dress all alone; but I made her understand that this would waste a great deal of time; that, moreover, being my mistress, it was not in the least improper, and that such was the custom between lovers. This was quite enough to convince her, and she yielded to circumstances with the best grace in the world.

"Her body was a little marvel of delicacy. Her arms, which were somewhat thin like those of every young girl, had inexpressible sweetness of line, and her budding breasts gave such charming promise, that none better developed could have sustained a comparison with them. She had still all the graces of the child, and already all the charm of the woman; she was in that adorable transition period when the little girl is blended with the young girl: a blending fugitive and impalpable, a delicious epoch when beauty is full of hope, and when every day, instead of taking something from your love, adds new perfections to it.

"Her costume became her extremely well. It gave her a little unruly air, which was very curious and diverting, and made her burst out laughing when I offered her the glass to let her judge of the effect of her toilet. I afterwards made her eat some biscuits dipped in Spanish wine, in order to give her courage and enable her better to support the fatigue of the journey.

"The horses were waiting ready saddled in the courtyard; she mounted hers with some deliberation, I bestrode the other, and we set out. Night had completely fallen, and occasional lights, which were being extinguished every moment, showed that the honest town of C—— was virtuously engaged as every country town ought to be on the stroke of nine.

"We could not go very quickly, for Ninon was no better horse-woman than she ought to have been, and when her beast began to trot she would cling with all her might to his mane. However, on the following morning we were too far away to be overtaken, at all events unless extraordinary diligence had been employed; but we were not pursued, or at least, if we were, it was in an opposite direction to that which we had taken.

"I was singularly interested in the little fair one. I no longer had you with me, my dear Graciosa, and I was immensely sensible of the need of loving somebody or something, of having a dog or a child with me to caress familiarly. Ninon was this to me; she shared my bed and put her little arms around my body to go to sleep; she most seriously thought herself my mistress, and had no doubt that I was a man; her great youth and extreme innocence preserved her in this error which I was careful not to dissipate. The kisses that I gave her quite completed her illusion, for her ideas went, as yet, no further, and her desires did not speak loudly enough to cause her to suspect anything else. After all, she was only partly mistaken.

"And, really, there was the same difference between her and me, as there is between myself and men. She was so diaphanous, so slender, so light, of so delicate and choice a nature, that she was a woman even to me who am myself a woman, and who look like a Hercules beside her. I am tall and dark, she is small and blonde; her features are so soft that they make mine appear almost hard and austere, and her voice is so melodious a warble that mine seems harsh in comparison. If a man had her he would break her in pieces, and I always feel afraid that the wind will carry her off some fine morning. I should like to enclose her in a box of cotton and wear her hanging about my neck. You can have no conception, my dear friend, of her grace and wit, her delicious coaxing, her childlike endearments, her little ways and pretty manners. She is the most adorable creature in existence, and it would have been truly a pity had she remained with her unworthy mother.

"I took a malicious joy in thus depriving men's rapacity of such a treasure. I was the griffin preventing all approach, and, if I did not enjoy her myself, at least no one else enjoyed her—an idea which is always consoling, let all the foolish detractors of egotism say what they will.

"I intended to preserve her in her ignorance as long as possible, and to keep her with me until she was unwilling to stay any longer, or I had succeeded in securing a settlement for her.

"In her boy's dress I took her on all my journeys, right and left; this mode of life gave her singular pleasure, and the charm that she found in it assisted her to endure its fatigues. Everywhere I was complimented on the exquisite beauty of my page, and I have no doubt that it gave many people a precisely contrary idea of what was actually the case. Several even tried to unravel the mystery; but I did not allow the little one to speak to anybody, and the curious were completely disappointed.

"Every day I discovered some new quality in this amiable child which made me cherish her more and congratulate myself on the resolution I had taken. Assuredly men were not worthy to possess her, and it would have been a deplorable thing if so many bodily and spiritual charms had been surrendered to their brutal appetites and cynical depravity.

"Only a woman could love her with sufficient delicacy and tenderness. One side of my character, which could not have been developed in a different connection and which was completely brought out in the present one, is the need and desire of affording protection, a duty which usually belongs to men. If I had taken a lover it would have displeased me extremely to find him assuming to defend me, for the reason that this is an attention I love to show to those whom I like, and that my pride is much better suited with the first *rôle* than with the second, although the second may be more agreeable. Thus I felt pleased in paying my little darling all the attentions which I ought to have liked to receive, such as assisting her on difficult roads, holding her bridle or stirrup, serving her at table, undressing her and putting her to bed, defending her if any one insulted her; in short, doing everything for her that the most impassioned and attentive lover does for a mistress he adores.

"I was insensibly losing the idea of my sex, and it was with difficulty that I remembered, at considerable intervals, that I was a woman; at first I often forgot myself, and unthinkingly said something that did not harmonise with the coat I wore. Now this never happens, and even when writing to you, to you who are in my secret, I sometimes preserve a useless virility in my adjectives. If ever I take a fancy to go and look for my skirts in the drawer where I left them—which I think very doubtful, unless I fall in love with some young spark—I shall find it difficult to lose these habits, and, instead of being a woman disguised as a man, I shall look like a man disguised as a woman. In truth, neither of the two sexes are mine; I have not the imbecile submission, the timidity or the littleness of women; I have not the vices, the disgusting intemperance, or the brutal propensities of men: I belong to a third, distinct sex, which as yet has no name: higher or lower, more defective or superior; I have the body and soul of a woman, the mind and power of a man and I have too much or too little of both to be able to pair with either.

"O Graciosa! I shall never be able completely to love any one, man or woman; an unsated something ever chides within me, and the lover or friend answers only to a single aspect of my character. If I had a lover, the feminine element in me would doubtless for a time dominate over the manly, but this would not last for long, and I feel that I should be only half satisfied; if I have a friend, the idea of corporeal voluptuousness prevents me from tasting entirely the pure voluptuousness of the soul; so that I know not where to rest, and perpetually waver from one to the other.

"My chimera would be to have both sexes in turn in order to satisfy this double nature: a man to-day, a woman to-morrow, for my lovers I should keep my languorous tenderness, my submissive and devoted ways, my softest caresses, my little sadly-drawn sighs, all the cat-like and woman-like elements in my character; then with my mistresses I should be enterprising, bold, impassioned, with triumphant manners, my hat on my ear, and the style of a boaster and adventurer. My nature would thus be entirely brought out, and I should be perfectly happy, for true happiness consists in the ability to develop freely in every direction and to be all that it is possible to be.

"But these are impossibilities, and are not to be thought of.

"I had carried off the child with the idea of deluding my propensities and turning upon some one all the vague tenderness which floats in my soul and floods it; I had taken her as a sort of escape for my loving faculties; but I soon recognised, in spite of all the affection that I bore her, what an immense void, what a bottomless abyss she left in my heart, and how little her tenderest caresses contented me! I resolved to try a lover, but a long time passed and I met no one who did not displease me. I forgot to tell you that Rosette, having discovered whither I was gone, had written me the most beseeching letter to go and see her; I could not refuse her, and I met her again at a country house where she was. I returned there several times, and even quite lately. Rosette, in despair at not having had me for her lover, had thrown herself into the whirl of society and dissipation, like all tender souls that are not religious and that have been wounded in their first love; she had had many adventures in a short time, and the list of her conquests was already very numerous, for every one had not the same reasons for resisting her that I had.

"She had with her a young man named D'Albert, who was at the time her established lover. I appeared to make quite a peculiar impression upon him, and at the very first he took a strong liking to me.

"Although he treated Rosette with great deference, and his manners towards her were in the main tender enough, he did not love her, —not owing to satiety or distaste, but rather because she did not correspond to certain ideas, true or false, which he had formed concerning love and beauty. An ideal cloud interposed between him and her, and prevented him from being as happy as otherwise he must have been. Evidently his dream was not fulfilled, and he sighed for something else. But he did not seek for it, and remained faithful to the bonds which weighed on him; for he has more delicacy and honour in his soul than most men, and his heart is very far from being as corrupted as his mind. Not knowing that Rosette had never been in love except with me, and that she was so still, in spite of all her intrigues and follies, he had a dread of distressing her by letting her see that he did not love her. It was this consideration that restrained him, and he was sacrificing himself in the most generous way.

"The character of my features gave him extraordinary pleasure, for he attaches extreme importance to external form; so much so that he fell in love with me in spite of my male attire and the formidable rapier which I wear at my side. I confess that I was grateful to him for the acuteness of his instinct, and that I held him in some esteem for having distinguished me beneath these delusive appearances. At the beginning he believed himself endowed with a fancy far more depraved than it really was, and I laughed inwardly to see him torment himself in this way. Sometimes, when accosting me, he had a frightened look which amused me immensely, and the very natural inclination which drew him towards me appeared to him as a diabolical impulse which could not be too strongly resisted. On such occasions he would fall back furiously upon Rosette, and endeavour to recover more orthodox habits of love; then he would come back to me, of course more inflamed than before.

"Then the luminous idea that I might perhaps be a woman crept into his mind. To convince himself of this he set himself to observe and study me with the minutest attention; he must be acquainted with every particular hair, and know accurately how many eyelashes

I have on my lids; feet, hands, neck, cheeks, the slightest down at the corner of my lips, he examined, compared, and analysed them all, and from this investigation, in which the artist aided the lover, it came out as clear as day (when it is clear), that I was well and duly a woman, and, moreover, his ideal, the type of his beauty, the reality of his dream;—a wonderful discovery!

"It only remained to soften me, and obtain the gift of amorous mercy, to completely establish my sex. A comedy which we acted, and in which I appeared as a woman, quite decided him. I gave him some equivocal glances, and made use of some passages in my part, analogous to our own situation, to embolden him and impel him to declare himself. For, if I did not passionately love him, he pleased me well enough not to let him pine away with love; and, as he was the first since my transformation to suspect that I was a woman, it was quite fair that I should enlighten him on this important point, and I was resolved not to leave him a shadow of doubt.

"Several times he came into my room with his declaration on his lips, but he dared not utter it; for, indeed, it is difficult to speak of love to one who is dressed like yourself, and is trying on riding boots. At last, unable to take it upon himself to do this, he wrote me a long, very Pindaric letter, in which he explained to me at great length what I knew better than he did.

"I do not quite know what I ought to do. Admit his request or reject it,—the latter would be immoderately virtuous; besides, his grief at finding himself refused would be too great: if we make people who love us unhappy, what are we to do to those who hate us? Perhaps it would be more strictly becoming to be cruel for a time, and wait at least a month before unhooking the tigress's skin to dress after the human fashion in a chemise. But, since I have resolved to yield to him, immediately is as good as later; I do not well understand those mathematically graduated resistances which surrender one hand to-day, the other to-morrow, then the waist and the neck, and next submit the lips to a lover's kisses; nor those intractable virtues which are always ready to hang themselves to the bell-rope if you pass by a hair's-breadth beyond the territory which they have resolved to grant on that day. It makes me laugh to see those methodical Lucretias walking backwards with the tokens of the most maidenly terror, and from time to time casting a furtive glance over their shoulder to make sure that the sofa on which they are to faint is quite directly behind them. I could never be as careful as that.

"I do not love D'Albert, at least in the sense which I give to the word, but I have certainly a liking and an inclination for him; his mind pleases me and his person does not repel me: there are not many people of whom I can say as much. He has not everything, but he has something; what pleases me in him is that he does not seek to satiate himself brutally like other men; he has a perpetual aspiration and an ever sustained breathing after beauty,—after material beauty alone, it is true, but still it is a noble inclination, and one which is sufficient to keep him in pure regions. His conduct towards Rosette proves honesty of heart, an honesty rarer than the other, if that be possible.

"And then, if I must tell you, I am possessed with the most violent desires,—I am languishing and dying of voluptuousness; for the dress I wear, while involving me in all sorts of adventures with women, protects me only too perfectly against the enterprises of men; an idea of pleasure which is never realised floats vaguely through my head, and this dull, colourless dream wearies and annoys me. So many women placed amid the chastest surroundings lead the most immoral lives, while I, by a somewhat facetious contrast, remain chaste and virgin like cold Diana herself, in the midst of the most disordered dissipation and surrounded by the greatest debauchees of the century.

"This bodily ignorance unaccompanied by ignorance of the mind is the most miserable thing in existence. That my flesh may have no cause to assume airs over my soul, I am anxious to know a man completely and all that his love is capable of. Since D'Albert has recognised me beneath my disguise, it is quite fair that he should be rewarded for his penetration; he was the first to divine that I was a woman, and I shall prove to him to the best of my ability that his suspicions were well founded. I would be scarcely charitable to let him believe that his fancy was solely a monstrous one.

"D'Albert it is, then, who will solve my doubts and give me my first lesson in love: the only question now is to bring the matter about in quite a poetical fashion. I am inclined not to reply to his letter and to look coldly on him for a few days. When I see him very sad and despairing, inveighing against the gods, shaking his fist at creation, and looking down the wells to see whether they are not too deep to throw himself into them,—I shall retire like Peau d'Ane to the end of the corridor, and put on my light-blue dress, that is to say my costume as Rosalind; for my feminine wardrobe is very limited. Then I shall go to him as radiant as a peacock displaying its feathers, with but a very low and loose lace tucker, partially unveiling those attractions which I usually conceal with the greatest care, and shall say to him in the most pathetic tone that I can assume—

" 'O most elegiac and perspicacious young man! I am truly a young and modest beauty, one who adores you into the bargain, and humbly asks to share your pleasures with you. Tell me whether this suits you, or if you feel any scruples in according her what she wishes.'

"This fine discourse ended, I shall let myself fall half-swooning into his arms, and, heaving melancholy sighs, shall skilfully cause the hook of my dress to come undone so that I shall still further disclose certain of my charms. The rest I shall leave to chance, and I hope that on the following morning I shall know what to think of all those fine things which have been troubling my brain for so long. While satisfying my curiosity, I shall have the further pleasure of making some one happy.

"I also propose to go and pay a visit to Rosette in the same costume, and to show her that, if I have not responded to her love, it was not from coldness or distaste. I do not wish her to preserve such a bad opinion of me, and she deserves, equally with D'Albert, that I should betray my incognito in her favour. How will she look at this revelation? Her pride will be consoled by it, but her love will lament it.

"Good-bye, most fair and good one; pray to heaven that I may not think as little of the pleasure as I do of those who afford it. I have jested throughout this letter, and yet what I am going to essay is a serious matter and something which may affect the rest of my life."

XVI

It was already more than a fortnight since D'Albert had laid his amorous epistle on Théodore's table, and yet there seemed to be no change in the manner of the latter. D'Albert did not know how to account for this silence; one would have imagined that Théodore had had no knowledge of the letter; the rueful D'Albert thought that it had gone astray or been lost; yet this was difficult of explanation, for Théodore had re-entered his room a moment afterwards, and it would have been very extraordinary if he had not perceived a large paper placed quite by itself in the middle of a table so as to attract the notice of the most inattentive.

Or was Théodore perhaps really a man and not a woman at all, as D'Albert had imagined to himself? or, supposing her a woman, had she so decided a feeling of aversion to him, or such a contempt for him that she would not condescend even to take the trouble of giving him a reply? The poor young man who had not, like ourselves, the advantage of searching the portfolio of Graciosa, the confidante of the fair Mademoiselle de Maupin, was not in a position to decide any of these important questions either in the affirmative or in the negative, and he was mournfully wavering in the most wretched irresolution.

One evening he was in his room, his brow pressed with melancholy against the window-pane, and was looking, without seeing them, at the already bare and reddened chestnut-trees in the park. The distance was bathed in a thick mist, a grey rather than black night was falling, and cautiously placing its velvety feet on the summits of the trees; a large swan was amorously dipping and redipping its neck and shoulders in the steaming water of the river, and its whiteness made it appear in the shadow like a large star of snow. It was the only living thing to give a little animation to the gloomy landscape.

D'Albert was thinking as sadly as a disappointed man can think at five o'clock on a misty autumn evening with a somewhat sharp north wind for music, and the wigless skeleton of a forest for a prospect.

He thought of throwing himself into the river, but the water seemed very black and cold to him, and the swan's example only half persuaded him; of blowing his brains out, but he had neither pistol nor powder, and he would have been very sorry to have had them; of taking a new mistress, or, sinister resolution, even two! but he knew none who would suit him, even none who would not suit him. In his despair he went so far as to wish to resume his connection with women who were perfectly insupportable to him, and whom he had had horsewhipped out of his house by his footman. He ended by resolving upon something much more frightful,—to write a second letter.

O sextuple booby!

He was at this stage in his meditations, when he felt a hand place itself on his shoulder, like a little dove descending on a palm-tree. The comparison halts somewhat inasmuch as D'Albert's shoulder bore a very slight resemblance to a palm-tree; but, all the same, we shall keep it in a spirit of pure Orientalism.

The hand was at the extremity of an arm which corresponded to a shoulder forming part of a body, which was nothing else but Théodore-Rosalind, Mademoiselle d'Aubigny, or Madelaine de Maupin, to call her by her real name.

Who was astonished? Neither I nor you, for you and I had long been prepared for this visit; but D'Albert who had not been expecting it in the least. He gave a little cry of surprise half-way between oh! and ah! Nevertheless I have the best reasons for believing that it was more like ah! than oh!

It was indeed Rosalind, so beautiful and radiant that she lit up the whole room, with her strings of pearls in her hair, her prismatic dress, her laces, her red-heeled shoes, her handsome fan of peacock's plumes, such, in short, as she had been on the day of the performance. Only,— and this was an important and decisive difference,—she wore neither gorget, nor chemisette, nor ruff, nor anything that effectually hid those two charming, unfriendly brothers, who, alas! have only too often a tendency to become reconciled.

A lovely, panting bosom, white, transparent, like an ancient marble, of the purest and most exquisite cut, projected boldly from a very low dress body, and seemed to bid defiance to kisses. It was a most reassuring sight; accordingly D'Albert was very quickly reassured and he abandoned himself in all confidence to his most disorderly emotions.

"Well! Orlando, do you not recognise your Rosalind?" said the fair one with the most charming smile; "or have you, perhaps, left your love hanging with your sonnets on some bushes in the forest of Arden? Are you really cured of the sickness for which you requested a remedy from me with such earnestness? I am very much afraid so."

"Oh no! Rosalind, I am more sick than ever. I am in extremity; I am dead, or very nearly!"

"You have not a bad appearance for a dead man; many living persons do not look so well."

"What a week I have spent! You cannot imagine it, Rosalind. I hope that it will be equivalent to a thousand years of purgatory to me in the next world. But, if I dare ask you, why did you not reply to me sooner?"

"Why? I scarcely know, unless it be just because I did not. However, if this motive does not appear a valid one to you, here are three others not nearly so good, from which you shall choose: first, because carried away by your passion you forgot to write legibly, and it took me more than a week to make out what your letter was about; next, because my modesty could not reconcile itself in a shorter time to such an absurd idea as to take a dithyrambic poet for a lover; and then because I was not sorry to see whether you would blow your brains out, or poison yourself with opium, or hang yourself with your garter. There!"

"Naughty banterer! I assure you that you have done well to come to-day, for perhaps you would not have found me to-morrow."

"Really! poor fellow! Do not assume such a doleful air, I should also be affected, and that would make me more stupid in myself alone than all the animals that were in the ark with the deceased Noah. If once I open the sluice for my sensibility, I warn you that you will be drowned. Just now I gave you three bad reasons, I now offer you three good kisses; will you accept them, on the condition that you forget the reasons for the kisses? I owe you quite as much as that and more."

As she uttered these words the fair infanta advanced towards the mournful lover, and threw her beautiful arms round his neck. D'Albert kissed her effusively on the cheeks and mouth. This last kiss had a longer duration than the others, and might have been counted as four. Rosalind saw that all that she had done until then had been only pure childishness. Her debt discharged, she sat down, still greatly moved, on D'Albert's knees, and, passing her fingers through his hair, she said to him—

"All my cruelties are exhausted, sweet friend; I took the fortnight to satisfy my natural ferocity; I will confess to you that I found it long. Don't become a coxcomb because I am frank, but it is true. I place myself in your hands, revenge yourself for my past harshness. If you were a fool I should not say this, or even anything else to you, for I do not like fools. It would have been very easy for me to make you believe that I was prodigiously shocked by your boldness, and that all your Platonic sighs and your most quintessential nonsense were not sufficient to procure your forgiveness for a thing of which I was very glad; I might, like another, have bargained with you for a long time and retailed to you what I am now granting you freely and at once; but I do not think that this would have increased your love for me by the thickness of a single hair.

"I do not ask of you an oath of eternal love nor any exaggerated protestation. Love me as much as heaven ordains—I will do as much on my side. I will not call you a traitor or a wretch when you have ceased to love me. You will also have the kindness to spare me the corresponding odious titles, should I happen to leave you. I shall be merely a woman who has ceased to love you,—nothing more. It is not necessary to hate each other all through life because of a night or two passed together. Whatever may happen, and wherever destiny may drive me, I swear to you, and this is a promise that can be kept, that I shall always preserve a charming recollection of you, and, that

291

if I am no longer your mistress, I shall be your friend as I have been your comrade. For you I have laid aside my male attire to-night; I shall resume it to-morrow for all. Think that I am only Rosalind at night, and that throughout the day I am and can be only Théodore de Sérannes——"

The sentence she was about to utter was stifled by a kiss followed by many others, which were no longer counted and of which we shall not give an exact catalogue, because it would certainly be rather tedious and perhaps very immoral—for some people; as to ourselves, we think nothing more moral and sacred under heaven than the caresses of man and woman, when both are handsome and young.

As D'Albert's importunities became more amorous and eager, Théodore's beautiful face, instead of being smiling and radiant, assumed an expression of proud melancholy which caused her lover some disquiet.

"Why, dear sovereign, have you the chaste and serious air of an antique Diana now, when we should rather have the smiling lips of Venus rising from the sea?"

"You see, D'Albert, it is because I am more like the huntress Diana than anything else. When very young I assumed man's attire for reasons which it would be tedious and useless to tell you. You alone have divined my sex, and, if I have made conquests, they have only been over women,—very superfluous conquests, which have embarrassed me more than once. In a word, although it is an incredible and ridiculous thing, I am virgin,—as virgin as the snow on Himalaya, as the Moon before she had lain with Endymion, as Mary before she had made the acquaintance of the divine pigeon, and I am grave as every one is when about to do a thing on which it is impossible to go back. It is a metamorphosis, a transformation that I am about to undergo: to change the name of girl into the name of woman, no longer to have to-morrow what I had yesterday; something that I did not know and that I am going to learn, an important page turned in the book of life. It is for that reason that I look sad, my friend, and not on account of any fault of yours."

As she said this she parted the young man's long hair with her two beautiful hands, and laid her softly puckered lips upon his pale forehead.

D'Albert, singularly moved by the gentle and solemn tone in which she uttered this long speech, took her hands and kissed the fingers one after another; then very delicately broke the lacing of her dress so that the body opened and the two white treasures appeared in all their splendour: upon the bosom which was as sparkling and as clear as silver bloomed the two beautiful roses of paradise. He pressed their vermilion points lightly in his mouth, and thus went over the whole outline. Rosalind submitted with exhaustless complaisance, and tried to return his caresses as exactly as possible.

"You must find me very awkward and cold, my poor D'Albert; but I scarcely know how to set about it. You will have a great deal to do to teach me, and really I am imposing a very laborious task upon you."

D'Albert made the simplest reply, he did not reply at all; and, straining her in his arms with fresh passion, he covered her bare shoulders and breasts with kisses. The hair of the half-swooning infanta became loosened, and her dress fell to her feet as though by enchantment. She remained quite upright like a white apparition in a simple chemise of the most transparent linen. The blissful lover knelt down, and had soon thrown the two pretty little red-heeled shoes into an opposite corner of the apartment; the stockings with embroidered clocks followed close after them.

The chemise, gifted with a happy spirit of imitation, did not remain long behind the dress; it first slipped from the shoulders without there being any thought of checking it; then, taking advantage of a moment when the arms were perpendicular, it very cleverly came off them and rolled as far as the hips whose undulating outline partially checked it. Rosalind then perceived the perfidiousness of her last garment, and raised her knee a little to prevent it from falling altogether. In this pose she was exactly like those marble statues of goddesses whose intelligent drapery, sorry to cover up so many charms, envelops them with regret, and by a happy piece of treachery stops just below the part that it is intended to conceal. But, as the chemise was not of marble and its folds did not support it, it continued its triumphant descent, sank down altogether upon the dress, and lay round about its mistress's feet like a large white greyhound.

There was certainly a very simple means of preventing all this disorder, namely, to check the fugitive with the hand: this idea, natural as it was, did not occur to our modest heroine.

She remained, then, without any covering, her fallen garments forming a sort of pedestal for her, in all the diaphanous splendour of her beautiful nakedness, beneath the soft light of an alabaster lamp which D'Albert had lighted.

D'Albert, who was dazzled, gazed upon her with rapture.

"I am cold," she said, crossing her hands upon her shoulders.

"Oh! pray! one minute more!"

Rosalind uncrossed her hands, leant the tip of her finger upon the back of an easy-chair and stood motionless; she gave a slight movement to her hips in such a way as to bring out all the richness of the waving line; she did not appear at all embarrassed, and the imperceptible rose of her cheeks was not a shade deeper: only the somewhat quickened beating of her heart caused the outline of her left breast to tremble.

The young enthusiast for beauty could not sufficiently feast his eyes on such a spectacle; we must say, to Rosalind's boundless praise, that this time the reality was beyond his dream, and that he did not experience the slightest deception.

Everything was united in the beautiful form standing before him —delicacy and strength, grace and colour, the lines of a Greek statue of the best period and the tone of a Titian. There he saw, palpable and crystallized, the cloudy chimera that he had so often vainly sought to stay in its flight; he was not obliged, in the manner he used to complain of to friend Silvio, to limit his gaze to a certain fairly well-formed part and not stray beyond it, on pain of seeing something frightful, and his amorous eye passed down from the head to the feet and ascended again from the feet to the head, and was ever sweetly soothed by a correct and harmonious form.

The limbs were proudly and superbly turned, the knees were admirably pure, the ankles elegant and slender, the arms and shoulders of the most magnificent character, the skin as lustrous as an agate, the bosom enough to make gods come down from heaven to kiss it; a torrent of beautiful brown hair slightly crisped, such as we see on the heads by the old masters, fell in little waves along an ivory back whose whiteness it brought out in wonderful relief.

The painter satisfied, the lover resumed the ascendancy; for, whatever love a man may have for art, there are things that he cannot long be satisfied with looking at.

He took up the fair one in his arms and bore her to the couch. In an instant he undressed and flung himself beside her.

The girl pressed herself against him and embraced him closely, for her two breasts were as cold and as white as snow. This purity of skin aroused D'Albert and excited him to the highest pitch. Soon she too became inflamed. He began to caress her most ardently and madly— chest, shoulders, neck, mouth, arms, legs. He longed to cover with a single kiss her entire beautiful body, which was melting into his, so close was their embrace. In this wealth of charming treasures, he did not know which to attain first.

All their kisses became one, and Rosalind's perfumed lips were joined to D'Albert's to make a single mouth. Their chests were expanded, their eyes half closed; their arms, exhausted by passion, no longer had the strength to press their bodies to each other. The divine moment approached. A supreme spasm convulsed the two lovers, and the curious Rosalind became as enlightened as possible on a matter which had so deeply perplexed her.

Still, one lesson, no matter how intelligent one may be, cannot suffice; D'Albert gave her a second, then a third. Out of consideration for the reader, whom we do not wish to humiliate and discourage, we shall not carry this description too far.

Our fair reader would possibly pout at her lover if we revealed to her the sum total of the lessons imparted by D'Albert's love, assisted by Rosalind's curiosity. Let her recall the best occupied and most charming of her nights, the night which would be remembered a hundred thousand days, did not death come before; let her lay her book aside and compute on the tips of her pretty white fingers how many times she was loved by him who loved her most, and thus fill up the void left by us in this glorious history.

Rosalind was prodigiously apt, and made enormous progress in that single night. The ingenuousness of body which was astonished at everything, and the rakishness of mind which was astonished at nothing, formed the most piquant and adorable contrast. D'Albert was ravished, distracted, transported, and would have wished the night to last forty-eight hours, like that in which Hercules was conceived. However, towards morning, in spite of a multitude of kisses, caresses, and the most amorous endearments in the world, well adapted to keep one awake, he finally found himself obliged to take some little repose. A soft and voluptuous sleep touched his eyes with the tip of its wing, his head drooped, and he slumbered between the breasts of his beautiful mistress. The latter contemplated him for some time with an air of melancholy and profound thought; then, as the dawn shot its whitish rays through the curtains, she gently raised him, laid him beside her, stood up, and passed lightly over his body.

She went to her clothes and dressed again in haste, then returned to the bed, leaned over D'Albert who was still asleep, and kissed both his eyes on their long and silky lashes. This done, she withdrew backwards, still looking at him.

Instead of returning to her own room she entered Rosette's. What she there said and did I have never been able to ascertain, although I have made the most conscientious researches. Neither in Graciosa's papers, nor in those belonging to D'Albert and Silvio, have I found anything having relation to this visit. Only, a maid of Rosette's informed me of the following singular circumstance: although her mistress had not slept with her lover that night, the bed was disturbed and tossed, and bore the impress of two bodies. Further, she showed me two pearls, exactly similar to those worn in his hair by Théodore when acting the part of Rosalind. She had found them in the bed when making it. I leave this remark to the reader's sagacity, and give him liberty to draw thence any inferences that he likes; for myself, I have made a thousand conjectures about it, each more unreasonable than the rest, and so absurd that I really dare not write them even in the most virtuously periphrastic style.

It was quite noon when Théodore left Rosette's room. He did not appear at dinner or supper. D'Albert and Rosette did not seem at all surprised at this. He went to bed very early, and the following morning, as soon as it was light, without giving any notice to any one, he saddled his page's horse and his own, and left the mansion, telling a footman that they were not to wait dinner for him, and that he might perhaps not return for a few days.

D'Albert and Rosette were extremely astonished, and did not know how to account for this strange disappearance, especially D'Albert, who decidedly thought that his behaviour on the first night had entitled him to a second. Towards the end of the week, the unhappy disappointed lover received from Théodore a letter, which we shall transcribe. I am afraid that it will satisfy neither my male nor my female readers; but the letter was in truth none other than that which follows, and this glorious romance will have no other conclusion.

XVII

"You are no doubt greatly surprised, my dear D'Albert, at what I have just done after acting as I did. I will allow you to be so, for you have reason. The odds are that you have already bestowed upon me at least twenty of the epithets that we had agreed to erase from our vocabulary—perfidious, inconstant, wicked,—is it not so? At least you will not call me cruel or virtuous, and that is something gained. You curse me, and you are wrong. You desired me, you loved me, I was your ideal;—very well. I at once granted you what you asked; it was your own fault that you did not have it sooner. I served as a body for your dream as compliantly as possible. I gave you what assuredly I shall never again give to any one, a surprise on which you hardly counted and for which you ought to be more grateful to me. Now that I have satisfied you, it pleases me to go away. What is there so monstrous in this?

"You have been with me entirely and unreservedly for a whole night; what more would you have? Another night, and then another; you would even make free with the days if need were. You would go on in this way until you were surfeited with me. I can hear you from this crying out most gallantly that I am not one of those with whom surfeit is possible. Good gracious! I am like the rest.

"It would last six months, two years, ten years even, if you will, but still everything must have an end. You would keep me from a kind of feeling of propriety, or because you would not have the courage to give me my dismissal. What would be the use of waiting until matters came to this?

"And then, it might perhaps be myself who would cease to love you. I have found you charming; perhaps, by dint of seeing you, I might have come to find you detestable. Forgive me this supposition. Living with you in close intimacy, I should no doubt have had occasion to see you in a cotton cap or in some ridiculous or facetious domestic situation. You would necessarily have lost the romantic and mysterious side which allures me more than anything else, and your character, when better understood, would no longer have appeared so strange to me. I should have been less taken up with you through having you beside me, in something like the fashion in which we treat those books that we never open because they are in our libraries. Your nose or your wit would no longer have seemed nearly so well turned; I should have perceived that your coat did not fit you and that your stockings were untidy; I should have had a thousand deceptions of this kind which would have given me singular pain, and at last I should have come to this conclusion: that you decidedly had neither heart nor soul, and that I was destined to be misunderstood in love.

"You adore me and I you. You have not the slightest reproach to make against me, and I have nothing in the world to complain of in you. I have been perfectly faithful to you throughout our amour. I have deceived you in nothing. I have neither false bosom nor false virtue; you had the extreme kindness to tell me that I was yet more beautiful than you had imagined. For the beauty that I gave you, you repaid me with pleasure; we are quits.—I go my way and you yours, and perhaps we shall meet again at the Antipodes. Live in this hope.

"You believe, perhaps, that I do not love you because I am leaving you. Later, you will recognise the truth of the contrary. Had I valued you less, I should have remained, and would have poured out to you the insipid beverage to the dregs. Your love would soon have died of weariness; after a time you would have quite forgotten me, and, as you read over my name on the list of your conquests, would have asked yourself: 'Now, who the deuce was she?' I have at least the satisfaction of thinking that you will remember me sooner than another. Your unsated desire will again spread its wings to fly to me; I shall ever be to you something desirable to which your fancy will love to return, and I hope that in the arms of the mistresses you may have, you will sometimes think of the unrivalled night you spent with me.

"Never will you be more amiable than you were that blissful evening, and, even were you equally so, it would still be something less; for in love, as in poetry, to remain at the same point is to go back. Keep to that impression, and you will do well.

"You have rendered the task of the lovers I may have (if I have other lovers) a difficult one, and no one will be able to efface the memory of you;—they will be the heirs of Alexander.

"If you are too much grieved at losing me, burn this letter, which is the only proof that you have possessed me, and you will believe that you have had a beautiful dream. What is there to hinder you? The vision has vanished before the light, at the hour when dreams return home through the horn or the ivory gate. How many have died who, less fortunate than you, have not even given a single kiss to their chimera!

"I am neither capricious, nor mad, nor a conceited prude. What I am doing is the result of profound conviction. It is not in order to inflame you more, or from calculating coquetry that I have gone away from C——; do not try to follow me or to find me again: you will not succeed. My precautions to conceal from you all traces of myself have been too well taken; you will always be for me the man who opened up to me a world of new sensations. These are things that a woman does not easily forget. Though absent, I shall often think of you, oftener than if you were with me.

"Comfort poor Rosette as well as you can, for she must be at least as sorry for my departure as you are. Love each other well in memory of me, whom both of you have loved, and breathe my name sometimes in a kiss."